Also Available From Elle Kennedy

MIDNIGHT REVENGE

A KILLER INSTINCTS NOVEL

ELLE KENNEDY

A SIGNET ECLIPSE BOOK

SIGNET ECLIPSE

Published by New American Library,
an imprint of Penguin Random House LLC
375 Hudson Street, New York, New York 10014

This book is an original publication of New American Library.

First Printing, February 2016

For more information about Penguin Random House, visit penguin.com.

ISBN 978-0-451-47443-8

Printed in the United States of America
10 9 8 7 6 5 4 3 2 1

Penguin
Random
House

To all the readers who have been waiting
so patiently for D's book—this one's for you!

ACKNOWLEDGMENTS

As always, I want to give a shout-out to the usual suspects who held my hand during the process of writing this book:

My editor, Laura Fazio, and everyone at New American Library/Berkley (especially Jess Brock!) for being so enthusiastic about this series.

Research whiz Travis White for helping me make every setting and mission come alive.

Vivian Arend, my own personal cheerleader and self-proclaimed hater of romantic suspense—yet she reads every single book in this series . . .

Brighton Walsh for beta-reading this project and for offering valuable feedback. And for IM'ing with me in the wee hours of the night to help me iron out plot points!

And of course, all the fans of the series! Your endless support and contagious excitement are what make this entire process worthwhile.

Chapter 1

Two months ago
Oaxaca, Mexico

"You need to pull him out."

Just as Derek "D" Pratt had anticipated, his blunt command caused silence to fall over the line. But making this call had been unavoidable. He'd held his tongue for months—fuck, almost four months now—and it was time to make sure the boss knew that one of their men had become a liability.

Still, it felt like he was ratting out Macgregor, and although D was many things, a rat was not one of them. He knew when to keep his mouth shut. Most days he preferred it. But if the choice came down to snitching on a teammate or staying quiet and watching that teammate get himself killed, then he'd sing like a fucking canary.

And people accused him of having no honor.

"Is it that bad?" Jim Morgan's gruff voice slid into D's ear, and he could picture the other man back at their compound in Costa Rica, sucking on a cigarette and pacing the stone terrace as he worked over the implications of this latest hiccup.

D took a drag of his own smoke, then blew a gray cloud into the night and watched it dissipate slowly. No breeze tonight. Not much humidity either. In fact, the temperature had taken a dramatic dip from afternoon to evening. Earlier it'd been so hot that he'd stripped off his shirt while waiting for the doc to treat Macgregor, and now he was in a threadbare hooded sweatshirt, wishing he hadn't forgotten his jacket in the chopper.

The small brick building that housed the clinic was three hours from Oaxaca and nestled at the base of the mountain, its isolated location making it the ideal place for an in-and-out patch job. D and the other men on Morgan's team of operatives had paid many visits to this clinic over the years. Sofia Amaro, the sole physician in charge, didn't bat an eye anymore when one of the mercenaries showed up bloody and broken and requiring a quick fix.

"It's bad," D confirmed. "He almost got both of us killed this morning, not to mention Ruiz, the fucking person we were supposed to be protecting."

"You told me Delgado's men engaged."

"They did. With the *ceiling.* One of them fired a warning shot after Ruiz said something that pissed off Delgado. The motherfuckers were trying to make a point." Aggravation bubbled in his throat as the morning's clusterfuck buzzed through his mind. "Macgregor shot and killed that guard, Jim. He lost his cool and snapped."

Christ, they'd been lucky to get out of there alive, which probably wouldn't have been the case if the meeting had taken place in cartel territory rather than at the neutral site chosen by the DEA. Morgan's team had been tasked with protecting Agent Joseph Ruiz while he negotiated with Delgado, a major cog in the cartel machine who'd been willing to cooperate with the DEA in exchange for . . . for who the fuck knew what, because they hadn't even reached the demands portion of the meeting. Because of Liam fucking Macgregor.

Thanks to pure, blind luck and their armory of skill, D and Liam had managed to keep Ruiz alive during the gunfight and shove him into the armored truck outside, and then D had floored it all the way back to Guadalajara.

Now the DEA was foaming at the mouth because of the botched meeting, and Liam was sedated in a hospital room because he'd taken a bullet to the shoulder and refused to swallow his pain meds. It was like dealing with a goddamn child.

"He's done," D told his boss, taking another deep pull on his cigarette. "This Sullivan thing has screwed with his head, and if you don't bench him—indefinitely— then he's going to get himself killed. He'll get us all killed."

Morgan sighed. "I was hoping sending him out on jobs might distract him."

"Bad call. Now he's just distracted in the field. Pull him out, or I'll drag him back to the compound myself and lock him in the tunnels."

A tired chuckle sounded in his ear. "And you wonder why everyone's terrified of you. You need to learn some diplomacy instead of forcing people to bend to your will."

"I don't force shit. I do what needs to be done."

There was a beat. "How's he doing? Did Sofia get the bullet out?"

"She did, and he's fine—physically anyway. Mentally, he's fucked. He's one bad decision away from hopping a plane to Dublin and shooting answers out of people."

"Shit. All right. The moment Sofia clears him for travel, bring him home. I'll call Ruiz and placate him, but the DEA is pretty fucking pissed. Might be the last time they contract us out."

"Who cares? Government jobs are a bitch anyway."

"Yeah, but government allies are an asset," Morgan countered. "We could've used Ruiz if the Sullivan thing ends up being connected to the cartels."

The Sullivan thing. Even though he was guilty of using the phrase himself, he hated that they were referring to their teammate's disappearance like that. Like it was no big deal. But it *was* a big deal, so big that Liam Macgregor was lying on a gurney right now with a bullet wound in his arm.

"Is that what you think?" D asked in a low voice. "That Sully might've gotten mixed up with a cartel? Because now you're reaching."

"I know I'm fucking reaching, but what the hell else am I supposed to do? It's been *four* months. Sully's gone off the grid before, but he's never stayed away this long without making contact." Morgan sounded as frustrated and confused as he'd been when D had called him from Dublin in October to tell him that Sullivan Port had gone AWOL.

"We'll find him, Jim."

After a split-second pause, Morgan said, "I know."

That nanosecond of silence, unnoticeable unless you knew Jim Morgan as well as D did, was enough to stiffen every muscle in his body.

Son of a bitch. The boss had given up.

After months of tapping every contact available to the team, months of following every lead and leaving no stone unturned, Morgan had given up on Sullivan. He didn't expect to find him. Or, rather, he didn't expect to find him *alive*.

The knowledge triggered a burst of anger in D's gut, along with a sickening rush of guilt that caught him completely off guard. He didn't experience that emotion often.

His past choices, the mistakes he'd made . . . He didn't dwell on them, because regret was a waste of time. When he made a decision, he was fully prepared for the consequences. If he took a life, he made peace with the action before he even pulled the trigger. And once the deed was done, it was fucking *done*. No looking back. No moaning and griping and feeling bad about it. Guilt and regrets were for weak men who couldn't stomach the choices they'd made in their lives.

But that was the problem with "this Sullivan thing." Because it *wasn't* the result of a choice D had made or an action he had taken.

And yet it was entirely his fault that Sullivan was missing.

Sucking hard on his smoke, he filled his lungs with nicotine, hoping to ease the sudden tightening of his chest. "I'll call you once we head out," he muttered.

He disconnected the call before Morgan could respond, and the ensuing silence was a relief. Although being part of a team meant he had no choice but to engage in conversations, undergo briefings, and sit through strategy sessions, he really hated it sometimes. Hated talking, hated the sound of his own voice.

He took one last drag, then stomped the cigarette out beneath his boot and stalked inside.

The fluorescent lighting in the clinic intensified the throbbing of his temples. He hadn't eaten all day, but that wasn't the reason for the headache. He'd spent three years in Delta, followed by three more with the Smith Group, the hush-hush black-ops agency he'd sold his soul to. Both gigs had ensured he could go for days without sleep or sustenance. What he *couldn't* handle were loose ends. They gnawed at him like hungry scavengers, evoked a powerless sensation that made him want to pull out his HK and unload a clip into the wall.

Sullivan was a loose end, damn it.

"He's asleep." The stern voice drifted toward him as he rounded the corner toward Macgregor's room.

Sofia Amaro stood outside the door, arms crossed over perky tits that were barely contained by her tight white tank. He instantly tensed—something about this woman always elicited that response.

Her I'm-ready-to-go-to-battle pose was one he'd seen dozens of times before. Sofia was a pit bull when it came to her patients, snarling at anyone who tried to ignore her orders. D had always held grudging respect for her headstrong nature, but it also triggered an unwelcome rush of lust each time he encountered her.

He put on an indifferent look as their eyes met, pretending that her perfect tits and insolent scowl didn't get his blood going. "Is he cleared for travel?"

D peered past her slender shoulders into Liam's room, studying the prone man on the bed. Good. Liam's face had some color again—it had been dangerously pale during the chopper ride from Guadalajara.

"No," Sofia said firmly.

He'd worked black ops long enough to know when someone was lying to him. Arching an eyebrow, he met her green eyes.

"Yes," she amended, a flush coloring her olive-toned cheeks. "But he needs rest. He was damn near exhausted when you brought him in."

D was already pulling his cell phone from his back pocket, ready to call their pilot.

"For fuck's sake, Derek," Sofia burst out. "Can't you give him a few hours? The bullet was a through-and-through. It'll heal. But he needs some fucking rest."

D's other brow joined its twin up near his hairline. Sofia was bossy as hell, but she rarely ever cursed, which told him she was genuinely upset about Liam's condition. His finger hesitated over the TALK button as he studied her worried gaze. After a beat, he tucked the phone in his pocket.

"Three hours," he said gruffly. "That's all I can spare."

"Can, or are willing to?" A note of challenge entered her voice.

"Can. Morgan needs him back at the compound."

"Morgan can wait. The health of his men should come before his need to work them ragged."

D's lips twitched. "Is that any way to talk about your benefactor?"

Sofia froze. Then, tucking a strand of dark hair behind

her ear, she slowly met his eyes. "What are you talking about?"

The chuckle slipped out. "Don't play games, Sofia. You're better than that."

Irritation flickered in her expression.

"I know my boss funds this place," he said with a shrug. "So the way I see it, you work for him just like the rest of us."

"I work for myself," she snapped. "And for the patients who come here. Morgan's money might keep this clinic open, but I'm not at his beck and call. He knows that."

D released another laugh, low and harsh. "Is that so?" He gestured around the deserted corridor. "Look around, baby. Listen. No staff. No voices. I called you from Guadalajara and told you I was bringing Macgregor, and you sprinted over here like the good soldier you are and opened up the clinic for us." D smirked. "You work for Morgan. Deal with it."

Those green eyes flashed, and something about her defiant expression stirred his cock.

Fuck.

Now was not the time to think about sex. And Sofia Amaro was not the woman to think about having sex *with*. She was on Morgan's payroll, and her services were invaluable to the team. No way would D risk losing their private physician for a chance to get off.

"You win, Derek. I'm another one of Jim Morgan's minions. Just like you." Then she spun on the heels of her hiking boots and disappeared into Macgregor's room.

D followed her, propping his shoulder against the doorframe as he watched her check the IV drip at Liam's side.

"You went to a lot of trouble for a bullet wound that'll heal," he said suspiciously.

Sofia spared him a dark look. "I told you—the bullet wasn't the issue. He's suffering from exhaustion and dehydration." She scoffed under her breath. "What, you couldn't be bothered to toss a canteen his way every couple hours? Not everyone is a robot like you are."

A robot? He thought it over, and decided that probably *was* the best way to describe him. He was a cold bastard. Ruthless. Violent. He'd been that way since he was eight years old, and if he'd ever had the ability to feel compassion or tenderness, then it had been beaten out of him a long time ago.

But he'd never made apologies for who he was, and he wasn't about to start now.

As Sofia tucked the thin blanket tighter around Liam's waist, D caught a glimpse of leather and metal around the man's wrists. "Did you restrain him?" he demanded.

Her eyes didn't convey even an ounce of remorse. "Damn right I did. He struggled like crazy when I tried giving him the sedative. Kept insisting he didn't need it and that he had to go find Sully."

D's stomach clenched.

Sofia sighed. "I take it you guys aren't any closer to finding him?"

"You fucking think? He disappeared without a goddamn trace, Sofia." D gritted his teeth. Even though his frustration was directed at himself rather than her, he didn't apologize for snapping at her.

Fortunately, she was unfazed by his sharp tone. "Do you think someone took him?"

"Yes."

Her brow furrowed. "Why?"

Because of me.

He swallowed the confession, same way he'd been doing for months. Because what was the point in telling people about his suspicion? There was no concrete evidence to support it. Nothing except the offhand remark of an Irish bartender.

But D knew, deep in his bones, that he was responsible. That Sullivan had been abducted because of *him*.

Something must have gone down at the end of that Dublin job, but even four months later, D was no closer to finding out what. When Sean Reilly had gotten tangled up with some very dangerous Irish gangsters, the team had flown to Dublin to help him out. The job had gone smoother than most and Reilly had come out on top, but somewhere between the end of the mission and the morning the team was scheduled to leave, Sullivan had fallen off the face of the fucking earth.

Security footage showed Sully in the hotel bar at two in the morning, talking to a dark-haired man whose face had been shielded from the camera. A few minutes later, he left the bar, and that was the last anyone had seen or heard from him.

Foul play was definitely involved. The security footage in the lobby and outside the hotel had been wiped clean, which meant someone had gone to great lengths to cover up whatever had happened in front of those cameras.

The team had run the stranger's profile—what little of it they had—through every facial-recognition program out there, but there'd been no hits. And nobody, not a damn person on their extensive list of contacts, had been able to identify the man. The bartender's account had been useless for the most part—he insisted he hadn't heard a word of Sully's conversation with the stranger, that it'd looked friendly enough, and that Sully had been sober and calm when he'd walked out of the bar alone.

The only red flag? The bartender hadn't referred to Sullivan as *Sullivan*—he'd called him *Mr. Pratt*.

As in Derek Pratt.

D didn't know why his teammate would have been using his name, but it stood to reason that if the bartender had believed himself to be in the company of Derek Pratt, then so had the stranger.

The intended target that night hadn't been Sullivan.

It had been D.

"Derek?"

Sofia's voice jerked him back to the present.

"I don't know why he was taken," D muttered in response. *But I intend to find out.*

His gaze drifted to the bed. Even injured and sedated, Liam Macgregor looked like a fucking movie star. Sometimes D found himself staring at the guy and wondering how Liam had ever worked for the DEA. A face like his was too damn memorable, which wasn't a characteristic you wanted in an undercover agent. Deep-cover operatives were supposed to blend. Liam Macgregor didn't blend—he stood out.

"He and Sullivan were close, huh?" Sofia asked.

Were. Her use of the past tense didn't surprise him. He was starting to suspect that most of his teammates believed that Sullivan was dead. Not Liam, though. The man refused to stop searching for his best friend.

Christ, D should've told Morgan to sideline the guy

months ago. He'd seen Liam spiraling, and he'd done nothing to try to stop it.

"Joined at the hip," he told her.

She glanced at her patient, her expression softening. "Sullivan's a great guy. I really hope you find him."

"You don't sound hopeful."

"Are you? Because in your line of work, four months is a long time for someone to go off the map. Usually that means they're no longer *on* the map."

He couldn't disagree. But fuck, he hoped they were wrong. Hoped like hell that Sully was alive and well out there, and not the unfortunate victim of a case of mistaken identity.

Sofia moved away from Liam's bed and strode back to the door, gesturing for D to follow her. His gaze unwittingly rested on her ass, round and firm beneath her faded jeans. She didn't dress like any doctor he'd ever met. No scrubs or white coat for her, but jeans, skimpy tops, and the occasional flannel shirt she threw on when it got cold.

The sight of her ass brought another ache to his groin, which only pissed him off again. Men like him weren't allowed to feel sexual desire for women like Sofia. Men like him didn't feel sexual desire, period. For D, sex was nothing more than a pent-up need that required an outlet every once in a while and in no way involved bullshit like intimacy or lust. Tension and release—that's all it was to him. To normal people, to women like Sofia, it was far more than that.

Usually, he avoided those women like the plague. But the awareness that hummed in his blood whenever he saw Sofia Amaro was impossible to control. She was so fucking spirited. And bossy. He'd always wondered what it would be like to fuck her.

But he wouldn't allow himself to find out.

Times like these—and it pained him to even think it—he missed Noelle. Morgan would rip D's throat out with his bare hands if he knew D was thinking about his wife in a carnal way, but he couldn't help it. His arrangement with Noelle had been exactly what he'd needed: hardcore fucking and nothing more.

"You're quiet tonight," Sofia remarked. Then she laughed. "Quieter than usual, that is. I swear, you're the most tight-lipped person I've ever met."

Shrugging, he glanced over at her. Well, glanced over and then down, because at six-one, he towered over her five-foot-two frame. And because of his height, he could also see right down her tank top, getting an eyeful of the creamy swells of her tits. She had great tits. He'd admired them on more than one occasion. It pissed him off how often he found himself staring at this woman.

This was the first time she'd ever caught him, though, and she rolled her eyes when she noticed where his gaze had traveled. "And instead of answering, he stares at my boobs. Classy, Derek."

He smirked at her. "On what planet could I ever be considered *classy*?"

"True." She tilted her head. "But I've never seen you check anyone out before."

Because normally he didn't. Or at least, he was usually more discreet. Sofia didn't seem put off by his behavior, though. If anything, she looked . . . intrigued. Fucking hell. She really needed to wipe that interested look off her face. After this morning's adrenaline rush, he was too damn primed for sex, and if she offered him an opening, he wasn't sure he could stop himself from taking it.

As they walked toward the back of the small building, he gave her a wary look. "Where are we going?"

"Outside." She frowned at him. "The last time you were here, you ignored my clear-cut instructions and took off while you had a concussion. I don't trust you not to whisk Liam away if I turn my back, and I don't trust you in the clinic."

He didn't bother trying to defend himself. Hell, part of him was still entertaining the idea of calling in their chopper and getting Liam out of here when Sofia wasn't looking.

They stepped outside through the rear doors. She seemed unruffled by the cool breeze on her bare arms, continuing forward at a brisk pace.

He walked alongside her, cursing himself the whole time. He needed to get *away* from her, damn it, not stay glued to her side. Usually he kept to himself when he was at the clinic. Found a room to crash in, or smoked out front. But he suspected that even if he'd wanted to do either of those things, Sofia wouldn't let him.

They followed the dirt path behind the clinic until the terrain grew hilly. It was the dry season, but the mountain elevation allowed most of the plants to remain green. A carpet of purple bougainvillea stretched out on both sides of the path, blooming wildly across the landscape.

A few more yards, and a single-story house with a

white exterior and sloped roof appeared in the distance. Sofia's house.

D experienced a prick of discomfort. Sofia had never invited him or any of his male teammates to her home before. Abby Sinclair, the sole female mercenary on the team, was the only one Sofia had welcomed into her private space, and that was during a dangerous storm. Which was damn ironic, because Abby was a terrifying motherfucker and not someone most people wanted to be alone with. D used to worry she might slit Kane's throat in his sleep, but since she'd given birth to their son, he considered the prospect less likely.

As they neared the house, a light flicked on over the rickety wooden porch. Motion sensor. He approved.

But then Sofia opened the front door without unlocking it, and his approval faded. Yes, she was isolated up here and hadn't encountered any trouble from the cartels since she'd opened the clinic, but safety was nothing more than an illusion.

"Your door should be locked," he said curtly.

"Wouldn't make a difference. That door is so old I could break it down just by tapping on it, even if it's locked."

He made a mental note to send in a contracting crew to rectify that. Sofia was a valuable asset to the team. Morgan wouldn't like having to replace her if she died during a home-robbery attempt.

"Want a beer?" She glanced over her shoulder as she strode into the house.

D hesitated in the doorway. He didn't do this kind of shit. Nope, hanging out with women was definitely not a regular experience for him. Well, except with the ones he'd been ordered to kill. During his agency days, he'd had no choice but to lay some groundwork with his female targets, and unfortunately, that had involved drinks and dinners and conversation he'd hated making.

"You can come in. I won't bite."

The mocking note in her voice made him sigh. Other than Noelle's operatives, Sofia was the only woman he'd ever met who wasn't afraid of him. Everyone else, men and women alike, shit their pants when he walked into a room. And that was the way he liked it.

He reluctantly stepped inside, watching as she wandered across the open-concept main room toward the kitchen. She grabbed two longneck bottles from an old refrigerator that was humming so loudly, D suspected it sucked up way too much power.

"Here." She walked over and handed him a bottle of cheap Mexican beer, then leaned against the work island separating the kitchen from the living area.

He knew from experience that this particular brand of beer tasted like piss and was weaker than water, but fuck, he had a few hours to kill, so he twisted off the cap and took a sip. Since it was hot inside the house, he set the bottle on the table next to the couch and stripped off his hoodie. That left him in a wifebeater, and he didn't miss the way Sofia immediately zeroed in on his bare arms.

She eyed his tats, her gaze traveling up his forearms to his biceps, then to the snake coiled around his neck. She'd never asked him about his tattoos in all the time he'd known her. Luckily, she didn't ask now.

As she sipped her beer, he stared at her long, graceful throat. Then their eyes locked, and his cock twitched again.

"I can't figure you out," she said thoughtfully.

He shrugged. "There's nothing to figure out."

"Your men say you're a coldhearted bastard. And honestly, I think they're secretly terrified of you." She slanted her head. "But I also think that's exactly what you want. For them to be afraid."

"If you brought me back here to psychoanalyze me, you're wasting your time." He took a menacing step forward, just because he was in the mood to see her flinch.

But she didn't. Instead she smiled. "See? You're doing it right now. Trying to scare me."

He took another step, and this time received a response. A hitch in her breath, almost inaudible, and he heard it only because he'd been watching her throat and seen the slight dip to it.

She wanted him.

He might not be good with all that romance bullshit, but he knew sexual arousal when he saw it. The reddish tint to her cheeks. The interest flickering in her eyes. The fluttering of her pulse at the center of her throat.

Screw it. He felt his body take over, his mind forgetting all about professional courtesy and ordering him to take her already. She wanted him. All he had to do was lay down some ground rules first, make sure she knew what this was—and what it wasn't.

"Don't worry. I get it," she said, her tone mocking him again. "If people fear you, then they won't try to get close to you. Right, Derek?"

She was one of the few people who called him that.

To everyone else, he was D. D, vague and unmemorable—
just the way he liked it.

As she offered a look of challenge, he stepped closer
and bared his teeth in a hard smile. "As much as I'm
enjoying this verbal foreplay," he said abruptly, "what do
you say we just skip to the part where you ride my dick?"

Chapter 2

Heat.

Sofia hadn't expected it, but holy hell, there it was. Flooding her body and pulsing between her legs as flames of arousal licked at her skin.

And Derek Pratt, of all people, was responsible for it.

Morgan's mercenaries flew in and out of her life every few months. They showed up bloody and hurt and in need of treatment, and she gave it immediately, because as much as she hated to admit it, D was right. Morgan *was* her boss. Yes, he understood that the patients she treated in the neighboring villages came first, but *she* understood that it was her duty to fix up his men.

She wasn't sure she could fix D, though. At least not in the psychological sense, because Derek Pratt might actually be unfixable. She'd seen him stand by and watch while she pried bullets out of his teammate's bodies, without even flinching, without showing an iota of concern. On the surface, he looked like he didn't give a shit if his men lived or died, but every so often Sofia caught glimpses of emotion behind his cold mask. He did care, but only sometimes and only about certain people.

Still, those infrequent slivers of compassion weren't enough to convince her that he was a good man. He might not scare her when it came to her physical safety, but he sure as hell frightened her in other ways. His hard exterior and complete lack of humanity were deeply unnerving.

So why were her breasts suddenly tingling in his presence? Why was her core throbbing with need? In the six years they'd known each other, her body had never shown any sexual desire for the man.

So where was this unexpected attraction coming from?

She stared at his chiseled features, his gleaming dark eyes. God, a man as dangerous as this one, as *cold* as this one, wasn't allowed to be so handsome. His appearance had always unnerved her too. That incredibly attractive face, those defined cheekbones, sensual mouth.

Her gaze lowered, and she became preoccupied with his body. Tall and muscular, his chest massive beneath his wifebeater, his long, powerful legs encased in snug cargo pants.

And the tattoos . . . they'd always fascinated her. The deadly samurai and diamondback snake engaged in a fighting pose on his left forearm. The gorgeous dragon on his right biceps, about to take flight off his shoulder. And the snake around the base of his neck . . . that one didn't fascinate her so much as terrify her.

"What's the matter?" he said mockingly. "You've got nothing to say to that? You're always so quick with the snappy comebacks, Sofia."

He was right. She usually was. But he'd caught her off guard with his crude suggestion, and now she couldn't stop picturing what it would be like to . . . to ride his dick.

She couldn't get the phrase out of her mind because, *God*, she wanted it.

"You know what? Maybe I'll ride *you*. I'll ride you hard," he drawled when she didn't respond. "I think I'd rather do that anyway."

She finally found her voice. "Who says I'm open to either option?"

He laughed. Except it wasn't *really* a laugh. His laughter, rare as it was, never seemed to be triggered by humor, only derision. "Are we playing games now? Because we both know you brought me here to fuck me."

Had she? No, she couldn't have. But . . . well, if that *was* the reason she'd invited him into her home, then it certainly hadn't been a conscious decision.

He raised one dark eyebrow. "Am I wrong?"

Sofia swallowed, thinking it over.

Oh God. He *wasn't* wrong.

When he'd stepped off that chopper earlier, with one muscular arm supporting Liam, her first thought had been— Okay, her first thought had been to take care of his barely conscious teammate. But her *second* thought? She'd wondered, just for a second, what it would be like to . . . well, fuck him.

She'd admired his looks before, but this afternoon had been the first time her appreciation had translated into actual awareness.

Into lust.

It's not him. It's because you haven't had sex in more than a year.

Yeah, she couldn't deny she was hard up. The mere thought of having a man inside her made her thighs clench. She liked sex. She liked it a hell of a lot, and ever since her affair with a doctor from the relief foundation had fizzled out, she'd been aching for it.

Now a sexy man was standing in front of her, and her libido had roared to life. And although she hadn't consciously planned to hit on him when she'd invited him inside, there was no point in denying the truth.

"No," she said.

"No what?"

"You're not wrong." Sofia sighed. "I guess I wouldn't mind getting laid."

His eyes narrowed as he advanced on her. Like a predator. Because he *was* a predator. A ruthless soldier, lethal and impassive, and yet right now, she didn't mind being the prey. If she were being honest, she preferred it. Day in and day out, she was the one in control, the one holding people's lives in her hands. But in bed . . . she submitted.

She used to hate that word—*submission*—because submission was associated with weakness, but over the years she'd learned to differentiate between the two.

"Do you want to get laid, or do you want to get fucked?" he rasped as he bridged the distance between them.

She raised her eyebrows. "Aren't those one and the same?"

"No."

Mere inches separated them. His muscular body dwarfed hers, dominated her personal space, and she gulped when one large hand curled around her throat, roughly skimming the delicate tendons there before the pads of his fingers rested on her pulse point. She knew he could feel the wild hammering of her heart, sense the way her body reacted to his nearness.

Her breasts were heavy and achy. And she was wet. God, Derek Pratt was making her wet. She had never, ever expected this.

"*Getting laid* implies a lot of shit I'm not interested in doing." His voice was harsh yet oddly seductive. "Lying down, for one—not gonna do that. Bringing each other pleasure . . . won't do that, either."

A strangled laugh popped out. "No pleasure, huh? Then what's the point?"

"Release," he said simply. "I'll fuck you, Sofia, hard enough that you'll feel it for days. I'll make you come. You'll make me come." His fingers slid down her throat to her collarbone, then lower, toying with the swell of her cleavage. "If you want seduction and drawn-out foreplay and someone telling you how fucking good it feels, you won't get that from me, so feel free to ask somebody else."

It was difficult to concentrate on what he was saying, because her brain had stopped working after the *I'll fuck you, Sofia* line.

God, she wanted that. She wanted an orgasm that didn't come from her own hand. She wanted to feel his powerful body tight to hers, his cock plunging inside her.

Her gaze lowered to the unmistakable bulge beneath the fly of his cargo pants. The sight sped up her pulse. Jesus, he was big. She wasn't sure why that surprised her. Every other part of him was big, so why not the part she wanted now?

"What'll it be?" His eyes remained shuttered as

always. "Do you want me to fuck you, or do you want me to walk away? But you should know I'll be walking away regardless, with or without the fucking."

Of course he would be. He didn't strike her as the type of man who stuck around. Who cuddled and kissed and enjoyed postcoital intimacy with his lover. This would be sex and nothing more, because that's all a man like Derek Pratt was capable of giving a woman.

Was she insane for even considering this? For wanting it? She knew the difference between sex and love, but she required at least *some* intimacy from a lover. A hint of tenderness, a moment of connection. That wouldn't happen with D, and it should bother her. It really should.

But holy hell, she wanted him. So much that her sex was throbbing painfully, clenching around emptiness, aching to clamp around *him*.

"Answer me, Sofia." A command. A taunt.

She let out a wobbly breath. "I . . . want you to fuck me—"

Before the last word even left her mouth, she found herself being spun around. Her belly pressed up against the counter, and her hands instinctively flew down to brace against the hard surface.

She wanted to turn and look at him, but his solid body kept her in place. Her breathing grew labored as his big hands landed on her waist, then traveled upward, sneaking beneath the hem of her tank top. Even if she'd wanted to move, she was no longer capable of it, because his touch was distracting, hypnotic.

No gentleness in the way he tugged her shirt up and over her head. He tossed it on the hardwood floor, and then his long fingers undid the button of her jeans. There was something dangerously erotic about not being able to see him. She heard his even breathing behind her, felt the heat of his body. One calloused hand splayed on her lower back while the other eased her jeans down her thighs. When the air met her bare skin, a full-body shiver rolled through her.

She heard the rustle of his clothing. He'd knelt down on the floor—his fingertips were now skimming down her legs to where the denim had snagged at her ankles. She hurriedly kicked off her boots, and when he rasped, "Lift," she obeyed. Lifting one foot, then the other, so he could remove her jeans and panties.

Naked. She was fully naked now and he was still fully clothed, the material of his pants rubbing her bare buttocks as he stood up and ground his hips against her.

"Oh God," she choked out.

"There's no God, Sofia. Just the devil. Just me."

He was right. He *was* the devil, doing sinful things to her body as he reached up and cupped one breast, squeezing hard enough to make her gasp. His palm brushed her nipple, which puckered in response, straining into his hand. When his fingers found that distended bud and pinched it, desire sizzled from her breast to her clit, summoning a moan from her lips.

She heard a zipper being dragged down, another rustling of fabric, then the unmistakable sound of a wrapper tearing.

He was putting on a condom.

God. She couldn't breathe. How had things escalated so fast? They'd gone from barely exchanging ten sentences to her naked against the counter with him about to fuck her.

"You want it bad," he remarked, and she moaned when his fingertip toyed with her opening. "Your pussy's soaking wet."

She was wetter than she'd ever been, in fact. She'd never felt this way before. Completely and totally dominated, and he wasn't even inside her yet.

D's finger slipped in an inch, then another, until it was lodged in deep. When her inner muscles squeezed around it, he made a guttural noise, and then his finger disappeared.

Sofia sagged forward in disappointment. Empty. She felt empty now. Frustration turned her hands into fists, tight to the counter. Why was he teasing her? Why—

The blunt head of his erection nudged her opening, and she realized he hadn't been trying to tease her. He just didn't want to waste time.

There was no tenderness, no foreplay other than that exploratory finger he'd used to test her readiness. Nothing but the sound of his breathing, her panting, and then his deep voice muttering, "Brace yourself."

She'd barely uncurled her fists and planted her palms down when he drove inside her. So hard she gasped. So deep she saw stars.

But it didn't hurt. Oh no, it felt . . . good. So fucking good. Her body stretched to accommodate his thick length, then clamped on tight as if to trap him inside her. Pleasure flooded her core, tingling in her fingers and buzzing in her toes. She'd never felt so *full* in her entire life.

He didn't start off slow; he was merciless from the word *go*. Slamming into her from behind in frenzied thrusts, hitting a spot deep inside that made her pussy throb. His fingers dug into the flesh of her hips, but the tiny sting of pain only sent another jolt of pleasure up her spine. Holy hell, she was *definitely* going to feel him for days. His cock stretching her, his marks on her skin.

She'd never been fucked like this before. D didn't let up his hard, relentless tempo. Didn't give her time to adjust or breathe or move. Over and over again, deep thrusts that brought moan after moan to her lips.

It shouldn't have felt this incredible, being manhandled this way. He was rough. He didn't say a word. He didn't even seem to care if she was enjoying—

Sofia moaned when he reached around her body and pressed his thumb on her clit. She was wrong. He *did* care if she was enjoying it. Because now he was rubbing circles over that swollen bud, slowing down his thrusts as he teased pleasure from her nerve endings.

"Oh *God*. Keep doing that," she begged, shocked by the throaty pitch of her voice, the wanton need ringing there.

"You gonna come for me, Sofia?" His breath fanned over the nape of her neck. "I'll come harder if you're squeezing my cock."

His wicked fingers played with her clit until she could no longer think clearly. Her vision became a blur of white dots, her body tightening with tension, pulsating with arousal, until the pressure broke apart and a blinding rush of ecstasy swept through her body.

Her surroundings faded away, the orgasm robbing her of breath. Behind her, D's thrusts got faster again. Faster, deeper, harder . . . And then he buried himself to the hilt and went still, and she felt his chest trembling against her back as he climaxed. He didn't make a sound, but his fingers pinched into her waist, the prick of pain mingling with the pleasure still floating inside her.

Her heart was beating uncontrollably. Her breathing was equally out of control. When D slowly withdrew from her core, she almost wept from the loss. From the emptiness.

Drawing a shaky breath, she found the courage to turn around. Expressionless eyes peered back at her. She wondered if he'd looked like that during the actual sex. Probably. The man didn't advertise what he was feeling, ever, and she suspected that extended to sexual desire as well.

"I . . ." She trailed off. For the first time in her life, she had no idea what to say. She'd just come harder than she'd thought possible. Derek Pratt had done that to her, and she couldn't wrap her head around it.

D rolled off the condom, and she got her first view of his cock. Long and imposing, still hard as a rock. He tucked it back in his pants, then walked to the sink, opened the cabinet beneath it, and tossed the condom in the little plastic wastebasket.

Without a word, he strode to the couch, reached into the front pocket of his sweatshirt, and pulled out a pack of cigarettes. He tapped the small cardboard box until one cigarette popped out, then shoved the smoke in the corner of his mouth but didn't light it. Instead, he watched her as intently as she was watching him.

A strange wave of tension rippled through the room. Not awkwardness. Not anger. Lingering awareness.

D narrowed his eyes. "You good?"

She nodded, surprised he'd even bothered to ask about her well-being.

Nodding back, he took a step toward the front door.

"You promised to give him three hours to rest," she called after D.

"He'll get his rest, Sofia. We're not leaving yet."

No, he was just leaving her house. Leaving *her*.

She was more dazed than upset as she watched him walk out the door. As she heard the creak of the porch steps and the soft thud of his footsteps moving away from the house.

Her body was still on fire. Still tingling and pulsing and *aching*. She hadn't expected this. Hadn't expected to enjoy having sex with D. Hadn't expected to want to do it *again*. But she did. God, she wanted to shout for him to come back and do it all over again.

But he'd gotten what he'd wanted and now he was gone, and she wasn't even angry about it, because she'd gotten what she'd wanted, too. Except the bastard had left her wanting more, damn it. She couldn't make sense of that. D was not a man you invited into your life *or* your bed, yet she'd done both tonight.

Gulping, Sofia ignored the discarded clothes on the floor and went to her bedroom, where she found an oversized T-shirt and slipped it on. Then she sat on the edge of the bed and ran a hand through her hair. Okay. She'd had sex with D. No big deal. They'd both enjoyed it, and now it was done.

With a sigh, she fell onto her back and closed her eyes, willing her body to stop tingling and her mind to quit conjuring up images of a repeat performance. *It was just a onetime thing,* she told her oversexed brain.

A yawn overtook her. She should probably sit up before she fell asleep, but . . . it felt so nice to lie down.

She hadn't slept last night because she'd been delivering a baby for one of the local women, and then she'd spent the entire day seeing patients and the entire night monitoring Liam Macgregor.

Crap, maybe she *should* sleep for a bit. Otherwise she'd be guilty of the same thing she'd accused Liam of doing: working herself to death.

She crawled up the bed and fiddled with the alarm, setting it to go off in an hour and a half. That would leave her time to check on Liam before D dragged him to that chopper.

A moment later, she was curled up on her side, fast asleep.

Sofia awoke to the deafening buzz of her alarm. Groaning, she reached over and slapped the snooze button, but the noise didn't go away. No longer buzzing, though. It was a different kind of noise, a rhythmic *rat-tat-tat* echoing beyond the open bedroom window.

She shot up, cursing loudly when she realized what she was hearing.

Helicopter rotors.

D was stealing her patient ahead of schedule.

Thoroughly outraged, she flew out of the bedroom and ran to the porch, where she anxiously peered through the trees in the direction of the helipad that Morgan had insisted on building behind the clinic. Blinking red and blue lights twinkled in the dark sky as a familiar military chopper made its ascent in the darkness.

"Fucking bastard," she muttered.

She didn't have to go to the clinic to know that they were gone, but she did anyway, just in case the helicopter had belonged to someone else. Which was a stretch, because the only aircraft that landed here belonged either to Morgan or the relief foundation, and the latter only showed up in the mornings.

She was right—that had been Morgan's chopper, all right. Because Liam's bed was empty when she stormed into his room.

Laughter bubbled in her throat as she stared at the sheets, which were still stained with Liam Macgregor's blood. Goddamn D. He'd only given her two hours instead of three.

He'd also given her the best sex of her life.

For some reason, that just made her laugh harder.

Chapter 3

Present Day
Turtle Creek, Costa Rica

"I, Ethan, take you, Juliet, to be my lawfully wedded wife . . ."

Weddings. D had no idea what the point of them was. Tax purposes, maybe? But nah, folks didn't need a wedding for that—a marriage license and a quick ceremony at the courthouse took care of all the paperwork required for taxes.

Symbolic, then? A way to declare undying love to each other in front of an audience?

Waste of fucking time, in his opinion.

This particular wedding was taking place at night, and the bluish water in the kidney-shaped pool cast an eerie glow over the manicured lawn. Morgan's housekeeper, Inna, had handled every detail herself—the neat rows of white wicker chairs on either side of the rose petal–strewn aisle. The tiny lights twinkling from the trees. The intricate altar she'd commissioned from one of the local carpenters.

But D was too busy pondering the reason for this circus to focus on his surroundings. He was the only person in attendance who wasn't sitting down, but rather standing in the back, his arms folded over the front of his muscle shirt. When Ethan had begged him to wear a suit, D had laughed in the man's face.

"I, Juliet, take you, Ethan, to be my lawfully wedded husband . . ."

The bride's throaty voice echoed clearly and earnestly in the clearing behind the compound. Ironically, this farce couldn't even be blamed on Juliet Mason, the thief–turned–assassin who worked for Morgan's wife, Noelle. According to Noelle, Juliet had resisted the marriage, but Ethan Hayes was the Boy Scout of the team, and just old school enough to insist on making things official.

D swept his gaze over the very small crowd. Morgan sat in the front row with Noelle on his right, and his daughter, Cate, on his left. Isabel and Trevor had flown in from Vermont. Luke and Olivia had made the trek from Aspen with their dog, Bear, who was sitting obediently at his master's side.

Kane and Abby's dogs were equally calm, which meant hell must have frozen over, because the three chocolate labs were fucking menaces. They were ridiculously protective of Abby, even more so now that she was carting around a baby all the time. And, yep, the damn baby was also present for the wedding, sleeping peacefully in his father's arms. The kid hadn't made a peep since the ceremony had started.

Christ. How was this his life? D wanted to strangle himself for allowing it to get to this point. His résumé was extensive—he'd been an assassin, a cleanup man, a soldier, and a criminal.

And now he was a goddamn wedding guest.

Sometimes he regretted joining up with supersoldier Jim Morgan after his self-imposed retirement from Smith Group. He could have disappeared, but he was built for action, and so he'd chosen to stay in the game. Except that meant going from a solo operative to a team player, and *that* meant he was now surrounded by people all the fucking time. Not just his teammates, but also Noelle's operatives, who'd not only joined professional forces with the team, but had become the wives and girlfriends of most of his men.

"You may now kiss the bride."

The minister was beaming like a fool as Ethan dipped his new wife and kissed the living shit out of her.

Juliet didn't seem to mind being mauled. The tall brunette looped her arms around Ethan's neck, her white dress fluttering around her ankles as she kissed him back.

Applause broke out. D didn't join in. He suddenly felt a huge rush of gratitude toward Kane and Trevor, who'd married their women in private and spared everyone from attending their weddings.

As his teammates went up to congratulate the newlyweds, D eased away from the excitement. He stalked past the refreshment table, which was piled high with champagne flutes and the fancy-pants hors d'oeuvres Inna had slaved over all day.

Christ, he could go for a beer. Or a bottle of Jack Daniel's. And a cigarette. Fuck, he needed a smoke.

His gaze landed on the stone terrace that overlooked

the yard, where Liam Macgregor stood like a statue, a beer bottle in his hand and a vacant look in his eyes. The man had refused to come down for the ceremony. D wasn't sure he blamed him. He didn't exactly feel like celebrating himself.

He was halfway to the flagstone path that led to the terrace steps when Olivia Taylor intercepted his path.

"You didn't congratulate them." Her tone wasn't chiding, but laced with disappointment. And her perceptive green eyes bored into his face, as if she were trying to tunnel her way into his mind.

He hated the way this woman looked at him. He'd met her in Manhattan a few years back, during a mission in which Luke had fallen hard and fast for the soft-spoken brunette. D, on the other hand, had been less than thrilled about her presence.

Luke's fiancée was too damn insightful, too compassionate. She saw things that other people didn't. And in New York . . . she'd seen *him*. They'd shared an awkward encounter, a hug that had left D shaken. Since then, he'd done his best to avoid Olivia whenever Luke happened to bring her to the compound, but the stubborn woman always seemed to seek him out.

"They've got enough well-wishers," he said with a shrug. "They don't need me."

Olivia shook her head. "It would make Ethan happy if you said something."

He stifled an angry curse. Fuck Ethan. *Fuck* these people. It wasn't his job to make them happy.

But the damned woman was staring at him as if it was, and her chastising gaze succeeded in making him feel guilty.

The only other woman who held this kind of power over him was Sofia. Except Sofia was even worse than Olivia, because once Olivia left the compound, she didn't linger in his mind. But Sofia . . . she fucking lingered.

She'd been messing with his head for two months now.

He hadn't expected to enjoy fucking her as much as he had. When he'd pulled out of her pussy, still rock-hard and wired with arousal, he'd been stunned to realize he wanted to screw her again. Hell, he probably would've screwed her all goddamn night if he hadn't walked away. But he'd forced himself to go, to avoid giving in to temptation and taking what he couldn't have. What he *shouldn't* have taken in the first place.

"Please, D," Olivia said softly. "Ethan respects you. He views you as an older brother. You know it would mean a lot to him if you went over there."

Goddamn it. His jaw went rigid, but he couldn't turn away from those big earnest eyes. After a beat, he found himself giving a curt nod and stalking back to the group.

He weaved his way toward the happy couple, ignoring the knowing looks from his teammates. Even the baby in Kane's arms seemed to be smirking at him, blinking at D with the honey-yellow eyes the kid had inherited from his mother. But when Jasper grinned that toothless grin of his, he was all Kane.

D marched up to Ethan and tapped him on the shoulder. The younger man turned around, his expression immediately filling with—damn that Olivia—pleasure.

"Congratulations," D muttered.

Ethan's mouth twitched. "On a scale of one to ten, how physically painful was that for you to say?"

D glowered at him.

Juliet untangled herself from Ethan's muscular arms and surprised D by throwing her arms around him—and kissing him right on the mouth.

The quick peck startled the shit out of him. He and Juliet weren't enemies, but they weren't best buds either. Her fiery nature didn't mesh with his serious one, and most of the time he found her tolerably annoying.

"You need to smile every once in a while," she whispered in his ear. "That scowl of yours is hot as fuck, but damn, D, life is good sometimes."

He swallowed a laugh. Yeah right. Life was *never* good. Sometimes it deceived you into thinking it was, but D knew the world for what it was. A cesspool of evil and violence. A living nightmare.

Though it might be nice to borrow those rose-colored glasses sometime and see what these people saw.

He leaned in, brushing *his* lips against *her* ear. "You hurt him, and I'll fuck you up."

Melodic laughter floated around him as Juliet stepped back into Ethan's waiting arms.

There. He'd wished them well. Time to get the hell out of here.

This time when he stalked off, he made sure to steer clear of Olivia, who was probably plotting a way to force him into socializing or some shit. He climbed up to the terrace in hurried strides, where Liam continued to stand at the railing, watching the festivities with a grimace.

"Look at them," Liam remarked when D came up beside him. "It's like they have no care in the world."

D lit a cigarette and followed Liam's gaze, taking in the same joyous scene. Luke's head bent over Olivia as he kissed her cheek. Abby and Isabel chatting on the far end of the aisle. Cate's dark blue eyes lighting up as she laughed at something the team rookie, Ash, had just told her.

Liam was right. No care in the world.

But another pair of blue eyes, these paler than a glacier, suddenly peered up at the terrace, and D wasn't surprised when Noelle's gaze locked with his. He swore the woman could read his mind.

The look she gave him spoke volumes. He could read her too, read her well, and he knew in that moment that she wasn't part of this happy charade. She was still looking for Sullivan, just like he was, and the slight nod she offered confirmed it.

Liam didn't catch it, though. He was too busy scowling, visibly offended by what he was seeing. "They don't give a shit that he's still out there," he mumbled, and there was no mistaking the pain in his voice. "Christ almighty, D. He's probably being tortured as we speak."

The guilt was back, a dull knife twisting his insides. He almost opened his mouth and told Macgregor about his suspicion that Sullivan had been abducted in his place, but he pressed his lips together to stop the confession from slipping out.

He didn't give a shit what people thought about him, but Liam was looking for someone to blame, and D couldn't afford to be on the man's radar right now. If he alerted his teammate to the fact that he might be responsible for Sullivan's disappearance, Liam wouldn't just hate him—he'd interfere.

D had feelers out. He'd tapped contacts that not even Morgan knew about. He *would* find out what happened to Sullivan, and when he did, he couldn't have Liam screwing up his plans. Macgregor wasn't right in the head. He was acting on impulse and fear, and his desperate need to find their teammate could very well put Sullivan's life at risk.

Unfortunately, D's silence only deepened the darkness in Liam's eyes. "You think he's dead, don't you?"

D looked at the other man, frowning at the hissed accusation. "No. I don't."

Liam's hostility dampened. Slightly. "Then why the fuck aren't you doing anything to find him?"

"Every contact I have is out there looking for him," D said coldly. "Same way your people are looking for him, and Morgan's, and Noelle's. We have nothing to go on, man. We combed every inch of Dublin—hell, Reilly and Bailey are *still* there, talking to anyone who'll listen. Noelle's girl Paige has been poring over every frame of security footage in that city, trying to locate him."

Liam slammed a hand on the railing. "How does someone just *disappear*? Who the fuck *has* him? And don't you dare give me that bullshit about how maybe he took off—Trevor tried selling me that earlier, and I'm not fucking buying it."

Neither was D. Sullivan had always been a nomad, but when he wasn't with the team, there was only one other place he'd be: on his boat. And the damned boat was moored in Portugal, where Sully had left her six months ago before heading to Dublin. D had examined the marina's security footage himself, which clearly showed that Sullivan hadn't stepped foot on his yacht since he'd docked her.

"Why don't they care?" Contempt dripped from Liam's voice as he stared at their colleagues. "Weddings? J.J.'s christening? Cate's graduation? What the hell is wrong with them?"

D laughed harshly. "The world doesn't stop when something bad happens, bro. Life goes on. But that doesn't mean they don't care about him."

"They think he's dead."

"Not all of them."

"Just one is enough. One person gives up and the rest fall like fucking dominoes."

Liam no longer sounded angry, but anguished. Visceral sorrow polluted the air around them, and D suddenly felt like fleeing. *This* was why you didn't get close to people. Liam had been fine before his friendship with Sullivan. Then he'd gone and formed a bond with the man, and now look at him. Hurting. Furious. Pathetic.

D liked his teammates. He respected them. He cared whether they lived or died, and he saved their asses when their asses needed saving. He even showed up for their fucking weddings and graduations. But truly caring about them? Enough to experience genuine grief if they were gone? No, he would never let himself get that close.

Finding Sullivan wasn't about having some deep emotional connection with the man. It was about righting a wrong. D was already going to hell for the sins he'd committed, but damned if he was going to burn for *this*. He refused to have a teammate's death on his conscience.

"You know what? Here." Liam shoved his beer bottle in D's free hand and stumbled away from the steel railing. "Finish this for me. Toast the happy couple. I can't stomach this."

As the other man staggered toward the French doors leading into the kitchen, D decided that Liam had the right idea. Maybe he'd head down to the basement, kill some time in the target range. Normally he preferred the outdoor range on the property, but he doubted the wedding party would appreciate the sound of his rifle going off in the middle of their celebration.

He took a final drag of his smoke, his gaze sweeping over the sprawling compound. The property had once belonged to a drug kingpin, and Morgan had bought it at government auction after their last compound had been compromised. Although the outbuildings, ranges, tunnels, and armory were absolutely to D's liking, the house itself was too damn luxurious. It boasted three floors of posh suites, along with a massive kitchen, a living room right out of a ski chalet, a game room, a theater, and dozens of other extravagances that D didn't give a shit about.

He didn't belong in a place like this, and he often wondered why he stuck around. He could easily live off-site like some of the other men, but for some fucked-up reason, he'd chosen not to.

D stubbed out his cigarette in the glass ashtray on the wrought-iron table, but before he could leave the terrace, his phone buzzed in his pocket.

He pulled it out, frowned at the unknown number, and answered with a brusque "Yeah?"

A raspy voice responded in Spanish. "I hear you're looking for someone."

The caller was male, but D didn't recognize the voice. Switching to Spanish, he barked out, "Who's this?"

"A friend of a friend."

Wrong answer. D didn't have any fucking friends.

"Be more specific," he snapped. "Three seconds, or I hang up."

There was a pause.

"One," D warned.

"The cash you promised Vic," the caller said hastily. His voice was no longer deep and growly, and although there was something familiar about it now, D couldn't place the guy. "I want it."

His eyes narrowed. Vic was one of his informants in Tijuana, a low-life drug dealer D hit up for information every now and then. He'd contacted the dealer a few months ago and promised a nice reward for any intel on Sullivan, but there'd been no word until now.

"Why isn't Vic calling me himself?"

"Because he's dead."

"Bullshit. I would've heard about it. I keep tabs on all my rats."

"He was killed this morning." Another pause. "I'm his brother."

An incredulous laugh popped out. "Jesus, is that you, Tonio?"

"Yes," the teenager admitted guiltily.

Oh, for fuck's sake. He was dealing with *Tonio*? Vic's little brother was a gangly seventeen-year-old, and, like his brother, a member of a two-bit gang that distributed cocaine in Tijuana. Stupid little boys who thought they were big, bad men.

"Where the hell is Vic?" D demanded.

"I told you. He's dead." A note of panic crept into Tonio's voice. "A drug deal went south this morning. He was gunned down by six Diablos Rojos."

Shocker. D had always known that moron Vic would eventually get himself killed.

"What, so now you need some cash to skip town?" D asked with a chuckle. "You thought you could feed me false intel and I'd send you a get-out-of-Tijuana ticket?"

"It's not false intel," Tonio protested. "Vic was going to call you after the deal. He told me so himself."

D frowned. "And you waited this long to get in touch with me?"

"I had no choice. Your number was on one of his burners, and those are all in his apartment. I had to wait for the heat to die down before I came back here. Had to make sure I wasn't being followed."

That gave him pause, because his internal lie detector was telling him the kid was being honest.

"I need that cash, Delta," Tonio pleaded, using the name D's informants knew him by. "Please. Wire it to the place you and Vic use."

"No," he said bluntly. "That's not how Vic and I operated. He gave me the intel, I sent him half. I verified the intel, he got the other half."

"I don't have that kind of time! I've got the entire Diablos Rojos organization gunning for me. Vic fucked them over big-time."

D stifled a sigh and mulled it over. Twenty grand was a huge chunk of change, but it meant nothing to him in the grand scheme of things. And if the intel led to a dead end, at least Tonio would have a chance.

Not that D gave a shit if the kid lived or died. Right now, he just needed a lead. A crumb. *Anything.* Sullivan had been gone for six months, and the ticking clock in

D's head was getting louder and louder the longer Sully stayed off the grid.

"I'll wire the full amount," D told the kid. "But first you cough up the intel."

The line went silent.

"That's my final offer, Tonio."

"All right, I'll tell you. But you've gotta promise to wire the cash the moment we hang up."

"I already said I would. Now, what did Vic find?"

"The guy you're looking for—Australian? Merc, right? Vic heard some whispers about someone fitting that description being taken captive."

D froze. "Who's the source?"

"I don't know. Vic didn't tell me. But you *know* my brother, Delta. He has—" Tonio stuttered, correcting himself. "He *had* eyes and ears everywhere."

Which was one of the reasons D had contacted him. Vic lived in the underbelly of Mexico's crime world. That slimy motherfucker knew everyone.

"Where's the Australian being held?" Although he was speaking Spanish, he still lowered his voice, because half the people currently milling on the lawn spoke the damn language. Hell, Isabel alone was fluent in a dozen languages.

"Isla del Rey," Tonio answered.

The stone floor beneath D's feet swayed.

Shit. Motherfucking *shit*.

So much for putting the past behind him.

Tonio added, "Mendez has him."

With those three words, D knew that if Sullivan wasn't already dead, it was only a matter of time before he would be.

Chapter 4

Six months ago
Isla del Rey, Mexico

He regained consciousness when the boat bumped the dock.

Maybe it was the sudden calmness of the water, the slower speed, the scent of earth and citrus that joined the salty air he'd been breathing for most of the trip. Years of sailing the world and living on his boat for months at a time had trained his senses to recognize every leg of a sea journey, and those senses alerted his subconscious now, drawing him from his sedated slumber to let him know they'd reached their destination.

Sedated.

Jesus Christ. How had he allowed that to happen?

Sullivan Port opened his eyes and blinked against the sudden onslaught of sunshine. When they'd thrown him in the back of that SUV, it had been dark. And rainy. In *Dublin*. But clearly they'd traveled far, far from Dublin since his captors had knocked him out at the hotel.

He tried to move, and it took a second to figure out why his body wasn't cooperating. His arms were yanked behind his back, wrists bound together and tied to the metal barrel he'd been propped up against. His legs were stretched out on the dirty deck of the fishing vessel, his ankles trussed up by a thin cable, just like his wrists.

The duct tape on his mouth rendered talking impossible, but he was able to turn his head, and when he did, he instantly spotted the man from the bar. The man with the neat goatee and dark eyes.

The man who'd abducted him because he thought Sullivan was Derek fucking Pratt.

Sully would've corrected the bloody bastard back in Dublin, but he hadn't been given the chance. The stranger's instructions had been more than clear, buzzing through Sully's head now as he regained his mental faculties.

"Walk out of the bar. Hands visible at all times. Step outside. No sudden movements, no funny business, or my men open fire on everyone in this hotel."

He supposed he could've called the man's bluff, but it had taken no time at all to confirm that the stranger did indeed have backup. Half-a-dozen suit-clad operatives positioned in the lobby, bar, and restaurant, ready to kill anyone unfortunate enough to be awake and roaming the hotel at two thirty in the morning. Granted, the civilian count had been low—six, maybe seven folks—but Sullivan hadn't wanted to risk it.

He'd figured he could neutralize the situation once he got outside and the civilians were out of harm's way, but he hadn't accounted for the needle. The shadow that appeared from nowhere and injected a tranquilizer into his bloodstream.

At least twelve hours must have passed since then, judging by the fact he was on a body of water that was most certainly *not* the English Channel, approaching an island that looked far too tropical for the UK.

If he had to hazard a guess, he'd say they were in Mexico, Latin America maybe. And with the time difference, that meant it was nine in the morning, maybe later.

The island wasn't huge. Just a flash of green on a backdrop of blue. Thick vegetation took up the far end, but the area surrounding the marina had been cleared away. It had a military feel to it, thanks to the tall guard towers and concrete airstrip a hundred yards from the dock. A gleaming white jet sat on the tarmac, along with a handful of smaller aircraft, including a military-grade Chinook helicopter.

Christ. What had he gotten himself into?

Or, rather, what had *D* gotten him into?

"Cut him loose," a voice said.

"Yes, sir."

The men were speaking Spanish, and it took Sully's foggy brain a moment to snap into translation mode.

A man with a shaved head appeared in front of him, a hunting knife in his hand. He reached behind Sullivan and slashed at the rope securing him to the barrel.

Sullivan sagged forward, then found himself being hauled to his feet as the man knelt down and sliced the cable around his ankles. Blood flow rapidly returned, making his legs tingle. He didn't give in to the urge to drop-kick anyone. There were six men on the boat, and in his loopy state, he wasn't sure he could take them all without getting a bullet in his head.

Bloody hell, that sedative had knocked him out for longer than he was comfortable with. He had no idea where he was or who he was dealing with. An enemy of D's, obviously. But who? Derek Pratt was a bloody enigma wrapped in a riddle. Sully knew nothing about D's past except that he'd been Delta at one point.

But these men weren't US military, and they definitely weren't on American soil right now.

He squinted in the sunshine, tensing when he glimpsed an olive-green Jeep with the top down approaching the far end of the dock. Shit. He needed a game plan.

Rough hands dragged him to the starboard side, where his goateed abductor had already hopped off the boat. From the dock, Goatee Asshole reached down and grabbed Sullivan's wrists.

"Off the boat," he snapped in English.

Sully stepped off the vessel, experiencing a rush of vertigo when his feet met solid ground. He blinked through the dizziness and conducted a quick sweep of the marina. His heart sank when he finished his security assessment. Four guards with assault rifles in each of the three towers. Six more positioned on the outskirts of the harbor. Several more in the cargo area.

He was on fucking Alcatraz.

As his worry heightened, he glanced at his wrists and discovered they were bare. His watch was gone. He hadn't been able to activate his tracking SOS at the hotel before the men had knocked him out, and clearly they'd stripped him of all electronics when he'd been unconscious.

A cloud of exhaust wafted toward him as the Jeep stopped at the end of the dock. Goatee Asshole promptly gripped his arm and barked, "Walk."

The entire walk down the dock, Sullivan kept his eyes on the Jeep. The man sliding out of the driver's seat was clearly a hired thug in a muscle shirt and fatigues, with a pistol aimed at the new arrivals.

The man leaving the passenger's seat was the one in charge. His attire was casual—khakis and a white polo shirt—and his bronzed skin had the leathery look of too many years spent in the sun. His face was clean-shaven, but his bare arms were hairy as fuck, and he had a thick mass of it on his head, too. Despite his country-club appearance, he was very obviously the boss. Commanding stride, hard expression, air of power and entitlement.

Sullivan had never seen him before in his life.

The sweet scent of tobacco replaced the odor of car exhaust, drawing Sully to the fact that the man was smoking a cigar.

"You don't say a word—you understand me?" Goatee Asshole hissed as the two men approached.

Sullivan rolled his eyes. He was gagged. How the fuck was he supposed to speak?

"Javier," the man with the cigar boomed, his tone not at all receptive. Dark, menacing eyes studied Sullivan before narrowing at the goateed man.

"Mr. Mendez," the other man—Javier—stammered. "Thank you for granting me an audience."

The smooth operative Sullivan had encountered in the hotel bar had transformed into a stuttering, panicky mess. Which made no sense, because Javier was a pro. Former military, if Sullivan had to guess. Maybe a mercenary, definitely an independent contractor. And his team was equally skilled, as they'd proven back in Dublin.

So why were they all so terrified of a man who'd shown up to a meeting with one measly bodyguard? There were five armed men on the fishing boat and Javier himself was armed, yet not a single man drew his weapon. Not a single man moved.

"You said this visit is regarding the Pratt job?" Mendez sounded impatient.

"It is." Javier gestured to Sullivan. "I found him."

There was a beat of silence.

"All right. And who is *this* man?" Mendez, now looking annoyed, raised the cigar to his mouth and took a puff.

"Derek Pratt."

The older man laughed, deep and hearty. "That's not Derek Pratt."

Javier blinked. Again and again. He looked at Sullivan, then Mendez, then Sullivan again, his gaze moving like a Ping-Pong ball between the two men. It would have even been comical if Sullivan weren't seconds away from getting killed. Because whoever this Mendez was, he'd wanted D, not Sully. And now that Sully's captors had brought Mendez the wrong man, Mendez would have no use for him.

Bloody hell.

"That was the name he was going by," Javier blurted

out, speaking so fast—and in Spanish—that it was difficult for Sully to keep up. "I've been tracking Pratt since you posted the bounty, and after months of dead ends, he finally turned up. A hotel room in Dublin was booked under his name." He glowered at Sullivan. "This man used Pratt's name in the bar. When I questioned him, he claimed to be Derek Pratt."

Interest flashed in Mendez's eyes. "Is that so?" He scrutinized Sullivan for a moment, then turned back to Javier. "What else did he tell you?"

"Nothing, sir. Just his name. We kept him sedated during the trip here, and he only regained consciousness ten minutes ago."

"I see." Mendez puffed on the cigar, blowing out a cloud of smoke before glancing at his thug. "The gag."

Without warning, the thug stepped forward and ripped the duct tape off Sullivan's mouth. As the warm air met his dry lips, Sully moistened them with his tongue, his gaze fixed on Mendez.

"Well, I know who you're *not*," Mendez said in English, a pleasant smile on his face. "So why don't you tell me who you *are*?"

Sullivan didn't answer. He'd been trained by the Australian Army, special ops. He wasn't saying a goddamn word.

"I'm telling you, he was using the name Pratt," Javier insisted.

"Jesus Christ, are you fucking deaf?" Mendez snapped. "This isn't Pratt."

"Well, then he knows Pratt! The hotel room in Pratt's name—there were two occupants in it. And this man knew the room number. He charged a drink to it. He *knows* Pratt."

Mendez frowned at Sullivan. "Who are you?"

He stared back and said nothing.

With a sigh, the man in charge addressed his thug. "Paulo, please give Javier his reward."

As the bodyguard reached into his back pocket, Sullivan didn't miss the flicker of horror that flashed in Javier's eyes. When Paulo's hand emerged with nothing more than a fat manila envelope, Javier released an audible breath of relief.

Before the guard could hand over the envelope, Mendez intercepted his hand. "Wait." He reached inside and removed four stacks of crisp American bills.

Sullivan studied the amount stenciled on the bands wrapped around the money. Twenty-five thousand. Mendez had just relieved the envelope of a hundred grand.

Smiling, the man in charge held out the envelope.

"You said two hundred thousand," Javier said petulantly.

"No, I said two hundred thousand to anyone who brings me Pratt, and one hundred for anyone who brings me information about Pratt. You did the latter." Mendez eyed the man as if waiting for him to challenge that.

Javier visibly gulped. Then he nodded. "Thank you, sir."

"It was a pleasure doing business with you, Javier." Mendez's jaw tightened. "Time to go now."

Sully's former captor didn't waste time. Didn't even spare Sullivan a backward glance as he bounded down the long dock toward the fishing boat.

The moment Javier was out of sight, Mendez gave Sullivan a thorough once-over, taking in every detail. The olive green cargo pants, the white T-shirt streaked in dirt, the scuffed black boots.

"Who are you?" he asked again.

Sullivan didn't answer.

"I see. You're planning on being difficult." Mendez smiled. "That's all right. We have ways of dealing with that."

The thug lumbered forward and curled a hand around Sullivan's upper arm. "The workshop or the dungeon?" he asked his boss.

Mendez paused. He seemed to be deep in thought, and when he finally spoke, it was as if Sullivan wasn't even there. "He's a soldier. American, maybe European. Level of skill unknown. I don't want to waste time in the workshop if he's black ops." His features hardened as he looked at Sullivan. "Here's what's going to happen, friend. Either you tell me who you are right now or my man will break each of your fingers, one by one."

Sullivan stared straight ahead.

"Paulo," Mendez commanded.

Smirking, the thug placed a hand on Sullivan's bound wrists and pried his left pinkie about an inch from his fourth finger.

"Are you sure you don't want to introduce yourself?" Paulo asked.

Sullivan realized the man was actually quite handsome. Tall and lean, with cropped dark hair and skin a lighter shade of brown than Mendez's. The emptiness in his brown eyes, however, revealed him to be a stone-cold killer.

When Sullivan remained quiet, Paulo gave a sharp twist and broke Sully's pinkie.

A jolt of pain traveled from his finger and up his arm, but Sullivan didn't even flinch.

"Highly skilled," Mendez said with a nod, as if confirming it to himself. Then he stepped forward and brought his cigar to Sullivan's left arm. The glowing tip hovered right above the skin.

The same skin that had been hit with shrapnel from a bomb in Dublin a few days ago. The same arm that now boasted a neat row of horseshoe-shaped stitches, courtesy of Liam Macgregor.

Heat radiated against his biceps, and Sully drew a breath in preparation. Damn that bloody Derek Pratt to hell. Who the fuck were these people?

"Who are you?" Mendez voiced what Sully had been thinking about him.

He clenched his teeth, steeling himself against what was bound to be a very painful—

The scorching end of the cigar touched the center of the shrapnel wound.

Bloody *hell*. Red-hot pain shot through Sullivan's arm, the stench of burnt flesh rising into his nostrils and bringing a gush of nausea to his throat.

On the surface, he stayed still. Calm.

His jaw ached from the tight clench of his teeth. His arm was on fire.

But he continued to stare straight ahead.

"The workshop will be wasted on him," Mendez announced.

The man lifted the cigar, leaving behind a circle of

oozing red flesh. Then he tossed the cigar into the water lapping against the dock and barked an order at his thug.

"Take him to the dungeon. We'll get started on him tonight."

Chapter 5

Present day

The moonlight guided his way through the rainforest. The silver beams slicing through the canopy of trees were faint, mere shadows even, but after months of darkness, it was like a spotlight blasting him in the face.

His pupils couldn't handle it. His arms and legs weren't working right, either. He was a big man—six three and more than two hundred pounds—but he felt like a gangly teenager as he stumbled forward.

One foot in front of the other. He could do this. He *could*.

Twigs and dirt and pebbles pricked the soles of his feet. He wasn't wearing shoes. But at least he had pants. A shirt. It was a relief, because he'd been naked for most of his imprisonment. Especially when . . . when *she* came. She'd wanted him naked.

One of the guards had taken pity on him and dressed him last night because the temperature had dropped and the window in his cell didn't protect him from the elements. No windowpane, just iron bars letting in the cold, making him shiver as the ocean breeze cooled his skin.

But that breeze was helping him now. His limbs might not be working at the moment, but his nose did. His nose smelled the salt. The ocean. He needed to find the water. It was the only fucking way off this hellhole.

One foot in front of the other—

Sullivan tripped over his own feet. He fell forward, landing in a tangle of undergrowth that scratched his bare arms. His brain became foggy again as he lay on the jungle floor. He knew he should be concentrating on something. The shore. The ocean . . . a boat. Right. Yes. Even if he made it to the water, he would need a boat.

There wouldn't be one. He'd be stranded and they'd find him and they'd drag him back to the cell and give him more drugs and—

His breaths flew out in panicky pants. No, he couldn't let them start the new cycle. The drugs were almost out of his system. He could *feel* them leaving his system. Yesterday had been bad. The day before that had been worse. He'd spent those days curled up on the floor of his cell, every muscle in his body screaming with agony. It was better now. Today was better.

His teeth chattered as shivers raced up and down his spine and goose bumps rose on his skin. Fuck, he had to stand up. If he didn't get up, they would find him.

Breathing hard, he forced his knees to bend, his legs to straighten. He was on his feet again. Christ, when was the last time he'd eaten? Mendez's people had made sure to feed him. To give him water. Just enough food, just enough water. So he wouldn't die of starvation or dehydration. But he wasn't able to eat during the with-drawal. He hadn't eaten since the withdrawal.

The boat.

For the love of Christ, he needed to focus on the boat. Where was the marina?

No, not the marina. He couldn't go there. The guards in the towers would see him.

Lord, he didn't even know which side of the island he was on. He hadn't stopped to orient himself when he'd escaped his cell. When he'd realized the guard's mistake.

A fluke. Six months of hell, and his freedom was the result of a fluke. Screams from the neighboring cell had caused his guard to run out. There'd been shouts, a gun-shot, then nothing but the whimpers of the girl in the other cell.

The key hadn't turned in the lock.

Sullivan had heard that key turn hundreds of times these past six months, but tonight it hadn't. His guard had forgotten to lock him up. He'd waited an hour. A whole hour, sitting there, waiting for the guard to real-ize his mistake.

But the door had stayed unlocked.

The details of his escape spun through his mind. Stepping into the hall. Getting blinded by the fluores-cent light. The dead guard on the cement floor. There'd been too much to register, too much stimuli after months of darkness and silence.

The girl's whimpers ran on a loop in his head, bring-ing another rush of sickness. He'd checked her cell. It had been locked, and he couldn't break down a steel door. Hell, even if it had been made of straw he wouldn't have had the strength to break it down. So he fled. He hadn't tried to help her. He wouldn't have been able to help her. He didn't have a weapon. Strength. Nothing.

He'd fled.

But he would send help for her. He *would*.

The queasiness transformed into gut-wrenching nausea that brought him to his knees again. His eyes watered as he leaned forward and vomited all over the jungle floor. His stomach contracted. It hurt. Everything fucking hurt.

Keep walking. Southwest.

The voice ordered him to move. He'd heard it when he'd left the prison, but he wasn't sure if it was *his* voice or someone else's. But maybe it didn't matter whose voice it was, because it rang with certainty. It told him to go southwest.

Minutes or hours later, he emerged from the trees, shoving palm fronds aside with his hands. He hissed when he glimpsed the ocean. A skinny wooden dock extended from the sand to the dark, calm water, four white motorboats moored on either side of it. The soldier in him said there were probably slips like these all over the island, escape routes for the monsters who lived here.

Another wave of shivers racked his body. His abdomen spasmed hard, but he breathed through the pain. Ordered himself to focus.

Then he stumbled toward the dock.

Wilmington, Delaware

"Is it done?" Pacing the gleaming parquet in his office, Edward Bryant absently brought his bourbon glass to his lips. The ice cubes clicked together as he took a sip, but he barely heard the sound they made. All his attention was focused on the phone sitting atop his mahogany desk.

An answering voice slid out of the speakerphone, offering the first piece of good news Bryant had heard in months.

"Affirmative, sir. He's gone."

"Good." A frown puckered his brow. "You planted a tracker?"

"Negative. He would have found it. Even if I implanted it under the skin, the guy's a pro. He would have taken it out with his own teeth if needed."

Either Bryant was imagining it or that was genuine admiration in his operative's voice. "But we've got eyes on him?"

"Affirmative. The team you dispatched already confirmed they have a visual. He won't be able to make a single move without alerting them. I assume from this point on you'll be dealing with them directly?"

"Yes. But I want you to continue checking in as scheduled. Alert me of any moves Mendez makes."

"When will I be extracted?"

"When the prisoner leads us to Pratt," Bryant snapped. "And no sooner."

The line fell silent.

"That was the deal you agreed to," he reminded the agent. "And that is the deal you're getting."

Bryant jammed his finger on the END button and drained the rest of his bourbon. Fucking operatives. It was like dealing with children sometimes. *Send backup. Extract me. Hold my hand.*

Boo-fucking-hoo.

When he'd founded Smith Group, he'd thought he was gathering the deadliest men on the globe. Qualified men, ruthless men. Men with grit and instincts. And most of them were, yes. But others . . . Freddie Jones, for example . . . Well, everything was peachy keen until you ordered them to do something that made their little tummies hurt, and suddenly they were goddamn crybabies.

Not Derek, though. Lord, that boy had been the best operative Bryant had ever employed. No matter the order, Derek had gotten the job done. Nothing was off-limits. Nothing was over the line.

And the ungrateful little shit had walked away from him.

Operatives didn't leave the Smith Group. Derek had known that. He'd signed away his life when he'd joined the agency, and Bryant would be damned if he let the bastard go unpunished for his treason.

Bryant settled in his desk chair and stared at the closed oak doors of his office. He could practically taste the victory. The vengeance.

After nine years, Derek was finally back on the grid— and the prisoner would lead Bryant right to him.

Chapter 6

D packed in a hurry, all the while wondering how he would make it out of the compound without anyone noticing or cross-examining him. Too many people lived here, damn it. It made him miss the days when he'd lived alone.

After he finished tossing gear into his go bag, he slung the duffel strap over his shoulder and swiped his trusty HK off the bed. He'd grab the bigger guns once he reached Mexico, but he felt naked without his pistol, so that he tucked under his waistband on his way out the door.

There was only one person he was interested in talking to before he left, but everyone was still out back, toasting to the newlyweds. Sighing, he pulled out his phone and texted the boss, telling Morgan to meet him in the tunnel. There'd be too many questions if he left through the gate.

Mendez.

The name continued to darken his mind like a thundercloud, and he quickened his strides as he hurried downstairs.

Jesus. Mendez had Sullivan.

The team had run dozens of scenarios about who could've nabbed Sully. Old enemies. Former clients. They'd even investigated a few special-ops soldiers Sully had had run-ins with during his stint in the Australian army. It hadn't occurred to anyone, D included, that the most powerful sex trafficker in the Western Hemisphere was the one responsible for their missing teammate.

How the hell had Mendez made a move without D's knowledge? D had kept tabs on the bastard ever since Smith Group had shut down, and he hadn't heard even a whisper that Mendez had figured out the alias he was using. But the name Derek Pratt had raised a red flag in Dublin, which meant Mendez knew its significance— otherwise he wouldn't have snagged Sullivan.

Despite the urgency tightening his gut, D couldn't help a smug chuckle. Mendez must have thrown a hell of a hissy fit when he'd realized the man his goons had brought him wasn't the one he'd been hunting all these years.

The humor faded fast, though, because it was damn lucky Mendez hadn't killed Sully on the spot. Or hell, maybe he had.

No. He wouldn't have. Mendez was smart. He recognized the value of having a live victim to interrogate instead of a dead man to bury.

D didn't even want to think about all the ways Sullivan had been suffering at those sadistic hands.

He was rummaging through a cabinet in the armory in search of extra clips when footsteps echoed in the cavernous concrete tunnel. A moment later, Morgan appeared, exactly three minutes after D had texted.

"What's going on?"

D shoved the spare ammo in his bag. "I've got something I need to take care of. I wanted to give you the heads-up that I'm taking off."

Morgan paused, then asked the question D had been expecting. "Sully?"

He shook his head. "Some personal shit came up."

The boss's dark blue eyes narrowed, probing D's face, but D had been a professional liar for most of his career. He'd been trained by both Delta and Smith, and trained well. Not even Jim Morgan, a man who could read any person he came across, was immune to D's considerable talents.

The trick was to sprinkle the truth into the lie. Just a few morsels, just enough so the person you were lying to could draw his own conclusions.

"An old friend got in touch," D said, because that was the truth. An old friend *had* gotten in touch. "Mr. Smith," he added, and that was the lie.

He could see Morgan quickly doing the math. The boss was one of the few people who was aware of D's background. The others knew he'd worked black ops, but didn't know the name of the agency, so while other people wouldn't even blink at the name Mr. Smith, Morgan immediately understood what it meant.

"Shit. You need backup?"

"Nah. I don't want to drag anyone else into this." D shrugged. "Actually, there's nothing to drag them into. It's a simple matter of tying up a loose end."

Morgan nodded. "Are you taking the jet?"

"No, I'll take one of the Cessnas. I'm not going far."

Even if he was, he still wouldn't take the jet, which was on standby at Morgan's private airfield outside of Turtle Creek, the town nearest to the compound. It made more sense to take one of the smaller aircraft in the hangar—he could fly those fuckers himself and avoid dealing with questions from their pilot, Sam.

"Keep your cell on you," Morgan ordered. "And send an SOS if you need us."

"Roger."

As the boss stalked off, D released a breath heavy with relief. Nice. That had gone easier than he'd anticipated.

He locked the armory and stepped into the corridor, following the fluorescent-lit space to the massive garage where the Humvees were stashed. He'd just hit the button to open the mechanical door at the tunnel's entrance when footsteps sounded again.

D stifled a curse when Liam marched into the garage.

Fuck. So much for easy.

"Where are you going?" Liam spoke sharply, forgoing any preamble.

"I have some business to take care of," he said coolly.

Liam searched his face. "You're going after Sullivan."

"No. It's a personal matter."

"Bullshit. You've got no family, no friends. There's no such thing as *personal* in your life."

"I told you, it's business. Personal fucking business. I had a life before I joined the team, all right? Not everything I do involves you assholes."

Liam advanced on him with military precision. "If you're going after Sullivan, I'm coming with you."

"I'm not going after Sullivan." D set his jaw. "Like I

told you before, I've got people looking for him. If they call, I'll let you know."

He headed for the driver's door, but Liam intercepted him, his hand moving at lightning speed toward the door handle to prevent D from opening it.

"Get the fuck out of my way," D said coldly. "I promise you, you don't want to do this right now."

"Do what? Find my best friend?"

"No, find my fist in your jaw. Because I'll fucking do it. I'll beat the shit out of you if you don't get out of my way."

Liam didn't move his hand.

"This has nothing to do with Sullivan." Frustration bubbled in his throat. "A ghost from my past is causing some trouble. I need to take care of it."

Liam eyed him uneasily. "I . . . don't believe you."

"Yeah, well, I don't give a fuck. I have to go." D struck like a rattlesnake, giving Liam's wrist a sharp twist and forcibly shoving it off the door.

Blue eyes blazed angrily at him, but D didn't care that his teammate was pissed. He didn't care that his teammate was *right*. Damned if he'd bring Liam along. The guy had gotten so out of control he'd needed to be benched, for fuck's sake. D refused to put him in the field again and possibly risk Sullivan's life.

"Look, talk to Morgan if you don't believe me," D muttered. "Tell him I give him permission to explain to you who I used to work for. Maybe that'll shut you up." He opened the Humvee door and threw his bag into the passenger's side. "Now go get some fucking sleep, Liam. You look like shit."

Before Liam could object, D slid into the driver's seat

and slammed the door. For good measure, he hit the power locks in case his teammate tried anything stupid. But the other man just backed away from the vehicle, arms tight across his chest as he glowered at D through the windshield.

Ignoring the contempt being aimed his way, D started the engine and sped out of the tunnel, leaving his angry teammate in the rearview mirror.

The terrain was bumpy on this side of the property, so he waited until he'd cleared the rocky hillside before reaching for his phone. His first call was to the airfield, ordering Morgan's pilot to gas up one of the planes. His second call went to his guy in Cancún, to arrange for a car to meet him when he landed.

The third call . . . it was to a number he hadn't used in years. He knew it was in service, though—he always made sure his contact numbers were up-to-date, no matter how much time had passed since he'd used them. It had been nine years since he'd dialed this particular number, and when a familiar male voice slid into his ear, D's shoulders went stiffer than boards.

"It's Jason," he rasped, the name burning his tongue as it left his mouth.

A hiss of shock filled the extension. "Is this a fucking joke?" was the answering sputter.

"Did you ever know me to joke?" D gritted his teeth. "Look. How about we skip the bullshit and hellos and where've-you-beens? I'll be in the neighborhood soon. We need to meet."

His former colleague was smart enough not to argue, because the man knew from experience what happened when you argued with Jason.

After a short silence, the caller said, "When and where?"

Doctors made the worst patients. Sofia hadn't thought the old saying applied to her, but that morning she discovered it absolutely did.

The nurse had left Sofia's chart on the desk. Other patients would have kept their hands to themselves and waited for the doctor to come in and go over the results with them. Sofia wasn't other patients.

The second the door closed behind the nurse, she snatched up the thin folder and popped it open.

Relief swept through her as she skimmed the first page. Gastroparesis had been ruled out, thank God. No intestinal problems. Nothing bacterial. Not the flu, but she'd already known that.

Since her only symptoms were nausea and vomiting, the first thing she'd done this week was take a pregnancy test, but it had come back negative. That was when the worrying *really* started. Worst-case scenarios had flashed through her head like scenes from one of those medical-anomalies reality shows. She'd envisioned all sorts of gory stomach conditions that had scared her enough to drive to the hospital in Oaxaca and get tests done.

She flipped to the next page and studied the lab results. Blood work looked good. No signs of—

She sucked in a breath.

What the *fuck*?

But . . .

The door swung open before she could make sense of what she was seeing. Sofia hurriedly closed the folder, but didn't manage to set it on the desk in time.

"Caught red-handed, Dr. Amaro." The silver-haired doctor held out her hand, wearing the expression of a schoolmarm about to slap a pupil's wrist with a ruler.

"The results are wrong," Sofia blurted out.

Dr. Bella Torres took the folder from Sofia's guilty hands, the corners of her mouth crinkling as she smiled. Although the doctor was more than twenty years older than Sofia, the two women were good friends. Sofia had referred many patients to Bella, who was a specialist at the hospital.

"Mmm-hmm," Bella mused, her smile widening. "The blood tests, the ultrasounds—they're all wrong, huh?"

Sofia bit her lip.

The woman's tone softened. "I see that this is a shock for you, but the results don't lie, Sofia. You're pregnant."

She ignored the panic shooting up her spine. "I took a test when the nausea started. It was negative."

"Well, *those* results were wrong." Chuckling, Bella consulted the chart. "According to this, you're eight weeks along."

Another protest rose. "I got my period. Twice. At the time it was supposed to come!"

"You know as well as I do that women can experience light bleeding during pregnancy, especially in the early stages. And if it occurs at the time you're expecting your period, it's easy to mistake it as such." The doctor's eyes narrowed in concern. "How heavy was the bleeding?"

"Not heavy at all. But I've always had light periods."

"Was it lighter than usual?"

"Yes, but—"

"But nothing. It wasn't your period." Bella set down the chart. "Are you experiencing any bleeding now?"

"No."

"Spotting?"

"No." It had stopped since her last "period."

God. How could this have happened? She'd peed on that stick only because she'd needed to rule out every possibility, and when the minus sign had appeared in the plastic window, it hadn't surprised her in the slightest, because she truly hadn't believed she was pregnant. They'd used a condom, damn it. And she was on the pill.

A hysterical laugh flew out. "*Two* methods of birth control and they both failed me. What are the odds?"

Unless . . . had the condom broken? D had been the one to dispose of it, and Sofia had taken out the garbage the next day without thinking to check it. But he would have told her if the condom broke, right?

Maybe he hadn't noticed?

Bella's tone went gentle again. "Do you know who the father is?"

If a stranger had asked her that, she might have bristled, but she'd known Bella for five years and considered her a friend. So she nodded.

"Okay." Bella paused. "Well, first things first. We're taking you off the pill. And I want you to go in for another ultrasound. If you plan on letting the pregnancy progress—"

"I do."

The swift response startled her. Sofia had barely had five minutes to absorb the news, but the second Bella voiced the word *if*, she knew there was no if about it. She was thirty years old. She was healthy. She had the financial means to support herself and a baby.

And she wasn't about to terminate the pregnancy just because . . . well, because the father was the scariest man she'd ever met in her life.

Jesus.

Derek Pratt was the father of her baby.

Panic clamped around her throat, making it impossible to talk. Bella was still talking, though. About ultrasounds and prenatal vitamins and—

"Stop," Sofia interrupted. She swallowed through the tightness in her throat. "Do you mind giving me a minute?"

Concern filled the doctor's eyes. "Sofia—"

"Please, I need to be alone for a minute. To let this sink in."

Despite the reluctance creasing her forehead, Bella nodded. "All right. I'll check in on my next patient and come back when I'm done."

"Thank you."

The moment Bella left the room, Sofia's heart rate doubled. Tripled. Her pulse drummed frantically in her ears, and the lump in her throat became massive. Suffocating.

She was pregnant. All thanks to a one-night stand with a hardened mercenary who she only saw a few times a year when he showed up with a new bullet hole in his body.

Not exactly Daddy of the Year material, was he?

Desperation weakened her hands, making them tremble. She could keep it from him. D didn't have to know about the baby. She could keep it a secret and—

Yeah, right. As long as Jim Morgan funded her clinic, his men would need to be patched up, which meant she was bound to run into D again. Maybe when she was seven months pregnant. Maybe when the baby was already born. He'd see her belly, or worse, he'd see the baby, and he'd wonder. No, he'd *know*. The bastard knew everything.

Sofia drew a shaky breath. Okay. She had to tell him, then.

And then what? They weren't in love. Hell, she wasn't sure Derek Pratt was even capable of loving a woman.

But was he capable of loving a child?

Did she want him in her child's life?

He lived a dangerous life—how could she trust him with her child's safety?

Her strangled groan echoed in the empty examination room. God, she needed to think, but her brain was on the verge of shutting down. Too many questions were racing through her mind. Too many decisions.

Sofia buried her face in her hands, breathing hard as her jumbled mind was finally reduced to only one thought.

Fuck.

Chapter 7

Cancún, Mexico

He hated this city. The crowds, the tourists, the bars. So many damn bars, packed to the rafters with college-age assholes who never failed to annoy him. Girls in so little clothing they may as well be naked. Dudes wearing T-shirts with idiotic sayings decaled on the front.

It was D's idea of hell, and being there brought back memories of all the unwanted time he'd spent in tourist traps like these. Cancún, Cabo, Cozumel, Puerto Vallarta—they all offered a plethora of stupid, drunken targets.

Mendez's MO had never been all that original. The man's organization specialized in kidnapping tourists and shipping them to Asia. His foot soldiers brought him the girls, and Mendez took care of the rest. For a short time, D had been one of those foot soldiers.

He scowled as he stood outside the bar. It boasted a bright yellow sign featuring a frog wearing a red crown. Christ, the last thing he wanted to do was walk in there.

He'd arrived in Cancún late last night, and this

morning and afternoon had been spent making calls
and preparations. His first order of business had been
arranging for a safe house. He hadn't wanted to use any
of Morgan's usual places or ones linked to his own
aliases, so finding a new place, totally off the books, had
taken some time. After that, he'd gathered the supplies
he'd needed, made some more calls, and tailed his target for six straight hours.

Now it was time to finish the job.

When he walked inside, the bar was packed with
warm, sweaty bodies, the overpowering stench of perfume, sweat, and alcohol permeating the air. D strode
up to the counter and ordered a Corona.

He'd cased the area ahead of time and cleared it of
threats, but he was armed and alert as he turned to study
the crowd. He couldn't lower his guard, couldn't be certain Caruso wouldn't betray him. But he was probably
being paranoid. Caruso would be stupid to cross Jason.
When D had helped the former federal agent disappear,
the only compensation he'd demanded was that Caruso
keep tabs on the Mendez family. For nine years Caruso
had been doing just that, and in exchange D made sure
the Feds stayed off the guy's trail. One phone call, and
Caruso's superiors would have his location—the man
would be a fool to take that risk.

Beer bottle in hand, D leaned against the counter
and did another sweep of the bar.

And there she was.

As his gaze collided with the dark-haired bombshell
across the room, he suddenly felt like he'd stepped into
a time machine. He was twenty-four again. Christ, he

almost expected to look over and find Gael standing beside him.

"Hola, *papi*." A young woman with huge tits and glassy eyes sashayed up to him. "You wanna get outta here and fuck me?"

D arched a brow. Shit, chicks were a lot less coy these days. They used to at least ask him to buy them a drink first, flirt a little before they offered to spread their legs. This one wasn't a whore, though—she lacked the trashiness of the whores that serviced this area. Not a tourist either. Which meant she was a local, and stoned out of her mind, from the looks of it.

"No," he said coldly.

She opened her mouth as if to argue, but it snapped shut when she saw the look in his eyes. Then she stumbled off without another word.

D kept his gaze trained on his prey. Angelina Mendez. The bitch hadn't aged. She'd be twenty-eight now but didn't look a day over twenty, and the youthful, carefree vibe she emitted had her fitting right in with the college crowd.

She was at a tall standing table surrounded by a dozen or so kids. More males then females, but Angelina seemed far more interested in the girls. Giggling with them, asking them questions, clinking her shot glass against theirs.

His jaw tightened. She was on duty tonight. Still working for the family business, then.

D knew the drill, remembered it as if it was yesterday. Chat 'em up. Find out where they were from, who their families were. Rich girls needed to be avoided, because their parents would stop at no expense to find their trust-fund brats. Middle-class or poor girls were preferred, as long as they didn't hail from big families. The ideal targets were loners, girls on the outs with their folks, women estranged from their loved ones. Those were the ones nobody ever looked for.

His chest was tight as he watched Angelina work. Her long throat tipped back as she downed a tequila shot with both her hands behind her back. The group cheered, and she wore a goofy grin as she accepted the high fives from the boys in the group. Her eyes shone like black diamonds, her body exuding the kind of sexuality that drew every male gaze in the room to her.

She'd always been better at the job than her brother. Sexy but sweet, wild but fun. Something about her made people hand over their trust like mints.

Gael, on the other hand . . . People had looked at him and seen a fuck-up, a nineteen-year-old punk with a hint of sadism beneath the surface. The girls hadn't trusted him, and they'd been right not to, because Gael Mendez had been a slimy motherfucker. A coke addict. A rapist. A sick fuck.

D would happily kill him all over again if he could.

It was ironic, though. The one time D had done the right thing, and it had caused all sorts of *wrong*. He didn't regret putting that bullet in Gael's brain, but the fallout had been a pain in the ass. He'd gone off script, and because of that, he'd made an enemy out of Mendez, out of his handler. He'd pulled that trigger, and life as he'd known it had ceased to exist.

Fighting his annoyance, he shoved the memories aside and forced himself to concentrate. Gael was dead, but Angelina was very much alive, holding court among those laughing, intoxicated girls who were oblivious to her sinister motives.

D was standing at the bar in plain sight, yet her gaze didn't once travel in his direction, and that made him want to chuckle. He could just imagine her horror if she spotted him. Hell, he almost willed her to look his way so he could see her reaction, but Angelina was wholly immersed in her task.

That had always been her problem—tunnel vision. She wasn't aware of her surroundings. She focused on one person, one task, and remained oblivious to the rest. It didn't surprise him that her instincts hadn't been honed in the nine years since he'd seen her. Angelina would always be the most self-absorbed woman he'd ever known.

D watched. Waited. He scanned the group, wondering which female had been targeted. The blonde with the pigtails, maybe. Or the one in the tube top. The Mendez organization went after blondes—the Asian market loved them. Redheads too, but not as much as the blondes.

He sipped his beer, battling a rush of impatience. Angelina remained oblivious to his presence, still focused on charming her new "friends."

Nearly forty minutes passed before she finally whispered something to one of the girls and excused herself from the table.

Her curvy body swaying through the crowd drew much attention, but it did nothing for D. He'd once dug his fingers into that round ass. Squeezed those big tits. Kissed those pouty lips. But it had been a job, a tool to get close to Mendez. He'd used Angelina as skillfully as he'd used her brother.

Across the room, Angelina headed for the corridor leading to the restrooms. D set down his bottle and made his move.

At first he was jostled left and right, but people began stepping out of his way once they noticed him. He knew he was a scary motherfucker. The tats. The scowl. Isabel and Juliet teased him that he needed to smile more often, claiming he had a million-dollar smile, but in his world, there wasn't much to smile about. He was fully aware that he was attractive, but that was simply another weapon in his arsenal.

A long line stretched out from the ladies'-room door. D could see Angelina only in profile, but the pout of her lips was unmistakable. The little princess wasn't happy about waiting in line, and for one brief moment, he glimpsed the real Angelina behind the college-girl facade. The spoiled bitch, the daddy's girl who'd do anything to please Raoul Mendez. Unfortunately for her, Mendez had only had eyes for his pride and joy—Gael.

Angelina, Gael's twin, had been an afterthought to Mendez, and D had happily exploited that as well.

She was engrossed in her cell phone as she stood at the end of the line, texting something on the keypad. Her lack of awareness only aided D's cause.

He reached into his waistband and extracted his HK, palming it against his thigh as he entered the corridor. A moment later, he stood directly beside her, yanking the phone out of her hand in one swift move.

"Hey—" Her outraged shout died abruptly when she felt the muzzle of his gun jam into her lower back. She was smart enough to know what that meant, and she froze on the spot.

"Not a word," D rasped as he tucked her phone in his back pocket. "You're going to follow me now. And you're going to keep your mouth shut."

Her head whipped up in shock.

"Jason?" she breathed.

"Not another word," he snapped. "Not here."

She still looked dumbfounded. Horrified. But her rosebud lips pressed shut as he used the barrel of his gun to nudge her forward.

She started to move, her gaze glued to his profile as they walked to the end of the hall and turned right. They passed two staff members on their way to the rear exit, but D ignored their startled exclamations and kept moving.

He was surprised Angelina hadn't put up more of a fight. He would've been happy to knock her out. Preferred it, even. But the woman remained silent. Obedient.

Only when they stepped into the alley behind the bar did she begin to struggle.

"You fucking *bastard*!" she screeched.

Two small fists shot up at him, one batting him in the chest, the other flying toward his jaw, but he was both faster and stronger than her. He slapped her fist away and pressed his gun to her temple, shoving her against the brick wall before she could strike again. They were hidden between two overflowing Dumpsters that stank to high heaven, but he still kept his voice to a whisper.

"Don't fight," he hissed in her ear. "I didn't come here to hurt you. But make no mistake, I will absolutely do it if you push me."

Dark eyes blazed up at him. "What are you *doing* here? You—you—*you killed my brother*! You killed

him and disappeared and . . ." The venom in her voice
was replaced by confused silence. Defeat.

"Yes, I killed him. I had my reasons, reasons you probably won't understand, but they were there," D said flatly.
"But I'm not here to talk about him. I'm here for you."

Something splashed his chin. The bitch had spat
at him.

At least she wasn't struggling anymore. Then again,
she couldn't struggle, not with his gun on her temple
and his thigh wedged between her legs, pinning her in
place. Fuck, he could snap her neck right now. It was so
damn tempting, he could hear the crack it would make
when he twisted.

But no. He had to stick to the plan.

"Does Papa know you're back?" she demanded.

Before he could answer, the back door creaked open
and then male voices echoed in the alley. Bar employees
stepping out for a smoke. D could smell the cheap tobacco
wafting toward the Dumpsters.

"You're coming with me to my car," he said softly.
"We won't get inside of it. I won't take you anywhere.
I'm not going to hurt you, all right? The only reason I
took your phone is so you don't call anyone until we're
done talking."

"Talking," she echoed, her expression skeptical.

"That's all I want. I promise. You're not in any danger, Angie."

Her breath hitched at his use of the nickname. The
nickname that only he had ever called her. In bed mostly,
when he'd fucked her to orgasm while she'd screamed
his name. Well, one of his names. And as she'd begged
Jason to screw her, to give it to her, he'd grunted her

name and faked pleasure and wondered when he'd be able to kill her.

"Please," he begged.

Begged, like a fucking dog, because that's what she needed. The trick with using people was to let them think they were using *you*. You figured out their weaknesses and exploited them, all the while making them believe *they* had the upper hand.

Gael's weakness had been cocaine and young pussy.

Angelina's weakness had been D.

"I can scream," she said tightly. "Mateo and David will hear me, come for me. They're nearby."

"They won't hear you."

Her eyes narrowed. "Why not?"

Because I killed them.

"Because you won't scream." D shrugged. "We haven't seen each other in nine years. I know you want to hear what I have to say."

Her features relaxed.

Christ, she was so damn naive. A woman who'd grown up the way she had should know that her bodyguards were dead. That the only way D could have gotten anywhere near her was if the guards had been eliminated.

Though *bodyguards* wasn't exactly the right word to describe the two men he'd killed. They were more like collection agents, tasked with transporting the tourists Angelina delivered from the bars. D and Gael had done the same thing back in the day. Find the targets, lure them away, and hand them over to the men who then delivered them to Mendez.

"I won't hurt you, Angie. I just need to talk to you," D assured her. "Please. Will you come with me?"

She blinked, looking even more confused now.

Then she nodded.

D hid a grin. It was so easy to play this woman.

He slowly dragged his gun down her bare arm and slid it back to her tailbone, but he didn't dig it into her flesh this time. He let her believe he'd loosened his grip. She needed to believe she wasn't in any danger.

They stepped out from the cover of the Dumpsters. The alley was empty now, the bar employees gone. Silence stretched between them as they took off in a brisk pace toward the street. He noticed her fingers clutching the strap of her purse, inching down the supple leather, but her hand froze when she caught him looking at her.

They passed two alleys, three, and then he directed her to the deserted passageway where he'd stashed his SUV. The moment they reached the vehicle, her hand zipped down toward the purse's opening.

D snatched the bag before she could access it and tossed it away. They both watched it land on the dirty pavement ten yards away.

"You'll get it back after we talk." He backed her into the passenger's door, injecting sincerity into his tone. "Don't worry—your gun will still be there."

She scowled at his knowing look.

"You'll get your phone back too. I promise."

Her hostility faltered, bewilderment taking its place. "You're really not going to hurt me?"

"Of course not." He thickened his voice as he stared at her, his gaze doing a slow, thorough sweep of her face. Her body. Those tits, big and round and barely contained by her flimsy top. The long legs extending from her tiny leather skirt.

"God." D made a choked noise. "You're even more beautiful than I remember."

Her eyes widened. The streetlamp in the distance allowed only the slightest sliver of light into the dark alley, just enough to reveal Angelina's flushed cheeks.

"Does Papa know?" she asked again, her tone softer now.

"If he did, I'd be dead already." D moved closer, pressing his body to hers as he buried his face in her neck and breathed in her perfume. She'd always worn too much fucking perfume. "I had to see you first."

"Why?" she whispered.

"Why the fuck do you think?" He nuzzled her neck, then dragged his tongue over her salty flesh.

A noticeable shiver shuddered through her.

So weak. This woman was so fucking weak when it came to him. She'd wanted him from the moment she'd met him, and it had been so easy to manipulate her back then. So easy to manipulate her *now*.

"Walking away from you was the hardest thing I ever had to do." D groaned as if he were in pain, and thrust his thigh between her legs. Her skirt was so short, her thighs were practically bare, and he knew she could feel the hard length of him straining against her flesh.

Her breath caught again.

Yeah, baby, I'm hard for you. He tried not to roll his eyes. Shockingly few people understood the concept of adrenaline boners. The erections of a soldier, the ones that stemmed not from arousal, but from danger. From risking your life, taking a life, escaping death.

"I missed you, baby," he mumbled. "So fucking much."

Sharp fingernails suddenly raked down his arms,

bringing a sting of pain. Angelina hissed like a rattle-snake as her furious voice heated his chin. "You killed my *brother*."

"I had no choice."

"There's always a choice!"

"Not back then." He dipped his head again, kissing her neck, moaning as if he couldn't get enough.

She flinched, then relaxed. Stiffened. Relaxed. It was like her body couldn't decide whether it wanted to welcome him or push him away.

"Why did come you back, Jason? Why now?"

"Because my past finally caught up to me." He licked the curve of her jaw, and she shivered again. "In a few hours I'm going to throw myself at your father's feet and beg for mercy. But we both know he won't show any. He'll kill me." He kissed his way toward her mouth. "I had to see you before that happened. I *had* to."

D ground his lower body against hers and lifted his head, pleased to see that her pupils were dilated. Her arousal incinerated the air. Confusion, too. And anger. But the arousal . . . that's what he capitalized on.

"Tell me you missed me, Angie. Tell me you missed *this*."

He cupped her breast over her shirt and squeezed it. Hard enough to make other women yelp, but not Angelina. She'd always liked it rough.

"Tell me you missed my dick inside this tight cunt."

He shoved a hand between her legs and squeezed just as hard.

A moan tore out of her throat. "You're so filthy."

"You missed that too." He laughed darkly. "Admit it."

Her eyes had glazed over with lust. Filthy, dirty lust, because she was a filthy, dirty woman. He still remembered how she would sneak into her father's dungeon all those years ago, hide in the shadows, and watch the guards beat the girls when they got out of line. Mendez had a strict rule about not touching the merchandise, but D knew Angelina would have liked to see the guards fuck the prisoners. She used to ask him to describe it to her—in vivid detail—when they were in bed together.

He grabbed her wrists and yanked them over her head, pinning them against the car as he rotated his hips so she could feel his erection. "Your father will find out I'm back. Soon. I want to fuck you before that happens."

She made a breathy noise. The wetness between her thighs was soaking the fabric of his cargo pants.

"Tell me you want me to fuck you," D ordered.

Angelina's pink tongue darted out to moisten her top lip. "I . . . want you to fuck me."

Triumph erupted in his gut, along with a flash of disgust. They hadn't seen each other in nine years—because he'd skipped town after murdering her *brother*—and yet she was so damn eager to spread her legs for him. It was almost enough to make him feel sorry for her. If she weren't such a twisted bitch.

He stared into her lust-drenched eyes, then lower, at the red lips quivering in anticipation. Keeping their bodies locked, he gave a husky chuckle and crashed his mouth over hers.

Angelina moaned the moment their lips touched, her eager tongue sliding out and chasing his into his mouth.

He let it, went through the motions of kissing—groaning, moving his lips, swirling his tongue with hers. But there was no desire burning in his blood. Inside, he was a block of ice. He was bored.

He released her wrists, and she rubbed up against him like a bitch in heat, her hands clawing at his chest and bunching the front of his T-shirt to pull him closer.

D deepened the kiss, curling one hand around her neck. He stroked the delicate tendons of her throat before settling his fingers at her nape, his thumb moving toward her windpipe. Slow and easy.

"Jason," she moaned against his mouth.

He took advantage of her parted lips and thrust his tongue past them. At the same time, he put pressure on her carotid arteries, his thumb pressing into one, his fingers tightening around her throat to pinch the other.

A surprised squeak flew out of her mouth. "Jason—"

Her expression became dazed in a matter of seconds, but there was no mistaking the gleam of accusation. Betrayal. Her eyes were screaming at him, *You promised not to hurt me!*

She should have learned by now that his promises meant shit.

Her hands slapped at him in a futile attempt to break free, but his grip was too strong, pushing deftly on those pressure points until Angelina finally went limp in his arms.

D easily caught her sagging body and opened the SUV's back door with his free hand. He heaved Angelina into the backseat, then reached for the roll of duct tape he'd left on the floor mat. After he'd torn off a piece and stuck it to her mouth, he made quick use of his zip ties, securing her hands and feet before straightening up and slamming the door.

In a heartbeat, the hairs on his neck stood on end, tingling wildly. D drew his weapon and aimed just as a familiar figure emerged from the shadows.

Liam Macgregor stared at him in disbelief. "What the *hell* are you doing?"

Chapter 8

Sofia had known Jim Morgan had a lot of money, but she hadn't realized the extent of his wealth. The man's compound in Costa Rica looked like it belonged to one of those criminal kingpins you saw in the movies. Bordered by the jungle on one side and a rocky hillside on the other, the sprawling Spanish-style home and numerous outbuildings were surrounded by not one, but *three* massive gates that she'd had to stop her car at in order to be buzzed in.

The security man who'd met her outside the house hadn't bothered giving her the grand tour. She'd been led into a gorgeous parlor with gleaming marble floors and twin spiral staircases, ushered down a corridor with expensive artwork on the walls, and brought into a living room that seemed more suited to a ski chalet than a Costa Rican estate. The room had impossibly high ceilings, wood-paneled walls with built-in bookshelves, and a stone fireplace she could walk into. Rustic luxury to the max.

She'd been ordered to sit, so Sofia was now fidgeting on one of the brown leather sofas, staring at the massive oak doors as she waited for Morgan to grant her an audience.

She already knew D wasn't here—the security guard had informed her of that when she'd arrived—and the pang of disappointment in her stomach refused to go away, gnawing at her insides. She desperately wanted to get this over with, but it had to be done in person, damn it.

She'd been calling him ever since she'd left the hospital yesterday morning, but his phone kept going to voice mail. Eventually her frustration had led her to call Morgan, who'd told her D was unavailable, but refused to say if D was at the compound. After Morgan's dodging, she'd finally decided to take matters into her own hands by flying to San José and making the drive to the team's property.

Sofia's shoulders tensed when footsteps sounded from the hall. That had better be Morgan out there. And he had better tell her where D was, because she was so not in the mood for his cryptic soldier bullshit right now.

When the heavy doors parted, it wasn't Jim Morgan who walked through them, but the most beautiful woman Sofia had ever seen. So beautiful that she was rendered speechless for a moment, which she suspected was the typical response this woman received from people.

Long golden hair cascaded over one slender shoulder as the blonde sauntered inside the room. Her features were perfection, her eyes the palest shade of blue. She wore all black, from the leggings hugging her shapely legs to the tank top clinging to her breasts, and although her bare feet should have made her appear casual, the blonde looked like a total badass as she marched toward Sofia.

"I have one question for you, Dr. Amaro—what the fuck kind of trouble are you in?"

Sofia blinked, taken aback by the woman's cold voice and even colder gaze. "I'm sorry, do we know each other? Who are you?"

The blonde perched her butt on the arm of the chair opposite the couch. "I'm the woman who's going to slit your throat if you've brought danger to my doorstep."

Her doorstep?

A snort sounded from the door, and Sofia breathed in relief when she spotted a familiar face.

"Leave her alone, Noelle," Abby Sinclair said with a sigh.

Noelle? Sofia's gaze flew back to the blonde. This was Morgan's wife—Ethan Hayes had told Sofia about her when he'd paid a visit to the clinic last year. According to Ethan, Noelle was a contract killer, and with the waves of menace rolling off her body, that was pretty easy to believe.

Abby walked into the room, holding a chubby-cheeked infant in her arms. "Sofia." She nodded in greeting. "Are you okay?"

"I'm fine." Sofia stood up and approached the redhead, her heart squeezing when the baby's tiny hand extended in her direction.

Swallowing the lump of emotion that rose in her throat, she lightly touched his teeny fingers and smiled at Abby. "Morgan had told me you were pregnant, but I didn't realize you'd already had the baby. Congratulations."

Abby's expression softened slightly, certainly not enough to completely eliminate the shrewd glint in her eyes. She was still the same terrifying woman Sofia had met several years ago when Abby had first joined Morgan's team. Clearly, motherhood hadn't changed that.

"Thank you." Abby absently ran her palm over the baby's fuzzy brown hair, and he immediately tipped his head back, gazing up at her in adoration. "This is Jasper. Or J.J., as the guys like to call him. It's short for Jasper Jeremy."

Another sharp pang clenched Sofia's heart when Jasper's entire fist surrounded her index finger. God, in seven months she would have her own little Jasper. She was going to be a mother.

The notion was still so surreal.

"As heartwarming as this little reunion is," Noelle spoke up, her voice icier than before, "I'd like to know why Dr. Amaro decided to pay us a visit." With a pointed look, she added, "Unannounced."

Sofia released the baby's hand and took a step back. "I need to speak to D."

Noelle's gaze sharpened. "Why?"

"Because I do." Irritation rose inside her. "Can you please tell me where he is? He's not returning my calls, and it's really important that I talk to him."

"Which leads me right back to the million-dollar question—what kind of trouble are you in?" Noelle crossed her arms. "Who's after you? And when can we expect them to show up?"

"I'm not in trouble," she replied through clenched teeth. "And nobody is after me. Do you really think I'd bring trouble to your door? This is Morgan's home—I wouldn't endanger him or anyone else living here."

Her gaze fell on the baby again, who still hadn't made a sound. He was calmly resting his cheek on his mother's breast, listening to the conversation almost as if he understood what was being said.

"There's no danger," Sofia repeated. "I just need to talk to Derek. It's a personal matter, okay?"

Suspicion darkened Noelle's expression. "Personal."

"Yes."

Noelle exchanged a look with Abby, then turned to Sofia with a shrug. "He's unavailable. Leave him a message and he'll call you back."

"If he was returning my calls, I wouldn't be here! Damn it, would you—" She hastily lowered her voice so she wouldn't upset the baby, but Jasper seemed unfazed by the tension in the room. "Just tell me where D is and I'll be on my way."

Noelle slid off the armchair and approached her, and Sofia tried hard not to flinch. Jesus. This woman actually scared her. Something about the way Noelle moved, the way her gaze cut right through you . . . How on earth did Morgan lie in bed beside her every night without worrying she'd kill him in his sleep?

"So." Noelle looked thoughtful. "Are you in love with him?"

Sofia blinked in surprise, shifting awkwardly. "No."

"All right, then. That leaves option number two." The blonde spoke in a blunt voice. "You're knocked up."

Now she *did* flinch. Which only made her angry, because she didn't even know this fucking woman. Who cared if Noelle was right on the mark? Sofia had no desire to discuss her private life with a stranger.

Abby's eyes flickered with interest. "You're pregnant?"

Sofia fought the urge to scream. "What is the *matter* with you people? There's this concept you need to learn—it's called boundaries. It's none of your damn business what I need to talk to Derek about."

"It is our business," Noelle corrected. "D works for my husband and lives on this compound. His business is our business. And his mistakes are our mistakes."

Mistakes. Was that what Noelle considered this pregnancy?

Well, the only mistake Sofia was willing to own up to was her stupid decision to come here. She'd thought she'd be speaking to Jim Morgan, who happened to be a reasonable man. If she'd known she was going to be interrogated by *Mrs*. Morgan, who was not at *all* reasonable, then she would have fucking stayed in Mexico.

"Where's Morgan? I want to talk to him."

"You just want to talk to everyone tonight, don't you, Doc?" Noelle's mocking blue eyes pierced into her. "Jim's in the jungle with his daughter. They won't be back until morning."

His daughter? Okay, Sofia wasn't even going to *touch* that one. But the second part of that sentence was perplexing enough to spark her curiosity. "Why are they in the jungle at this time of night?"

Abby gave a dry laugh. "He's teaching Cate how to track prey in the dark."

Sofia suddenly felt light-headed. God. Morgan was traipsing around in the jungle, teaching his kid how to "track prey"? Who the hell *were* these people?

Maybe she *shouldn't* tell D about the pregnancy. If he happened to notice her bulging stomach or see her with the baby, she could just pretend he wasn't the father. Say it was Chris's, the doctor she'd been dating before him. And if the baby ended up looking like a mini D, then she could play dumb, pretend she didn't notice the resemblance, that it was a coincidence—

Okay, she wasn't that stupid, and neither was D. They were adults, and they needed to sit down and talk about this.

Which might actually happen if these women stopped grilling her like she was on the damn witness stand.

"I've had enough of this bullshit," Sofia announced. She addressed Noelle rather than Abby, because it was clear who called the shots in this house. "You got me, all right? I'm pregnant. Eight weeks along, and the baby is Derek's. If you want proof, then I'm sure I can arrange for a paternity test once the timing is right," she added sarcastically. "Until then, just give me his address so I can speak to him in person. I don't want to do it over the phone. I don't want to do it via a goddamn letter. So for the love of God—"

"Go get Ash," Noelle told Abby.

The abrupt interruption—no, the *dismissal*—made Sofia's jaw drop.

And she'd been absolutely right about who called the shots, because Abby responded with a nod and left the room in brisk strides.

Sofia opened her mouth, only to get interrupted again. "What's your phone number?" Noelle barked out.

"What does that have to do with—"

"Jesus Christ. What's your phone number, Doc?"

Still confused, Sofia recited the digits. When she finished, Noelle removed a cell phone from the front pocket of her black pants, which were so tight Sofia couldn't figure out how they even *had* pockets.

As Noelle dialed, Sofia watched in disbelief, wondering what the hell was going on. Why wouldn't they tell her how to reach D? She wasn't asking for the codes of the president's nuclear football, for Pete's sake. She needed one measly address.

"Hey, it's me," Noelle said into the phone. "The app you downloaded for Macgregor? Download it to this number, too." She rattled off the number Sofia had just given her, then hung up.

Sofia raked a hand through her hair, officially exhausted. "What is happening right now?"

"One of my girls is setting up a tracking program on your phone. It'll show you D's location in real time."

Her eyebrows shot up. "Are you serious? Does he know you're tracking him?" When Noelle shrugged, indignation surged through her. "You're doing it without his knowledge?"

"Lose the high-and-mighty routine, Doc. You're getting what you want, no?"

"Why are you suddenly so eager to help me?" she demanded.

Noelle smiled. "Who says I'm helping you?"

Sofia narrowed her eyes, understanding dawning. "You're helping yourself," she said slowly. "Why? What do you gain from me going after D?"

Before Noelle could answer, a tall dark-haired man strode into the room. He looked young, twenty-five maybe, but his voice was deep and masculine as he addressed the blonde.

"Abby said you needed me?"

Noelle nodded, then gestured to Sofia. "Have you met the doc?"

He shook his head.

"Sofia Amaro," Noelle introduced. "She runs the clinic just outside Oaxaca. Fixes you boys up when you need fixing."

"Nice to meet you." He extended a hand. "I'm Ash."

He spoke with a slight Southern drawl, and there was genuine pleasure in his vivid green eyes as he shook her hand and smiled at her.

"You're going to accompany the good doctor to Cancún to meet with D," Noelle told Ash. "Make sure she stays safe."

He nodded as if the request was perfectly normal. "When do we leave?"

"Now. Macgregor's already there." Noelle's gaze flicked toward Sofia. "Excuse us, Doc."

Sofia didn't have a chance to respond, because the two of them were already stepping into the hall, the doors closing behind them.

What the hell was going on? Noelle had gone from not wanting her anywhere near D to offering her a personal escort to go see him.

Hushed voices came from behind the doors, but Sofia couldn't make out what they were saying. A moment later, Noelle returned. Alone.

"Ash is gathering his gear. He'll meet you outside in ten minutes, then take you to our airfield and get you to D."

Sofia was utterly dazed. "Thank you." When Noelle started to turn away, she blurted out a question. "That's it?"

"Is there anything else we need to discuss?"

"You tell me." Frustration churned in her stomach, along with an unwelcome rush of nausea.

God, no. Please don't let her throw up right now. Her morning sickness wasn't restricted to the mornings. It hit her the hardest at night, and the stress of this entire encounter was finally taking its toll on her.

"How come you're suddenly okay with me going to him?"

Noelle arched one perfectly shaped eyebrow. "Why wouldn't I be?"

Lord, this woman was the most enigmatic person Sofia had ever met. It made her want to scream.

"Because clearly you're Derek's personal protector." She couldn't stop the sarcasm. "What, you're not going to warn me not to hurt him?"

That got her a mocking laugh. "Oh, honey, you're not capable of hurting him." Noelle's amused gaze locked with hers. "He's going to hurt *you*."

Sofia gulped. It hadn't sounded like a threat. More like a promise. And the conviction in Noelle's voice, the twinge of unmistakable pity, caused Sofia's stomach to churn even harder.

"I hope you know that," the other woman continued. "And if you didn't, then start wrapping your head around it, Doc. My husband likes you. He won't want to see you hurt."

My husband likes you. Noelle couldn't have made her opinion of Sofia any clearer if she'd spray-painted it on the walls. But Sofia didn't give a shit what this woman thought of her. She didn't care what anyone thought of her.

She just wanted to talk to D, damn it. She just wanted to tell him about the baby.

And then what? a bleak voice asked.

Who fucking knew? Sofia certainly didn't. What she *did* know was that she and Derek had a lot of decisions to make.

Liam Macgregor gaped at his teammate, wondering if maybe he'd wound up in an alternate dimension. A planet where *Derek Pratt* exuded sex appeal, where Derek Pratt flirted and kissed and fondled beautiful women like he was Don frickin' Juan.

The only thing that made sense about what Liam had just witnessed was D rendering the woman unconscious, because that was exactly what a ruthless motherfucker like D would do. But everything before the knocking-her-unconscious part? The kissing and the grinding and all that groping?

Mind-boggling.

"What are you doing here?" D snapped.

"What do you think?" Liam snapped back. "Did you really believe I'd let you go after Sully by yourself?"

Annoyance flashed in D's coal black eyes as he lowered his weapon. "I already told you, this has nothing to do with Sullivan."

"Yeah, you did tell me that, and you were lying through your teeth." Liam raised a brow. "I believed you up until the moment you called me Liam, asshole."

He couldn't help but feel smug when he saw the amazement on D's face, as if the man truly hadn't realized his slipup. The other men called Liam by his first name all the time, but D had only ever referred to him as Macgregor or Boston, the not so clever nickname Sullivan had given him because he was from, shocker, Boston.

"You're here because of Sully," Liam accused in a low voice. "I know it and you know it, so please have the decency to stop lying to me."

"How did you find me?" D demanded.

Liam shrugged. "That doesn't matter. I'm here now, and I'm not going anywhere." He glanced at the tinted window of the SUV. "Who is she?"

Silence.

"How is she connected to Sullivan?" Liam pressed. "Or do you just go around knocking out innocent women for fun?"

"Innocent?" D gave an uncharacteristic snort. "The bitch isn't innocent, Macgregor." His features hardened as he opened the driver's door. "I'm not standing around and talking about this. I need to go."

"Fine. Then let's go." Liam rounded the car and threw open the passenger's door.

"I don't need you, Boston. I can handle this alone."

"Fuck you. And get in the fuckin' car." Liam slid into the SUV and slammed his door.

It took several seconds before D got behind the wheel, visibly pissed off. Then he started the car and pulled out of the alley without a word.

Liam used the silence to twist around and peer at the unconscious brunette in the backseat. She was undeniably gorgeous, the kind of woman who'd turn heads wherever she went. And D had been grinding up against her in a wholly familiar way.

Had they been lovers?

He almost laughed out loud at the thought. Lovers. Right. Liam doubted D had ever *made love* to anyone in his life. The man *fucked*. He fucked hard and then he left, at least according to the other guys on the team, who'd known D a lot longer than Liam had. But there was no denying that D had transformed in that alley. He'd been . . . magnetic. Sexual. A completely different man.

Liam shifted around in his seat. It didn't matter who the woman was. D wouldn't have grabbed her if she wasn't connected to Sullivan's disappearance, and Liam wasn't leaving D's side until he got the truth out of the man.

Christ, every time he thought about Sully, it felt like someone was scraping his chest with a hot blade. He'd been racked with fear and guilt since the moment Sullivan had turned up missing in Dublin, and the fact that D was shutting him out of the mission—whatever the hell the mission even was—made Liam want to put a bullet in D's goddamn kneecap and *force* him to talk.

"You're a real son of a bitch, you know that?" Liam spat out. "You should've just told me you were going after him. Then I wouldn't have had to waste more than a day tailing your ass. We could've been working together."

D didn't answer. His gaze remained on the road as he made a right turn and drove away from the tourist strip. It was Saturday night, and the streets were crawling with college kids who would no doubt be out partying until the wee hours of the morning.

A trio of drunken guys in Hawaiian shirts stumbled

along the crosswalk as D stopped at a red light. One of
them tripped over absolutely nothing, his hand landing
on the hood of their SUV with a thump as he attempted
to steady himself. Bloodshot eyes peered at the windshield, a slurred apology drifting in through D's half-
open window just as the light turned green.

Rather than acknowledge the kid, D hit the gas and
sped through the intersection, nearly clipping the drunken
party boy in the ribs.

"Where's Sullivan?" Liam demanded when D still
didn't speak. "Who has him?"

His teammate finally looked over. "I don't want you
involved in this."

Fury burned a fiery path up his throat. "Well, too
fuckin' late! I *am* involved."

He'd been involved from the moment he'd met Sullivan Port, the cocky Australian who'd snuck through
Liam's defenses and somehow become his closest friend.
Thanks to his stint in the DEA, Liam didn't have many
friends. He had colleagues. He had rivals. But friends?
Not so much. He'd spent his entire career in deep cover,
cozying up to bad guys and taking them down, but it
wasn't until he'd started contracting for Jim Morgan,
until he'd become part of a team and connected with
Sully, that he'd realized what true friendship really was.

And then he'd gone and ruined it. He'd had the best
friend he could ever hope for, the one person in this
world who he trusted implicitly, who he'd lay down his
life for, and he'd blown it.

It *killed* him that his last memory of his friend was
rooted in anger. That last night in Dublin, Sullivan had
accused him of not giving a shit about their friendship,

of letting a case of misguided lust sever the bond they'd formed.

Lust. It fuckin' ruined everything, didn't it? Liam hadn't expected to be attracted to his friend. He hadn't expected Sullivan to reciprocate those feelings. But it had happened, damn it, and Sully had been smart enough to know that acting on it would screw up their friendship. And instead of agreeing, Liam had pushed him. He'd pushed and pushed until his friend had eventually stormed out of that hotel room.

He grew sick to his stomach as he remembered Sully's furious strides, the slam of the door. It was his fault. If he hadn't picked a fight, Sullivan wouldn't have gone down to the bar. Sullivan wouldn't have been distracted. Because that was the only way a man like Sullivan Port would have allowed himself to get captured—if he'd been distracted.

An anguished groan ripped out of Liam's throat. "Don't you get it?" he mumbled. "It's my fault he's missing."

D turned with a sharp look.

"He was distracted because we argued. Someone got the drop on him because his head wasn't where it should've been, and that was because of *me*." Liam clenched his teeth. "It was my fault."

"No." D cleared his throat. "It was mine."

Chapter 9

D parked in the gravel lot behind the three-story apartment building on the outskirts of the city. The building wasn't the nicest, its pink concrete exterior cracked and dilapidated, but it suited D's needs. The six apartments were mostly used as short-term rentals for tourists, and D had rented out the two on the ground floor. He'd verified that the other four were occupied by spring breakers, which was good, because he didn't consider them a threat. The kids would get plastered at the bars every night, drag themselves home in the mornings, and pass the fuck out, oblivious to what was happening downstairs.

The real threat at the moment was Liam Macgregor.

Damn that bastard for crashing the job. D was pissed at himself for being careless, for that stupid slipup with Liam's name, for not realizing that Liam had been tailing him. Yeah, Liam knew how to remain invisible, but D was usually more aware. He couldn't remember the last time someone had snuck up on him, which told him that this Mendez thing was really messing with his head.

He glanced at the backseat, where Angelina was still out like a light. She'd be waking up soon, though.

He'd need to give her a sedative. The job would go a lot more smoothly if the bitch remained unconscious the entire time.

"Stay with her while I clear the safe house," D ordered. "You can bring her inside when I give you the all clear."

For once, Liam didn't argue. In fact, he hadn't said a word since D had slipped up yet again and admitted that Sully's disappearance had been his fault.

D had expected the Spanish Inquisition after that, but Liam had simply clammed up. They hadn't exchanged a single sentence in forty-five minutes, and he was anticipating a hell of a blowup when Liam finally decided to talk.

Swallowing a sigh, he got out of the car, drew his weapon, and approached the dark archway at the building's rear. A passageway ran through the ground floor from front to back, and rickety metal staircases on either side of the run-down exterior led to the upstairs apartments. No lobby, no intercom, no security whatsoever, which was one of the reasons D had chosen the location. That, and its numerous exit points—front and back doors, side windows in both apartments.

He did a sweep of the building and surrounding area, then cleared the apartments before signaling Liam. He stood in the archway, watching as his teammate opened the back door and hauled the unconscious brunette in a fireman's carry.

"So now I'm doing your grunt work?" Liam muttered as he stalked up, Angelina slung over his broad shoulder.

"You wanted to be part of the job. This is the job."

D marched into the apartment on their left and

flicked the light switch. The open-concept main room offered sparse furnishings—a couch, a coffee table, and a dinette set.

"Put her on the couch for now."

Liam carried Angelina to the beige sofa and deposited her on the scratchy cushions, while D unzipped his go bag and pulled out his field med kit. A zippered case inside the kit held syringes and several vials of heavy-duty sedatives, enough to keep Angelina out of commission for as long as he needed.

He could feel Liam frowning at him as he knelt in front of the couch and grabbed Angelina's right wrist. He checked her pulse. Steady, strong. Her eyelids twitched when he touched her, her breathing changing slightly. Fuck, she would wake up soon.

Without delay, D tapped the veins at the inside of her elbow, then injected the sedative and quickly zipped up the case.

"Are you going to tell me what's going on, or should I start guessing?" Liam's tone was flat.

D's cheeks hollowed in displeasure. Goddamn it. The last thing he needed was Macgregor screwing everything up for him. Now that Angelina was in his custody, D needed to handle the rest of this op with extreme caution.

"Who is she?" Liam demanded. "What are you planning?"

"An exchange," D said tightly.

Liam's breath sucked in. "Her for Sullivan?"

He nodded. He was reluctant to continue, but hell, Liam was here now, so it was time to suck it up and adapt. "Her father has Sullivan. Should be an easy trade."

Yeah fucking right. Nothing was easy with Raoul

Mendez. And their history? Not at all *easy*. Even if the exchange went as planned, Mendez would never stop hunting D. Which meant that after this, D would need a new identity.

Derek Pratt would have to die.

"If it was so easy, you wouldn't have gone Lone Ranger on us," his teammate retorted, seeing right through the lie. "You're expecting complications."

"I always expect complications."

Liam narrowed his eyes. "Why did you say it was your fault that Sully was taken?"

"Because he used my name at the bar. It alerted the wrong people, and they took him, thinking he was me."

"Wouldn't they know what you look like, these mysterious people who are after you?"

"The thug at the hotel? No. I've never seen him before in my life. He's never seen me. I think it was just the name that tipped him off. He probably didn't realize he had the wrong guy until he brought Sullivan to the boss."

"And who would that be?" There was an edge to Liam's voice.

"Nobody you need to concern yourself with."

"Don't you fuckin' give me that shit. I need to concern myself with every detail of this bullshit op you're planning. This is Sullivan's *life* we're talking about."

D cursed under his breath. "You're on a need-to-know basis, Macgregor, and I've told you everything you need to know."

"Fuck you."

"Uh-huh. Great comeback." He stalked to the door. "I'm grabbing supplies from the car. Watch her. If she wakes up for some reason, knock her out again—trust me when I say you don't want this bitch opening her mouth. It's better if she stays quiet."

He turned the knob and stepped into the walkway just as a shadowy figure approached the door.

In a heartbeat, D had his HK drawn and his elbow in the intruder's neck, slamming the solid male body against the concrete wall. There was a choked sound as he dug his forearm into the man's windpipe.

"D," came a strangled voice. "Jesus, it's me."

A rush of anger spiraled through him when he recognized the voice. The face. The green eyes of the team rookie, conveying a silent plea for D to stand down.

Mother*fucker.*

D eased the pressure on Ash's throat, but didn't remove his arm. If his hair had been long enough to pull, he would've ripped it out by the roots. Every fucking hair on his own goddamn head.

"What the hell are you doing here?" he snapped, struggling to control the rage coursing through his blood.

"Noelle sent me," the rookie sputtered. "She asked me to escort Sof—"

"Let him go, Derek," an annoyed voice commanded.

He abruptly released Ash and spun around to find another pair of green eyes staring back at him. A darker green than Ash's, surrounded by thick black eyelashes and gleaming with indignation.

Sofia.

D drew a breath, but it didn't calm him down. It only made his lungs burn.

He turned back to Ash, his voice coming out low, measured. "What. Is. She. Doing. Here."

"*She* is standing right here," Sofia retorted. "So you can direct that question to *me*."

He kept his gaze on Ash. If he looked at Sofia right now, he might actually lose his shit. He was in the middle of a delicate op, where a single mistake could mean the difference between Sullivan's life and death. And now not only did he have Liam's interference to deal with, but Ash's? *Sofia's?*

D pushed Ash out of his path and stormed inside. His blood boiled as he advanced on Liam, grabbing the man by the collar and shaking him.

"You involved Sofia?" he hissed out. "What the hell were you thinking?"

Liam planted both hands on D's chest and shoved him away, and it took all of D's willpower not to shove back. Not to smash his fist into the other man's chiseled jaw.

"I have no idea what you're talking about. I didn't involve—" Liam stopped in shock as Ash and Sofia entered the apartment.

But Liam's shock was nothing compared to the gasp Sofia gave when her gaze landed on the couch. Or rather, on the bound, gagged, and unconscious woman lying there.

Horror flooded her expression, and then she whirled around, her accusatory gaze burning D's face. "Oh my God! Did you kidnap an innocent woman?"

He took a breath.

Then another one.

And then he started to laugh.

Deep bellows of laughter that caused every pair of eyes to widen in alarm. But he couldn't stop it. His nice and tidy solo op had turned into a clusterfuck of monstrous proportions. First Liam showing up. Then Ash. Sofia. And if one more person used the word *innocent* in conjunction with Angelina Mendez . . .

Another hearty laugh flew out of D's mouth. Innocent, his ass.

"Is he laughing?" Ash asked Liam.

"I think so? I mean, I've never heard that sound come out of his mouth before."

His teammates looked worried about him. Sofia just looked outraged.

"You think this is funny?" she exclaimed, racing over to the sofa before he could stop her. She dropped to her knees and pressed two fingers to Angelina's neck, checking for a pulse.

D's misplaced humor faded rapidly. "She's not dead," he muttered.

Sofia ignored him. She gently pried Angelina's eyelids open, studied her pupils, then glowered at D over her shoulder. "What did you give her?"

Rather than answer, he turned to Ash. "You said Noelle sent you?"

The younger man nodded.

"And I'm guessing Noelle is the one who gave you my location?" D asked Liam, who nodded in response. "How?"

Liam frowned. "How what?"

"How did she know where I was?"

Liam gestured to the tactical watch strapped to D's wrist. "I'm assuming she used the SOS tracker."

"No, she didn't." Because D didn't *have* an SOS tracker—he'd disabled the GPS in the watch two hours after Morgan had given it to him. And since his location registered only when the SOS button was triggered, the security men monitoring the grid had no idea that D's tracker wasn't operational.

Noelle must have found another way to track him, then. His clothes, maybe? Boots? No, too many variables involved with that. He could ditch his clothing at any moment and the tracker would be useless. Which meant . . .

He pulled his cell phone out of his pocket, damn near glaring at the thing. How long had Noelle and Morgan been tracking the team's phones? It had to be a recent development, because D swept his gear for bugs before every job, and everything had come up clean before the gig in Guadalajara two months ago.

He was tempted to crush the phone beneath his boot, but the tracker could come in handy now that Sofia was here.

And fuck.

Sofia. Was. Here.

Why, damn it?

Now that he was feeling calmer, he finally took the time to study the woman he'd fucked two months ago. She wore a blue tank top and faded jeans with a hole in the knee. Her dark hair hung in a long braid over one shoulder. And when she rose from the floor and approached the men again, she looked noticeably tired. Drained.

"Why did you come here?" D asked gruffly.

Her expression grew even wearier. "Because I needed to see you."

He clenched his teeth so hard they hurt. Liam and Ash were both staring at him, eyebrows raised, as if they were waiting for answers of their own, an explanation for . . . for what? For why Sofia would need to see him? For why he'd abducted an "innocent" woman?

Well, he didn't have to explain shit.

"Why?" he asked again, searching Sofia's face.

Liam answered before she could. "You know what, D? *Enough*. You're not allowed to ask any more questions— not to me, not to her, not to anyone. Not until you cough up some answers of your own."

"He's right," Sofia said, her gaze straying toward Angelina again. "Why is that woman tied up and sedated? And I swear to God, if you don't have a good explanation, I'm calling the police. Her family could be looking for her! She could be—"

"A sex trafficker," D interrupted, his voice coming out in a loud boom, because holy fucking shit, he'd had it up to here with everyone tonight. "She could be a sex trafficker, Sofia, and she *is* a sex trafficker, so don't go feeling all sorry for her, all right? And her family will *definitely* be looking for her—you're right about that. Because guess what? Her father is a sex trafficker too. He sells women as sex slaves, and he's very, very rich because of it. Oh, and by the way, he's currently holding Sullivan captive at the moment. So get off your fucking high horse. All of you."

Sofia's face went stricken.

Next to her, Ash's jaw dropped in astonishment. "Wait—you know where Sully is?"

"Yes," D muttered. "And I'll get him out."

When Liam cleared his throat pointedly, D almost strangled the man.

"*We'll* get him out," he corrected irritably. "Me and

Macgregor." He glared at Ash. "And you . . . you're going to walk out the door, put Sofia on a plane, and take her home."

"No," Sofia protested, sounding as frustrated as he felt. "Damn it, Derek. We need to talk first."

"I don't have time to talk. I'm in the middle of a rescue mission to save a man you happen to know, a man you claim to like. So for the love of God, just *go*. It's too dangerous for you to be here."

"But it's not dangerous for *you*?" she shot back.

"I'm always in danger, and I can handle myself."

"And I can't?"

Was she actually arguing with him right now? Jesus Christ. He'd never felt so aggravated in his life.

"How are you connected to these people?" Liam jerked his head toward Angelina. "How do you know her and her father?"

He pressed his lips together. Inhaled through his nose. "I'm not discussing this in front of the doc."

Now Sofia was the one laughing, even more hysterically than he had. She rubbed her temples as she shook with laughter, buried her face in her hands for a moment, then dropped her arms and stared at D.

"I'm in a shit-box apartment in Cancún at the moment, standing five feet from the woman you *abducted*. Sorry, the *sex trafficker* you abducted." She shook her head in disbelief. "So if you're afraid of upsetting my delicate sensibilities, don't be. And if you think you're shielding me from your big, bad self, then you should know that ship sailed a long time ago. I know you're not a saint, Derek. I've always known that."

She was right—he'd never pretended to be a saint—

but that didn't mean he felt comfortable telling her about his past. Telling any of them, for that matter. But they were all glaring at him, their gazes burning with accusation, as if he'd fucking *wanted* Sullivan to get captured.

"You need to tell me exactly what's going on," Sofia ordered. "I want to know what I've just become an unwitting accomplice to so I can decide whether to kill you, call a lawyer, or both."

And this, *this* was why he preferred to work alone. Because he didn't like answering to anyone but himself. Because everyone around him was a stubborn motherfucker who didn't know when to let things lie.

Unfortunately, he suspected that staying silent right now would only create more headaches than if he simply told them the truth.

"Her name is Angelina Mendez," he said reluctantly. "Her father is Raoul Mendez."

Surprisingly, of the three people in the room with him, the only one who recognized Mendez's name was the nonoperative of the bunch.

"Isn't he a gangster?" Sofia asked, wrinkling her forehead.

"I told you, he's a human trafficker. He dabbles in cocaine smuggling as well, but sex is his bread and butter." D rubbed the stubble dotting his jaw. He hadn't shaved since he'd left Costa Rica, and his face was starting to itch. "He specializes in the tourist trade. His people abduct female tourists, usually teenagers or college girls. Girls without families, the kind of girls that nobody notices when they turn up missing. Then he ships them off to Asia, where they're sent to whorehouses or private buyers."

Sofia's face paled. "How do you know this man?"

"I had dealings with him in the past."

"You *worked* for him?" she said in horror.

"No. I worked covert ops and went undercover in his organization."

"For Delta?" Liam said sharply.

D shook his head. "For someone else." He didn't elaborate, because talking about the Smith Group was a can of worms he refused to open.

Liam, of course, didn't let it go. "Who?"

"Doesn't matter who. It was black ops, completely off the books." He quickly went on. "Mexico was my assigned region. The agency I worked for set up a cover for me the day I signed on, and I used that cover for three years—Jason Hernandez, drug distributor. I dealt mostly with the cartels, but you can't be a criminal in Mexico without running into Raoul Mendez at least once or twice. So I knew him—not well, but enough that the agency assigned me to him after he pissed off the wrong people."

"Pissed them off how?" Ash asked.

"By kidnapping the wrong fucking tourist." D offered a scornful look. "After *that* debacle, he set up a thorough vetting process to make sure the tourists he was grabbing weren't going to be missed."

Liam nodded. "So who did Mendez grab?"

"His people unknowingly kidnapped a US senator's daughter when she was in Cabo on spring break. Once Mendez realized who she was, he shipped her off, but it was too late—the girl's father was already raising hell, demanding that something be done. There was no evidence connecting Mendez to the kidnapping, so the government had to go through black channels."

"They sent you in to find the girl?" Sofia spoke up.

The sound of her voice brought a strange clench to his stomach. Damn it, he hated that she was here listening to all this.

What he hated even more was that he couldn't stop remembering the night he'd screwed her.

Usually after he had sex with a woman, he didn't think twice about it. Didn't look back, didn't want more. But Sofia's mere presence was making his dick throb. He couldn't even blame it on adrenaline. He was hard because of *her*. Because every time he looked at her, he remembered how tight she'd been, how willing, the way she'd moaned when he'd slammed into her.

"Derek?" she prompted.

He bristled, annoyed to discover he'd spaced out. That he'd literally gone silent as he'd fantasized about being inside Sofia Amaro again.

"They wanted you to find the girl?"

D cleared his throat. "That was one of the objectives, yes. My cover was already in place. Mendez knew me and we'd already established a small level of trust. So I set up a meeting and told him I needed work, and he paired me up with his son. Gael." D's gut twisted at the memory. "I found out early on that the girl had been sent to Hong Kong. The next step was figuring out who the buyer was, but those details weren't available to me yet. I had to prove myself first, so I worked a few jobs with Gael to show my loyalty."

Sofia gasped. "You kidnapped tourists for that man?"

"I had a part to play," D said curtly. "I gave the Feds intel about every girl we dealt with, but it wasn't my job to save them. My job was to find the senator's daughter and kill Mendez."

"Did you find the girl?" she said warily.

D shook his head.

"And you didn't kill Mendez, either," Liam mused. "You failed at both objectives. Why?"

"The op went south," he admitted. "After I killed Gael."

"The son?" Ash asked in confusion. "Why did you kill him?"

"Doesn't matter. It happened, and my handler was unhappy with it. So was Mendez." D stifled a laugh. Unhappy? Understatement of the fucking year. "So I had to pull a disappearing act. I went underground, set up a new identity, and eventually joined up with Morgan. But Mendez has been looking for me ever since, and he must've figured out I was going by the name Derek Pratt now. His people took Sullivan because Sully made the mistake of using my name." D released a tired breath. "Any other questions?"

A frown puckered Liam's brow. "Tell me about Mendez. You worked for him. What's his MO? Torture?"

"He's got a torture chamber, yeah. Calls it the workshop. If he thinks a beating or a lost limb will make the prisoner talk, then he'll use the workshop."

Sofia was even paler now.

"But he's a master at reading people," D went on. "He can usually tell if a prisoner is able to withstand traditional torture—"

"Traditional?" Sofia blurted.

"So in the event of that, he resorts to more creative methods. Sully was trained not to reveal anything under torture. I bet Mendez figured that out pretty fast."

Liam's voice could have frozen an ocean. "Creative methods. What does he consider *creative*?"

"Everything," D answered reluctantly. "He experiments with different drug cocktails. Psychological games. Sensory deprivation. All sorts of shit."

Liam looked sick for a moment. Then his gaze sharpened, resting on Angelina. "Does she matter to Mendez?"

D nodded. "The only people he gives a shit about—other than himself—are his children. And one of them is already dead."

"Because of you," Liam said darkly.

"Because of me," he agreed. "And trust me, if I threaten to kill his daughter too? Mendez will do whatever it takes to get her back. So like I said, it should be an easy trade."

"Then make the fuckin' trade," Liam snapped.

"That was the plan. And it was moving along splendidly until you assholes decided to show up and slow me down." He scowled at Liam. "If you insist on sticking around, fine, then your job is to watch our hostage and keep her sedated." He shifted the scowl to Ash. "And your job is to get the fuck out of here, and take Sofia with you."

At the sound of her name, Sofia's head snapped up, her stricken gaze focusing on D. She was looking at him as if she'd never seen him before in her life, and he wanted to laugh again. She'd been more than willing to screw him when she'd thought he was a mysterious mercenary with a big cock, but one peek behind the curtain and she was recoiling in horror.

All these people . . . his teammates, Noelle, Sofia—they thought they knew him, but they didn't. They didn't know shit.

He bit back a curse. "There. You got your answers," he told her. "Now can you please let Ash take you back to the airfield?"

Sofia's features grew pained, and D frowned when he noticed the greenish tinge to her cheeks. She was also swallowing repeatedly—he could see her throat bobbing, working hard with each gulp.

"I . . ." Her eyes suddenly widened, and she clapped a hand over her mouth. "I'm going to be sick."

Chapter 10

Sofia barely made it to the bathroom in time. She didn't even close the door, just dove in front of the toilet and threw up the meager amount of crackers she'd eaten on the plane, all the while cursing her stupid body. Why couldn't she be one of those lucky women who didn't suffer from morning sickness? Or at the very least, actually have *morning* sickness, instead of all-hours-of-the-day-and-night sickness.

The only upside was that the nausea didn't last long. She always felt better right after she threw up, and the queasiness was all but gone as she flushed the toilet and went to the sink to rinse her mouth.

She was drying her face when D appeared in the doorway. She hadn't even heard his footsteps in the hall—suddenly he was there, his dark eyes fixed on her face, his powerful arms crossed over his chest.

God, she shouldn't have come. She'd thought it was important to tell him in person, but showing up here and finding an unconscious woman in the apartment? Listening to him describe how he'd worked for a human trafficker and kidnapped tourists? Because "it wasn't his job to save them"?

Who *was* this man?

She legitimately had no answer for that, because Derek Pratt wasn't even Derek Pratt. It was simply an identity he'd created after he'd stopped being Jason Hernandez. And who the hell knew who he'd been before that.

It bothered her that she didn't know his real name. No, it scared her. It fucking *terrified* her that she knew nothing about the man who'd fathered her baby.

"You good?" he said roughly.

Those were the same two words he'd voiced after they'd had sex in her kitchen, and the memory made her feel queasy again.

She managed a weak nod. "I'm fine."

D walked over to the sink and grabbed a hand towel. He ran it under the cold water for several seconds, then held it out. "Here. You looked flushed. Maybe this'll cool you down."

Sofia might have been touched by the gesture if there'd been any sort of tenderness behind it. But his tone was impersonal, his eyes grim. He didn't come closer, didn't wipe her forehead for her or tuck her hair behind her ear. That's what Chris, the doctor she'd been dating last year, would have done, and not just because he was a medical professional, but because he'd *cared* about her. Sure, their romance had fizzled, but during their time together, Chris had been sweet and gentle and kind. He'd been good to her. Good *for* her.

But there was nothing sweet, gentle, or kind about *this* man. Derek Pratt—or whatever his name was—was hard and cold and dangerous. And he was *not* good for her.

Sofia fought to control the panic skittering inside her. She dabbed her hot cheeks with the towel, avoiding D's gaze.

"You need to go," he told her.

"I know," she said dully.

Silence fell over the bathroom.

"Look, I . . ." He shifted his feet, visibly awkward. "I know you didn't like what you heard back there, but I'm not going to apologize for what I did in the past. Undercover work sometimes requires certain actions to be taken, whether you like them or not. And don't feel sorry for Angelina. Believe me, she's done worse things than I ever have. And she also happens to be Sullivan's ticket to freedom."

"I don't care about her, Derek," Sofia answered tightly. "I understand, okay? Trading her to Mendez is the only way to get your teammate back."

His eyes narrowed. "Five minutes ago, that plan literally made you sick."

"That's not why I got sick." She exhaled in a rush, deciding to get her secret out in one go. "I got sick because I'm pregnant."

When genuine shock washed over D's features, Sofia found herself fighting back laughter. It figured. The man was an emotionless robot 99.9 percent of the time, and *this* was what roused a reaction from him.

"It's yours," she added, when he still hadn't said a word.

That got her a curt nod.

It was her turn to shift awkwardly, because she truly

had no clue what was going through his head right now. If he even believed her.

"Before we had sex, I hadn't slept with anyone for more than a year," she confessed. "And I haven't been with anyone else since you."

Another nod.

She gulped. "If you don't believe me, we can get a test done."

"I believe you."

His raspy answer startled her. "You're just going to take my word for it?"

"Yes."

"Why?" she couldn't help but ask.

"Because your word is enough."

He ran a hand over his close-cropped hair, and the slight tilt of his head drew her attention to the tattoo around his neck. That damned snake seemed to move, undulate, with each breath he took, giving him a deadly vibe that set her nerves on edge.

"Is that why you came all this way—to tell me in person?" His tone was impossible to decipher.

"Yes," she said miserably.

He studied her face. "Are you keeping it?"

This time her voice was clear, ringing with conviction. "Yes."

Except maybe the answer to that question should be *no*. Maybe terminating the pregnancy was the smarter option. If she kept the baby, that meant she'd be tying herself to this man for the rest of her life. This incredibly dangerous man, who led an incredibly dangerous life.

But even knowing that, and even though it scared her, the idea of *not* keeping the baby was unacceptable.

"I'm keeping him," she said firmly, more to herself than to D.

He blinked. "Isn't it too early to know the sex?"

"Yes, but . . ." She shrugged. "I don't know. I kind of hope it's a boy, and I don't like saying *it*, so I'm saying *him*."

Another pang of nausea tickled her insides, but she didn't feel like throwing up again. This imposing man standing in front of her was making her nervous. He'd gone quiet again, his expression utterly impenetrable.

Would it kill him to give her *something*? A sliver of emotion? Anger, reluctance, joy, disgust— anything was better than *nothing*.

Sofia breathed through the queasiness. "Did I ever tell you about my family?"

D gave a slight shake of the head.

"Well, I didn't have one. My mother OD'd when I was three. My father went to prison for armed robbery and manslaughter while she was pregnant, and was killed two years into his sentence by another inmate. I lived with my grandparents in New Mexico until I was ten, but they were deported when Immigration found out they were illegals."

She slowly sank onto the closed toilet lid and rubbed her tired eyes. "They were shipped back to Mexico, but I was an American citizen because both my parents were. My grandparents thought I'd have a better life in the States, get a better education, so they left me behind with friends of theirs, a nice couple who took good care of me."

Bitterness rose in her throat. "When I was thirteen, my grandparents died within months of each other, and their friends kicked me out the second the money stopped coming in. After that, I stayed with a friend from school, but then her family moved, so I had to move too. I stayed with another friend, and then another and another. I pretty much moved from house to house, taking handouts, until I was old enough to live alone."

Her hand involuntarily drifted to her stomach, and D's gaze followed it. Another glimmer of emotion peeked through his shuttered mask—uneasiness.

"I want a family," Sofia said softly. "That's what I've always wanted. And that's why I'm keeping this baby."

D said nothing.

It was like talking to a brick wall. She really hoped this wasn't an omen of what it would be like when . . . When what? When they raised a child together? He hadn't given her any indication that he even wanted to be in the baby's life.

"We need to figure stuff out. I need to know how involved you want to be in his life."

He looked startled. "You want me to be?"

Did she? She had no fucking idea. But she wasn't the kind of woman who would keep a father from his child. D's life was dangerous, yes, but they could work around it. Abby Sinclair's baby was already living on that compound. If the place wasn't safe for a child, then Abby and Kane wouldn't continue living there. That ought to reassure her, right?

"If you want to, I'm sure we can figure out a visitation schedule that suits your needs," Sofia answered. "But I won't lie—your life worries me. I'd need to know that your place in Costa Rica is secure. You know, if he's ever there for a weekend, or a summer, or whatever we work out. I mean, I guess we should decide if we want joint custody or . . ."

She trailed off. There was too much to digest right now. Too many decisions to make. And if it was too much for *her*, she could only imagine how overwhelming it was for D. She'd known about the pregnancy for a day and a half. He'd just found out about it ten minutes ago.

"You can take some time to think about it," she said quietly. "I'm only two months along, so we have time to figure everything out. I just wanted you to know."

No response.

She waited for him to ask another question, to comment on the pregnancy, the future, *anything*, but all she got was a harsh command.

"You need to go." He stepped toward the door. "It's too risky for you to be here. I'm going to take care of a few things, reach out to Mendez and set up the exchange, but once that's finalized, you and Ash are leaving. Understood?"

His dismissal stung, but she wasn't about to argue with him. "Understood."

He hesitated in the doorway, keeping his back to her. "You can lie down in one of the bedrooms if you want." His voice was hoarse, softer than she was used to. "You're . . . pregnant. You should, ah, probably get some rest."

Then he was gone.

Pregnant.

D's mind spun like an out-of-control carousel as he hurried into the living room. Liam and Ash glanced up at his approach, concern etched into their faces.

"Is Sofia okay?" Ash asked.

"She's fine," he mumbled, heading straight for the door. "I need to make a few calls."

He stumbled onto the walkway and sucked in an unsteady breath. The humidity had tempered, and the breeze in the air had a slight chill to it, adding to the bone-deep panic plaguing his body.

Christ, how had this happened? They'd used a *condom*. He would have noticed if the condom had broken.

Well, no matter how it happened, he hadn't been lying when he said he believed Sofia. Sure, he could've called her bluff and demanded a paternity test, but there was no point. Sofia was the most honest woman he'd ever met, and he was a walking lie detector, for fuck's sake.

She was telling the truth.

She was actually having his baby.

D didn't lose his cool often, but right now, his composure was nonexistent. He staggered through the archway, doubled over, and dry-heaved in the parking lot, feeling like someone had gutted him with a sledgehammer.

He wasn't father material.

He couldn't be a father, damn it.

As his insides twisted, he sank to the ground and leaned against the concrete wall, furious with himself for not taking precautions sooner. Why hadn't he gotten a vasectomy years ago? He'd toyed with the idea, but it had seemed unwarranted at the time. He always used protection, and he only fucked when the tension became unbearable. He could go for months without sex. Years, almost.

His breathing grew labored as he fished out his phone. He needed to make calls. He needed to call . . . Morgan. No, Morgan would only tell Noelle and—

D's spine stiffened as something occurred to him. With shaky fingers, he pulled up his contact list.

"You knew," he growled when Noelle picked up. "You *knew* she was pregnant and you still fucking sent her here."

"I was wondering when you'd get in touch," Noelle drawled.

D was so pissed off he was surprised he wasn't foaming at the mouth. "I understand why you sent Liam my way," he hissed. "But Sofia? In her condition?"

"She's not dying, D. She's pregnant."

"And you decided it would be a good idea to involve her in this mission?"

"I was hoping it might snap some sense into you." She sounded irritated. "You might be able to fool my husband, but I knew from the second you left the compound that you were going after Sullivan. It's not wise to play the lone wolf on this, D. You need backup."

"I don't need anyone."

"Yes, you do."

He choked back his fury. "Did you really think sending Sofia here would make me abort the op?"

"No, I thought it would remind you of the stakes. That whether you live or die matters to someone other than yourself, you fucking asshole. You want to pretend you don't care about your team? Fine. But they care about *you*. It's utterly stupid to go all renegade when you have soldiers ready and willing to back you up."

"You are not my fucking boss, Noelle."

"Yeah, well, neither is Morgan." She laughed humorlessly. "That's just the illusion you grant him. But we both know you're your own boss. You're your own worst enemy too. And you'll be your own goddamn down-fall."

He swore.

"Brilliant comeback, Derek." He could picture her face, those beautiful features twisted in annoyance. "Now quit being a jackass and get your head on straight. Send Sofia home—she achieved her purpose. Let Macgregor and Ash back you up. And bring Sullivan back in one piece."

Click.

The bitch had hung up.

He almost whipped the phone to the ground, tempted to watch it shatter to pieces, but he resisted the urge and took another breath instead. All right, so his mission was getting more complicated by the second. But he refused to let Sofia's bombshell distract him from the objective.

She was pregnant? Fine. She wanted to keep the baby? Fine. That didn't mean he had to play Daddy. Didn't mean he had to make a single decision right now.

The only thing that mattered at the moment was rescuing Sullivan from Mendez's island of horrors.

D exhaled in a slow, even rush. Time to get his head in the game.

He dialed another number and waited for an answer. It took six rings before he got one.

"Who is this?" No hello. No pleasantries. Just the wary voice of a man D hadn't seen in almost ten years.

Despite the pounding of his heart and the lost composure he couldn't seem to find, D managed an unaffected tone. "Raoul." He paused. "Long time."

Silence crashed over the line.

"What, no response?" D said mockingly. "And here I thought we were old friends."

"Friends?" Contempt dripped from Raoul Mendez's voice. "I always knew you had a big set of balls on you, but you truly have the nerve to call me up under the guise of friendship? We are not friends, you son of a bitch."

"Oh, but we are. You have something I want. I have something you want." He chuckled. "That makes us best friends."

"You have nothing I want, Jason." Mendez chuckled too. "Well, except for your head. On a spike."

"Trust me, you want something other than my head." He clicked his tongue in disapproval. "Your men are slacking, Raoul. I assumed you would have been alerted by now."

"Alerted to what?" Mendez asked suspiciously.

"That I have your daughter."

The answering hiss made D laugh again.

"I see I've got your attention. Good." D leaned his head against the wall and rubbed his stubble-covered jaw. "So, best friend. Why don't we get down to business?"

Chapter 11

Five months ago

For the first time in weeks, Sullivan could think clearly. Before that, he'd been in a twilight state for what felt like an eternity, conscious but not, dreaming but awake.

He was almost disappointed in his captors. Did they really believe injecting him with so-called "truth serum" would garner results? Sodium pentothal didn't work in real life the way it did in the movies. Or maybe it didn't work that way on *him*. Maybe the minds of the prisoners who'd graced this cell before him had been so impaired by the anesthetic that they'd actually talked.

It had been seventy-two hours since his last injection. They'd left him alone for three glorious days, the guards entering his cell only to deliver food and water, and Lord, it was a beautiful feeling, being able to think again. Not having to listen to the constant flow of questions.

Who do you work for?

How do you know Derek Pratt?

Where is Derek Pratt?

Days. No, weeks of hearing the same questions, over

and over and over again. Usually Paulo was the person doing the asking, but sometimes Mendez interrogated Sullivan himself, probably when he had a few hours to kill.

No matter how loopy and disoriented the drugs had made him, Sully knew he hadn't said a word. Otherwise they wouldn't keep coming back. Otherwise he would already be dead.

He didn't mind the sodium pentothal. His brain was strong enough to resist it, and it numbed the pain, clouded reality just enough that he didn't have to focus on the fact that he was a prisoner here.

Still, it did feel bloody nice to have his mental faculties back.

He wearily glanced around the cell. The cinderblock walls. The iron shackles bolted into the wall and floor—one set for his arms, the other for his legs. The chains gave him about five feet of leeway, allowing him to move around and use the only modern fixture in the room: the dirty metal toilet in the corner.

Now that his senses had returned, he realized that his clothes reeked. And look at that—his arm had healed. The cigar burn was still red and puckered, but they'd pumped him full of antibiotics to prevent infection. Mendez was taking every precaution to ensure Sullivan remained alive.

Good. That was good. It meant he'd be alive when the team found him.

Because the team *would* find him. He'd been clinging to that truth since the moment Mendez had thrown him in this cell. They might not be able to track his location using the SOS system, but his mates were smart.

They were skilled. They would follow the trail from Dublin and they would *find* him.

All he had to do in the meantime was hold on. Keep his mouth shut and hold on.

But Christ, he was tired. The cell was perpetually dark. Even when the sun was out, the barred window was too small and set too deep for more than a shaft of light to peek through. Every time it came, that tiny bit of light, he would crawl across the stone floor and lie in that one sunbeam. Pretend he was lying on the deck of *Evangeline*.

They'll find you.

Holding on to the internal reassurance, he swallowed past his dry throat. Yes, they would find him. *Liam* would find him. Liam would never give up on him.

The thought of his best mate brought a deep ache to Sully's already sore chest. A few of the guards had knocked him around last week after his lack of response had annoyed Mendez. The man had ordered the beating not as a form of torture, but as punishment for Sully being a stubborn son of a bitch.

Yeah, he was stubborn, all right. He'd displayed that same stubbornness back in Dublin, when Liam had begged him to explore the attraction between them.

Sullivan's heart squeezed at the memory. He hated that the last time he'd seen his friend, they'd been arguing. The moment he got out of here, he would make things right with Liam.

And fine, maybe there was sexual awareness between them, but screw that. Ignoring it was the only way to hang on to the most important relationship in Sully's life. He hadn't cared about anyone, *truly* cared about them, in years. Not since—

Footsteps in the hall cut off his thoughts.

He instantly tensed, his hands curling on instinct into tight fists, but it made no difference. He was in chains. Bloody hell. He was *chained*, like a prisoner in some medieval dungeon.

The key turned in the lock, and then the cell door opened with a creak.

Paulo entered first, trailed by two guards whose names Sullivan didn't know or care to know. They were faceless monsters to him, and their rotations changed on a whim—he'd studied the shift changes, tried to figure out their routine, but Mendez was smart. There *wasn't* a routine, at least not one Sullivan could use to plan his escape.

The drugs, unfortunately, had impaired his mind, prevented him from being able to formulate any escape plans, but now that they were out of his system, he was on the alert again. Searching for any weakness he could exploit.

"Evening, soldier," Paulo said brusquely.

He always referred to Sullivan as *soldier*, and there was an odd note of respect in his voice each time he said it.

Of all the guards, Paulo was the hardest to figure out. He seemed to be Mendez's number two, obeying the man without question. He seemed to be as sadistic as Mendez was. And yet Sullivan had heard him shouting at another guard before, his tone laced with disapproval and disgust as he reamed the man out for touching the "merchandise."

Sullivan didn't have to be a genius to figure out what the merchandise was. He'd heard the female sobs echoing through the halls of the dungeon. He'd heard the guards talking about the girls they were transporting. Which meant he was smack-dab in the middle of a sex-trade operation.

"Are you feeling clearheaded?" Paulo's hand absently stroked the gun butt poking out of his hip holster. "The drugs should be out of your system by now."

Sully didn't answer.

Paulo nodded at one of the guards. "Check his pupils," he ordered in Spanish.

The guard knelt in front of Sullivan and peered closely at him. "He's good." Then he stood up and rejoined Paulo.

"So. Are you ready to tell us where Derek Pratt is?" Paulo asked pleasantly.

Sullivan stared at him.

That earned him a heavy sigh. "I thought you might say that." Paulo nodded at the second guard, who briskly disappeared through the open doorway.

No one spoke. Paulo tapped his foot, a bored expression on his face. The guard at his side didn't move.

A startled yelp echoed from the hall.

A female yelp.

Sullivan's stomach went rigid. Jesus. Looked like the game was about to change.

A moment later, the guard returned, dragging a dark-haired woman inside the cell. He gave her a hard shove, and she went sprawling to the floor, landing four feet from Sullivan's chained ankles.

His heart stopped when he noticed Paulo's smirk.

Oh Christ.

Forcing himself to remain stone-faced, he flicked his

gaze at the woman. Her hair was a mess, tangled and greasy and sticking up in all directions. The red dress she wore was ripped in several places, and streaks of dirt covered her bare legs.

She suddenly shifted her head and a pair of fearful dark eyes met Sullivan's. There was blood caked on her left temple. Her bottom lip was swollen, thanks to a red cut on the edge of her mouth, but even in her disheveled state, he could tell she was pretty. Beautiful, even.

As she silently stared at him, he almost opened his mouth to reassure her, to tell her everything would be all right. He tried conveying it with his eyes instead, but clearly he failed, because her expression didn't change.

If anything, she looked even more afraid, because someone else was now entering the cell.

Mendez.

Once again dressed in khakis and a polo, the man looked like he'd just stepped off the golf course of a country club. "Good evening." He greeted Sullivan with a smile. "I see you've met our guest. We grabbed her off a resort in Cabo last week. She's been in the cell next to yours since then. I bet you didn't even know you had company, did you?"

Sullivan's jaw tensed.

Mendez's smile widened. "We've decided to try something new today. Your resistance is impressive. It truly is, and I admire you for it. It's a sign of strength." He sighed. "You'd be surprised by how many weak men I encounter on a daily basis. It makes me sick, really. But while I appreciate your willpower and your loyalty to Mr. Pratt, it's time you told me how you know him and where he is. I've spent a lot of money and wasted a lot of man-power on Pratt, and I'm afraid I'm growing impatient."

Sullivan said nothing.

"I'm going to give you one last chance to tell me where I can find him. If you do, my men will release you."

Bullshit. Sullivan knew he was never walking out of here alive.

Mendez must have read his mind, because he clucked in disappointment. "You don't believe me. I guess I don't blame you." He glanced at Paulo. "Paulo, am I a man of my word?"

"Yes, sir."

"See?" Mendez told Sullivan. "I'm a man of my word. I have no issue with you, and I don't fear you. If I release you, I'm not afraid of you finding your way back here and exacting your revenge. No one approaches this compound without my knowledge, and nobody steps foot on it without my permission. So no, you're not a threat to me. Only a potential source of information."

Sullivan closed his eyes. He was so damn tired of these games.

"Open your eyes," Mendez said irritably. "Or else I'll order my men to pry them open for you. I want you to see what happens next."

Sullivan reluctantly obeyed.

Mendez gestured to the bulkier of the nameless guards, who promptly hauled the woman to her feet.

She cried out again, her husky voice cutting into Sullivan like a knife. He didn't look at her, though. He *couldn't* look at her. Because whatever was about to happen, whatever reason they'd brought her here, it wasn't going to be good.

"She's lovely, isn't she?" Mendez admired the curvy body beneath the torn dress. "Do you think she's a virgin?" He raked his gaze over her again. "No, I don't think so. Usually when a woman dresses like a slut, she *is* slut, right?" He shrugged. "But her pussy will probably still be tight." He chuckled at the guard, a stocky man with a thick neck and massive arms. "You think her pussy is tight, Ricardo?"

The man grinned. "I would very much like to find out, sir."

The girl let out a breathy wheeze. Her gaze sought out Sullivan's again, and this time he couldn't look away.

Mendez smiled. "Let's see what our prisoner has to say first." He raised a brow at Sullivan. "Here's what's about to happen. If you don't tell me where Derek Pratt is, Ricardo here is going to fuck our sweet guest. Right in front of you."

The brunette made a panicked sound.

Sullivan swallowed, his heart constricting painfully.

"So." Mendez slanted his head. "Where is Pratt?"

Goddamn it, he wasn't going to talk. *He couldn't fucking talk.*

"I'm not bluffing," Mendez said coldly. "Ricardo . . ."

The guard forced the woman to her knees, then gave her a forward shove so she had no choice but to land on both hands. Ricardo slowly slid her dress up and leered at her bare backside.

"No panties," Mendez remarked. "See? I told you she was a slut. That doesn't matter to the buyers, though. I send more than enough virgins their way. Sometimes they like the ones who know their way around a man's cock."

When Ricardo undid his zipper, Sullivan's stomach dropped. Acid burned his throat, ripped his insides apart.

"Please," she whimpered. "Please don't do this to me."

She'd spoken in English, and her accent told Sullivan she was American. Mendez had said he'd grabbed her from a resort. She was a tourist, then. The perfect prey for a sex predator.

"Me? *I'm* not doing this to you." Mendez jabbed a finger at Sullivan. "He is. *He* is going to let this happen to you." The man smirked. "All he has to do is give me the information I require, and your whore pussy will be spared." A pause. "Ricardo . . ."

Sullivan's throat clamped shut. Ricardo was undoing his pants.

"Where is Derek Pratt?" Mendez asked.

Sullivan bit his tongue so hard that blood filled his mouth. The coppery flavor slid down his throat and made him want to throw up.

"Where is Derek Pratt?"

Sullivan's teeth dug into his cheek now. He was seconds away from shouting out D's location, and it took all his willpower to control the reckless urge. He couldn't do it. Because there was more at stake here than just one woman.

Mendez hollowed his cheeks in annoyance. "Fuck her," he told the guard.

Ricardo locked eyes with Sullivan.

Waited.

When Sully remained quiet, the man's hips began to move.

Oh Lord. He was going to be sick. He . . .

He should give D up.

Sullivan opened his mouth—

No. You keep your fucking mouth shut, soldier!

He wouldn't just be endangering D if he talked. D wasn't the only one living on the compound, goddamn it. Liam lived there too. Cate. Ash. Abby—God, Abby had been ready to pop when Sullivan had gone to Dublin. She must've given birth by now. She and Kane had a *baby* now.

Sullivan watched.

He sat there. And he watched. And he didn't say a fucking word.

Liam. Cate. Ash. Abby's baby.

He focused on the people he loved, the people he had to protect at all costs, even if it meant . . . even if— he'd officially gone numb. He watched without really seeing. He heard without really listening.

He was going to hell. Oh Christ, he was going to hell. But at least the people he loved would be safe.

Sullivan clenched his fists. He kept watching.

Mendez and his men also watched. They watched *Sullivan.* Who was going to hell. Who was sitting there and . . . and . . . he gasped for air, but it didn't fucking matter. He couldn't breathe anymore.

Ricardo finished, standing as the woman collapsed on her stomach.

Mendez knelt beside her with a tsking noise. When he touched her shoulder, she recoiled. "Everything that just happened here?" he murmured to the trembling girl. "It was *his* fault. He did this to you."

Sullivan's throat closed up. He'd done this to her.

He had done this to her.

Paulo moved toward the girl, but Mendez stopped him with a sharp command. "Leave her. Let him see what he did to her. Maybe it will teach him to act differently the next time we visit."

The four men marched out of the cell without a backward look, leaving the woman behind.

The door shut. The lock clicked.

Silence. Deafening silence.

Sullivan desperately wanted to see her face, but she'd turned her cheek the other way. Tears stung his eyelids as he opened his mouth, and for the first time in more than a month, he finally heard his own voice.

"I'm sorry." He made sure to disguise his Aussie accent, using an East Coast American one instead. His voice was so hoarse, it was hard to talk. "I'm sorry," he repeated.

Her head turned, and the look she wore . . . defeat. Not anger, but pure and total defeat.

"It wouldn't have mattered if you said anything," she whispered. "It's not the first time they've done that to me."

"I . . ." A choked sob broke free, a rush of shame so powerful he keeled over on his side, unable to support his own weight anymore.

It hurt to talk. To think. He almost wished the drugs were still in his system. That way he wouldn't have to think about what had happened. What he'd *let* happen.

"I . . . Jesus Christ . . . I let him rape you. I . . ." He was a mess. A crying, blubbering mess. Racked with guilt and shuddering uncontrollably, his vision a blur of hot tears, his stomach contracting with each painful gulp of oxygen he sucked in.

There was a rustling sound and suddenly his head was no longer on the cold ground but resting on a soft, warm lap. She'd pulled him there. She was holding him.

Sully gagged. "I'm sorry. I'm so sorry."

"Hey . . . Hey, it's okay."

Okay? It was *okay*? He'd sat there and *watched*. He could have stopped it but he hadn't. *He'd sat there and watched*.

He would never be able to forgive himself for what he'd just done.

Sully wasn't sure how long he lay there, crying in her lap. The whole time, she petted his hair, stroked his cheek, murmured reassurances, and it was so bloody ironic because he was the one who needed to offer comfort. He'd allowed them to hurt her. He should be comforting *her*.

Time passed. Minutes. Maybe hours. Eventually his breathing slowed. His sobs subsided. But she didn't release him. She held him and stroked him, and that tiny shred of human contact was the most soothing thing he'd felt in so fucking long.

"I was on winter break."

Her soft voice drew him to the present. He didn't lift his head, but he was hanging on to her every word.

"Some friends from UCLA talked me into it. I didn't want to come at first." She exhaled audibly. "My parents died. When I was a kid. So the holidays are always the hardest. I like to be alone for them. But my friends convinced me it would be fun to go to Cabo." She gave a scornful laugh. "They said it would be *fun*."

"I'm sorry," Sullivan whispered. "I'm so sorry."

"Stop saying that. I already told you—it's nothing that

hasn't happened before. I've been here for a week. You must have heard my screams."

He hadn't. But he'd also been drugged out of his mind.

"It must be important."

"What is?" He sat up, but he was too ashamed to look at her. Too humiliated that he'd broken down and allowed her to comfort him after what he'd done to her.

He clumsily leaned back against the wall, resisting the urge to crack his own skull on the concrete behind it. Put himself out of his bloody misery.

"It must be important to you, keeping that man safe," she clarified. "Darren Pratt, or whatever his name was. The man they were asking you about." Her brow furrowed. "They really want to find him, I guess."

Sullivan swallowed.

"Did you ever . . ." Her tone went sad. "Did you ever think people like this actually existed? Sick, cruel people . . ."

"This isn't the first time I've witnessed cruelty," he said roughly.

In the back of his head, a warning alarm went off. A swift order not to reveal anything else.

He went quiet again.

So did she.

He watched, almost hypnotized, as she began using her fingers to untangle the knots in her hair. Something felt wrong. But he couldn't pinpoint what it was. He'd been in this stinking prison for so long that his brain-power had slowed. His mind had gone from a sharp blade to a dull butter knife.

"You're lucky," she mused. "I wish I'd witnessed

cruelty before. If I had, I would've been more careful. I wouldn't have let that man flirt with me or convince me to leave the resort to go to a bar in town. I would've been *careful*." Unshed tears sparkled on her lashes.

Sully spoke past the lump in his throat. "It wasn't your fault. Men like these . . . they're smart. It's a business to them."

She looked sick. "Kidnapping women . . . *raping* women . . . is a business?"

"A lucrative one."

"How do you know?" Her fingers tackled another knot at the bottom of her long hair. "How do you know so much about these people? Who *are* you?"

"I'm just someone who knows."

The prickly feeling at the back of his neck intensified as he watched her slender fingers pick at the knot. What was bothering him, damn it?

"Why are you letting them do this to you?" Her eyes rested on his shirt, the bloodstains at his side, then widened when she caught sight of his upper arm. The stitches, the cigar burn. She worked harder at the knot in her hair. "Why don't you just tell them what they want to know? Why—"

Sullivan launched himself at her.

She screeched in shock as he knocked her on her back, straddling her thighs and pinning her down. The shackles around his wrists rattled loudly as the chain stretched tight across her throat.

"Who the *fuck* are you?"

"What are you talking about?" she squeaked.

Growling, he moved the chain away from her neck and grabbed one of her hands. He gripped her fingers and held them up for her to see. Perfectly manicured fingers. French tips.

Every other inch of her was filthy and disheveled. The blood on her temple. The dirt on her legs. But her nails were perfect. They were fucking *perfect*.

"These aren't the fingernails of a woman who's been locked in a cell for a week," he spat out, squeezing her fingers until she yelped in pain. "You would've clawed at the walls. Clawed at the guards. You would've fought and your nails would be broken and bloody and dirty. *So who the fuck are you?*"

Her head shot up without warning, butting him hard in the nose. As pain jolted though his nostrils and blood poured out of them, the brunette rolled out from under him, stumbled to her feet, and sprinted to the door.

His chains restricted him from going after her. He sat up, wiping blood from his nose and spitting out the droplets that had slid into his mouth. Fury sizzled through his veins as the woman rapped her knuckles on the door.

A second later, one of the guards entered the cell. Not just any guard. Ricardo.

The man who . . .

The man who'd pretended to *rape* her.

Pretended.

A dizzying combination of horror and relief swept through Sullivan's body. A trick. It had all been a trick. A staged rape, a ploy to get him to talk.

Before he could fully absorb how sick and twisted that was, Mendez reappeared in the doorway, and the woman's tone immediately grew repentant as she addressed him in Spanish.

"I'm sorry. He figured it out."

Mendez's dark eyes shifted from Sullivan to the brunette. "He gave you nothing useful? Nothing?"

"Based on the accent, I'd say he's American." She pouted like a little girl. "I'm sorry, Papa. I tried."

Papa?

Bile rose in Sullivan's throat. Was this Mendez's *daughter*? Had the man actually stood by and watched his own daughter . . .

Sully bent over and threw up all over the floor.

The laughter of Mendez and his daughter was the last thing he heard before the door slammed shut and the lock slid into place.

Chapter 12

Present day

Sullivan regained consciousness to the sound of a soft, persistent thumping.

Everything was dark. He remembered being on the water at dawn, the sun creeping up from the horizon line and casting a pink and orange glow over the waves. Had he made it to shore? He remembered seeing land. He'd *seen* it. And it had been dawn when he'd approached it, so it should be morning now. Bloody hell, it should be morning.

Why was it dark again?

Had he made it to shore?

He was so bloody confused. The worst of the withdrawal had come at the five-day mark. It had to be at least day seven now. He was no longer shaking, no longer feeling like he was being stabbed from the inside out, but he was still dizzy. Still nauseous.

Oh Lord, he wanted a fix. He *ached* for it. He craved it more than anything else in the world.

Somehow he found the strength to sit up, and realized

what was causing the thumping. The motorboat was stuck, bobbing against a log or a boulder or whatever was trapping the small craft against the muddy bank.

He was lucky. He must have lost consciousness when he'd reached the shore, and if the boat hadn't gotten stuck, he might be floating in the middle of the ocean right about now. A coast guard patrol could have found him. Mendez could have found him.

It was so fucking dark out. Not even a shred of light— the moon must be hidden behind the clouds. And he was so cold. Shivering now, and he didn't know if it was because of the temperature or the withdrawal. As his teeth chattered wildly, he groaned and curled himself into a ball, praying that the shaking spell would pass.

He needed to find a phone. Civilization. He had no idea where he was, what country he was even in. When he'd first arrived on the island, he'd thought he might be in Mexico, but that had been six months ago.

His body shook even harder.

He'd been in that hellhole for *six months*.

As a wave of sickness overtook him, Sully shot into a sitting position, bent over, and vomited all over the side of the boat. But there was nothing to vomit. Just bile . . . and blood. Jesus, he could taste blood in his mouth.

Every muscle, every cell in his body, shrieked in agony. Everything *hurt*.

Ignore it. You need to get out of here.

The urgent voice in his head was right. Mendez's people would be looking for him. They could be speeding up in a boat at this very moment. He had no idea how long he'd been out for. At least twelve hours. Maybe more. Maybe days.

Sullivan had never felt so weak in his life as he tried to stand up. Shit. Bad idea. Not just because the boat was moving, but because his head was spinning. A wave of vertigo hit as he attempted to lift his foot and step onto the grassy sliver of land in front of him.

Everything swayed and bobbled and teetered and tilted, and suddenly he toppled over, landing back in the boat. Water splashed over the edge and doused him in the face.

Sully moaned. Goddamn it. He was a soldier. He was one of Jim Morgan's soldiers, for Christ's sake. He could do this.

He. Could. Do. This—

His head went foggy the second he tried sitting up again.

And then everything went black.

Sofia woke up at five thirty in the morning, shooting out of bed as if someone had lit a fuse in her ass. Either she'd dreamed it or she'd just heard a woman screaming. Screaming bloody murder. A high-pitched shriek laced with outrage and—

Nope, she hadn't been dreaming. She could still hear the screams. They were blasting toward the guest room from the front of the apartment, which told her that Angelina was awake. Awake, and clearly livid about her current predicament.

". . . *kill* you for this . . . hear me, Jason? He'll *kill* you!"

D's hostage was spewing threats now, bringing a tremor of fear to Sofia's stomach. The moment she stepped toward the door, the screams stopped and the apartment went silent. Eerily silent.

The men must have sedated Angelina again. Or maybe they'd knocked her out using a fist or a karate chop or some other form of violence.

God. How was any of this actually happening?

She rubbed her weary eyes as she glanced around the spare bedroom she'd slept in last night. D had wanted her and Ash to leave yesterday, but she'd been too exhausted to get on another plane so late at night. Eventually he'd relented and had let them stay until morning, claiming they were safe for the time being. Apparently D had already contacted Angelina's father, but Mendez had refused to agree to a trade until he verified D's claim.

The claim being that D was holding the man's daughter hostage.

D was holding someone *hostage*. Sofia had known he was a dangerous man, but seeing that danger in action was an entirely different story. She wanted to go home, damn it. Back to her safe little house in the mountains, back to her clinic, her friends in the village.

Swallowing a groan, she ducked into the hall bathroom and washed up, then examined her wrinkled clothing and tangled hair. She hadn't packed any toiletries or a spare set of clothes—she honestly hadn't expected to spend more than a few hours in Cancún.

She made do by running her fingers through her hair to brush it, then braided it over her shoulder and stepped into the hall. She jumped when she found D waiting there.

He wore cargo pants and a black muscle shirt that emphasized every hard ridge of his chest, which triggered a surprising spark of heat deep in her core.

How was she still attracted to him? After hearing

him describe his history with Mendez last night, she shouldn't want to touch him. Or kiss him. Or spread her legs for him again.

But damn it, that was exactly what she wanted. Her entire body *ached* for him. Ached to be filled by him. Maybe it was just the pregnancy hormones? Yeah, that had to be it. That was the only reason she could actually still desire this man.

"We need to talk," he said in a gravelly voice.

Nodding, she followed him to the spare room, where he closed the door and leaned against the wall. He folded his arms, drawing her gaze to his perfectly formed biceps. Her lips tingled with the urge to kiss them. To part so she could drag her tongue over those roped muscles and taste his skin.

What was the *matter* with her?

"How are you feeling?"

His gruff question startled her. "Uh. I'm fine. A bit hungry."

"I sent Ash to grab some breakfast. You can eat before you go."

Gee, he was giving her permission to eat? What a prince.

His arms dropped from his chest and rested against his sides. "You'll be contacted by a lawyer in the next few weeks."

She frowned. "What lawyer?"

"My lawyer. He'll bring some papers for you to sign." His gaze remained shuttered. "I'm transferring some money to you."

Suspicion tugged at her belly. "Why?"

"So you'll be taken care of."

Sofia couldn't stop the bite to her voice. "In case you die during the exchange for Sullivan?"

D shrugged. "You'll get the money either way. It's more than enough to support yourself and the kid for the rest of your lives."

Insult prickled her skin. He was offering her money? No, not even offering. He was straight-up *giving* it to her.

For some reason, that bothered her. A lot.

"I don't want your money," she said stiffly.

"Tough shit. You're still getting it."

Sofia stuck out her chin. "Then I won't sign the papers."

"I thought you might say that, which is why I instructed my lawyer to bring the same amount in cash and leave it on your porch if you refuse to sign. And if you want to be stubborn and give it to charity, go ahead. Because I also set up a trust fund that my lawyer will manage until the kid turns eighteen, at which point he'll have access to it."

The kid.

Not *the baby*. Not *our child*. It was just *the kid* to him. And the fact that he was offering money and nothing else spoke volumes.

"You don't want to be in the baby's life," Sofia said flatly.

"Trust me, you don't want me in your life. In either of your lives. I'm fucking poison."

Sorrow twisted in her chest. It wasn't like she'd been gung-ho about co-parenting with this man, but she hadn't thought he'd dismiss the pregnancy—dismiss *her*—so callously.

"You could really turn your back on your own child?" Her heart lurched as she voiced the bleak question.

"He'll be well taken care of," D muttered.

"Babies don't need money, Derek. They need *parents*." A lump obstructed her throat. "They need love and support and guidance."

"And he'll get all that from you." D's expression remained thoroughly indifferent.

"So that's it?" Sofia bit her lip. "Your final decision is you want nothing to do with this baby?"

"Yes."

That one blunt syllable was like a blow to the jugular. Her throat squeezed tight enough to restrict airflow, and her hands shook in response, trembling so hard she had to lace her fingers together and press them against her belly.

"Okay, then," she mumbled. "If that's what you want."

"It's better this way."

"Sure, Derek. If you say so." She forced herself to meet his gaze. "What's going on with Mendez?"

"Sofia—"

She interrupted him. "The parenting portion of this conversation is over, D. I want to know what's going on with Mendez."

After a second of silence, he cleared his throat and said, "We've set up a meeting."

"When?"

"An hour. There's an airfield three miles west of here, completely off the books. He's sending a chopper to pick me up and take me to his island."

Worry slammed into her. "What do you mean, *you*? You're going alone?"

"That was his one stipulation. He wants a face-to-face with me."

Sofia wasn't a seasoned operative, but she'd seen enough crime shows to know that attending a high-risk meeting without backup was *not* the way to go.

"You said you killed his son," she accused.

D nodded.

"And he wants a face-to-face with his son's *murderer*? Jesus, Derek. He'll kill you the moment he has his daughter back."

"Which is why I'm not bringing Angelina with me."

She blinked in confusion. "You're not?"

D offered a low chuckle. "I'm not an amateur, Sofia. If I show up with Angelina, of course he'll kill me on the spot. He'll kill Sully, too."

At the mention of Sullivan, Sofia searched D's face. "Is Sullivan alive? For sure?"

"Mendez claims he is. But that's another reason I'm going solo—I need to verify that before I give up Angelina. She's our insurance policy." He paused. "Macgregor will watch her while I meet with Mendez, and once we have confirmation that Sully is alive, I'll get him off the island and Macgregor will hand over Angelina at a prearranged location."

Doubt scurried through her. "You really think Mendez is just going to let you and Sullivan leave the island?"

"He won't have a choice. If Macgregor doesn't hear from me in twelve hours, he has orders to put a bullet in Angelina's head."

Sofia gulped down a rush of sickness. "And Liam will actually do it? Kill an unarmed woman, just like that?"

"For Sullivan? Macgregor will do anything." D noticed her expression and sighed. "You need to stop feeling sorry for this woman, Sofia. If anyone deserves to die, it's her."

"Nobody *deserves* to die," she argued, but in the back of her mind, she knew that wasn't true. She'd disproved that statement herself once, when she'd held a man's life in her hands, a very bad man, and she'd chosen to let him die rather than save him.

But the doctor in her, the woman who'd taken an oath to save lives, wanted so badly to believe that D's callous assessment of humanity wasn't true.

"I never took you for naive, baby." He cocked a brow in challenge. "What about Hitler? Are you telling me that if that maniac was standing in front of you and you had a gun in your hand, you wouldn't kill him? If he was unarmed, tied up, begging for you to save him, you really wouldn't pull the trigger?"

She clenched her teeth instead of answering.

D laughed again. "See? Some people *do* deserve it." He moved toward the door. "All right. It's time to go."

"I don't like this plan," she blurted out.

"You don't have to like it. You're not a part of it. You're going to the airport, remember?"

He paused in the doorway, his mocking gaze sweeping over her, and even while wearing that scornful expression, he was still the most attractive man she'd ever laid eyes on. His features looked like they'd been chiseled out of stone, and the dark scruff on his jaw was sexy as hell.

She didn't understand him. Didn't understand *herself* for being so attracted to him. Derek Pratt represented everything she hated in a man. He was aloof, dispassionate, insensitive at times. He wasn't boyfriend material. Hell, he wasn't even first-date material.

Her gaze slid up his corded throat to his mouth. That mouth had no right being so damn sensual. He hadn't kissed her the night they'd had sex. If anything, he'd made an effort to not even look at her. Taking her from behind while he was fully clothed . . . it was as impersonal as it could get.

The father of my baby, ladies and gentlemen. A man who can't even look a woman in the eye when he fucks her.

Along with a deep burn of resentment, her heart also ached with regret. There *had* to be more to this man. Nobody could be this cold and indifferent. Her gut told her that something had *made* him this way, and if she just took the time to find out what it was, then she could . . . what? Fix him?

God. Yes. Maybe she *did* want to fix him. Because that was what she did—she fixed people, damn it. And it drove her crazy that she couldn't seem to reach D, no matter how hard she tried. For years their paths had kept crossing, over and over again, yet she knew as much about him now as she had back then. Which was nothing. She knew *nothing*.

"Ash will drive you to the plane in ten minutes," he told her, then paused, visibly uncomfortable. "Make sure you go to all your doctor's appointments. Take care of yourself and the kid."

When he started to turn away, she hurried toward him. "Derek. Wait."

The wariness in his eyes barely took root before she was reaching up to cup his cheeks. He flinched the second she touched him. She ignored the response. She suspected he didn't like to be touched, but she didn't care. She swept her thumbs over the stubble on his jaw and locked her gaze with his.

"Be careful," she said softly.

Then she stood on her tiptoes and pressed her mouth to his.

His lips didn't move. Not at first. His discomfort showed in the stiffness of his body, and if she hadn't clasped her hands around his neck, she knew he would have pulled away.

She brushed her lips over his, slowly, gently. When she tried to deepen the kiss, he stiffened again, just for a moment, before his mouth opened ever so slightly and his tongue touched hers. Her pulse exploded as anticipation surged through her blood, but one fleeting taste was all she got. The softest, sweetest brush of his tongue, and then he wrenched their mouths apart.

"Good-bye, Sofia," he said gruffly.

She stared at the empty doorway after he'd left it, her heart beating fast. Why did he always leave her wanting more? She didn't know him. She wasn't sure she *liked* him. Yet she always wanted more. Another lay. Another kiss. Just . . . *more.*

Sofia stood frozen in place as she listened to the male voices wafting from the main room. D had said something to his men, and now they were engaged in muffled conversation. Then she heard footsteps. The front door shut. A moment later, the faint sound of a car engine, and then voices again. Liam and Ash, talking among themselves.

D had left.

Good-bye, Sofia.

Her insides twisted into a tight knot. His good-bye had sounded way too final. Like they were never going to see each other again.

She was probably worried about nothing. D had said so himself—Angelina Mendez was his insurance policy. As long as the woman was in Liam's custody, her father wouldn't dare kill D.

But . . . what if he did? What if D was wrong and Mendez didn't give a shit about his daughter? The man was a human trafficker—how much loyalty could he really have?

Sofia was still running worst-case scenarios in her head when Ash appeared. "Ready to go?" he asked.

With an absent nod, she followed him to the living room. Her gaze immediately homed in on the sofa, but the cushions were empty. "Where's Angelina?"

"Bedroom," Liam answered from the kitchen counter. "She got a little handsy this morning, so we had to tie her up. The bed frame seemed sturdy enough."

Sofia blanched. "Did you really have to do that? And does she really need to stay sedated?"

"You heard her earlier, right? The screams?" Liam made a derisive sound. "Well, those screams came with a pretty solid head butt. That chick is *strong*."

He drifted away from the counter, and Sofia experienced a spark of alarm when she noticed the swelling beneath his left eye.

"Let me take a look at that," she ordered, but when she stepped closer, he tried ducking out of her path.

"It's fine. Just a bruise."

"Humor me." She ran her fingertips along his cheekbone, gauging to see if it was fractured. He was right—

he'd taken a good hit and he would have a bruise, but other than that, he was fine.

"Here." Ash handed her a croissant and a bottle of water. "D said you need to eat before we go."

"And we always do what D says, right?" she said bitterly.

"Yes. He's leading this op, he calls the shots. Now *eat.*"

As much as it pained her to take a bite and give D the satisfaction of being her lord and master, she had a baby to think about, and she couldn't deny she was starving. She practically inhaled the croissant, then grumbled a request for another one, which Ash handed over with a grin.

Once she'd finished eating and chugged the entire bottle of water, he gently took her arm. "Time to go."

Again, Sofia didn't bother putting up a fight. She'd achieved her purpose in coming here—she'd told D about the pregnancy. There was nothing left to do but go home.

She felt oddly numb as they left the apartment. It was still so early that the temperature was slightly cool, but the sun was rising higher in the sky, hinting at another hot, humid day. She'd already arranged for one of her on-call doctors to cover the clinic for a few days, which meant she could go home, soak in the tub for a couple hours, then spend the rest of her week making plans for the future.

Good-bye, Sofia.

She wondered when D's lawyer would show up, which only brought another wave of resentment. Did he really think throwing money at her would make everything better? Make things right? She didn't need his oodles of cash. She made a decent living, more than enough to support herself and a child. So no, she didn't need his goddamn money. She needed . . .

Fuck, it didn't even matter what she needed. He'd made his position clear. He wasn't interested in being a father to their baby, and it shouldn't bother her that he didn't. She should be relieved.

But . . . it really, really bothered her.

She settled in the passenger's seat of the white Range Rover and waited for Ash to get behind the wheel. He'd just started the car when a curse left his mouth. "Shit. I forgot my phone."

Sofia pointed to the phone he'd dropped in the cup holder literally two seconds ago. "It's right there."

"My other phone," he explained, as if carrying more than one cell phone was the most natural thing in the world. But she supposed it was when you worked for Jim Morgan. "I'll be right back."

He left the car idling as he hopped out, and she absently watched his broad body stalk toward the building.

Good-bye, Sofia.

Damn it. Did he not expect to come back? D had said the face-to-face wasn't a big deal, but she couldn't fight the gnawing fear that he'd gone to that meeting expecting to die.

Her gaze strayed back to the apartment building in time to see Ash disappear through the entryway. Then she glanced at the keys in the ignition.

Don't even think about it.

Right. She was panicking for no reason. There was no need to rush after D. He was a soldier, for fuck's sake. No, he was more than that. He'd worked black ops. He'd *killed* people. Even if she did catch up to him, she doubted she'd be able to talk him out of going after Sully.

He'd said the airfield was three miles west . . .

You're being crazy right now, Amaro. Certifiably crazy. You can't talk him out of it.

But maybe she could. Maybe she could help him come up with another way to handle the exchange. Because showing up *alone* to meet with the father of the man he'd killed . . . it was fucking suicide.

She glanced at the building again. Ash still hadn't reappeared.

D had only a ten-minute head start. And he'd said the chopper wasn't arriving for another hour. She had plenty of time to drive there and convince him to abandon this foolish plan. They could leave the airfield before the helicopter showed up and find another way.

As the panic in her gut intensified, Sofia unbuckled her seat belt and climbed into the driver's seat.

Chapter 13

D arrived ahead of schedule, but made no move to approach the airfield. Instead, he called in a favor from a friend in the CIA to request satellite images of the area. Then he waited.

The airport was privately owned. It had one runway and one hangar, and catered mostly to locals, particularly those operating on the wrong side of the law. When D's contact came through for him ten minutes later, the images D received were less than an hour old. They also clearly revealed the heat signatures of the men Mendez had dispatched.

One sniper on the roof of the hangar, another one in the wooded area on the outskirts of the airport.

He decided to take care of the man in the woods first. He stashed the car a mile out, then trekked through the brush with his rifle in hand, which turned out to be unnecessary, because Mendez's crew had evidently gotten sloppy. The camo-clad man didn't even hear D approach him from behind, and one outraged growl was all the sound he made before D snapped his neck like a twig.

As the lifeless body sank to the earth, D helped

himself to the dead man's military-grade sniper rifle. Then he chuckled. Pathetic. Not only had Mendez's goon lacked any instincts whatsoever, but he sucked at choosing vantage points, too. Any soldier worth his salt would've picked a spot that allowed the second sniper to maintain a visual on him in case trouble arose. But the idiot had hidden himself from both the airport *and* his cohort's sights.

Which meant D had a perfect view of the second sniper's head—and the guy was completely oblivious to him.

He peered through the scope, resisting the urge to roll his eyes. Jesus. Mendez *really* needed to hire some new thugs. The man on the roof was a sitting duck up there. Flat on his belly, his rifle aimed at the open gate of the airfield as he waited for D to arrive.

D settled in the blind that the dead goon had so graciously left for him and positioned the rifle to his needs. The target was about eight hundred yards away. D could easily shoot twice that distance. He adjusted the stock so his eye was in the scope's center. Tested the grip, then frowned. It wasn't the rifle he would've chosen for this particular shot, but it would have to do.

He made some more corrections, adjusting for the direction of the wind and the elevation. The side of the sniper's head offered a perfect target, but he needed to hit it just right or he would risk revealing his location.

His finger hovered over the trigger as he took a breath. No. Not quite right. He frowned again, making one last correction.

Then he took the shot.

Perfection. A clean hit through the sniper's left temple. Barely a trace of blood as the man sagged forward onto his rifle.

Abandoning the blind, D reached into his pocket for his phone and dialed.

"If you're calling to change our terms, they're non-negotiable," came Mendez's frigid voice. "My men are already en route."

"Good," D replied. "I'll be here waiting for them. I just wanted to let you know I unwrapped the presents you left for me."

Silence greeted his ears.

"What—you thought I believed you when you assured me nobody would be here to ambush me?" D chuckled.

"It wasn't an ambush. It was a precaution." Mendez sounded annoyed. "The one lesson I learned from our former association is that the word of Jason Hernandez means shit."

"Your word's not exactly gold either. But it's all right, Raoul. I forgive you this transgression. The meeting will go as scheduled."

D hung up and checked his watch. The chopper would be landing in thirty minutes. He used his second phone to send Macgregor a brief message: "Going dark now. Will make contact once terms are reached."

Then he crushed the phone beneath his boot, kicked away the broken pieces, and covered them with dirt. The body he left in plain sight. He didn't give a shit who found it.

He checked the battery of his last remaining cell phone, the one that nobody but he and Mendez had the number of. He'd already ditched the phone with Morgan's tracking device. He'd just destroyed the one that could lead anyone back to Liam. Which meant he was all set. Only thing left to do was get on the chopper.

Once he got to Isla del Rey, he'd have to play it by ear.

Fuck, the thought of going back there made him edgy. He'd hated every single second he'd spent on that godforsaken island, all the insufferable socializing he'd been forced to do. His favorite thing about his Jason Hernandez persona had been that the man was known to be antisocial. Jason didn't make friends or have beers with "the boys." He distributed drugs, period. He was all business, all the time.

Gaining access to Mendez's inner circle had required he change it up. Raoul Mendez was all about excess. Lavish parties on his yacht, an endless parade of women, a perpetual flow of champagne—aka D's idea of a living nightmare. He'd had no choice but to play along, though. He'd attended the parties. Fucked the women. Drunk the champagne.

Christ, he'd hated it.

Slinging the rifle strap over his shoulder, he rose from the blind and hiked back to the SUV. It took five minutes to drive to the airfield, and when he pulled up in front of the hangar, a mustached man in brown coveralls strode out of it, greeting D with a frown.

"You Hernandez?" the man called out.

D nodded.

"Your ride will be here shortly." Still frowning, the man turned around and walked back in the hangar.

D lit a cigarette and tilted his head to the sky. It was clear and blue, not a single cloud in sight. Shit. A beautiful sunny day . . . always a bad omen.

As he smoked in silence, his mind drifted to Sofia and the good-bye they'd shared at the safe house. The kiss.

His stomach roiled just thinking about it. The feel of another person's mouth on his . . . it made him queasy. He'd never kissed a woman without it being part of a mission. He hadn't kissed Noelle. Hadn't kissed any of the others he'd slept with.

But when Sofia had kissed him, it had evoked a strange sense of longing. For one fucked-up moment, he'd truly wished he could give her more. That he could be the kind of man who actually stood by the woman he'd knocked up.

D sucked hard on his cigarette. Jesus. In seven months there'd be a kid with his DNA out there in the world.

He swiftly banished the thought before he repeated last night's pathetic failure and threw up again. He was doing the right thing, staying as far away as he could from that child. Sofia would be a good mother—he had no doubt of that. She was smart, compassionate, resourceful. She'd be just fine without him.

Besides, her concerns about Mendez killing him? One hundred percent valid. The moment he'd set up the meeting, D had known he probably wouldn't walk away from it alive. He knew how Mendez operated, and he also knew exactly what the man would demand: a package deal. Sullivan in exchange for Angelina *and* D.

D was fully prepared to give him what he wanted. Self-preservation had always been his number-one priority, but not at the expense of a teammate. Sullivan's life was worth a hell of a lot more than his, and D was willing to pay the ultimate price to save his teammate.

A rumble of sound made his shoulders stiffen. For

a second he thought it was helicopter rotors, because he was expecting a goddamn helicopter, and it took a second to register that it was a car engine. He cursed when a cloud of dust rose in the distance. A moment later, a vehicle sped through the gate.

A white Range Rover.

Ash had shown up in a white Range Rover last night.

Son of a *bitch*.

What the fuck was the rookie doing here?

D drew his pistol and aimed it at the approaching car. He didn't care if he had to put a bullet in Ash's knee. The kid wasn't coming on that chopper with him. No fucking way would he let—

D growled an expletive when the driver's face came into view.

Sofia.

Jesus Christ. Sofia was behind the wheel.

A rush of panic nearly knocked him off his feet, then propelled him forward. His mind was spinning as he raced toward the Range Rover. Why hadn't Ash or Liam called to warn him she was coming?

Fuck. Because he'd gone dark. Because he'd ditched his goddamn phone and they didn't have the number to his burner.

He reached the vehicle and threw open the driver's door before Sofia had even put the car in park.

"Turn around," he snapped. "Right fucking now, Sofia. Turn around and drive back to the safe house."

"Only if you come with me," she blurted out.

Her green eyes shone with concern, but it was nothing compared to the concern—no, the *fear*—coursing through his blood at the moment. The chopper was landing in twenty minutes. He had to get her out of here before that happened. She couldn't be here.

She. Couldn't. Be. Here.

"I saw your face when you left." Her voice rang with urgency. "I *saw* it. You're not planning on getting out of this alive, are you?"

"You can't *plan* whether you live or die," he shot back. "You either do or you don't."

"But you expect to die."

"I expect to reunite with an old enemy. Anything more than that, I don't fucking know. So please, just *go*. You need to go right now, Sofia."

Anguish clung to her voice. "He'll kill you."

"Then I'll die. But Sullivan will live, and that's good enough for me. It should be good enough for you, too. Or do you *want* him to die? Is that it?"

"No," she stammered. "But—"

"But nothing. The trade will go down how it goes down. I can't see the future. I don't know what Mendez will do. But I know what *I'm* going to do, and that's get my teammate out of the hellhole he's been trapped in for six fucking months." Frustration burned a path up his throat. "The helicopter will be here soon." He growled again. "What the *hell* possessed you to think coming here would be a *good idea*?"

She let out a breath. "Okay. You're right. In hindsight, it was a really bad decision."

"You fucking *think*?"

His incensed tone made her flinch. "I'm sorry. I . . . panicked. I was worried about you—"

"You don't need to worry about me!" he roared. "What you need to do is *leave*. Now."

No sooner had the words left his mouth than his burner phone rang.

Shit.

"Wait," he commanded, before she could put the car in drive.

Sofia froze.

The fear in his veins flowed faster, got colder. Trying to control his breathing, he answered the call with a curt, "Yes?"

"Who is she?" Mendez asked.

D's stomach dropped.

A flash of movement from the hangar caught his peripheral, and D turned to find the man in the coveralls emerging from the shadowy space. There was a Bluetooth device lodged in his ear and a rifle in his hands, aimed directly at the Range Rover.

The man belonged to Mendez.

Self-directed fury slammed into D's chest. Damn it. He'd slipped up. He should've taken care of the asshole before he'd approached Sofia's car, but he hadn't been thinking. He'd been too busy freaking the fuck out, and now Mendez had been alerted to Sofia's presence.

"She's nobody," D said coldly. "Just some bitch who needed directions."

Sofia winced again.

"I see." There was a pause, the muffled sound of voices, and then Mendez returned. "My associate informed my men that the conversation seems very heated for someone who's just looking for directions."

"Your associate is wrong. That's all this is."

"All right. Well, then you won't mind taking care of it, will you?"

Fuck.

"Because my helicopter will be arriving shortly, and I'm afraid there can't be any trace of this pickup," Mendez said. "She needs to be taken out. Would you like to do it, or shall the honor fall to Diego?"

D's free hand curled into a tight fist. He looked at Sofia, whose wide eyes were glued to the man by the hangar. Damn this woman. *Damn* her. He'd never had anyone give a shit about him before, and it infuriated him that her misguided concern had brought her here.

"You got me," he muttered into the phone. "She's a colleague."

Sofia's gaze flew to his, her mouth parting in a startled O.

"That's what I thought." Mendez chuckled. "She comes with you, then."

D swallowed, desperately trying to think of a way out of this clusterfuck, but Mendez went on before he could say a word.

"Please don't think about doing anything foolish, Jason. Diego has an open line to the chopper. If anything happens to him, they'll know, and then I might decide to kill my prisoner. You know, the prisoner you're so eager to get your hands on? And if anything happens to the men on my helicopter, *I'll* know, and then I'll absolutely kill the prisoner. So, like I said, don't be foolish." Mendez paused. "She comes with you."

Mendez hung up.

D drew another ragged breath. He'd considered that very option—killing Diego, sending Sofia away, and boarding the chopper. But now his hands were tied.

He stared at Sofia, making a valiant effort to control

his anger. Nope, he couldn't throttle her. She was a woman. She was *pregnant*. But she'd just complicated his life more than she would ever know.

"Get out of the car," he ordered.

She didn't move.

"Get out of the fucking car." His breathing went shallow. His mind worked overtime, seeking solutions. But there was no escape. Short of killing Diego and then every man on that bird—and effectively killing *Sully*—he had to play the new hand he'd been dealt.

"Why?" Sofia whispered.

"Because he wants you to get on the chopper with me."

Her cheeks turned ashen.

"You think I like this?" D hissed out. "Because I don't. You shouldn't have come here, but here you are, and now we're *fucked*. So for the love of God, get out of the car."

Sofia's entire body trembled as she shut off the engine and slid out of the SUV. D grabbed her arm to steady her, then brought his mouth close to her ear. "You need to go along with every single word I say, understand?"

She nodded, looking even paler.

"Now take a deep breath. You look like you've seen a ghost. You look weak." His sharp accusation made her eyes blaze. "Good, get angry. *That's* how you should look. You're a government operative, you hear me? You're not scared of these men. You're not scared of anyone, got it?"

Her breasts rose beneath her tank top as she inhaled deeply. The fear in her expression dissolved, and when fortitude took its place, D couldn't help but be impressed. He'd known Sofia Amaro for years. She was tough as nails when she needed to be.

And right now, he needed her to be.

"If you follow my orders and play along, there's a chance we'll get out of this alive. If you don't, then we're as good as dead. Do you understand?"

She nodded.

He shifted his stance, angling his body just slightly so that it wouldn't be noticeable to the man at the hangar. "Now take the gun out of my waistband and slide it under yours. Slowly. No sudden movements."

Sofia did as she was told, her small hand grabbing hold of his spare handgun. D watched Diego the entire time, satisfied when the man's expression didn't change. Mendez's people would know Sofia was armed, but that didn't matter. They'd expect it. D just needed to make sure she was, for his own peace of mind.

"You know how to use a gun?" he demanded.

"Yes."

"Good. If you need to use it, you don't hesitate. You shoot to kill. Understand?"

She offered a nod in response.

D clenched his teeth. "I need to hear you say it."

"I understand," she said firmly.

"Good," he said again.

Their gazes held for one long moment, and then they walked toward the landing strip to wait for the helicopter.

Chapter 14

Liam was pacing the master bedroom of the safe house when his phone rang. He dove for it like a frickin' Olympian, breathing in relief when he saw Ash's name on the display. For the past thirty minutes he'd been telepathically ordering the rookie to call him back with some good news.

"She got on the chopper with D," Ash reported.

So much for good news.

"Jesus Christ! How did you let that happen?" Ash had been tailing Sofia in Liam's SUV, using the GPS in Sofia's Range Rover. He should have caught up with her long before she'd reached the airfield.

"I couldn't go in."

"Why the hell not?"

"Because critical shit was going down. Some thug was holding a gun to them, D got a phone call, and the next thing I know, he and Sofia are walking to the helipad. I would've jeopardized them, jeopardized *Sully*, if I engaged."

Liam's chest tightened at the sound of Sully's name, but he forced himself to focus. "Wait—D had his phone on him? He said he was going dark. Why the fuck didn't he pick up when we called to tell him Sofia was gone?"

"No clue." Ash paused. "So what now?"

He gritted his teeth, then said, "Now we stick to the plan. D will take care of Sofia. We'll watch the hostage until D secures Sully's release. Get your ass back here."

"Roger that."

Liam disconnected the call and glanced at the bed, where Angelina Mendez lay on her back with one wrist handcuffed to the bedpost. The woman's skirt had ridden up and was bunched around her upper thighs to reveal long, tanned legs. She really was smoking hot. He wondered if D had tapped that. It had sure looked that way last night when he'd been mauling her up against the car.

Liam wasn't interested in following in D's footsteps, though. He didn't give a shit how hot the woman was— Angelina Mendez was nothing but a means to an end to him. And it was time the two of them had a little chat.

He sat at the edge of the mattress and lightly slapped her cheek, hoping to stir her from the sedation. He'd given her only a small dose earlier, enough to knock her out for an hour, two max. He was fully aware that he was going against D's instructions, but he didn't give a shit about that either.

His best friend had been missing for six months. This woman had been an accomplice to that. End of story.

"Wake up," he murmured.

Her eyelids twitched beneath his fingertips.

"That's it, darling. Wake up for me."

A soft sigh escaped her lips. For several seconds her eyelashes fluttered, until finally her eyes slitted open.

He watched her face as she became cognizant of her

surroundings. Of *him*. When her mouth parted in outrage, he slammed his palm over it.

"Uh-uh, you're not going to scream. And if you try to head butt me again, I'll head butt you right back this time. I've been told I have a thick skull, so we wouldn't want that perfect nose of yours to shatter. Would we?"

She frowned.

"Now I'm going to take my hand off your mouth, and you and I are going to talk. *Quietly.* Sound good?"

He slowly removed his hand, and his eardrums were happily greeted by the sound of silence. Liam grabbed the water bottle from the bedside table and twisted off the cap.

"Here. Drink."

She dutifully swallowed the water he poured into her mouth, but didn't look happy about it. "Where's Jason?" she demanded.

Liam set the bottle aside. "He and your father are discussing the terms of your release."

Angelina snorted. "Papa won't discuss a damn thing with Jason. He'll kill him on sight."

He raised a brow. "At your expense?"

She mulled it over for a second. "Yes."

Which was like a punch to the gut, because if Mendez's daughter believed her own father would forsake her just to get revenge on D, then that was a grim omen about Sullivan's fate.

Liam tamped down his rising apprehension. "I want to know what your father did to him."

"Jason?" Her features twisted in anger. "Papa treated him like a *son*. He welcomed him into his home, gave him a job—"

"Not Jason. Sul— The prisoner." Liam quickly corrected himself, not wanting to endanger Sullivan's life by revealing his identity. "The man your father was holding in his dungeon."

Angelina smirked. "I have no idea who you're referring to."

Frustration had his hand shooting out and curling around her throat. "Don't play games with me right now, darling. Trust me, I'm not exactly feeling . . . *stable* at the moment." He tightened his grip. "Piss me off and I might lose control, snap this pretty neck of yours."

Even with his fingers around her windpipe, she didn't look at all afraid. "You won't kill me. You *can't* kill me. Jason needs me alive."

"Jason will kill you in a heartbeat if it turns out our man is already dead." Liam smiled humorlessly. "So why don't you give me the inside scoop? What will Jason find when he gets to the island—a dead man, or a living, breathing one your father will trade for you?"

"I already told you, my father won't make a trade," she said scornfully. "Jason stole the most important person in Papa's life. His perfect son. His heir. I'm nothing to him. Not the way my brother was."

"Is our man alive?" Liam repeated through clenched teeth.

"You look like a movie star," she remarked, ignoring the question. "Has anyone ever told you that?"

Sullivan told him that all the time.

Sullivan, who had been tortured by this woman's father.

"Tell me what your father did to him. Tell me if he's alive."

Her dark eyes twinkled. "Oh, *querido*, look at you, all worried about your little friend. Are you a soldier or are you a pussy? I'm leaning toward pussy."

He closed his hand tighter around her throat. *"Tell me."*

Angelina started to laugh, the sound low and wheezy, thanks to the obstruction of his hand. "You *are* worried. You poor thing. Will it make you feel better if I told you he enjoyed every second of what we did to him? What *I* did to him?"

Liam loosened his grip. "He's alive?"

She didn't answer for a moment, and he could see her brain working, as if she were trying to decide whether to say more. She must have reached the conclusion that whatever she said couldn't hurt her, because she laughed again, high and melodic this time.

"He begged for it, you know."

"Begged for what?" Liam said warily.

"Me." She was positively beaming now. "He couldn't get enough, that sweet, beautiful man. He *is* beautiful, no? Not like you, not so . . . *perfect*. But that face." She shivered. "Rugged. Masculine. And his cock . . . Your friend is hung like a stallion. Did you know he had a big cock? He's a big man, so I suspected it, but suspecting and seeing are two very different things, aren't they?"

His breathing got choppy.

"I won't lie, though," she said, her tongue darting out to moisten her lips. "He didn't like it at first. But that was all right—it's more fun when they fight it. But, *querido*? He grew to *love* it. I'd put my mouth on that big cock and he'd *beg* for more." Angelina's rosebud mouth curved. "Do you want me to tell you the sounds he made when he was inside me?"

The bitch was lying. There was no way Sullivan would screw this woman. No way he would *beg*.

Unless he had no other choice. Unless it meant staying alive.

Liam grew sick to his stomach. Sullivan could have done it. Slept with this vile creature in order to survive. Either that, or the bitch had raped him.

Didn't matter, though. It didn't fucking matter, because Liam had officially heard enough.

Somehow he managed to stand up, despite his wobbly legs.

Angelina watched him as he grabbed the black case from the table. "Aw, *querido*, did I upset you?"

"Shut up," he muttered.

"But why?" She batted her eyelashes. "I thought you *wanted* to talk. Did you not?"

He unzipped the case and extracted a clear vial and a syringe.

"Did you not ask me to tell you what I did to him?" she taunted. "But I see you don't like what I have to say. You don't like knowing that I fucked your friend. Many, many times. And he *loved* it—"

Liam jammed the needle into the side of her neck. "Shut. Up."

But the bitch kept talking. The sedative would take a minute to kick in. A minute was plenty of time to allow her to spew more filth, to mock him, hurt him.

"Would you rather we discussed the waterboarding? Or maybe the drugs? I can tell you all about the drugs, Mr. Movie Star. All about how we broke him and played with him and—"

Liam slammed the bedroom door and stumbled into the hall, raking both hands through his hair. Christ, how could a person take so much joy from describing the torture of a man? D was right. Angelina Mendez wasn't innocent. She was poison.

The sound of the front door opening had him hurrying to the main room. He must have looked as stricken as he felt, because Ash's expression flooded with concern the moment he saw Liam's face.

"What happened?"

"Nothing." He swallowed the bile coating his throat. "I was checking on the hostage. She's still down for the count."

Ash nodded. "Any word from D?"

"No. It'll probably be a couple hours before he—"

Liam's ringing phone cut him off midsentence. His pulse sped up when he glimpsed the unknown number.

"Or not. I think this is him." He wasted no time answering the call. "D?" he barked.

Heavy panting filled his ear.

"D?"

There was a soft groan, barely audible, but clear enough that Liam's spine turned into a steel rod. "D. Talk to me, damn it."

"It's . . . not D, mate," a voice croaked.

Every muscle in Liam's body coiled tight.

No.

This couldn't be happening. He was hallucinating that voice. His mind had conjured up the memory of it and—

"Boston, you there?"

A shocked breath shuddered out. *"Sully?"*

*   *   *

Isla del Rey was stunning. A true slice of paradise. Beyond the protected marina and airstrip were endless miles of unspoiled beauty—white sand beaches on the coast, rocky elevations inland, and lush vegetation as far as the eye could see. From her seat in the helicopter, Sofia admired the gorgeous island, for a moment forgetting that she was not coming here by choice.

All it took to remember her current predicament was the sharp voice of the man in the pilot's seat.

"Preparing for descent."

She bit her lip and gave D a sidelong look, but he didn't look back.

He hadn't said a word to her since they'd boarded the chopper, and she didn't blame him. She'd screwed up. She shouldn't have given in to panic and chased after him. She should've known that just because they had time before the helicopter arrived didn't mean that nobody would be watching the airfield. But in her over-powering concern for D's well-being, she hadn't once stopped to consider they might not be alone.

And now that one foolish mistake had cost her. Big-time.

Her stomach churned as the helicopter began to descend. Her hand instinctively flattened over her lower belly, which finally garnered a reaction from the man beside her. D gave a slight shake of the head, his lips pursing in a frown. Sofia hastily removed her hand and laced her fingers together instead.

Message received. He didn't want her to advertise the pregnancy.

Hell, *she* didn't want to either. She just hoped she didn't get sick in front of Mendez.

Dread gathered in her chest when the helicopter touched down. One of the three camo-clad men on board opened the door, then ordered her and D to get out.

After that, it was utter silence. D still didn't speak. Neither did the men.

Sofia inhaled deeply as they were ushered toward a waiting Jeep. The salty scent of the ocean filled her nostrils, along with the fragrant aroma of mango, coconut, and guava. She tried not to flinch when one of the men shoved her toward the backseat of the Jeep. Instead, she donned a bored expression to match the one D wore.

A moment later, they were driving inland. Mangrove trees stretched out from either side of the dirt path, which was narrow and bumpy, causing the Jeep to bounce hard enough to make her queasy again. She swallowed the nausea and breathed in the sickly sweet scent of the golden trumpet flowers along the path, willing herself not to vomit.

If you follow my orders and play along, there's a chance we'll get out of this alive. If you don't, then we're as good as dead.

D's blunt words continued to buzz in her mind, relentless, urgent. She had to trust that he would get them out of this. He *had* to get them out of this.

The drive took twenty minutes, each passing second heightening her nerves. A luxurious house came into view, perched high in the landscape with its red Spanish-tile roof gleaming in the morning sunshine. It was a sprawling, gorgeous home with a modern hacienda feel to it, offering panoramic views of the ocean and rainforest. As opulent and over-the-top as Morgan's place in Costa Rica, except this one actually *did* belong to a criminal.

As the driver killed the engine, the thug in the passenger's seat hopped out and yanked open the back door. "Get out," he snapped.

She and D obeyed without question, but Sofia could tell that following orders was not something D enjoyed. His profile was harder than stone, his jaw twitching as if he were trying to restrain himself from snapping back.

"Mr. Mendez is waiting for you on the terrace. I need your weapons now."

This time, D *did* respond. "No."

"You can't see him if you're armed," the thug said tersely.

"Fine, then I guess we won't be seeing him." D bared his teeth in a smile. "Take us back to the chopper."

"*Or*"—the guard drew his gun and pointed it at Sofia's chest—"you can give me your weapons."

She felt the color draining from her face as the gun barrel focused on her heart.

D's eyes flashed, but he didn't put up a second argument. He simply handed over his sleek black pistol, then gestured for Sofia to do the same.

Maybe it made her the wimp of the century, but she felt slightly better without the weight of the gun in her waistband. She hated guns. Hated violence. Which was ironic, because she was currently surrounded by the former, and probably about to endure a lot of the latter.

The thug handed their weapons to the driver, then nodded at them to follow him. Sofia swallowed as they walked past the stone courtyard and rounded the side of the Mediterranean-style home. The path was lined with orchids, some as high as eight feet tall, their beautiful white petals offering false security to the island's visitors. This wasn't a beautiful place. This wasn't a *safe* place.

God, why hadn't she told D about the baby over the phone? Why hadn't she stayed home, damn it?

The path ended at a set of wide stone steps leading up to a massive terrace with a regal iron railing. Sofia fought a burst of panic when a man appeared above them, his hairy arms resting on the rail.

Dark eyes gleamed at them. No, at *Derek*. The man's gaze was focused solely on D, and a sneer twisted his lips as D climbed the steps with an easy gait, as if he had no care in the world.

"Jason, how good of you to visit." Mendez's cold features belied his pleasant tone. "I was about to sit down for breakfast. Join me."

Sofia had no clue if the invitation included her, but the armed guard was behind her on the steps, so she had no choice but to follow D. The terrace smelled like a greenhouse, probably because of the dozens of potted flowers filling up the space. At the far end was another set of steps that led to an infinity pool that sparkled amid a natural setting of boulders and fronds.

"Kiwi?" Mendez held out a serving plate laden with the green fruit as they approached a wrought-iron table at the edge of the pool.

Sofia hated him already. He was pompous and phony, her two least-favorite qualities in a person. The man hadn't seen D in nine years, for fuck's sake. What was the point in this gracious-host act when he was obviously seething inside?

Clearly, D was as irritated by the charade as she was. "I don't want your damn kiwi, Raoul. I want my man. That's all I came for, and that's all I'm willing to discuss."

Mendez's nostrils flared. "Is that any way to treat an old friend? With such hostility?" He signaled his guard. "Leave us."

Once the thug disappeared, Mendez gestured to the table. "Sit."

D remained standing. Sofia followed his lead.

With a grumble, Mendez lowered himself into a chair and crossed his ankles. The epitome of casual. He finally turned his curious gaze to Sofia, who met it head-on. She prayed she looked calm and in control. God knew her heartbeat was the farthest thing from in control.

"Introduce me to your colleague, Jason."

D didn't even glance at her as he said, "Esmé, meet Raoul. Raoul, Esmé."

All righty then. Apparently she was Esmé now.

"It's a pleasure to meet you, Esmé," Mendez said graciously.

Her expression remained indifferent. "Where's our man?"

Holy shit, she'd just sounded like a total badass. She was tempted to sneak a peek at D and check if he was impressed, but she didn't dare risk it.

Mendez let out a hearty laugh, his eyes moving back to D. "I was really hoping we could catch up before we got into all the messy stuff. However, I see I'm going to meet resistance. From both of you." He leaned back in his chair. "Sit, my friends. Please. We have a lot to discuss."

Sofia once again allowed D to make the decision, and when he grudgingly pulled out a chair and dropped into it, she did the same. The moment her butt landed on the seat, her legs began to tremble, fear replacing the bravado she'd displayed. At least she'd managed not to shake like a leaf when she'd been standing in front of Mendez. And as long as he didn't peek under the table, he wouldn't be able to see how rattled she truly was.

"Let's get to it, shall we?" An ugly scowl marred Mendez's mouth. "I want to know how you did it, and why you did it."

D's unruffled expression didn't alter, but an incredulous note entered his voice. "You want to know how I kidnapped your daughter? For fuck's sake, old man, is that really a pressing issue at the moment?"

Anger colored the other man's eyes. "I'm not talking about my daughter. My daughter will be fine." Malice dripped from his tone as he continued. "I'm talking about my son, you reprehensible bastard. I want to know why you murdered my son."

Chapter 15

The call finally came in. *Finally*. Bryant had been waiting for a report ever since the team leader in Cancún
had informed him that the prisoner was on the move.
But the man had been completely useless for nearly
forty-eight hours. A puking, sniveling mess, taking his
sweet-ass time contacting his colleagues.

No wonder he'd gotten captured. If he'd been a trained
Smith operative, he never would've wound up on that
fucking island to begin with.

"He made a phone call," the leader of Bryant's ground
crew reported.

Triumph surged through him. He stalked to the wet
bar in the corner of his office and poured a glass of Scotch
as he addressed his man. "Any idea who he contacted?"

"Negative. He used a pay phone in a town near the
beach. Too far away for us to hear what was being said,
but we can contact the phone company and trace the
call if you'd like."

Lord, there were still pay phones in existence? Bryant had figured cellular technology would have rendered them all obsolete.

"Don't bother. Whoever he called, he'll be leading you right to them. Focus on tailing him. Check in the moment he makes contact with his people."

"Roger that."

Bryant hung up and took a deep swig of his Scotch, but it wasn't alcohol he tasted—it was victory. Mendez's prisoner was going to lead him straight to Derek.

He basked in the satisfaction of that, of knowing he would see his former operative soon. Derek Pratt had made a mockery of what the agency stood for. He'd taken everything Bryant had so willingly given him, and then thrown it back in Bryant's face.

Ungrateful bastard.

His phone rang again, interrupting his thoughts. Jones was checking in. Good. It was crucial that Jones keep a watchful eye on Mendez now that the prisoner was free.

"We've got a problem," was the first thing Jones said.

"Has Mendez left the island?"

"No. But Derek Pratt just showed up."

Bryant froze. The glass in his hand shook as he absorbed the shock.

"Are you serious?" he hissed into the phone.

"As a fucking heart attack. He landed about ten minutes ago. Him and some woman." Jones cursed softly. "Shit is about to explode, sir. I'm talking Hiroshima-level explosion here."

Bryant didn't get rattled often, but *son of a bitch*, he was rattled right now. Derek was on Isla del Rey? How the *fuck* had that happened? How had Derek surfaced without landing on the radar of a single one of Bryant's people?

He took a breath to calm himself. "Has Mendez seen him yet?"

"They're meeting as we speak. From what I've managed to learn, Pratt abducted Mendez's daughter. He wants to trade her for the prisoner."

The prisoner that Jones had let go.

Shit. Things were absolutely about to explode.

"Mendez is scrambling," Jones went on. "He's got every available man combing the mainland for the prisoner. The island too."

"You're telling me that after two days of searching the island, the idiot still thinks there's a chance the prisoner didn't make it to the mainland?"

"Mendez is a stubborn motherfucker." Jones snorted. "Look at how long he kept him hostage, doing everything in his power to break him. Six goddamn months, for nothing. Mendez can't admit defeat."

Bryant drained the rest of his Scotch, then slammed the glass on the desk. "If Pratt took the man's daughter, that means he believes Mendez still has the prisoner," he said slowly. "Which means Mendez will try to stall."

Jones voiced his agreement. "He thinks he'll be able to recapture the hostage before Pratt grows wise to it. But he can't stall forever, sir. Pratt is smart—he'll see through it eventually."

Derek was smart, all right. Too smart for his own damned good, and resourceful enough to have been able to pull a disappearing act right in front of Bryant's eyes.

Damn it, why hadn't he given Jones the order to release the hostage sooner? Or hell, to delay it? It was just his luck—Derek voluntarily coming out of the woodwork to save his colleague *two fucking days* after Bryant had released him.

"Whatever you do, don't let Mendez kill him." Bryant sank into his chair. "I don't care what it takes—you make sure Pratt stays alive."

"Sir, that could mean blowing my cover."

"I just said I don't care what it takes!" he boomed, slapping a hand on the desktop. "Nobody touches Pratt, you hear me? Nobody kills Derek Pratt but me."

Mendez was stalling.

And D didn't fucking like it.

From the second that Mendez held out that kiwi plate, D had known something was amiss. Raoul Mendez didn't make small talk or offer his guests fruit. He usually got right down to business.

D stared into the older man's eyes, which were awash with bitterness. Mendez's demand hung in the warm morning air, but D was in no hurry to address it. He was more interested in gauging his old enemy, figuring out if and how the man had changed.

Mendez had hardly aged a day in the nine years since they'd last seen each other. His bronzed skin was more leathery now, far too tanned and not at all healthy-looking, but there were no new wrinkles on his face. No hair loss. He was as fit and commanding as ever.

D's gaze shifted to Sofia, who hadn't said a word since they'd sat down. She was handling the encounter a lot better than he'd expected. Her gaze hard and focused, her body language deceptively relaxed.

The sight of her at this compound made him want

to vomit. Damn her for involving herself in this. It was too dangerous for her to be here.

"Tell me," Mendez repeated, his visibly clenched jaw telling D that the man was losing patience.

"Not until you tell me where my man is," D answered, casually resting his hands on the glass tabletop. He might not be armed, but he didn't feel threatened. He'd been trained in hand-to-hand combat; he could snap Mendez's neck like a stick if it came down to it.

"Is that how you want to play it?" Mendez's jaw relaxed. "All right, Jason. Let's do it your way. I'll answer your questions. Then you'll answer mine."

D shrugged. "Where's my colleague?"

"In the dungeon." Mendez reached for the water glass in front of him and took a delicate sip. "You remember the dungeon, don't you?"

Oh, he remembered. Mendez's son used to drag him down there so the sick bastard could toy with the girls. Gael hadn't touched them, of course—the merchandise was off-limits—but he'd sure as hell enjoyed playing mind games with them, making them believe he *would* touch them.

As much as D hated the idea of Sullivan being in that stone prison, he was relieved to hear that Mendez hadn't sent him to the workshop.

"Is he alive?"

"Yes."

It was hard to tell whether Mendez was lying or not. D's internal polygraph wasn't picking up any dishonesty on the man's part, but something about his expression was . . . *off.*

D set his jaw. "I want to see him."

"Later." Mendez waved a hand. "It's my turn to ask questions. Why did you kill my son?"

D had been prepared for this, so the lie flowed smoothly from his mouth. "Because I was ordered to."

The table fell silent. Mendez watched him carefully, as if he were employing his own internal lie detector. "Why?"

"Why what? Why was I ordered to kill him or why did I follow orders?"

"Both," Mendez snapped.

"I had a job to do." D crossed his arms over his chest. "What, you think I did it out of malice? Some personal vendetta against Gael—"

"Don't you *dare* speak his name in front of me!"

D chuckled. "What would you like me to call him, then? Because this conversation revolves around him."

Mendez's breathing got heavier. He sucked in a breath, reached for his water again. After a hurried sip, he said, "Who wanted my son dead and why?"

"They killed him because of you. You know that."

"*You* killed him!" Mendez growled. "*You*, not *they*! Take some responsibility for your actions, you fucking bastard."

"I was an operative and I followed orders." D arched a brow. "If it makes you feel any better, I didn't enjoy it."

Mendez's face turned redder than a tomato. "My boy *loved* you. He respected you, looked up to you!"

"I had no ill feelings toward him, Raoul. He was a good kid." The lie burned D's throat on the way out. "That's the reason I aborted my mission. Because of Gael."

Suspicion colored the other man's tone. "You just told me the mission *was* Gael."

"No, I said the mission was *you*. You abducted a senator's daughter. I spent six months trying to squeeze her location out of you, and when you continued to keep me in the dark, my superiors decided it was time to amp up the pressure. They ordered me to kill your son to show you we meant business. But . . ." He feigned a sigh. "I felt bad."

"You felt *bad*? You goddamn son of a bitch!" The man shot forward as if to pounce on D, then sagged back in the chair a nanosecond later as he realized the grave mistake he'd been about to make. "You felt bad," he echoed dully.

"Yes."

D didn't look at Sofia as he answered. He'd confessed at the safe house that killing Gael hadn't been part of the mission. And he did *not* regret it. But he hoped like hell her expression didn't reveal the truth.

"Like I said, he was a good kid. I didn't enjoy pulling the trigger. I hope you believe that." He offered another shrug. "Afterward, I checked in with my handler, and he had another order for me. He wanted Angelina dead too. And I couldn't fucking stomach it. I couldn't be some brainless hired gun anymore for people who would sell me out in a heartbeat if it came down to it. But these people . . . they're smart. Ruthless. You don't retire from the agency—you're terminated. My only choice was to run."

Mendez studied D's face, his expression conveying nothing.

"For what it's worth, I spared you and Angelina."

A laugh of disbelief flew out of the man's mouth. "How generous of you."

"I could've killed you. We both know that. But I didn't. I knew you would never stop hunting me, but I owed you a debt for killing your son. You kept your life. That was how I repaid you."

Mendez's jaw fell open. "You've got some balls, Jason. I'll give you that."

With a chuckle, D glanced at the silent woman beside him. "How you doing, Esmé? Bored yet?"

"Thoroughly," Sofia replied, looking annoyed. "Can we please skip to the part where we verify that our colleague is alive?"

"Impatient, isn't she?" Mendez reached for his water again. "This is why women should not be tasked with such delicate jobs. They don't have the necessary attributes for it."

Sofia gave him a sweet smile. "Yeah? Well, I have the necessary skills to kick your ass, old man."

D hid a smile of his own. She was getting into character. Good. That was good. As long as she continued to convey no fear, he might be able to get them out of this alive.

"She's got backbone," Mendez remarked to D. "I do admire that. Now, where were we?"

"We were done," he said pleasantly. "I told you why Gael had to die. There's nothing left to say."

"Oh, but there is."

Goddamn it, why was Mendez stalling?

D suspected he already had the answer to that, but he refused to let the thought surface. If he did, that would mean admitting defeat. Admitting that he'd failed. Admitting that because of him, Sullivan Port was—

"Who were you working for?"

Mendez's question served as a much-needed interruption from his bleak thoughts. D rested his hands on his thighs and said, "Smith Group."

Mendez sneered. "Never heard of it."

"Of course you haven't. We're ghosts, Raoul. Or rather, we *were* ghosts. The agency shut down after I left it."

"US government?"

"Loosely affiliated with it. *Very* loosely."

"Black ops," Mendez mused.

"Obviously." D rolled his eyes. "The man you want? The one who ordered me to kill your son? His name is Edward Bryant. He was the big gun at Smith Group, ran the whole show."

"Selling out your former boss, Jason? You *are* feeling generous this morning." Mendez chuckled softly.

"I have no loyalty to Bryant or Smith Group anymore. You wanted to know why your son died? Well, Bryant is the reason. Do what you will with that intel. I don't give a shit." D scraped back his chair, and Sofia quickly followed suit. "I want to see my man now."

Mendez went quiet. He remained seated, but the air had changed, thickened with tension. Danger. "Is my daughter alive?" he finally asked.

"Of course she is. I'd never hurt Angie." D cocked a brow. "Well, unless I had no choice."

"I want proof of life."

He laughed. "Funny. We've been asking for that very

thing since we got here." His humor faded. "Here's the deal, Raoul. Esmé and I are the only two people on the planet who know where Angelina is. Make that three, actually, because if something happens to either one of us, our colleague has been given very clear instructions. If he doesn't hear from us in twelve hours, he'll put a bullet in Angelina's head."

"Proof of life," Mendez repeated.

"You first. Take us to our man."

After a beat, Mendez rose from his chair. He stood several inches shorter than D, not much taller than Sofia, in fact. But the man carried himself like he was the biggest, baddest dude on the planet. It made D want to laugh again.

Mendez brought his fingers to his lips and whistled sharply, and two armed men appeared without delay. "Get the car," he barked at his thugs. "We're going to the dungeon."

Relief flooded D's belly. He spared a glance at Sofia, who didn't look at all relaxed. Hell, he wasn't either. He might be relieved, but his instincts were on high alert, humming ominously.

Mendez gestured to the stairs and offered a broad smile. "Shall we?"

Chapter 16

The "dungeon" turned out to be a square building that was both above and underground, an imposing concrete structure that sent a cold shiver up Sofia's spine. She didn't like this. *Any* of it. Mendez gave her the willies. Her skin hadn't stopped crawling since they'd joined him on the terrace, and now the sick feeling had gotten worse. Much, much worse.

She wanted to whisper in D's ear and beg him to stop them from going inside the building. He was a soldier, damn it. He could grab a gun from one of the thugs and kill Mendez. Kill them all.

God, where was this bloodlust coming from? As a doctor, she wasn't supposed to wish anyone dead, but right now, nothing would make her happier than to see every single man on this island meet his grisly demise.

But D didn't make a move against the men. She knew he wouldn't act until he saw Sullivan, and she didn't even blame him for it. If he killed Mendez and it turned out Sullivan was being held somewhere other than this island, then the chances of finding Sully might possibly die with Mendez.

A bulky guard unclipped a heavy key ring from his belt and unlocked the steel door at the building's entrance. Mendez entered first, then D and Sofia.

Blood.

After years of smelling blood in its various states, her nose immediately registered the scent. Fresh blood was more metallic, letting off a sweet, sometimes fruity scent as it began to dry. The older it got, the mustier it smelled, sour even. The odor in the dungeon fit the latter description; it had the faint but unmistakable stench of dried blood. She didn't know whether she felt relieved or terrified.

Mendez led them down a narrow hallway with a gray stone floor and rusted metal doors on both sides. Sofia counted fourteen doors before they finally came to a stop at the last one in the corridor.

The guard didn't reach for his key ring. He just turned the knob, and the door opened with a loud creak.

Sofia didn't need to peer inside to know the cell was empty. The fact that it had been unlocked said it all.

"You son of a bitch," D hissed, lunging forward.

Two assault rifles shot up before he could reach Mendez, who laughed in delight.

"Oh, Jason, did you really think he'd still be alive? After all these months?" The man laughed harder, nodding at one of the guards.

The bulky one grabbed Sofia's arm, and she squeaked in indignation when he shoved her into the cell. The other guard did the same to D, whose eyes were flashing with disgust.

"Your daughter's as good as dead," he spat to Mendez. "I hope you realize that."

"No, my daughter will be released as agreed," the man corrected. "See, I now have *two* hostages to use as leverage. Lucky me." He barked a command at the bulky guard. "Take his phone."

Sofia watched in dismay as the guard stripped D of his phone. Why wasn't D fighting back, damn it? He was standing there like a statue, letting Mendez toss them in a cell. Letting these men steal his only connection to Liam and Ash.

"I have some other business engagements to attend to," Mendez said cheerfully, "so you and the lovely Esmé will have the afternoon to relax. Once I return, we'll discuss the terms for my daughter's release." He offered Sofia a gracious smile. "I hope your colleague on the mainland is more fond of you than he is of Jason, because only one of you will be leaving this island, and I'm leaning toward you, *querida*."

Bullshit. He wasn't letting either of them go. Sofia knew that without a shred of doubt.

Oh God. They were going to die on this island.

"Have a seat. Relax. I'll see you both soon." Mendez smiled broadly as he stepped to the door. "By the way, your former colleague stayed in this cell for, oh, about three months. So I'm sure you'll feel right at home here."

The door creaked shut behind the men, and Sofia's heart sank when she heard the lock snap into place. She stared at the door for a second, took a breath, then spun around.

"What the *hell* was that?" she shouted.

D didn't even blink. "What the hell was what?"

"You're supposed to be some kind of supersoldier!

Why did you let them bring us here? Why did you let them put us in this cell? Why didn't you *fight* them?"

"Because they would have killed us," he said flatly. "And if I did eliminate Mendez and his men and we somehow made it back to the helicopter? Then the men at the airfield would have killed us. You saw the guard towers. This island is crawling with armed guards." He made a scornful sound. "Not even a supersoldier like myself could take down an entire army."

"You . . ." She took a breath. "But you didn't even try."

"I know when to pick my battles."

"So what now? What the hell do we do now?" She paced around the cell in a panic. "How do we get out of this?"

D shrugged. "I'm thinking on it."

Disbelief slammed into her. "You're thinking on it? *You're thinking on it?* I swear to God, Der—" She instantly halted, realizing she'd almost said his real name. Or one of his names. Whatever. Lowering her voice, she scanned the cinder-block walls and low ceiling in search of camera equipment. "Can they hear us?"

D shook his head.

"How can you be sure?"

"Because Mendez doesn't believe in cameras."

Doubt flickered through her. "He doesn't believe in cameras," she echoed.

D slid his powerful body down the wall and moved into a sitting position. "He's old school. The island is rigged with motion sensors and explosives, but there isn't a camera in sight. Didn't you notice?"

Had she noticed? No. Because she wasn't a goddamn

soldier. She wasn't on the lookout for things like cameras and motion detectors and security protocols.

"Security footage can be used against you," D said, shrugging again. "The wrong person gets their hands on it, and suddenly all your crimes are right there in Technicolor for the world to see, evidence that can be used to take you down. He doesn't leave a digital trail either. Doesn't even own a computer."

She reluctantly lowered herself next to D, keeping two feet of space between them. "How does he do business, then?"

"Good, old-fashioned pencil and paper." D snorted. "Every transaction is recorded by hand in a ledger, and every deal is made in cash, which then goes to offshore bank accounts that can't be traced back to him. Like I said, old school."

Sofia's gaze landed on a dark stain three feet from her hiking boots. Dried blood. Was it Sullivan's? God, she hoped not.

D was looking at it, too, his profile going hard.

"Do you think Sullivan is really dead?" she whispered.

He didn't answer.

"Derek."

That harsh gaze focused on her. "I have no fucking idea, okay? I knew Mendez was hiding something when we sat down with him, so yeah, there's a chance Sully is dead. But there's also a chance he's alive."

Worry rolled up her spine. "What do we do now?"

"I told you, I'm thinking." He went silent again, those dark eyes shifting to the wall ahead, fixing on the dusty, cracked stones.

He was thinking. Great. She wished he would tell her

what he was thinking. It was impossible to read this man, and she hated that he never gave her a shred of insight, a tiny clue that might help her figure him out.

"Why did you kill Gael Mendez?"

She saw his jaw twitch, but his mouth remained shut in a tight line.

"I know you weren't ordered to do it. You told me so yourself." The need for insight grew stronger. "So why? Why did you kill that man, D?"

His silence seemed to last forever, but just when she thought he wouldn't answer, his gruff voice echoed in the cell.

"He tried to rape a child."

A shocked breath flew out of her mouth. "What?"

D shifted his broad body so he could look at her, and what she saw in his eyes floored her. Distress. Anger. Sorrow. For a man who didn't usually reveal his emotions, he was broadcasting some pretty intense ones at the moment.

"He liked to fuck young girls," D spat out. "Really young ones—like eight, nine years old."

Horror coated her throat. "You . . . *saw* him do that?"

D shook his head. "Not before that night. He would talk about it, though. All the fucking time. Talk about how tight their pussies were, how much he loved looking into their eyes when he screwed them. He liked seeing how afraid they were, how much pain he was inflicting. I figured it was just talk at first. I spent months at that bastard's side, and he never once hurt a child in front of me. But the night I killed him . . . he grabbed a little girl off the street."

Sofia's breathing grew unsteady. "He raped her?"

"Tried to. I stopped him." Unmistakable pain thickened D's voice. "It was almost midnight. I don't know why she was even out on the street at that time of night. She couldn't have been older than ten, and she was walking down the fucking street at *midnight*. Gael and I were in the car, heading back to his place in Cancún after trolling the bars. And he . . ." D trailed off.

Sofia slid closer, resting her palm on his knee. He flinched, as expected, but she didn't remove her hand. She squeezed his kneecap and asked, "He what?"

"He slowed down and rolled down the window, started saying shit to the girl. I ordered him to cut it out, but he wouldn't stop. He just kept up with the disgusting come-ons, invitations to get in the car—that sort of thing." D's expression twisted in repulsion. "She got spooked and started running, and that's when he stopped the car and ran after her. He was nineteen, she was ten. The asshole caught up to her in five seconds flat. He grabbed her and dragged her into an alley."

Sofia gasped. "Oh God."

"I already told you, there isn't a God," D muttered. He let out a breath. "I looked the other way about a lot of the shit Gael pulled, but I couldn't turn the other cheek that night. I just couldn't. So I ran after them. Reached the alley in time to see him straddling the little girl. He'd gotten her on her stomach and pulled down her pants, and he was taking out his dick when I showed up." D cursed angrily. "He smiled when he saw me. Asked me to help hold her down."

Rage infused Sofia's blood. She'd witnessed plenty

of gruesome things over the years, seen what people were capable of doing to each other, but she couldn't imagine standing by and watching a grown man rape a child.

"The girl was crying, trapped there like an animal. It reminded me of . . ." He suddenly cleared his throat, and whatever he'd been about to say didn't come to fruition. "I snapped. I stared at his smug face and *snapped*. I put two bullets in his head."

She inhaled. "What happened to the girl?"

"Gael's body fell on top of her, pinning her down." D sounded sick. "I heaved him off her. Christ, she was covered in blood. Drenched in it. I asked her where she lived, and she said right around the corner, but when I came near her, she started screaming and took off running."

"You didn't go after her?"

"I had to clean up the scene. She made it home okay—trust me, I checked. Her parents filed a police report the next morning, but the cops had no suspects or leads. I made sure Gael would never be found."

Sofia swallowed the horror, but not the pride she felt. The pride she let surface. "You did the right thing," she said quietly. "You saved that girl's life."

D glanced over in surprise. "You're actually commending me for killing a man in cold blood?"

"For killing a *child rapist*, Derek. You did a service to the world." She meant every word. The thought of Gael Mendez trying to rape a little girl made her want to throw up.

"Yeah, well, Mendez would disagree with you. His son could do no wrong in his eyes."

They went silent again. She wanted to ask him what

he was thinking, what he was *planning*, but her mind was stuck on that one teeny detail he'd almost revealed.

Before she could stop herself, she reached out and touched his cheek. His face stiffened beneath her fingers, his wariness unmistakable.

He didn't like to be touched. She'd noted that the first time she'd ever treated him. It had been six, maybe seven years ago, and he'd arrived at the clinic with a gash on his chest, courtesy of a machete. Every time her hands had made contact with his skin, he'd winced, and not from the pain.

"What did it remind you of?"

D tried to ease his head away from her palm, but she curled her fingers around his jaw, cupping his chin.

"You said that seeing the girl like that—trapped—reminded you of something," Sofia pushed. "What was it?"

His muscular chest sagged on a deep exhalation. "Leave it alone, Sofia."

"No."

"Why not?" D glowered at her. "What the hell does it matter?"

"Because it does. It *matters*." She stroked the dark stubble on his cheek and gazed at him, but he was still refusing to meet her eyes. "It matters to me, okay? For once in your life, can't you let someone in?"

He began to laugh. Low, humorless laughter that brought a chill to the already cold cell. "You think if you know what happened to me you'll magically be able to figure me out? Fix me? Baby, nobody can fix me. I'm broken beyond repair."

It was the first honest thing this hard, elusive man had ever said to her.

"I still want to know," she insisted.

D rolled his eyes.

She found herself begging. "Please, Derek. Just . . . please. Tell me who you are."

"You know who I am. I'm a soldier. I'm an asshole."

Frustration lodged inside her. Sometimes she truly hated him. She hated how closed off he was, how little he cared about others. About *her*. They were currently sitting in a prison cell, and he couldn't be bothered to reassure her or comfort her or even confide in her.

Under normal circumstances, she wouldn't have pushed him any harder. But these were not normal circumstances. These could be the last moments of their lives. They could fucking *die* in here.

"You were raped as a child," she said bluntly. When he didn't respond, her tone went even sharper. "Am I wrong? Because I don't think I am. I think someone abused you. I think someone took advantage of you and made you feel unsafe and stole your ability to trust. And I think it was someone close to you. Someone close to you *broke* you, broke your trust."

His eyes narrowed.

"Am I wrong?" Sofia repeated.

Several seconds ticked by. Minutes. And then a soul-sucking breath shuddered from his chest. "No. You're not wrong."

Her heart squeezed painfully. "Who was it?"

"Who the fuck do you think?"

"Your father?"

"Yes." D made a disgusted sound. "But my mother joined in too."

Sofia's breath hitched. "Your parents . . . *both* of them?"

"Most families only have one sick fuck to contend with, huh?" He chuckled. "I was lucky enough to have two."

"Derek . . ." She had trouble speaking past the lump in her throat. "I'm so sorry."

"Don't be. It was a long time ago."

His careless answer worried her, because she didn't believe it was false. He truly didn't *care*. It truly wasn't a big deal to him, at least not anymore.

"How old were you?" she whispered.

"I was eight when it first started. Lasted until I was fourteen."

Six years. Jesus Christ. His parents had sexually abused him for *six* years. And he was sitting here reciting the details as if he were reading from a manual.

"Why . . ." She wasn't sure how to phrase the question.

"Why did they do it?" he filled in knowingly. "Because they liked it. They liked screwing their little boy. Well, my father did—he was the one who did all the screwing. My mother just liked to watch."

Sofia's gag reflex almost kicked in. "She . . . watched."

"At the beginning she would hold me down for him," D said, shrugging. "That was back when I thought struggling would make a difference. But I realized pretty early on that fighting them only got them more excited, so eventually I stopped trying. That made my mother happy." His jaw tightened against Sofia's hand. "It gave her time to sit in the chair next to the bed and touch herself."

It took some serious effort not to throw up. Tears stung Sofia's eyes as she tried to tamp down her nausea. She wanted to throw her arms around him. She wanted to comfort him. But she was scared he would push her away.

"She would watch me the whole time. She got off on seeing my pain."

Sofia blinked rapidly, trying hard not to cry. "What happened when you turned fourteen? What made it stop?"

"I ran away. Lived on the streets for a few years, then enlisted in the army."

"And your parents? What happened to them?"

D's gaze finally locked with hers. The animalistic gleam there sent fear trickling down her spine. "I killed them."

Sofia gulped.

"The night before I left for basic training, I went back to that house—no, that hellhole—and I killed them." He smiled. "Him first, of course. Because she liked to watch, remember? So I made her watch. I gutted him like a goddamn fish and made her watch every second of it. But once it was her turn, I didn't drag it out. I slit her throat and left her on that chair like the piece of garbage she was."

Deafening silence crashed between them.

Sofia didn't know how to respond. How to react. He'd just revealed himself to be the bloodthirsty monster she'd always secretly believed he was. His macabre description of killing his parents should have appalled her.

And yet she wasn't recoiling from him.

She . . . God, she didn't blame him. His *parents* were

the monsters. His parents had brutally victimized an eight-year-old boy. How could she ever blame that boy for slaying the monsters when he had the chance?

"What, no response?" D said mockingly. "No horror? Judgment? I just confessed to slaughtering two people, Sofia. *That* is who I am."

He startled her by holding out his right wrist, drawing her attention to the two lines of black text tattooed there. Two dates. The first dated back more than twenty years ago. The second was about ten years after the first.

"See these tats? They spell out exactly who I am." D laughed harshly. "The first date? That's the first time my father shoved his cock in my ass. That's the day I saw the world for what it was. And the second one? It marks the night I killed them, those people who called themselves my parents. I'm *proud* of that one, Sofia. I think back to that night and I feel pride for what I did. No regret, no shame. I would kill them all over again if I could."

Her throat worked with each desperate swallow. But her hand . . . her hand stayed on his cheek, her fingertips continuing to stroke his scratchy beard growth. Tenderly. God, what was wrong with her? Why wasn't she afraid of this man? Why wasn't she horrified by his confession?

"Still no response," he mused. "How much more do you hate me now, baby?"

Sofia's fingers trembled on his face. She slowly dropped her hand. "I . . ."

"You what?" He was taunting her again.

"I killed someone once," she blurted out.

D looked startled by that. Then he snorted. "Good one, Doc."

"It's true." Unlike him, she *did* feel shame, bone deep and merciless. "A woman came to the clinic with her two kids, a five-year-old and a seven-month-old infant. Her husband . . . he beat them."

D frowned. "When was this?"

"Three years ago." She bit her lip. "They lived in a small town about twenty minutes from the clinic. The father worked in an orchard. Picked fruit during the day, and drank himself stupid at night. I guess he got drunker than usual that night, and he totally lost it. Because his dinner was *cold* when he got home."

Sofia battled a burst of disbelief. "His fucking dinner was cold, so he decided to punish his wife by beating the shit out of her. And when she tried to take the kids and run, he hit the five-year-old girl, then snatched the baby boy from her arms and threw him against the wall."

D hissed out a breath.

"The wife grabbed a knife from the table and stabbed him in the arm. Not a lethal wound by any means, but he ended up tripping and cracking his head on the table. Knocked himself right out. She took the kids and ran all the way to my clinic on a broken foot."

"How bad were their injuries?"

"Bad. The mother had a broken jaw, broken foot, fractured ribs, black eyes, dislocated shoulder. The five-year-old got off the easiest—a few bruises and a bloody lip. And the baby . . ."

Sofia swallowed. "He suffered a skull fracture when his head connected with the wall, but that wasn't even the biggest concern. His spleen had ruptured, and there was nothing I could do to fix it. I'm not equipped to operate in the clinic, and even if I were, I have no experience operating on babies. So I called the medevac and had the family airlifted to the hospital. The baby died on the helicopter, though. Too much internal bleeding."

"Shit."

"Yeah." Her heart ached at the memory, then hardened when she remembered what happened next. "The husband showed up at the clinic the next morning, wanting me to treat his arm."

"Are you fucking kidding me? Why wasn't he arrested?"

"Because his wife refused to press charges, and the police couldn't be bothered to arrest him themselves. You know how the cops in that region operate—if it's not a slam-dunk case, they don't bother. Without the wife's testimony, they didn't see the point in building a case against him."

"What'd he do when he showed up?" D suddenly frowned. "Did that bastard lay a hand on you?"

"No. He was more concerned with the infection in his arm. His wife had stabbed him with a dirty kitchen knife, and the wound was badly infected." Sofia's teeth dug into the inside of her cheek. "I refused to treat him. I told him I knew what he'd done and that I'd rather die than help him. So I sent him away, and a couple days later, I found out he died from septicemia. The infection poisoned his blood and he *died*."

D's voice contained a twinge of satisfaction. "Good."

"I took an oath to save people," she said miserably. "But I didn't save him. I *couldn't*."

"He didn't deserve saving."

A choked sound flew out. "I attended the funeral for the infant the week after I let that man die. Have you ever seen a baby's casket, Derek? Do you know how small it is? It's fucking *tiny*. I went to the funeral and stood there next to the baby's mother, all the while knowing that I let her husband die. But I didn't feel guilty about what I did. Because you were right the other day—some people *do* deserve to die."

It was the first time she'd ever told anyone about that incident. She'd almost told Chris about it once, but she'd been too afraid he would judge her. That he'd look at her differently. But she wasn't worried about any recrimination from D.

Neither of them spoke for a while. Faint sunbeams sliced into the cell through the barred window, forming a pattern of lines on the dirty floor. Dust motes danced in the air, and Sofia watched them swirl in the light, wondering if Sullivan had done the same thing when he'd been here.

She prayed he was still alive. She'd always liked the guy, no matter how many times he shamelessly flirted with her. Despite his cocky exterior, he seemed like a truly decent man. One of the good guys.

"I don't like kissing."

D's abrupt confession made her jump.

She turned to look at him. "Um. Okay." Where the hell had that come from?

"I've never liked it. Having someone's face so close to mine. And their mouth . . . and tongue . . ." His voice went gruff. "It makes me uncomfortable."

"Oh. Okay." She had no idea how else to respond.

"When you kissed me at the safe house earlier . . ."

His pants rustled as he shifted, and suddenly his intense gaze pierced her face. "It felt . . . nice."

Even in their current predicament, her heart still did a little flip.

"I wanna do it again."

The defensive set of his jaw brought a smile to her lips. He looked like he was waiting for her to argue.

But instead she let out a laugh. A strangled, slightly hysterical laugh that caused D's eyes to flash.

"Hearing how I indirectly killed a man *turned you on*?" she blurted out. "Seriously?"

"No. It's an idea I've been entertaining since this morning."

An idea he was entertaining? Gee. He made it sound *so* romantic.

Then again, they were in a cell at the moment, the last place where romance could ever thrive. Yet her heart was somersaulting faster now as honest-to-God anticipation rose inside her.

Which, for some reason, only made her laugh harder.

"Whatever," he muttered. "If you don't want me to kiss you, I won't."

Sofia's laughter died. His expression had become downcast, his jaw softening in defeat. She was stunned to realize she'd actually hurt him.

"No," she said quickly. "I *do* want it. I . . . I really want it."

His gaze found hers again. "I might not like it," he said awkwardly.

And for the first time in seven years, Sofia witnessed genuine vulnerability in his eyes. It was enough to send her heart soaring, enough to spur her into his lap before she could stop herself. He looked startled by the sudden movement, stiffening as her thighs straddled his, but she didn't give him time to back out.

"Kiss me," she ordered.

D's throat dipped.

She swept her fingers along the hard edge of his jaw. "Kiss me, Derek."

"Ah . . . all right."

Using the word *adorable* in relation to this man hadn't seemed possible, but right now, it was the only one to describe him. Adorable and awkward, the polar opposite of the cold, self-assured D she'd come to know.

He cupped her chin with one large hand, and she shivered from the feel of his callused fingertips scraping her skin. Dark eyes studied her face, more thoughtful than she'd ever seen them. His lips parted slightly as he rubbed her bottom lip with his thumb.

Sofia sat motionless in his lap. Waiting. Anticipating. Something was happening. Something new and strange and scary, tangling in her stomach and speeding her pulse, but she resisted the urge to put a stop to it. She wanted to know—no, she *needed* to know what intimacy with D would feel like. Which was ironic, considering they'd already had sex, the most intimate act there was.

But that night two months ago hadn't been intimate. It had been meaningless fucking.

This, right now, meant something.

D cleared his throat. "Uh . . ." His hand shook against her face. "I think this might be a bad idea—"

Sofia pressed her mouth to his before he could finish that thought.

Yep, she was being proactive.

The moment their lips met, he froze again, the same way he'd frozen this morning. She kept her eyes open, saw that his were too, and gently eased her mouth back half an inch.

"Don't think," she whispered. "Just . . . feel."

When their mouths met again, his lips were no longer hard and unyielding. They molded to hers, soft and sweet, the heat of his mouth searing her whole body. He kept one hand on her cheek. The other rested lightly against her hip, then tightened as she parted her lips to welcome his tongue.

The first stroke was tentative. Curious, even. He tasted like peppermint and coffee and something seductively male, and the flavor of him suffused her taste buds, made her dizzy with desire. As their tongues gently moved against each other, her lower body rolled instinctively, seeking friction.

D made a husky sound that vibrated against her lips. She felt him harden beneath his cargo pants, swell and thicken until his long erection pressed against her core. The knowledge that he was not only kissing her but also getting aroused by it was the most thrilling feeling she'd experienced.

"Are you okay?" she murmured.

His eyes were heavy lidded, burning bright. "I'm good. You?"

"I'm more than good." She cupped the back of his head to pull him close again, and the short bristles of his hair scratched her palms.

She kissed him again and was rewarded to see his eyelids flutter shut. She closed her own eyes and lost herself in him. In the warmth of his mouth and the sudden hunger of his tongue as it tangled with hers. He chased her tongue into her mouth, thrusting greedily, groaning as he drove the kiss deeper.

He clamped both hands around her waist and gave an upward rocking of his hips, his clothed erection sliding over the seam of her jeans. The delicious friction made her gasp, but he swallowed the breathy sound with another kiss. And then another. And another. Deep, drugging kisses that stole her sanity and had her panting for more.

"D . . ." She wrenched their mouths apart, a sense of urgency overtaking her. "All that stuff you told me . . . about your parents . . . You wouldn't have told me all that if . . ." She drew a much-needed breath. "You think we're going to die, don't you?"

A part of her had hoped he'd contradict her, but D simply sighed and said, "Yes."

Chapter 17

Sofia's mouth was wet and swollen from his kisses. For some reason, D couldn't tear his gaze off it. He . . .

He liked kissing her.

Actually, no. If the rock in his pants was any indication, he fucking *loved* kissing her.

And even with his bleak answer hanging in the air between them, he was still aroused. Still stunned that Sofia's lips had evoked such a visceral response in him. He was thirty-two years old, and this was the first time he'd gotten hard while making out with a woman. The first time he'd been content to *just* make out. He didn't feel the overwhelming urge for release, that ball of tension that only hard-core fucking or a rough blow job could sate. He just wanted to keep kissing her.

"You don't have a plan?" Sofia asked quietly. "No thoughts about how we can get out of this?"

"No." He'd never lied to her before, and he wasn't about to start now. They were screwed. Undeniably screwed.

But . . . there might be a way to save *her*. The *we* part, as in both of them escaping with their lives? That ship had sailed long before he'd even reached out to Mendez. For all his talk about Bryant being responsible for Gael's death, D knew that Mendez wouldn't be satisfied with getting revenge against the man who'd "ordered" D to kill his son. D had pulled the trigger, and D would pay the price for it. He'd accepted that.

Sofia, on the other hand . . . He could still save her. Maybe. It was unlikely that Mendez would agree to release her, but if D played his cards right, Sofia might stand a chance.

"Okay, then," she said, sounding resigned.

Then she climbed off his lap and unbuttoned her jeans.

It was difficult to catch him off guard, but with that one flick of a button, Sofia Amaro succeeded in making him gape.

"What are you doing?"

She kicked off her boots, then eased her jeans and panties down her shapely legs. "If we're going to die, then we may as well make good use of the time we have left."

His mouth ran dry as he stared at her pussy. The narrowest strip of dark hair covered her mound, while the rest of her was bared to his gaze. He was so captivated by the sight that he barely noticed her remove her shirt and bra. Then she was naked, settling on his lap again as her delicate fingers reached for his zipper.

"Sofia . . ."

"What?" She sounded amused as she yanked on the metal tab. "Do you have a better suggestion for how we should spend our time in here?"

He didn't know whether to laugh or curse. He'd always

appreciated her take-charge attitude, but fucking was the last thing on his mind right now. He needed to stop this, pronto, before things got out of hand.

His cock, however, had other ideas. It sprang into Sofia's waiting palm the moment she undid his pants, and when she squeezed the shaft, a jolt of heat sizzled right down to his balls.

"You left too soon that night," she said with a sigh.

He swallowed. "I did?"

She nodded. "I wanted you again right after it was over. I was disappointed that it only happened once. I've thought about you . . . about *this*"—she squeezed his cock—"for two months, Derek. I want you inside me again."

Christ. If she kept saying shit like that, he would come long before he even got inside her. And forget about not letting things get out of hand. They were very much *in* hand. In *her* hand, as she stroked his cock so skillfully it brought stars to his eyes.

"I can't die without feeling you inside me at least one more time." Her voice took on a throaty pitch. "So don't fight me, okay?"

She pumped his dick, one fast stroke, and a groan ripped from the back of his throat. "Ride me," he rasped.

Arousal darkened her eyes to a smoky hunter green. Gripping the base of his cock, she rose slightly, then lowered herself down on him. Her tight warmth surrounded his tip. Just the tip. Fuck, he needed more. He needed all of her. But she was teasing him, easing down a millimeter at a time. So agonizingly slow as she kept her gaze on his.

The eye contact triggered the familiar rush of unease,

a queasy pull on his insides, but when he clamped his eyelids shut, the heat of her pussy disappeared.

"Look at me," she commanded.

He reluctantly opened his eyes. "It's better if I don't," he mumbled.

"No. It's better if you do."

She leaned in and brushed her lips over his, and he surprised himself by deepening the kiss before she could pull away. Greedy and demanding, shoving his tongue through her parted lips in a desperate thrust. He wanted to swallow her up, to fucking *drown* in her. He didn't understand it and he hated himself for his weakness, for this unexpected need she'd unleashed inside him. Not tension, not the carnal urge to empty his seed somewhere, but real, bone-deep *need*. For another person. For *her*.

"I'm not just a nice, warm place for you to stick your dick," she whispered, but she didn't sound angry or critical. "I'm here, right here with you, and you need to be here with me too. I know why you don't want to look at me. I know why you don't want me looking at *you*."

His throat burned. Of course she knew why. He'd spilled his entire wretched history to her. Sofia was smart, perfectly capable of connecting the dots and figuring out why he kept his distance, why the thought of fucking someone and having them stare at him made him want to throw up.

Don't fucking say it, he wanted to shout at her.

But Sofia didn't voice the words. She simply cupped his cheeks and gave him another fleeting kiss. "I need you to be here with me," she repeated. "Otherwise it means nothing."

D inhaled a shaky breath.

"Can you do that for me?"

Several seconds passed before he managed to make his head move in a jerky nod.

"Thank you." Two soft words, followed by an even softer kiss as she guided his cock back to her opening.

He moaned when she seated herself fully, shocked by the burst of pleasure that rippled around his cock before shooting up his spine. She was tighter than he remembered. And wet. So fucking wet. His hips shot up instinctively, burying him deep, but when she let out a husky cry, he froze.

"You're . . . pregnant," he croaked. Fuck, he'd been so distracted by the tight grip of her pussy that he'd forgotten all about her condition. "Maybe we shouldn't . . ."

"We should. Oh God, we really should." She moved over him in a slow rhythm, soaking his shaft with her wetness.

"You sure?" he said roughly.

She ground harder against him, and his cock damn near exploded. "It's . . . God, it's *so* good. Sensitive but good."

Good didn't even begin to describe how she was making him feel. Each wet glide over his dick sent him closer into oblivion. Their surroundings faded. He wasn't aware of anything but the heat clamping around him, the smooth skin beneath his palms.

He slid his hands up Sofia's slender hips and cupped her tits, groaning when their heavy weight filled his palms. His eyes remained open as he toyed with her nipples, watching her gaze grow hazy, her lips part to release a soft sigh. He wished he were naked so he could feel her skin on his, the tight points of her nipples scraping his bare chest.

Was this how sex was supposed to be? Was his heart supposed to be pounding this hard? His chest was tight and achy, pulse careening dangerously as unfamiliar sensations traveled through his body.

No. Goddamn it. It was too fucking intense.

His hands fell from her breasts, his mouth opening so he could put a stop to . . . to *this*. But Sofia spoke before he could.

"Stay with me," she urged, locking her hands around his neck. "It's just you and me here, Derek."

Some of the panic in his chest dislodged. "Talk to me." His voice was hoarse. "Remind me you're here. Please."

"Okay." She ran a reassuring hand over his cheek. "Okay. But you need to look at me. Keep looking at me, all right?"

He nodded, his heart hammering faster.

Sofia rocked her hips again, her inner muscles squeezing him tight. "Do you like being inside me?"

"Fuck. Yes."

"I like it, too. I really . . . really . . . like it." Each word was punctuated by the rise of her body, followed by a downward descent that drew his cock deep into her. "I feel full. I feel . . ." She moaned when his hips snapped up again. "That's it, Derek. That's what I want. Fuck me just like that."

He gave her what she wanted, utterly transfixed by the look on her face. Raw passion. Lust. But *healthy* lust. The kind he saw in the eyes of his teammates and their wives. Pleasure without pain. Arousal without malice or perversion.

"I want to come," she begged. "I want you to make me come."

He watched her intently. "How can I get you there?"

"Touch me." She yanked his hand off her waist and brought it to the juncture of her thighs, pressing his thumb to her clit. "Here."

He rubbed that swollen bud, fascinated by her responses. Light strokes made her moan. Circular ones made her gasp. He applied more pleasure and was rewarded by a low cry that had her spine arching.

"Oh, like that. Just . . . like . . . that . . ."

Sofia's tits rose and fell rapidly with each hurried breath, and his gaze gravitated to her nipples, pink and puckered with excitement.

D leaned in and licked one, and she jerked as if he'd struck her, another wild moan leaving her lips. He sucked the rigid bud deep in his mouth, his cock growing impossibly harder when he felt her nipple pulsing on his tongue. He continued to stroke her clit, rubbing faster.

He stopped sucking on her nipple only when she began to shake with release. He lifted his head so he could see her face, and the sight of her took his breath away. Flushed cheeks, parted lips, green eyes glittering like brilliant emeralds.

He was so busy watching her come that his own orgasm caught him by complete surprise. Pleasure surged through him in hot, pulsing waves, burning him from the inside out. He wrapped his arms around her and buried his face in her breasts, breathing hard.

What the *fuck* had just happened?

"D." Her palm gently ran over the back of his head, her touch strong and soothing. "Look at me."

He weakly lifted his head. "Jesus," he choked out.

Her mouth twitched before curving in a smile. "That wasn't so bad, huh?"

Before he could stop it, a laugh flew out. Bad? Christ, he was still harder than granite, his cock recovering within seconds from that mind-shattering climax.

Sofia's eyes widened when he gave a slight thrust. "Wow. Okay. Did I just create a monster?"

The laughter continued to pour out, even as he gently moved them forward so his body covered hers. He kept his hands beneath her back, creating a barrier between her bare skin and the cold floor. He didn't give a shit if the cracked stones scraped up his knuckles. He needed her again. Now.

"Are you sore?" he asked gruffly.

"No." Her eyes twinkled. "Are you?"

"No." He withdrew his cock, then slid back in. She was still so wet. God, this woman was going to kill him. "I want you again. I . . . need you again."

Her hand rose, fingers skimming his cheek. "Then take me."

Sofia couldn't believe what she was witnessing. Derek Pratt had completely transformed. The man who'd screwed her from behind in her kitchen two months ago was now lying on top of her, his hungry gaze fixed on her as if he couldn't get enough. As if he wanted to memorize every inch of her face so he could refer to it later.

His body was warm and solid. She should've felt

trapped, crushed, but she didn't. She felt safer and more content than she ever had in her life, and her own body was already coming to life again, melting beneath him as delicious dampness crept between her legs.

She needed him again too.

"Take me," she repeated as she peered up at him.

He answered not with words but with action, plunging deep as his mouth crashed over hers. A thrill raced up her spine. He was kissing her again, so passionately that she didn't even have a chance to come up for air. But oxygen was overrated. She didn't need it. Didn't need to breathe, not when he was filling her again, reawakening the pleasure inside her.

He didn't beg her to talk this time. His mouth stayed glued to hers as his hips flexed and retreated, his cock driving into her with urgent strokes.

Sofia's hands traveled down his back. He was still fully clothed, damn it. She wanted to strip him naked, run her fingers over every hard inch of flesh, but she settled for sliding her hands beneath his waistband and squeezing his taut ass. God, his ass was perfect. Round and muscular, quivering beneath her hands as he fucked her.

The pregnancy had turned her body into a hypersensitive bundle of nerve endings, heightening every sensation so that every stroke of his cock was a blinding rush of ecstasy. And her breasts had never felt heavier or as achy as they brushed against his chest.

"Come for me again," D rasped against her mouth. "I want to see it again."

"See . . . what?" she managed to choke out.

"The look on your face." His hand moved between them. "It was fucking *beautiful*, Sofia. I want it again."

He pressed his thumb on her clit and rubbed. Teased and toyed and stroked until the pressure in her core detonated in a dizzying blast of bliss.

"Yeah. That's what I wanted," D groaned, slowing his pace as he stared at her face. "Fuck . . . *fuck*." He thrust one last time, a shudder rocking his powerful body as he came again.

Sofia could barely catch her breath. It was like a tornado had flown through the cell and knocked her off her feet. She'd always known that Derek Pratt was a force of nature, but holy hell, when the man let go, he really *let go*.

"Are you okay?" He carefully slid his hands out from under her and sat up.

"I'm—" She gasped when she saw his knuckles. "Oh shit. Your hands."

D seemed unconcerned by the bloody scrapes. "I'm fine."

She was touched when she realized he'd kept his hands beneath her to protect her back. God, just when she thought she'd gotten a handle on this man, he flipped it around and showed her a new side of himself.

Sofia picked up her discarded clothing and hurriedly threw everything back on, then snapped into doctor mode as she knelt beside D. She used the bottom of her shirt to sop up the blood, which was all she could really do at the moment. She had no gauze or antiseptic, nothing but the clothes she was wearing.

Chuckling, he moved his hands out of her grasp. "I'm fine," he repeated.

Men. Why did they always act like everything was no big deal? The last time she'd treated D for a serious

concussion, he'd said the same damn thing—*I'm fine.*
Yeah fucking right.

"You're the one I'm concerned about," he added, discomfort creasing his features. "Are you sure the, ah, sex
didn't hurt the . . ." His gaze rested on her stomach.

"The *baby*, Derek. Saying the word doesn't mean
you're signing a contract to be in his life."

The bitterness appeared out of nowhere, bringing a
sharp bite to her tone. In all the chaos since she'd shown
up at the airfield, she'd completely forgotten about their
talk this morning. About how his *lawyer* would be visit-
ing her, giving her money, because D was uninterested
in being a father to their child. Not just uninterested,
but adamantly against it.

"Sofia . . ."

She sighed. "I'm sorry. I shouldn't have snapped
at you."

He didn't answer for a moment. Then he sighed too.
"You're angry at me."

"No." *Yes.*

"It's all right. You can be angry." D slid toward the
wall and leaned his head against it, his demeanor revert-
ing back to what she was used to—hard and detached.
"I wish I could say the words you want to hear. I really
do. But that's not who I am. I . . ." He slowly met her
eyes. "I can't lie to you."

Pinpricks of pain stung her heart. "It's . . . fine. It
really is. It's not like we planned this. I can't expect you
to be happy about the pregnancy when—" Her body
suddenly went cold as panic fluttered up her spine.

"Sofia?"

Her throat got too tight to speak through.

"What's wrong?" D demanded.

"I won't be in his life either," she blurted out. "He won't *have* a life."

The panic turned into a full-blown anxiety attack, causing her to sag forward and bury her face in her hands.

"Mendez is going to kill us. He'll kill *me*. And the baby . . ." Her breathing went shallow. "The baby will die with me. Oh God."

Sickness spiraled up her throat. She gagged, stumbling toward the metal toilet in the corner of the room.

She heard D's footsteps behind her as she doubled over and emptied the meager breakfast she'd eaten earlier, her eyes watering as wave after wave of nausea crashed over her.

D knelt behind her and pulled her braid off her shoulder, then smoothed a few loose strands of hair away from her face. He didn't say a word as she threw up. He simply held her hair back and patiently waited until she'd finally stopped retching.

Sofia wiped her mouth with her shirt, nearly gagging again when she smelled D's blood on the thin fabric. Then she groaned softly and turned to look at him. "I'm not afraid of death," she admitted.

He blinked. "Ah, okay."

"Are you?"

"No."

She searched his face. "What scares you, then?"

There was a beat, and then he said, "Nothing."

A miserable laugh slid out. "Bullshit."

"It's the truth." His voice was quiet. "I've already experienced almost every horror you can imagine, and the ones I haven't experienced, I've witnessed. So, no. Nothing scares me." He swallowed visibly. "What scares you, Sofia? If not death, then what?"

She swallowed too. "Being abandoned."

D looked startled by her very candid answer. "Oh."

"Everybody I've ever loved has abandoned me. My dad was thrown in jail. My mom chose to shoot heroin instead of taking care of me, and then she OD'd. My grandparents were deported and then died. Every person I lived with left me behind. My last boyfriend left me to take a doctor post in Africa." She stared desperately at him. "Everyone leaves me, Derek."

She could tell she was freaking him out, making him uncomfortable again, but she couldn't stop the words from exiting her mouth.

"I never would have left this baby," she whispered. "I would have been there for him every day of his life."

His gaze softened. "I know you would have."

"But now I won't be able to because we're going to fucking *die* here."

"C'mere."

D reluctantly held his arms open, and she hesitated for only a moment before sinking into his embrace. She buried her face in his neck and fought back tears. She'd never felt so damn powerless in her entire life.

"I'll figure something out." His touch was tentative as he stroked her back, his voice hoarse as he spoke again. "I promise you, I'll do everything in my power to get you out of here, Sofia."

You. Not *us*. She didn't miss the distinction, but she

was too exhausted to argue. "Sure, Derek," she said numbly. "If you say so."

It felt like someone was using his intestines as marionette strings, pulling and tugging them in all directions. As his abdomen contracted with each sharp yank to his gut, Sullivan breathed through the pain and tried not to scream in frustration.

The withdrawal shouldn't hurt this much anymore—it had been almost a week since his last fix. So why did it still hurt *so bloody much*? And it wasn't just the nausea and the shaking and the bouts of ice-cold shivers that plagued his body. It was the cravings.

They weren't going away.

They were getting stronger. Pulsing in his blood and pounding in his chest, reducing his thoughts to *want, want, want.* He *wanted* it, damn it. So fucking bad he could taste it, and yet if someone had asked him to describe the high, he wasn't sure he could do it justice.

A full-body orgasm.

No, a thousand orgasms. Pure and utter euphoria that surrounded you in a warm blanket and held you tight and—

Snap out of it, mate.

Sullivan sucked in another breath, willing away the craving. He had to get his shit together. Ash was coming to get him. Liam had said so.

Oh Christ, he was going to see Liam again.

He'd burst into tears when he'd heard his friend's voice on the phone. Bawled like a bloody baby. He couldn't even remember what he'd said. Hell, he couldn't remember how he'd made it to the pay phone in the first place, because time no longer had meaning. The days and hours and minutes were a dizzying blur of pain and euphoria and sex and desperation.

He had the vague recollection of stumbling across a beach and crawling through a forest. Hearing the rumble of car engines and seeing the ocean. Startled faces focused on him. His trembling fingers dialing a number he knew from memory.

And now he was here, ten yards from a beat-up gas station, staring at a dusty road as he waited for the rookie to pick him up.

He tensed when a black SUV appeared at the end of the road, and the mere act of his muscles tightening brought another gut-wrenching jolt of agony. Please, let that be Ash. It had to be. All the other vehicles he'd seen were rusted over, falling apart. It had to be Ash.

The SUV stopped and the driver's door opened. Heavy boots hit the dirt, and then a familiar figure rounded the front bumper.

Relief nearly knocked Sullivan on his ass.

"Sully," Ash called, hurrying over with urgent strides. His concerned gaze swept Sullivan from head to toe. "Sully. You okay?"

He managed a nod.

Ash hesitated, still scrutinizing. Sullivan couldn't even begin to imagine what the other man was seeing. He hadn't looked in a mirror in six months. He knew he had a beard—it scratched his hands every time he rubbed his face. He knew his clothes were stained with blood, maybe even torn. He knew he must look ravaged.

He *felt* ravaged.

"C'mon," Ash said, his voice gruff. "Let's go."

Sullivan swayed on his feet as he stepped forward, and when the rookie gently took his arm, he flinched as if someone had stabbed him with a needle.

Ash immediately let go. "Ah . . . sorry. I . . . uh . . ." He stopped talking, shook his head as if he were fighting an internal debate, then reached for Sully again. This time, his grip was strong. "Let's go."

Sully allowed his teammate to guide him to the car. His legs were weak as he swung them into the seat, and his fingers were shaking so badly that Ash had to buckle his seat belt for him. A moment later, the rookie got behind the wheel and put the gas station in their dust.

"Where are we going?" Sully mumbled.

"Safe house. Liam's waiting for us there." Without glancing over, Ash touched his ear to activate a nearly invisible transmitter, and when he spoke a second later, Sully knew he was addressing Liam. "I've got him." Ash paused for Liam's reply. "Yeah. He's safe." Another pause. "I know. We'll figure it out."

Ash cut the comm.

As out of it as he was, Sully didn't miss the groove of worry in the younger man's forehead. "What's going on?" he demanded.

"Nothing. It's all good, Sully."

"You're lying." He swallowed. "What's wrong? Is Liam . . . Boston's okay, right? And D?" He drew a shallow breath into his lungs. "Tell me what's going on."

Ash looked over, visibly unhappy. "Just a little hiccup. It'll be fine, man."

"What hiccup? Tell me!" Panic shot through him. *"Is Boston okay?"*

"He's fine. I promise, Liam is *fine*. We've got a minor issue with D, that's all. You don't need to worry about it."

"Tell. Me."

The rookie sighed. "D went to get you."

"What do you mean?"

"He's meeting with Mendez to discuss your release."

He froze. "What? Where? Where did he go?" Tremors rattled his hands as an icy gust flew up his spine. "Did he go to the island? *Is he on the island?*"

Ash hesitated again. Then he nodded.

A strangled roar tore out of Sullivan's mouth. He lunged for the steering wheel. "*No*. Bloody *no*! We have to get him. He can't be there."

The car swerved wildly, making Sully's head spin. With a frantic curse, Ash slapped Sullivan's hands away and straightened the vehicle a nanosecond before it clipped the side mirror of a neighboring car. Loud honks blasted all around them. They sounded like deafening trumpets in Sullivan's head, and he covered his ears with his palms.

"Shut them up," he burst out.

Ash's expression swam with worry as he regained control of the SUV. The honking stopped, but Sullivan's ears continued to ring.

"Sully. You need to calm down."

"He can't be there," Sullivan whispered. "It's . . . a bad place."

"I know it is, man." Ash's voice was quiet. "But he's already there, and there's nothing we can do to change that right now. Reinforcements are already on the way. We'll get him off the island, I promise."

He nodded weakly. His head hurt. Everything fucking hurt.

The rest of the drive was plagued by silence. Sully closed his eyes, but he didn't sleep. He couldn't sleep. D had gone to the island. D was going to die.

His tired brain was capable of producing only those two thoughts.

D is on the island. D will die.

He wasn't sure how long they drove for, but when Ash finally slowed the car, Sullivan could no longer smell the salty breeze of the ocean through the open window. They were inland, then. In a city. He gazed out the window and saw run-down buildings. Bodegas. Pawnshops. Yeah, a city.

"This is it." Ash pulled into a small parking lot and killed the engine.

Sullivan stared at the pink apartment complex. "Liam is in there?" he said slowly.

Ash nodded.

They got out of the car, and once again Ash had to steady Sullivan before he keeled over. Each jerky step brought him closer to the entranceway. To the teammate— no, the *friend*, the best friend he hadn't seen in months.

"He's inside," Ash said when they reached a paint-chipped door. "I promise."

Sully breathed deeply and followed the other man inside.

The apartment was empty.

Just as disappointment flooded his gut, Ash called out, "Boston?" and then a muffled response came from the corridor. "I'm back here. Just giving our guest some water before she goes to sleep again."

Guest?

Sullivan stared blankly at the rookie, who shrugged and said, "Don't worry about it."

The halfhearted assurance didn't ease him. He staggered toward the hallway, his pace quickening as he heard the faint sound of Liam's voice. He had to make sure his friend was all right. *He* wouldn't be all right until he made sure that Liam was.

Sully skidded to a stop in front of an open doorway. Broad shoulders filled his line of vision. Familiar shoulders.

Liam.

He sagged forward in relief. "Boston—" The greeting died in his throat when he spotted the figure on the bed.

Dark eyes stared back at him.

Then blue eyes, as Liam turned his head and sucked in a sharp breath.

Dark eyes, gleaming at him as recognition dawned in them.

Blue eyes, swimming with shock and joy.

Then they both turned red. Everything turned red as the woman on the bed released a throaty laugh and said, "Is that you, *querido*?"

A growl of outrage sliced the air. Had it come from him? He had no clue. He had no awareness, no restraint.

Just a thick red haze where his vision used to be, as he lunged at Angelina Mendez and wrapped his hands around her throat.

Chapter 18

Four months ago

She came back to visit him. Two weeks after she'd begged a man not to rape her and then let Sullivan cry in her arms, she returned to the cell with a carefree spring in her step and greeted him with a broad smile reserved for old friends.

"Good evening, *querido*. You look well rested."

Sullivan clenched his teeth. "Get out."

Her delighted laughter echoed in the air. "I missed you too, baby."

She'd cleaned herself up since the last time he'd seen her. Her chocolate-brown hair was loose, shining as bright as her eyes. A slinky green sundress draped over her ample curves, swirling around her firm thighs as she moved closer.

"David," she called over her shoulder.

The guard of the day entered with brisk efficiency, carrying a large bucket, which he placed at Angelina's feet. He handed her a washcloth, then drew a six-inch hunting knife from the sheath on his hip.

"I thought you could use a bath," Angelina said with another smile. "It's been, what? Two months since you washed up?" She glanced at David. "Cut his clothes off."

The guard was about to step forward when she touched his arm.

"You might want me to hold that." She gestured to his rifle.

Without a word, David handed over the weapon. Then he knelt in front of Sullivan.

Sullivan didn't move a muscle. He tracked the movement of the knife as the guard brought it to his collar. Even with his hands shackled, he could have grabbed the knife, slashed David's throat and watched the man bleed out. But there was no point, not when Angelina had a rifle trained on him.

She laughed again, as if reading his mind. "Don't kill poor David," she clucked. "He's just trying to help you."

David made a clean slice down the center of Sullivan's shirt, then several more strategic cuts until the fabric lay in pieces on the floor.

His bare chest made Angelina's eyes widen in approval. "Now the pants," she ordered.

Sully tensed when the guard unlocked one of the iron cuffs on his ankles. He resisted the urge to scissor his legs and capture the bastard's neck, twist until he snapped the bloody thing. Instead, he sat silently as the man removed his pants.

After Sully was shackled again—and buck fricking naked—David rose to his feet and accepted his rifle from Angelina.

She nodded at the door. "Leave us now."

Once they were alone, her expression grew decidedly seductive, her gait even more so as she sauntered toward him. When she realized that her fuck-me walk had no effect on him, irritation flickered in her eyes.

"I'm sorry for what happened the last time we were together," she said as she settled on her knees. "It was my father's idea to let Ricardo fuck me in front of you." She shrugged, dipping the washcloth in the bucket. "It's proved successful in the past, but I had a feeling you wouldn't bite. You seem like a very smart man, *querido*."

She brought the sudsy, wet cloth to his chest and swiped it over his skin. Water rolled between his pecs and dripped down his stomach, and her eyes followed the path of the soapy drops, flaring with heat as she studied his groin.

"You have a big cock."

Sully said nothing. Though he couldn't deny that the hot water dribbling down his body felt bloody glorious. He remained utterly still as she washed him, basking in the first feeling of warmth he'd experienced since he'd gotten here. Not the warmth of her touch, but the water. It was heavenly. And the soap smelled so fucking good.

"Ah, you like this, don't you, baby?" Her teasing voice made him nauseous. "I'm glad. I want you to like me. I want you to feel at home here."

She wrung out the cloth and soaked it in the bucket again, then proceeded to clean every inch of his body with damn near reverence. His chest and shoulders. His stomach. His legs. She saved his groin for last, giggling as she ran the soapy cloth over his cock and balls. She spent a long time in that region. A minute. Five minutes. A bloody eternity.

Sully ground his teeth together. He wanted to kill the

bitch for how much enjoyment she was receiving from this, but at least his body wasn't responding. He was softer than pudding down there, no matter how many times she stroked and petted him.

When her expression grew annoyed again, he hid a satisfied smile.

"This won't do." Angelina's hand slid into her cleavage and emerged with a tiny white pill that she held up in front of him.

Sullivan felt sick again.

"But this will help." She brought her hand to his mouth and danced her index finger along the seam of his lips.

It would serve her right if he bit that finger right off, but he forced himself not to act on his bloodlust.

"Open for me, *querido* . . ." The tip of her finger teased his lips. When she felt the tight clench of his teeth, she smirked. "Would you rather I call David back so he can hold your mouth open while I shove this pill down your throat?"

Sullivan knew when to admit defeat. Reluctantly, he parted his lips, nearly gagging when she gently pressed the pill on his tongue. He didn't want to swallow it, but it turned out there was nothing *to* swallow. The tiny tablet dissolved almost instantly on his tongue, filling his mouth with a sickly sweet taste. Bloody hell. What had she given him?

"It should only take ten minutes to kick in. Until then . . ." She bent her head and dragged her tongue over his flaccid shaft. "I'll just amuse myself."

Sullivan didn't feel humiliated often. There was nothing about sex that could make him blush, that could make him feel cheap or used or shamed. But sitting there while a woman he loathed with every fiber of his being licked his unresponsive cock? It was the most degrading experience of his life.

She didn't seem to mind his lack of interest. Her tongue toyed and prodded as breathy noises of pleasure left her mouth and heated his groin. He didn't know how long she kept at it, but eventually his body began to betray him. The pill had taken effect and he was stiffening, an unwanted erection forming beneath Angelina's greedy mouth.

"Oh, *querido*, *that's* what I like to see."

She sat up and wiped her swollen mouth with a dainty hand, then lifted the bottom of her dress. He bit his lip when he noticed she wasn't wearing any panties.

Laughing, Angelina settled on his lap. "Now it's time for the fun part."

Chapter 19

Six months since he'd seen his teammate, and Liam didn't even get six *seconds* to bask in the joy of reuniting with Sullivan. One moment Sully was standing in the doorway, the next he was throwing himself on Angelina Mendez. Two hundred-plus pounds pinning her down as strong hands went for her throat.

"Sully!"

Liam lunged for the bed, horror flooding his gut when he saw Sully squeezing Angelina's windpipe. The woman gasped for air, her arms and legs flopping like a fish out of water as the big Australian choked her. She tried batting at Sullivan with her fists, but the man didn't budge.

Liam grabbed hold of Sully's massive shoulders and yanked, but to no avail. Sully was panting like a rabid animal, his knuckles turning white as he tightened his grip around Angelina's neck.

"Sullivan! *Stop!*"

Jesus Christ, Liam couldn't pull him off her. Sullivan was an immovable wall of unchecked rage.

Hurried footsteps sounded from the door. "What the hell?"

"Ash!" Liam yelled. "Come here and *help* me!"

The younger man flew across the room, wasting no time locking his arms around Sullivan's chest while Liam frantically tried prying Sully's hands from Angelina's throat.

Sweet Jesus. He wouldn't budge. Two grown men were attempting to pull Sullivan off the woman, but he'd developed superhuman strength. He was the fuckin' Hulk, his torso impossible for Ash to move, his hands glued to Angelina, leaving no room for Liam's hands to slide underneath them.

The noises she made were inhuman. Choking and growling, growing softer and softer. Blood vessels popped in her eyes, making them bulge and redden.

"Sullivan, we *need* her!" Ash shouted, the muscles in his face straining as he wrapped himself around the other man. *"Let. Her. Go."*

Liam's panic exploded when Angelina's eyes glazed over. Her arms dropped to her sides, her body twitching as she fought to breathe.

But Sully couldn't be stopped. Wild grunts rumbled from deep in his chest, and his fingers dug into the woman's throat until she finally went silent. Until her eyes became lifeless.

Only then did Sullivan release her, so abruptly that the brute force Ash had been using on him caused both men to topple backward off the bed.

Liam struggled to contain his panic as he bent over the motionless woman. Oh Jesus, she couldn't be dead.

She was their insurance policy, damn it. Her very existence was the only thing keeping D and Sofia alive.

He checked for a pulse and cursed loudly when he found none. Fuck.

Fuck, fuck, *fuck*.

"Get him out of here," he snapped at Ash.

He barely registered their footsteps as they left the room. He was too focused on performing CPR on Angelina Mendez. He started with chest compressions, hoping to restore blood circulation, to restart her heart, but when that didn't garner a response, he switched to rescue breathing. Prayed to every higher power there was. Begged the bitch to breathe, to open her eyes. To not be *dead*. But he was wasting his breath. Literally *and* figuratively.

Angelina was gone. Sullivan had strangled her to death.

Jesus.

"Boston!" Ash's frazzled shout sounded from the other room. "I need you!"

Liam sucked in a breath and stumbled off the bed. His gaze rested on Angelina's bloodshot eyes. Dead eyes, glaring up at him in accusation. D had asked him to do *one* thing—keep the woman alive—and he'd failed. He'd fuckin' failed.

His heart pounded as he sprinted to the adjacent bedroom, where he stopped in his tracks. Sullivan was pacing the room in a mad rush, his muscular body lumbering around in circles as Ash stood against the wall, watching warily.

Liam's heart ached. His friend was . . . wrecked. Blood

and dirt streaked his torn, wrinkled clothes. His blond hair had grown out nearly to his chin, and his beard was thick and unkempt. He looked like he'd been marooned on an island for years.

But the change was more than physical. His mental and emotional states were . . . alarming. He was mumbling to himself as he stalked around the room, unintelligible nonsense that stopped the moment Liam appeared.

"Liam." Sully's voice rang with misery as he staggered toward him.

He caught Sully around the waist, steadying the other man before he keeled over. Sully pressed his face on Liam's shoulder, his broad shoulders quaking.

"I didn't mean to kill her. I didn't mean to. I'm . . . not thinking clearly."

Liam's throat closed up. "I know," he said gruffly. "It's okay."

He met Ash's eyes over Sullivan's head and the two of them exchanged a guarded look. Because it *wasn't* okay. Angelina had been their hostage. They'd needed her. D and Sofia needed her.

Sullivan started panting again. "I know what'll help, Boston. You can find it anywhere. Send Ash." His desperate gaze sought out the rookie. "Go find some and I'll get better. I promise I'll get better."

"Get what?" Liam said slowly, growing sick to his stomach.

Before he could blink, Sullivan slammed both hands against his chest and pushed him away. "Heroin! Smack. H. Whatever you want to bloody call it! *Please*. Just go find some!"

A chill seized Liam's spine. Heroin?

Jesus Christ.

They'd gotten him addicted to heroin?

Terror clenched in his gut as he stared at his friend. Oh hell. Liam had been DEA. He'd interacted with enough drug dealers and junkies to be able to recognize the signs of withdrawal. The shaking, the shivers, the way Sully was now clutching his side as if his abdomen was being split open like a watermelon.

Liam's blood went ice-cold as he remembered one of their last nights in Dublin, when Sullivan had described his life on the streets, how he'd dealt drugs to survive . . . how he'd gotten hooked on the shit he was selling.

"Please, Liam." Sully's eyes had gone glassy, his breathing low and choppy. "One fix. It'll help with the withdrawal. It'll make me feel better so we can finish the job."

Liam raked his hands through his hair, took a breath, and fixed Sully with a hard look. "I will not, nor will I ever, get you heroin."

Anger blazed in his friend's eyes. "It'll *help*."

"It won't help a damn thing. And if you were thinking clearly at the moment, you'd know that."

Sullivan moaned again. He rubbed his temples over and over again. Then he staggered forward and clutched the front of Liam's shirt. "Please do this for me. Please, Liam. Everything hurts. It fucking hurts, and it's been hurting for months. I *need* to feel better."

His heart cracked in two. "Sully—"

"*Please*. Just one fix and I'll feel better." The man was pleading now. "I'll do whatever you want. Anything you want."

Liam yelped when Sully reached for his zipper. "What the fuck are—"

"I'll suck your dick," his friend blurted out, sounding panicked. "How about that? That's what you wanted in Dublin, right? I'll suck your dick and you'll get me a fix and then I'll feel better."

Liam's gaze shot toward Ash, whose jaw had gaped open.

"I still don't think it's a good idea," Sully mumbled as he tried to drag Liam's zipper down. "But I'll do it, okay? I'll do whatever you want."

Liam grabbed his friend's hand before it slid inside his pants. "Sully. Jesus Christ! Stop!"

He gave the man a hard shove, then regretted it instantly, because Sullivan lost his balance and went tumbling to the floor. Before Liam could lean forward to help him up, Sully shot to his feet, his gray eyes burning with malice as he advanced on him again.

"What kind of bloody friend are you? I'm in *pain*. I'm *hurting* and you . . . you . . ." He started shivering again, his expression conveying pure agony.

Liam looked at the rookie. "Ash . . ."

The younger man read his mind. He withdrew his nine mil from his holster and carefully walked over, but Sully was oblivious to Ash's approach. He was too busy panting and shaking and trying to hit Liam, who easily blocked each weak strike of Sully's fists.

Ash came up behind their teammate, reluctance etched into his features.

Then he raised his Glock and slammed the butt on the back of Sullivan's head in one sharp motion.

Their teammate went out like a light.

Liam could scarcely breathe as he and Ash caught Sully's unconscious body and lowered it on the twin bed. He stared at the person who mattered most to him in this world, and for one horrifying moment, he truly didn't recognize him. He'd just seen Sullivan choke the life out of a *woman*, but as alarming as that'd been, it hadn't evoked the same level of terror he was feeling now.

"The guys are showing up in a couple hours," Ash said quietly. "One of them can take Sully back to the compound."

Liam nodded.

"Morgan will want to send him somewhere." Ash shifted his feet, awkward. "Rehab, I guess."

Liam gave another nod. Then he cleared his throat. "Listen . . . that stuff he said . . . about Dublin . . ."

The rookie's cheeks took on a reddish hue, but despite his visible discomfort, his tone remained business-like. "He wasn't thinking clearly," was all Ash said.

Liam's gaze strayed to his unconscious best friend. "Yeah." He swallowed. "He wasn't thinking clearly."

Everyone leaves me, Derek.

D couldn't stop thinking about Sofia's dejected confession. It ran in his head on a loop, making him feel things he hadn't expected to feel. Sorrow, first and foremost. He actually felt *sad* that everyone Sofia had ever cared about had abandoned her. He felt . . . sympathy. Not pity or indifference, which was what other people's sob stories usually evoked, but genuine sympathy.

And then there was fierce determination, incredibly odd in its urgency. Saving her had already been a priority for him, but now it was a necessity. He refused to let Mendez kill her. He fucking *refused* to let that happen.

She'd been asleep in his lap for hours, her soft breathing tickling his thigh through his pants. D had been fighting the strangest urge to take her hair out of its braid and stroke those silky, dark strands. He'd seen Kane do that to Abby before, absently stroke her hair when they were nestled together on the couch, or hell, even during a briefing. The act had always brought a serene look to Kane's face.

D wondered if tangling his fingers through a woman's hair would achieve the same result in him. If it would soothe him, ground him.

He didn't dare find out, though. He was afraid it might cause him to grow more attached to her. He was surprised by how attached he'd already become.

He liked Sofia a helluva lot. He respected her. He enjoyed her company. He . . . *desired* her. She'd been right earlier—she was more than a warm place to stick his dick, more than a simple outlet for release. The way he was starting to feel about her wasn't simple at all. It was complicated as fuck, and he didn't like it.

"D?" She stirred in his lap, her sleepy gaze finding his as she lifted her head. Within seconds, that gaze became alert. She shot into an upright position. "Why did you let me fall asleep?"

"Because you were tired," he said gruffly.

She rubbed her eyes, then glanced at the window. When she realized the sun had gone down, her features were no longer relaxed, but taut with worry. "It's *evening*? Why hasn't Mendez come back yet? How long is he going to leave us in here without food or water?"

"Not long. He'll show up soon."

"How do you know that?" Her mouth quivered. "What if he doesn't come back at all? What if he lets us starve to death?"

"He won't."

Mendez would never dream of letting his old enemy die of natural causes when his trusty workshop could do the trick. D was already anticipating it. Being strapped to that metal table while Mendez and his goons treated his body like a game of Operation. It was an inevitability.

"How can you be so certain—" She stopped talking when a creak sounded from the door.

D stifled a sigh. Awesome. Let the games begin.

One of the guards entered first. Lean and muscular, with light brown skin and a harsh mouth that tightened at the sight of the prisoners.

Mendez was next, decked out in white pants and a thin V-neck sweater, a tuft of dark hair peeking out of the V.

"I hope you've been enjoying your visit," Mendez said. "I had to take a short trip to the mainland and attend to some business, but I've really been looking forward to this." His gaze flicked from Sofia to D. "So, which one of you would like to visit the workshop first?"

"Me," D announced.

Sofia looked over, startled.

Mendez was equally surprised. "So eager to volunteer. Interesting."

"Don't come in your pants just yet," D cracked. "I want something in return."

He rose to his full height and approached the men. The guard's hand immediately snapped up, aiming a .45 Beretta at D's chest.

"Relax," D said in a mocking voice. "I'm only interested in making a deal."

"A deal?" Mendez chuckled. "You're not in any position to bargain with me, Jason. But all right, I'll hear you out."

He nodded in Sofia's direction. She'd stood up too, but stuck close to the wall. "You let Esmé go, and in exchange you'll get your daughter back." D locked eyes with the other man. "And you'll get me."

Sofia's breath hitched.

"You can do whatever you want to me," he added with a shrug. "Whatever form of revenge you've got in mind, go nuts. I'll accept my punishment without giving you any trouble."

Mendez looked intrigued.

"Just put Esmé on a chopper first. My colleague will collect her, and when I receive word that she's safe, I'll order my man to release your daughter. And once Angie is back in her father's loving bosom"—D couldn't stop the sardonic jab—"you can concentrate on what matters most to you—killing me."

Mendez slanted his head, a pensive gleam in his eyes.

"What do you say?" D coaxed. "Me and your daughter . . . and all you have to do is release my colleague here." He gestured to Sofia again. "She's got nothing to do with this, Raoul. I contracted her for this exchange three days ago. She wasn't involved in the op that killed Gael."

The older man was quiet for so long that it worried D. When he finally responded, it was with low, astonished laughter that worried him even more.

"She means something to you." Mendez shook his

head in amazement. "I didn't realize you were capable of loving someone other than yourself, Jason."

D bristled. "She means nothing to me. Not outside a professional context anyway. But she's innocent in all this. Let her go, Raoul. You don't need her."

"You're right. I don't." Mendez pursed his lips as he studied Sofia. "She's too old to ship off to my clients. I suppose I could give her to the guards as a gift, but they prefer younger pussy, too."

D risked a glance at Sofia, and his stomach clenched when he noticed how green she looked. Fuck. He hoped she didn't throw up again. She'd confessed before falling asleep that her nausea was worse in the evenings.

"No, it's obvious what needs to be done." A smile stretched Mendez's mouth. "Paulo?"

The guard at his side shifted the trajectory of his weapon.

From D to Sofia.

D spoke up sharply. "Raoul—"

"Shut up," the man hissed. "You're done talking, Jason. You want a deal? Well, *here's* the deal. I'm going to blow this bitch's head off right in front of you. Because I want to, and because I *can*. And after her brains are spattered at your feet, you're going to call your man and order him to release my daughter. *Then*, once Angie is 'back in her father's loving bosom,' I'll give her the honor of having the first go at you in the workshop. And we both know she'll enjoy it, don't we?"

Uncharacteristic panic scurried up D's spine. The hard glint in Mendez's eyes revealed there would be no bargaining with the man. He wouldn't let Sofia go.

"Come here," Mendez snapped at Sofia.

She stayed frozen in place, her distraught gaze seeking D out.

"Don't look at him, bitch. He can't help you." Mendez crooked his finger at her. "Now get the fuck over here."

Her jaw set. She still didn't move.

Annoyance flashed across Mendez's face, but then he chuckled. "Fine. You know what? Stay right there." He held up his hands and formed a square, as if he were framing a shot for a movie. "The gray stone will make a nice backdrop for your blood and brains. I'll be sure to take a picture of it afterward." His tone sharpened. "Paulo."

The guard stepped forward.

D's shoulders tensed. Screw it. He was taking the bastards down.

"Any final words?" Mendez asked Sofia.

D couldn't look at her. He was too busy planning his attack, working over the possible snags. Disarm Paulo. Shot to the head. Shot to Mendez's head. That was the easy part.

Outside the cell, who the fuck knew. D didn't have an exact head count of the guards in the prison, but he knew there was a damn army posted at the marina and airstrip. He and Sofia would get shot down, no doubt about it.

But he'd rather take a bullet during an escape attempt than watch Sofia get executed right in front of him.

"Nothing to say?" Mendez clicked his tongue. "Well, that's your right, I suppose." He focused on D. "Turn around, Jason. I want you to see this."

D obeyed only because it put him side by side with Paulo. It'd be easier to twist the man's wrist from this position, pry the gun away without taking a bullet to the face.

He adjusted his stance, his peripheral vision fixed on the barrel of the silver forty-five. Sofia's slender frame against the wall was out of focus, but he saw that she'd closed her eyes. And she'd crossed her arms over her belly.

The protective pose broke his fucking heart. Christ, he hadn't realized he still *had* a heart. But apparently he did, and it hurt like a motherfucker. Hurt even worse when he caught the slight movement of Sofia's palms stroking her stomach.

"Do it," Mendez ordered.

Paulo cocked the weapon, then homed in on his target: Sofia's forehead.

D drew a steady stream of air into his lungs. Relaxed his body and emptied his mind. It was time to end this bullshit.

He didn't get the chance, because Paulo's hand suddenly moved at lightning speed.

Deft fingers squeezed the trigger, and a blast of gunfire shook the walls as the man put two bullets in Raoul Mendez's head.

Chapter 20

Sofia had heard gunshots before, but hearing them fired in a small cell at close range was a whole other experience. It was like an explosion in her eardrums, momentarily deafening her before leaving behind an earsplitting ringing that muffled the shouts flying out of Paulo's mouth.

It sounded like he was ordering her and D to move, but she was rooted in place. At D's feet, Mendez's body lay faceup, blood pouring from the holes in his forehead, trickling down his nose and chin in two gruesome lines.

Paulo had killed Mendez.

Why the hell had Paulo *killed* Mendez?

Shock paralyzed her body as she stared at their dead captor, but suddenly a dark shadow filled her line of vision. D, grabbing her arm to tug her forward.

His urgent voice penetrated the fog. "*Sofia*. We have to go."

She was too numb to argue, too confused to question him. As her pulse shrieked like a banshee, she stumbled after him toward the door. Paulo was in the lead as the three of them raced down the brightly lit corridor, which was eerily empty.

"Where the fuck is everyone?" D demanded.

"He clears the prison during an interrogation," Paulo answered without turning around. "He doesn't like witnesses."

Present tense. The guard was speaking about Mendez in the present tense, after he'd just . . .

God, what the *hell* was going on?

"Faster," Paulo barked.

Sofia's lungs burned as she sprinted after the men. D had let go of her arm, but she felt his gaze on her, heard his even breathing. Their footsteps pounded against the stone floor, halting when they reached the exit.

Paulo checked the clip of his weapon before addressing D. "Stay behind me. I cleared the area beforehand, but some of his men might still be lurking around."

"Why are you doing this?" D hissed out. "Who are you?"

The other man cocked the gun and reached for the door handle. "I'm one of the good guys." Anger colored his tone. "And I just blew my goddamn cover to save your ass, so how about you stop asking questions and start following orders?"

"Not until you tell me who the fuck you are."

Testosterone thickened the air as the two men stared each other down for so long it brought a spark of panic to her gut. Snapping out of her numb state, Sofia grabbed D's sleeve and spoke in a sharp voice.

"It doesn't matter who he is. He's helping us, and that's all that matters right now."

D narrowed his eyes.

"One crisis at a time," Sofia snapped. "First, we get off this fucking island, *then* we question the man who decided to help us. Okay?"

After a beat, D nodded. "Okay." He scowled at Paulo, who looked impatient as hell. "Lead the way, savior."

The man's nostrils flared in irritation. Then he raised his weapon and threw open the door.

Sofia's heart pounded as they crept outside. The dirt courtyard was empty, save for the Jeep parked twenty feet away. No guards. No alarms blaring in the distance. Relief swept through her like a flash flood, but it died the moment they reached the vehicle.

Her gaze flew back to the prison as something occurred to her. "The other cells," she blurted out. "Is there anyone in them?" She suddenly felt sick. "Girls . . . the girls Mendez kidnaps?"

Paulo was quick to shake his head. "The latest shipment went out three days ago. The prison is empty."

This time the relief was bittersweet. The *shipment*. God, how could he talk about human beings that way? Those girls were living, breathing—

Not the time! an aggravated voice chastised.

Sofia sucked in a breath. Right. It wasn't the time to rebuke this man about his views on sex trafficking, even internally.

"Get in," Paulo commanded.

D helped her into the passenger's seat, then hopped in the front next to Paulo. She noticed his gaze never left the other man. No, the other man's *gun*. D's eyes stayed on the weapon the entire time, as if he were contemplating disarming Paulo and shooting him in the head.

An engine roared to life, and Sofia flew back in her seat when Paulo abruptly stepped on the gas. The Jeep shot forward as he floored it.

The ride was bumpy, jarring her body as they sped off in a dizzying rush. She fumbled for the seat belt and realized there wasn't one, so she held on to the center console. Held on for dear life as mangroves and palm fronds flashed by in her periphery.

He was going the wrong way. Alarm bells went off in her gut as she realized Paulo was driving east rather than south, moving in a direction that wouldn't take them back to the house or the marina.

D noticed too, his outraged curse slicing through the hissing wind. "Where are you taking us? That's not the way to the marina!"

"The marina is suicide," Paulo shouted over the wind. "I'm getting you off this island, asshole."

Why? Why was he helping them escape? Why had he killed Mendez?

Sofia's mind kept getting stuck on that one word. *Why.* She didn't trust Paulo, but what other choice did they have? The man had just killed Raoul Mendez. He'd saved Sofia's life. She had to believe he wouldn't have gone to all that effort just to later kill her and D.

The moonlight illuminated the path as the Jeep moved at breakneck speed, the scent of salt growing stronger with each mile they placed between them and the prison. The ocean. She could smell the ocean.

A deep pothole in the road had her bouncing in the seat, and she grabbed the back of D's seat to steady herself. He twisted around to check on her, his eyes softening for a moment before going hard again. She knew he didn't like this. She didn't either. But she sure as shit hadn't liked being locked in a cell, so if her ticket to freedom required having to trust Paulo, then so be it.

She was thrown forward when the vehicle came to a grinding halt on the side of the path. Paulo hopped out and barked another order. "Move. Now."

D held out his arm for her, and Sofia's legs shook uncontrollably as her feet hit solid ground.

"I've got a boat stashed beyond those trees," Paulo told them. "The slope to the beach is steep. Watch your footing."

He took a step toward the thick brush, but D's voice stopped him.

"We're not going anywhere until you tell us who you are."

Paulo turned, his expression shining with impatience. "Jesus, Pratt, do you have a fucking death wish? I'm trying to *help* you."

"Why?" D growled. "Who do you work for?"

"Who do you think?" the man shot back. "Who else would send me undercover to infiltrate a human-trafficking ring?"

D eyed the other man for a moment. "The Feds? You're a fucking Fed?"

"Ding, ding, ding. Give the man a prize." Paulo looked disgusted. "Can we please go now?"

"Not until I call my people."

"You'll make your call when we get to the mainland."

D crossed his arms.

"For Christ's sake, we're on borrowed time here, you stubborn fool." Paulo shoved aside a low-hanging vine with the barrel of his gun. "You know what? I don't give a shit. Stay here, for all I care. I, on the other hand, am getting the hell off this island."

Sofia's jaw dropped as the man disappeared through the thick vegetation.

"Derek," she pleaded. "He has a boat. We *need* him."

D dragged a hand over his scalp, then muttered an expletive. "I don't trust him."

"Neither do I, but we're all out of options. The marina is guarded like a fortress. We'll never make it to a boat without getting killed. Same goes for the airfield. And I don't know about you, but I'm not in the mood to die tonight."

His reluctance was obvious, digging a line into his forehead.

"He's just one man, D. You can take him." She spoke in a ruthless tone she'd never heard herself use before. "Use him to get to the mainland and then take him out. Slit his throat. I don't fucking *care* what you do to him, okay? I just want to go home!"

Her voice cracked on the last sentence, and it was that desperate wobble that spurred D to action. With a nod, he grabbed her hand and tugged her toward him, pressing his lips to hers for one brief moment.

Then he twined their fingers together and the two of them raced after Paulo.

Liam had known that Morgan was sending backup his and Ash's way, but he hadn't expected the frickin' A-Team to show up. He'd figured the boss would dispatch Castle or a few of the other contractors.

Yet here they were, the most highly trained soldiers

on the team, hauling their gear into the small apartment
and slapping Ash on the back as they trudged inside.

Luke was grinning from ear to ear as he glanced
around the living room. "The OGs, back together!"

Next to him, Kane offered a dry smile. "OGs?"

"Original gangstas, dude." Luke beamed. "It's been
fucking *ages* since we were all on the same rotation."

Trevor and Ethan rounded out the small group, and
Liam couldn't deny he was happy to see them. He'd
worked with these men enough times to trust them
implicitly. Between the six of them, he was confident
they could save D from whatever torture Mendez had
chosen for him.

Between the seven of you, a voice in his head corrected.

The reminder made him gulp. Right. With Sullivan,
they were a group of seven. Except Sullivan was out of
commission at the moment, sedated in the guest room
after he'd *murdered* their fuckin' hostage.

"Where's Sully?" Trevor asked, his dark eyes searching the room.

"He's in the bedroom," Ash answered. "We, uh, had
to sedate him."

The four newcomers wore identical frowns. "What
the hell for?" Kane demanded.

"Is he all right?" Ethan said warily.

Liam and Ash exchanged a look.

"He . . ." Liam trailed off.

Fuck, he didn't want to tell them. It was ripping him
up inside, knowing what Sullivan had gone through. Not
just knowing, but *seeing*. Seeing his friend fly into a blind
rage, then break down as he begged and pleaded for a fix.

"He's got a little problem," Ash finally admitted.

The others didn't appreciate the vague response.

"What kind of problem?" Kane sounded annoyed.

"Just a . . ." Ash stopped, then mumbled under his breath. "A heroin problem."

Shocked silence greeted Liam's ears.

"I'm sorry." Luke blinked. "Did you just say *heroin problem*?"

Ash nodded, his voice taking on an awkward note. "And, uh, a murder problem."

More silence.

"I'm sorry." Trevor's brows were drawn tight as he echoed Luke. "Did you say *murder problem*?"

Liam fought a groan of irritation and joined the conversation. "Yes," he said tersely. "He's fucked up, all right? He strangled our hostage to death and he's going through heroin withdrawal."

Four stricken faces stared back at him.

"Shit," Kane muttered.

"Those fuckers got him addicted to *smack*?" Luke burst out.

Liam gave a tired nod.

"What's the sitrep on D?" Trevor asked, looking incredibly upset.

"No word from him," Ash said grimly. "A bird took him and Sofia to Isla del Rey this morning, and we haven't heard from them since."

Ethan spoke up, his voice uneasy. "How did Sofia get caught up in all this?"

"She showed up in Costa Rica, demanding to talk to D," Ash replied. "Noelle ordered me to escort her here."

"Why would Noelle do that?"

Luke snorted. "Are we really going to waste our time analyzing Noelle's motives? Because that's an entire semester of grad school right there."

"What about the hostage?" Ethan asked. "Where's the body?"

"Master bedroom," Ash told him. "We still need to take care of that."

Luke was quick to volunteer. "On it." He grinned at Kane. "What do you say, OG? Wanna dump a body with me?"

Kane rolled his eyes. "Were you always this annoying?"

"Yup."

Trevor spoke in a brisk voice. "Morgan wants me to take lead on this one, so here's what's going to happen." He looked at Luke and Kane. "You two are on cleanup. Ethan, check in with Morgan. Tell him about Sullivan's, uh, issues. Ash—"

"I'm going to check on Sully," Liam blurted out.

The abrupt exclamation raised every eyebrow in the room, but he didn't care. He couldn't stand around, talking and making plans, when his best friend was lying there unconscious in the other room.

"Macgregor," Trevor called as Liam marched toward the back hall, "we need to formulate an extraction plan—"

"You guys figure it out," he muttered without changing course. "Fill me in after."

He stumbled into the corridor, where he stopped for a moment, leaning against the wall and sucking in a ragged breath. He knew he should be focusing on rescuing D, but he couldn't. Not right now. Not when D wasn't the only one who needed rescuing.

Sullivan was still out cold when Liam entered the room. He closed the door behind him, then approached the bed the way one would approach someone on their deathbed. His chest ached. His heart ached.

The man on the bed *looked* like his best friend, but it wasn't, damn it. Sullivan Port didn't beg or scream in desperation. Sullivan Port didn't offer to suck someone's cock for smack. Sullivan Port didn't strangle unarmed women.

"What the hell did they do to you?" Liam mumbled.

Sully didn't move. Didn't open his eyes.

Liam wasn't sure he wanted him to. Eventually he'd need to start asking the hard questions and find out what Sullivan had endured on the island so that Liam could determine how to help him. But right now, Sully needed time. And rest.

Fuck, *he* needed rest. Liam hadn't slept since he and D had brought Angelina to this safe house. It felt like someone had shoved grains of sand in his eyes, and his temples were throbbing, sending shooting pains through his skull.

He rubbed the bridge of his nose, then let out a heavy breath and moved closer to the bed. He swept his gaze over the chiseled planes of Sully's face. The curve of his bottom lip, the dark blond beard shadowing his square jaw.

After a moment of hesitation, he sat on the edge of the mattress and ran his fingertips over Sully's thick beard growth, stroking gently as he watched the soft rise and fall of his friend's chest.

When he heard footsteps, he snatched his hand back as if he'd touched a hot stove, twisting toward the door just as Trevor appeared.

"How's he doing?" the team leader asked.

Liam answered in an absent voice. "Good, I guess." Yeah, right. Sullivan was not *good*. He was the farthest thing from *good*.

There was a moment of silence.

He reluctantly tore his gaze off Sully, and was uncomfortable to find that Trevor's expression had softened, almost to the point of tenderness.

"You know what?" Trevor said slowly. "Don't worry about the extraction, all right? Just stay here with Sullivan, and we'll take care of the rest."

Embarrassment heated his face. Fuck. Trevor had obviously glimpsed something Liam hadn't wanted him to see.

"Maybe you should get some sleep, too." Trevor cleared his throat. "You look like shit, Boston." With that, he backed out the door, then closed it.

Liam could still feel his cheeks scorching. Damn it. First Ash, hearing Sully's reference to what had happened in Dublin. And now Trevor, finding Liam at Sully's bedside like a tormented lover.

Fuckin' hell.

He shifted his attention back to Sully. Then he sighed. Screw it. He *did* need to sleep. He just needed to close his eyes and shut out the world and pretend that his friendship with Sullivan Port hadn't turned into the most complicated clusterfuck of his life.

Marina was too generous a description for the place to which Paulo steered the speedboat twenty-five minutes after their escape from Isla del Rey. D's instincts hummed unhappily as the man who'd killed Mendez eased on the throttle and slowly guided the boat toward a small inlet, where a rickety wooden dock offered only a handful of boat slips. Beyond the dock was a gravel parking lot shrouded in darkness, and a ramshackle log hut with a weathered sign that advertised boat rentals.

But there were no other boats. No signs of life or civilization, except for a black SUV parked in the lot.

Damn it. He didn't trust this man. And he didn't believe for a second that Paulo was FBI.

"The rendezvous point is nearby," Paulo said as he lined the boat up with the side of the dock and tossed a rope around one of the rotted posts. "My team is waiting there for us."

"We won't be rendezvousing with your team," D answered sharply.

Grabbing Sofia's hand, he helped her out of the boat. Their boots hit the dock with a thud, causing the boards to creak.

Paulo's forty-five snapped up as he joined them. "You're not going anywhere until my superiors debrief you."

D chuckled. "You really want to keep playing this game? You're not a Fed—we both know that. So why don't you tell me who you're actually working for?"

Paulo offered a chuckle of his own. "Does it really matter? I have my orders. Who's issuing them is inconsequential." He cocked his gun. "Walk to the car."

D raised a defiant brow. "Or what—you'll shoot me? You have your *orders*, remember? And clearly those orders are to keep me alive."

"Yes, but nobody said anything about keeping *her* alive." Paulo shifted his aim to Sofia.

Rolling his eyes, D immediately stepped in front of

her to shield her with his body. "If you want her, you'll have to go through me. Which we've just determined you can't do. So walk away, asshole. Go back to your bosses and tell them I died on the island during our escape. I'm sure they won't fault you for it, because, hey, you tried, right?"

An angry flush rose in Paulo's cheeks. "Walk to the car."

"No."

The man took a menacing step toward them. "Walk to the fucking car! Now!"

D smiled. "No."

Sheer frustration darkened Paulo's eyes, making his entire body tremble. But his gun hand remained steady. "Jesus Christ! Are you always this fucking difficult? No wonder he wants you dead!"

As entertaining as Paulo's temper tantrum was, D was growing tired of this exchange. "Who's *he*? Who wants me dead?"

"Who the fuck do you think? Bryant!" Spittle flew out of Paulo's mouth as his anger continued to spill over in palpable waves. "He's invested nine years of his life looking for you—nine years of *my* life—and I swear to God, if you don't walk to the motherfucking car right now, I won't give him the honor of killing you! I'll do it *myself*!"

Bryant.

The name made D freeze, the rest of Paulo's rant muffled by the sudden pounding of his heart.

Edward Bryant.

He wasn't even surprised. He'd always known his former handler would track him down eventually. D had covered his tracks after he'd left Smith Group, but Bryant was the most resourceful man he'd ever met. Former CIA and a legend in the black-ops community, at least before his agency's reputation had been blown to smithereens. He also had a very long memory. If you crossed him, he never, ever forgot it.

"Do you realize what I've had to do these past nine years?" Paulo shouted. "I've seen things, done things, that I can never come back from! Because of *you*, you goddamn piece of shit! I worked for that sick fuck Mendez for nine years! I sold his girls and fucked his whores and tortured his enemies, waiting for *you* to show up. No, *praying* for you to show up! Who do you think helped your buddy escape? I did!"

D blinked in surprise. "My buddy?"

"The blond guy," Paulo spat out. "Mendez's prisoner. I risked my ass to let him go, just on the off chance that he might lead us to you—"

D was past listening. *The blond guy.*

Sullivan?

Sullivan was alive?

"Well, I'm done waiting for you. You're going to do what I fucking say, you hear me?"

D ignored the burst of hope that soared in his chest. Tucking the thought of Sully aside, he focused on Paulo's enraged face and asked, "Why?"

That stopped the other man cold. "Why what?"

"Why would you put yourself through deep cover for so long?" D furrowed his brow. "How much is Bryant paying you?"

Paulo's jaw fell open. "I'm doing my job, you fucking moron. The same job *you* used to do, before you betrayed your country and sold our secrets to foreign enemies."

D laughed. "Oh, shit. Is that what Bryant told you I did?" He was beginning to put the pieces together, and the gravity of what Edward Bryant had done triggered a rush of pity toward the infuriated Paulo.

"Now you're going to get in that goddamn car and pay for your crimes," Paulo hissed. A red vein appeared in his forehead, throbbing visibly. "You're not going to screw this up for me, you hear me? I was promised retirement. I deserve it after everything I've had to do in service of finding you."

The pity in D's stomach intensified. "Retirement? For fuck's sake, man, there's nothing to retire *from*."

Paulo blinked.

"The agency was shut down nine years ago," D clarified.

Silence crashed over the dock.

Paulo's jaw opened, then snapped shut. He cocked his gun, but his hand shook as he did it. "You're lying," he said coldly.

"Sorry, but I'm not. The government disbanded Smith Group after my last gig with them."

"Stop lying to me."

"Mendez kidnapped that senator's daughter, remember?" D met Paulo's uncertain gaze. "Remember how the senator raised hell? Well, he raised even more of it after the job went south. Got the president on his side, and our commander in chief brought down the wrath of fucking Lucifer on the special-ops community. All the intelligence agencies were scrambling to protect themselves, but the senator wouldn't rest until there was a head on the chopping block. Bryant took the heat."

Paulo's face went pale. "Bullshit."

"Our boss broke the number-one rule of black ops—he put his agency in the spotlight. And you know what happens when covert operations are no longer covert. If you can't do it discreetly, then why do you exist?" D shrugged. "The president decided Smith Group no longer deserved to exist."

"Bull. *Shit.*"

"Bryant went underground after his forced retirement. There were rumors that he'd gone private, but his name never came up in association with any contracted jobs or operations around the globe. I haven't heard a peep about his activities since Smith Group was shut down." D had to laugh. "I always wondered what he was up to, but . . ." Another laugh. "Christ, I didn't hear about his activities because there *were* none. He was too busy hunting me. And he used you to help him."

Paulo's breath caught.

"He lied to you," D told the man, unable to control his laughter.

The soft squeeze of Sofia's hand on his lower back killed the humor, reminding him of the stakes.

"Bryant pretended that Smith Group was still operational so you'd follow his orders and go undercover. Because a Smith agent doesn't turn down an order, does he? And a Smith agent reports to no one but his handler, so you really had no way of knowing the agency was disbanded." D grinned. "You're a fucking idiot, Paulo—or whatever your name is. Not Paulo, obviously."

Pure anger reflected back at him in Paulo's eyes.

"You got played, bro. And of course you did. He dangled retirement under your nose?" D snorted. "Shit. You should've known better, though. Even if Smith Group was still around, you know it doesn't let its agents retire. We know too much, which makes us too big of a threat. Which makes us expendable. Bryant never would've let you go. But that doesn't even matter. He *played* you."

"You're lying," Paulo said again.

D shook his head. "He had no authority to assign you to Mendez, but he did it anyway. And why? Just so you could twiddle your thumbs for nine years *in case* Mendez found me before Bryant did? Jesus, man. I actually feel bad for you."

Paulo made a strangled sound. "Shut up. Just . . . shut the fuck up." His hands shook uncontrollably. The gun swayed, winks of silver catching in the darkness.

D's shoulders tensed. Crap. He'd gone too far. Paulo was a heartbeat away from losing his shit.

"You know what? I don't even care if you're lying," Paulo said abruptly. His arm flew up, the barrel of his gun moving from D's chest to his head. "I'm done with this bullshit! I'm done with this job, I'm done with you, I'm just fucking *done*—"

A hiss sliced through the air, the faintest crack of a rifle, and Paulo dropped like a sack of bricks.

Sniper. Jesus Christ.

D barely registered the thump of the body, barely heard Sofia's horrified gasp.

One second D was upright. The next he was throwing himself at Sofia and covering her body with his. Waiting for the sniper to take his next shot.

Chapter 21

Sofia's heart nearly burst through her rib cage as the wind was suddenly knocked out of her. The heavy weight of D's body crushed her spine, pressing her chest into the wooden platform beneath her. Blood. She smelled blood. Paulo's, she realized. He'd just been shot in the head.

The marina was scarily silent. No gunfire. No voices or footsteps. Nothing but the soft whisper of the wind.

"Why isn't he shooting at us?" Sofia's voice sounded muffled to her ears. Probably because D's body was stretched on top of her like a two-hundred-pound blanket.

"Because Bryant wants me alive," he murmured, his breath fanning over her ear.

"You think the sniper belongs to Bryant?"

"Has to. No one else would have been tracking Paulo. The sniper would've called it in, too—we'll probably have company pretty fucking soon."

Sofia drew a breath, but not a single trace of oxygen reached her lungs. "D, I can't breathe. You're crushing me."

He shifted his position slightly, redistributing his

weight to his elbows so his chest wasn't flat against her back. Sofia inhaled deeply, then said, "What do we now?"

"We make a run for the car."

Alarm raced through her. "He'll shoot at us if we run. Maybe we should start crawling."

"It's a lot harder to hit a moving target, baby. We run. No, we fucking *sprint*. On my count, okay?"

Okay? No, *not* okay. She'd almost faced execution by firing squad not even an hour ago. There was no way she was placing herself in the path of another bullet.

But D's tone brooked no argument. "On three, we're going to get up. Keep your head down and stay on my right, understand? We're running to the passenger side of the car. Not the driver's side, not the front bumper— the fucking *passenger side*, all right? And I want you to hit the ground the moment you get there."

Fear lodged in her throat. "I don't like this."

"Neither do I, but we're sitting ducks here and Bryant's men are gonna show up any second. We don't have a choice, Sofia." His tone became brusque. "On my count."

She sucked in a breath, fighting to control her racing heartbeat.

"One."

They were absolutely going to die.

"Two."

Sofia drew another breath.

"Three."

D yanked her to her feet and they took off running. His right side—he'd told her to stay on his right. And to keep her head down. God. It was impossible to see where she was going when she was ducking her head. Fifty yards. The car was only fifty yards away.

The frantic slap of their boots on the gravel matched the wild hammering of her heart. They were halfway to the SUV when gravel exploded at her feet, flying up into her face. The sniper had taken another shot. Holy hell, they were really going to die.

"Run," D growled.

His strides were so much longer than hers that every sharp tug of his hand on her arm nearly sent her airborne. Her lungs burned as she tried to move faster. Damn it, why couldn't she be taller? Why were her legs so fucking short?

Sofia was panting for air by the time they reached the car.

They'd actually *reached* the car.

She dove for the passenger's side and hit the ground just like D had ordered. Sharp pebbles sliced into her palms as she braced them on the gravel. Another burst of fear ignited her belly when she realized D wasn't beside her anymore. He was crouching near the front tire, one hand snaking beneath the undercarriage of the vehicle, while his feral expression focused intently on the tree line beyond the parking lot.

"Derek," she whispered. "What the hell are you doing?"

"Grabbing the key. Just stay down."

A moment later, his hand emerged—with nothing in it. Sofia bit back her panic when D slowly crept toward the front bumper.

"Derek. Goddamn it, don't leave me."

He didn't answer. He was already gone, and from her perch on her stomach, she couldn't see what he was doing or where he was going. Her heart rate tripled, thudding in her blood and shrieking in her ears until it was all she could focus on. Her entire world had been reduced to deep, pulse-pounding fear.

She jerked when a door slammed. Oh God, had Bryant's people arrived? She hadn't heard a car engine. She didn't hear voices, either.

Except D's, low and commanding as the door above her head suddenly flew open.

"Get in. Head down."

Holy shit, he was inside the SUV.

Sofia threw herself into the passenger's seat and slammed the door, then huddled as low as she could get. "You actually found a key?" she blurted out as D hit the gas.

"Magnetic box under the bumper."

The car lurched forward, and Sofia braced herself, anticipating gunshots, a shattered windshield, *anything*. But nothing happened. The sniper wasn't shooting at them. Why wasn't he shooting at them?

"How did you know the keys weren't in Paulo's pockets?" she said in amazement.

"Because he was undercover," D answered, as if that explained everything.

"So?"

"So he wouldn't be stupid enough to carry around keys for a car Mendez didn't know about. It would raise too many red flags." D sped up, his hands firm and steady on the wheel. "You can sit up now. We're good."

She raised her head, worried when she glimpsed nothing but blackness through the windshield. He hadn't turned on the headlights. "Where are we going? Back to the safe house?"

"Too risky."

"Then we need to find a phone. Let Liam know we're all right."

"Not yet."

"Why?"

D didn't seem at all concerned as he drove at a dangerous speed down the dark road. "We need to switch cars first."

"Why?"

He glanced over. "Anyone ever tell you that you ask a lot of questions?"

"Anyone ever tell *you* that answering questions with two-syllable responses is *annoying*?"

An honest-to-God grin filled his face, and despite the fear still surging through her veins and the uneasy suspicion that they were still in grave danger, Sofia found herself grinning back.

"What do you mean, they're gone?" Bryant screamed into the phone.

"They took off before we got there, sir."

"What about Jones?"

"KIA. He snapped, sir. He was two seconds from pulling the trigger on Pratt—Hawk had no choice but to take him out. But you said you wanted Pratt alive, so Hawk didn't engage."

Frustration sizzled in his blood. "He should have shot Pratt in the fucking leg, then!"

Christ, was he working with amateurs here? Hawk was a trained Smith operative, the best marksman Bryant had ever employed. The man was perfectly capable of a strategically placed shot meant to injure rather than kill.

"He didn't have a shot," Tanner reported. "Pratt isn't some two-bit hack, sir. He knows what he's doing."

Bryant fought the urge to whip the phone across the room. He drew a calming breath, but just before he could respond, Tanner spoke up again.

"We'll be able to track him no problem. Sanderson just checked in with some good news."

Sanderson was running point for the contractors Bryant had dispatched to tail the prisoner, but so far his reports had been uneventful. The prisoner had rendez-voused with two soldiers at an apartment building out-side Cancún, and there'd been no notable activity since then.

Bryant perched on the edge of the desk, wrapping the fingers of his free hand over a crystal paperweight, using the circular stone as a stress ball.

"Four mercenaries showed up about thirty minutes ago. Sanderson recognized one of them."

"Who?"

"Kane Woodland. Former Navy SEAL, left the teams about eight years ago to work in the private sector. For James Morgan."

Bryant frowned. He knew Morgan only by reputation—but it was quite a reputation. Ranger, black ops, and now a soldier for hire. The man was known for getting shit done, particularly hairy extractions overseas.

Derek was a merc now?

The thought was like a slap to the face. He'd trained the bastard, turned him into an efficient killing machine, and now Derek was a soldier for hire? Rescuing kid-napped CEOs and taking out rebels?

"Order Sanderson and his men to pull back," Bryant said slowly.

"You're terminating the surveillance?"

"No. Not a full retreat. I want them to give the mercs a wide berth. We don't know what Jones may have said before he died. If he admitted to releasing Mendez's prisoner, then Pratt will warn his team that they're possibly being watched. And if they work for Morgan, then they'll be smart enough to make a tail."

"Roger that."

"But the moment Pratt makes contact with them, your orders are to move in, understood?" Bryant squeezed the paperweight until his knuckles where whiter than the crisp dress shirt beneath his blazer. "And this time, if it looks like he might be able to escape? Shoot him down like a fucking dog."

Forty-five minutes later, D pulled up to a cheap motel with a neon pink flamingo–shaped sign.

Sofia breathed in relief when the car finally came to a stop. They were now in a beat-up pickup truck that D had hot-wired in the parking lot behind a grocery store, because it turned out her supersoldier was paranoid as hell; they'd switched cars four times since their escape from the marina, pulling over every ten minutes so D could secure them another ride.

She'd quit complaining after the third switch. Truth was, she appreciated his caution. Adrenaline still burned in her blood from all the unwanted excitement she'd had to deal with today. She couldn't believe that it had been less than twenty-four hours since she'd followed D to the airfield. And since then, she'd faced death more times than she could count.

"You'll need to check us in," he said as he parked in front of the motel office.

She gulped. "Why do I have to do it?"

"We need to keep a low profile." D gestured to the tattoos peeking from his collar and sleeves. "I'm not exactly low-profile."

Sofia couldn't help but snicker. "How did you ever work undercover, then?"

"This *was* my cover," he said gruffly. "The tats came with the job."

"Oh."

He handed her the wad of cash she'd found in the glove box of their first vehicle—Paulo's SUV. The man might be dead now, but she had to commend him for the thorough preparation he'd put into his exit plan.

"It'll be fine," D assured her. "Nobody tailed us. But make sure to use a false name."

He was right. Renting the room was no trouble at all. In the guestbook, Sofia scribbled the first name that came to mind—the very original Jane Johns—and five minutes later, she was back at the car, dangling a room key in front of D's open window.

He slid out of the car, unfolding his six-foot-plus frame and rising to his full height. He walked ahead of her to their room, withdrawing his weapon as he approached the door.

"Stay out here," he ordered.

He turned the key in the lock and disappeared through the shadowy doorway, returning less than a minute later and gesturing for her to come inside.

Sofia barely had time to examine her surroundings before D moved back to the door. "Where are you going?" she squeaked in alarm.

"I'm just hitting the discount store across the street. Figured we needed a change of clothes. And food. You definitely need food." His dark eyes rested on her belly, and then he awkwardly glanced away. "Lock the door behind me. I'll be back before you know it."

A moment later, he was gone, and even though she'd locked the door, Sofia didn't relax until D returned twenty minutes later, carting two plastic shopping bags inside.

The food selection was far from a gourmet feast—a dozen packages of ramen noodles, a box of crackers, and a stack of chocolate bars.

"That's all they had," he muttered when her lips twitched in amusement.

Luckily, the motel room had a kitchenette with a small microwave, and Sofia wasted no time heating up the noodles. She and D ate in silence. When her mind wandered back to everything Paulo had said before he'd died, she finally spoke.

"Do you think Sullivan is alive?" she hedged. "Paulo said he released him, remember?"

"I remember." His eyes revealed nothing.

"You think he was lying?"

D took a sip from his water bottle, then said, "I think that unless I see Sullivan for myself, I need to operate under the assumption that he's dead."

"Isn't it better to operate under the hope that he's alive?"

"Hope is a waste of time, baby. Just leads to disappointment."

Her heart squeezed. God, what a sad way to live. She couldn't imagine living her life without ever experiencing hope.

She chewed her last cracker, then stood up and threw out their empty containers. "I think I'm going to take a shower."

D stayed at the table, nodding in response.

Sofia headed for the bathroom door, but hesitated before walking through it. Uncertainty washed over her as she turned to look at D. He was expressionless, his shoulders rigid, and she suddenly found herself longing for the man who'd held her so tenderly in that cell. Who'd moved inside her while watching her with what she could only describe as reverence.

"Do you . . ." She swallowed. "Do you want to join me?"

His head lifted in surprise. And then a spark of heat lit his eyes. "Yes," he said hoarsely.

Neither of them spoke as they entered the bathroom together. Sofia had never been self-conscious about her body, but she was oddly nervous as she stripped off her sweaty tank top and dirt-streaked jeans. D had seen her naked before, so why were her hands trembling like she was about to lose her virginity?

Without meeting her eyes, D yanked his T-shirt over his head, then undid his pants and let them drop to the tiled floor. Holy shit. He was naked. This was the first time she'd ever seen him naked, and her gaze ate him up, frantically trying to memorize every detail.

He was . . . fucking *beautiful*. Long limbs and toned muscles, his skin sleek and golden, at least where it wasn't covered with ink. The tattoos, especially the snake at the base of his neck, gave him a feral look. When he turned toward the shower, she saw the tattoo on his back and her breath hitched.

Unable to fight her curiosity, she came up behind him and traced her fingers over the black tribal eagle spanning his upper back from shoulder to shoulder. Then she frowned, because beneath the majestic bird were tally marks. Black lines in groups of five, and one group of three. Forty-three in total.

He flinched when she swept her fingers over the marks, and she quickly bit her tongue to stop herself from asking what the tally signified. After hearing about the significance of the dates on his wrists, she didn't want to push him about this particular meaning. She was too afraid to know the answer.

D turned on the water and stepped into the tub, tilting his head toward the spray. She stood there for a moment, watching the water slide down his powerful body. Her gaze landed on his backside. Jesus, even his ass was muscular, taut and round, the indentations at the sides of his buttocks revealing how strong of an ass it was.

Desire pooled between her thighs. Her breathing quickened as she joined him under the spray and tugged the shower curtain closed. He turned around, his gaze locking with hers for a beat, before he reached for the bar of soap in the ceramic dish built into the wall.

Sofia didn't say a word as he lathered up his hands, but when those big palms suddenly touched her skin, she couldn't stop a moan from slipping out. God, was he seriously going to—yes. Yes, he was.

D ran his soapy hands down her arms, gently kneading her tingling flesh as he washed the day's dirt and grime off her body. She would've called his touch methodical, professional even, if it weren't for the heat burning in his eyes, the raw arousal that caused goose bumps to rise all over her body.

He was hard. His thick erection jutted from his groin, the tip pressing into her belly, leaving streaks of his arousal in the sudsy rivulets traveling down her body.

Before she could stop herself, she reached out and wrapped one hand around his cock, and he jerked as if she'd struck him.

"I'm trying to be a gentleman." His rueful voice was muffled by the rushing water.

The pressure between her legs was so intense she could barely speak. "By running your hands all over my naked body? That's not something a gentleman does, Derek. It's something a tease does."

"*I'm* the tease?" he countered, lowering his gaze to where her hand was gently stroking his shaft.

"Do you want me to stop?" she asked, tightening her grip.

He made a husky noise. "No." His eyes glittered with arousal. "I want you to make me come."

Sofia's thighs clenched, the dampness between them slicking her core. She wanted to make him come too. So badly that her mouth tingled with the urge to take him inside. But she was too transfixed by the look in his eyes. If she got on her knees, she might miss the way his eyelids went heavy when she squeezed the crown of his cock. She might miss the glow of heat that shone in his eyes each time she rubbed the sensitive underside with the pad of her thumb.

She stayed on her feet. The soapy water made it easy to glide her fist up and down his thick length, but she maintained a lazy tempo, smiling when he tried to thrust harder, faster. His flesh was satiny smooth, the heat of him searing her hand.

His coal black eyes burned hotter, lips parting slightly as he stared at her. Not through her, the way he'd done so often in the past, but *at* her. He wasn't watching what her hand was doing to his cock; he was watching *her*.

Sofia's heart soared at the knowledge that they'd reached another pivotal point. In the cell, she'd had to beg him to look at her. Now he was doing it freely, intensely.

"Squeeze my dick, Sofia. Hard. I like it hard."

She felt the raspy command between her legs. Her clit was tight and swollen, throbbing painfully as it screamed for attention. She ignored the plea and grasped him tighter, pumped harder. The wet slap of her hand traveling over his cock mingled with the sound of the water rushing from the showerhead.

D's features creased as if in pain, his muscular forearm flexing as he braced it against the wall. His hips started to move, a fast, frantic snap as he thrust his cock into her fist.

Sofia swallowed a moan when she saw the pleasure swimming in his eyes. "Tell me how much you like it," she choked out. "Tell me what I do to you, Derek."

His voice was as choked as hers. "You make me . . . *feel*." A growl flew out, echoing in the air. "My cock is so full it feels like it's going to explode." He groaned when she pressed her thumb on his tip and swirled it over the moisture seeping out of it. "My balls are aching. I . . ." Another groan.

Sofia brought her other hand into play, kneading his tight sac as she pumped his shaft. "I want you to come. And I want you to look at me while you come."

It was a pointless request, because he wasn't looking anywhere else. His gaze was glued to her face. He looked savage, agitated, completely out of control as his hips moved faster.

"I'm coming," he ground out, his features twisting in pleasure.

God, he was. Soaking her hand with his release, his broad shoulders quaking as he climaxed with a groan that sent a thrill shooting through her. She'd broken his restraint, pushed her way through his steely defenses and made him come apart, and her reward was *seeing* him. Seeing him for the first time, seeing that guarded edge disappear from his eyes, seeing raw, unsullied emotion take its place.

"Jesus." D shook his head, looking disoriented and visibly shaken. "What the fuck do you do to me, Sofia?"

I make you feel.

Her heartbeat stuttered as she absorbed the thought. He'd said it himself—*You make me feel.*

Maybe it made her the cockiest bitch on the planet, but she realized in that moment how true it was. She affected this man in a way nobody else ever had. For some inexplicable reason, she had power over him.

"Come on," she said softly, reaching for his hand. "The water's getting cold."

He was noticeably wobbly as they stepped out of the

shower. Struggling to gain her composure, Sofia grabbed two clean towels from the rack and handed him one. The notion that she affected D was unsettling, because it came with another realization: he affected her too.

She felt safe with him. She felt . . . at ease. Which was all kinds of fucked up, because nothing about this man should make her feel at ease. His hard personality, his dangerous profession. Everything about him should make her want to run far, far away, and yet she could honestly say that she'd never felt more at peace than when she was with him, even when they were outrunning bullets or locked in a prison cell.

What the hell did that mean, damn it?

"Sofia."

He mumbled her name as they left the bathroom. She stopped at the foot of the bed, turning to look at him. "Yeah?"

"Can I go down on you?"

She blinked, fighting equal doses of shock and humor. Had he seriously just asked her that?

"I, uh, don't usually like foreplay," he added when she didn't answer. His expression was sheepish. "Mostly because I've never cared about making anyone else feel good."

"Oh. Um . . ."

"But it's different with you."

He shrugged, and droplets of water slid from his throat to his pecs. His very defined pecs. God, the man was *ripped*.

"I want to make you feel good," he finished.

Holy hell, Derek Pratt was . . . cute. So fucking cute that it summoned a laugh from her throat.

His expression darkened. "It's funny that I want to lick your pussy?"

The crude words made her heartbeat race. Oh wow. Just when she thought he was cute, he turned around and became wicked.

"No, it's not funny." She swallowed. "It's . . . God, I want you to do that. Do it. Please."

Chapter 22

D's mouth ran dry as Sofia untucked the front of her towel and let the terry cloth drop to the floor. She put her naked body on display for him, and holy fuck, what a display it was. Endless stretches of perfect curves and smooth, bronzed skin, and her tits looked fuller to his eyes, making him wonder if that had something to do with the preg—

He banished the thought before it could surface, refusing to let his mind wander in that direction. He'd been making a pointed effort not to think about it, not to second-guess the decision he'd made about not being part of the kid's life.

"Derek?" She raised one eyebrow. "Aren't you supposed to be making me feel good?"

The naughty twinkle in her eyes made his cock twitch. There were so many other matters he should be concentrating on at the moment. Contacting his team. Making arrangements to get out of Mexico.

But right now, all he wanted was to bury his face between Sofia's legs.

"Lie down," he rasped.

Her hips moved seductively as she went over to the bed, where she stretched out on her back, her dark hair fanning over the fluffy pillow beneath her head.

"Lift one knee up."

She did what he'd asked, and his throat went even drier. He now had a perfect view of her pussy, pink and delicate and glistening with excitement.

His cock responded again. His balls began to tingle, but not as badly as the way his mouth tingled, his tongue pulsing with the need to taste her.

He ditched his own towel and strode naked to the foot of the bed, not missing the way Sofia's gaze zeroed in on his erection. He almost reached down and gave his dick a stroke or two, just to ease the growing ache in his balls, but he resisted the urge. Instead he slid down to his knees, circled both hands around Sofia's shapely ankles, and gave them a tug.

She squeaked as he dragged her down the mattress so her ass was right at the edge. So her pussy was inches from his mouth.

"Slow?" he asked, searching her passion-drenched eyes. "Fast?"

"I don't care. Just make me come."

Her bossiness triggered a grin. He'd always appreciated that about her, the way she didn't mince words or play games. She spoke her mind and made her intentions known. Made her *demands* known.

D rested one hand on her left thigh, absently sweeping his palm over it. Her skin quivered beneath his touch. Her eyes grew hazier.

"Tease," she mumbled in accusation.

Still grinning, he lowered his head and licked a firm

line from the top of her slit to her opening. Then he shoved his tongue inside her.

Sofia's hips shot off the bed, a startled cry leaving her lips. "Oh my *God*."

Fuck, she tasted good. The softest trace of soap, and something addictively feminine. Bracing his hands on her thighs, he pushed his tongue deeper, then swirled it around her opening before licking his way back up. When his lips brushed over her clit, she moaned and reached for his head, clamping her hands around his scalp to trap him in place.

Chuckling, D easily slipped out of her grasp and started kissing her inner thigh.

"*Totally* a tease," she whispered.

"You fucking love this," he whispered back. Then he bit her thigh and was rewarded with a delighted gasp.

Jesus, he was harder than he'd ever been, yet in no rush to bury himself inside her. He was enjoying himself too much. Enjoying the silkiness of her skin under his tongue, the slick folds beneath his lips. And the sounds she was making. The breaths and the gasps and the purrs. He fucking loved it.

He teased her for as long as his patience allowed, which wasn't long at all, because he was dying to suck on her clit. So he did. Deep, hungry pulls that had Sofia squirming on the bed, begging for more, groaning for him not to stop, never to stop.

As he suckled her swollen clit, he pushed one finger inside her, then another, filling her with both. Fucking her with them as he flattened his tongue and started licking her clit in earnest.

"Oh God, you are way too good at this." Her voice came out as a croak, shaky with excitement.

She tasted like heaven. She *felt* like heaven. And when she cried out and came all over his face, he was *in* heaven. Which was fucking mind-boggling, because there was no such place. No heaven. Only hell, painful, fiery hell. That was what he'd always believed, because he'd never known anything different.

Until tonight.

Until right fucking now, as Sofia's pussy pulsed against his mouth and clutched his fingers. As she moaned with abandon and convulsed in pleasure.

When she finally grew still, he climbed up her body and lay on his back beside her, the taste of her on his lips. In his blood.

His cock rose, slapping his navel and leaving a wet streak on his abs. Christ, he wanted to fuck her, but that hadn't been on the agenda. He'd wanted to make *her* feel good, not himself.

Except Sofia had other ideas.

Cheeks flushed and eyes glittering, she crawled on top of him and gripped the base of his cock. "You should have done this when I was coming," she whispered, and then she sank down on him, impaling herself on his dick.

Holy fuck, yeah, he *should* have. Her pussy was swollen, soaking wet and tight as a glove, and he cursed himself for missing out on feeling it spasming around him as she'd climaxed.

But this was good, too, the wet heat surrounding him, the slow grind of her pussy along his shaft as she started to move.

D gripped her hips as he stared up at her. Her hair

was still damp, the long, dark strands falling over her shoulders and swaying above her rigid nipples as she rode him.

"I'm five seconds away from coming," he warned her, and it was the honest-to-God truth. Licking her had turned him on like a motherfucker.

"Good. I want you to."

She bent forward and kissed him, and the hard points of her nipples scraped his pecs. One puckered bud rubbed his own nipple, and it was that tiny bit of unexpected friction that sent him over the edge.

His lips were locked to hers as the orgasm shot through his body and fragmented his brain. Gasping for air, he broke the kiss and continued to thrust upward, fucking his way through the orgasm, which only made it stronger, painful almost, but damn it, he couldn't stop. He couldn't pull out. Couldn't leave the warmth of her body.

Sofia collapsed on top of him, her breathing tickling his chest as his thrusts eventually slowed, then ceased altogether.

D rested his hands on her lower back and struggled to regain his breathing. When her lips skimmed over the tattoo on the base of his throat, he stiffened slightly, but didn't push her away.

"So this snake was part of your cover?" She sounded thoughtful as she kissed the red-and-black ink on his flesh.

"Yeah."

He left it at that, but just as he'd expected, Sofia didn't let it go. "Was it a gang thing?" she asked curiously.

"Kind of. A cartel thing." He stopped, reluctant to continue, but he knew she'd keep pushing if he didn't.

"The tats on my arms I got after I joined Smith Group. I was assigned the Jason Hernandez alias, and Hernandez was supposed to be a hardened criminal, just out of jail."

"Have you ever been to jail? The real you, I mean?"

"No. Have you?"

Her laughter heated his chest. "No."

D felt a smile tug on his mouth. He was glad she couldn't see him, because hell, he'd smiled way too much for his comfort tonight.

"Anyway, my first assignment was to off this cartel scumbag—Hector Domingo. Or Hector *el serpiente*, as he liked to call himself."

She snickered. "Hector the Snake? Doesn't that imply that he's, well, a snake?"

"He *was* a snake. Double-crossed his business partners, killed his rivals, added toxic chemicals to the drugs he distributed. Not exactly a prince."

D slid his hand up her back, awkwardly playing with the ends of her hair. It felt weird lying down with her like this. And he was still inside her. Semihard, but his cock was still and relaxed, almost as if it was simply content to be where it was.

"I needed to infiltrate Hector's crew, but in order to do that, I had to prove myself."

"How?"

"By doing lots of shit you don't need to know about. But I did it and I proved myself. Except there was one last thing to do before I was officially welcomed into the fold. I had to get the cartel symbol tattooed on my neck. Every member of the crew had the tat."

Sofia rose, straddling his thighs as she peered at him

in dismay. "You were willing to get a *snake* permanently tattooed on your neck for a job?"

"Didn't have much of a choice. Once you agreed to work for Smith Group, they owned you. They owned *me*." Reluctance seized his throat for a moment. "You saw the marks on my back under the eagle?"

"Yeah. I saw them." She hesitated. "What does the tally mean? Forty-three what?"

"Forty-three kills. Each time I completed an assignment, I'd have to report to headquarters for debriefing. This building in Wilmington—"

"Virginia?"

"Delaware. It was a consulting firm, but that was just a front. Inside, it was like the fucking Pentagon. I'd go in and get debriefed, and before I left, they'd ink another tally mark on my back. They liked to remind us operatives that every life we took belonged to Smith, that *we* belonged to Smith."

Sofia looked so upset that D forced a chuckle. "Hey, the snake's not so bad, is it? Abby says it makes me look like a badass."

Her mouth twitched. "Yeah, I guess it does." A thoughtful glint entered her eyes. "So, did you kill Hector *el serpiente*?"

"Of course."

"How?"

"I cut off his head with a machete."

Sofia gasped, her cheeks going pale. "Jesus Christ, Derek."

"Hey, you asked."

After a beat, she burst out laughing. "You're right, I did. I guess that one's on me." Her expression went serious again. "Do you have *any* good memories? Did you have any moments in your life where you experienced actual joy? You know, one of those perfect moments where everything is right in the world, where your heart is so full it feels like it's going to explode, and you're so happy you can't stop smiling?"

She sounded profoundly sad as she voiced the questions.

D thought it over, and a massive lump rose in his throat, obstructing his airway. "Not before tonight."

She wrinkled her forehead. "Tonight?"

"Yeah. Tonight. Right now." His voice sounded hoarse to his ears, like his throat was lined with gravel. "This is the first time everything in my world has felt right."

And, Jesus Christ, that scared him.

So much he clamped his lips together, refusing to say another fucking word. Sofia Amaro was dangerous. She was too damn dangerous, and he couldn't believe he was only recognizing that now. He should've heeded the warning signs the night he'd fucked her two months ago, the night he'd left the warmth of a woman's body actually wanting more.

But he'd ignored those alarms. He'd ignored them, and now he was *in bed* with the woman. Caressing her. Talking to her. Revealing things he had no business revealing.

As if sensing that he was shutting down on her, Sofia slid off his lap, off his *cock*, and D almost wept from the loss.

"I had one of those perfect moments when I was seven," she admitted, stretching out on her side next to him. She didn't comment on the confession he'd just let slip, and he was grateful for that. "It was when my grand-parents and I lived in New Mexico, before they got deported."

When she trailed off, D broke his recently decided no-talking rule and asked, "What happened?"

"Nothing, really. My *abuela* packed a picnic lunch, and the three of us went to the park. It was the most gorgeous day. Clear and sunny and beautiful. My *abuelo* was pushing me on the swings, and everyone was look-ing at us."

D turned his head to find her grinning.

"He had a lot of tattoos," she explained. "Way more than you have. Full sleeves, all over his legs, even on the backs of his hands. People always looked at him funny when he walked by, but I didn't see the ink. I saw the man. He was a really good man. And we had so much fun together, that day especially."

Her tone grew wistful. "I just remember swinging higher and higher, feeling like a bird, free and happy and soaring, and every time I looked down, I would see my grandmother smiling at me from the picnic blanket and feel my grandfather's hands on my back as he pushed me higher. Everything was right in the world that day."

Something hot and unfamiliar traveled through D's chest and settled in his heart. When he noticed Sofia's expression collapsing, the warmth turned into a deep ache.

"I never understood why they didn't take me back to Mexico with them when they got deported. They insisted I would have a better life in the States, but that was bull-shit, Derek," she said angrily. "How was moving around from house to house better than living in Mexico with people who actually *loved* me?"

He had no answer for that. He had no answers for anything, actually. Only questions. Lots of fucking questions.

How had he allowed Sofia Amaro to get under his skin like this?

And what the hell was he supposed to do now?

Liam was wrenched from sleep at four in the morning by a hard kick to the shin. He instantly went on the alert, his hand shooting for the end table where he'd left his gun, only to falter when he realized he wasn't under attack.

The kick had come from Sullivan, who was lying next to him on the bed, arms and legs thrashing as he moaned in his sleep.

Sully was having a nightmare. A bad one, from the look and sound of it.

Liam hesitated, then touched the other man's shoulder. He gave it a soothing squeeze, hoping the gesture would ease his friend.

It did the opposite.

Sullivan shot into a sitting position, and even in the darkness, Liam could see the sheer panic in his eyes. Sully's fists flew up in a defensive posture, his breath coming out in sharp pants.

"Sully." Liam slid up to his knees. "Hey, it's okay. You're safe."

The other man whirled his head around. "Boston?"

"Yeah, it's me. Everything's cool, man. Just go back to sleep."

The mattress started to vibrate as Sullivan broke out in wild shivers. "What are you doing in here?"

"I needed to sleep. You needed someone to watch over you." He shrugged. "Decided to kill two birds with one stone."

Sullivan gingerly lowered himself onto his back, but the shaking spell didn't cease. His torso continued to shudder, his breathing shallow now. "Fuck," he groaned. *"Fuck."*

Swallowing, Liam lay back down as well. After a moment of hesitation, he reached for his friend. "C'mere."

Sully stiffened, then began trembling again, so hard that Liam forcibly yanked Sully toward him. Sully's head fell against Liam's chest, and then the man curled up next to him, both arms tucked toward his own chest as shivers rolled through him.

"I want it so bad I can taste it."

Sully's breath tickled Liam over the thin fabric of his T-shirt, and now Liam was shivering, too, because Sullivan's body was like a block of ice.

This time he didn't hesitate—he wrapped one arm around his friend's broad shoulders and held him tight. A lump rose in his throat and his heart ached.

"I know," Liam said softly. "But you're going to get through it—I promise. You just need some good, old-fashioned detox. I'll take you to a facility myself after the extraction."

Sullivan's voice was muffled against Liam's right pec. "D is still on the island?"

"We think so." He awkwardly smoothed his hand between Sully's shoulder blades. "But you don't need to worry about that, okay? Trevor is leading the op. The boys will bring D home safe."

Silence stretched between them. Liam stared up at the ceiling, then moved his hand along Sully's spine and cupped the back of the man's head. Sullivan's hair was soft beneath his palm, bringing a strange tightness to his chest. It felt so fucking strange holding another man like this.

"I'm not sorry I killed her."

Sullivan's anguished confession broke the silence.

"She deserved to die, Boston. She deserved it."

He gulped. "Do you . . . ah . . . want to tell me what she did to you?"

"No." The response was swift and empathic. "Don't make me talk about her."

He was quick to offer reassurance. "You don't have to. You can tell me when you're ready. Or don't tell me at all. It's fine." He threaded his fingers through Sully's hair. "Go back to sleep."

"I . . . can't." His friend sounded tormented. "Every time I close my eyes, I think about that bloody cell. And *her.* And the cycles."

Liam's forehead creased. "The cycles?"

"That's what Mendez called it." Sullivan was barely audible now. "Cycles. I just finished the third one before I escaped. Three weeks of"—his voice cracked—"of the most incredible high you can ever imagine. Euphoria. So fucking perfect. And then they took it away. The high went away and everything hurt."

Christ almighty, everything *did* hurt. Liam's entire body was riddled with pain as he listened to his teammate's description of what those bastards had put him through.

"And when I was hurting, they'd come in and wave it around, taunt me with it and say I could have some if I told them where D was. But I didn't talk." A note of pride rang in the bedroom. "Not one fucking word, Boston."

Liam ran a hand over the nape of Sully's neck, and his friend shivered in response. Just one shiver this time, not the incessant trembling from before.

"It would go on for a week. A whole week of agony." A pause. "Have you ever gone through withdrawal?"

"No," Liam said hoarsely.

"*That's* torture. They could've sawed my bloody arm off and it wouldn't have come close to the pain of not having a fix." Sullivan shifted, his cheek sliding over Liam's shoulder before settling on his pec again. "But I wouldn't talk, and then the next cycle would start. That high . . . That bloody high . . ." He groaned again. "I can't talk about it anymore. I want it too much."

Liam kept his gaze on the ceiling. Shadows danced across it, thanks to the sliver of moonlight coming in from the crack between the curtains.

"You talk," Sullivan ordered. "I want to hear you talk. Tell me what's been going on."

"With what?"

"With anything. Everyone. Did Abby have the baby?"

"Yeah, she did." Liam smiled in the darkness. "Jasper Jeremy Sinclair Woodland. Mouthful, huh?"

"Jeremy . . . after her foster father?"

"I think so. And Jasper was the name of Kane's grandfather. His mother insisted on it, and Kane and

Abby caved. Abby said it was better than arguing with Kane's mom."

Sullivan's weak laughter heated Liam's collarbone. "What else have I missed?"

He thought it over. "Ethan and Juliet got married a couple months ago. And Luke and Olivia set a date for their wedding—June, I think. Isabel caught baby fever after Abby had Jasper, and Trevor says he's planning on knocking her up soon. Cate turned nineteen."

"Huh, she's almost legal now. I bet the rookie's happy about that."

"Naah. Ash knows he can't touch her without losing a hand, or worse. The boss would kill him."

"What about you?" Sullivan asked abruptly. "What have you been up to?"

Liam took a breath. "Looking for you."

Sully froze. "That's it? Six months have gone by and that's all you've done, mate?"

"Yes."

Tension thickened the air, and it was so suffocating that Liam quickly lightened the mood. "My family's on my ass again," he admitted.

"Yeah? What's the Macgregor clan upset about now?"

"My ma's ragging on me about not coming home. She's harassing me about Robbie's baptism—Robbie's my new nephew. My sister Maggie had another kid." He fought a rush of guilt. "When Ma said Robbie's name, I honestly couldn't remember which of my sisters he belonged to. I swear, my sisters and my brother's wives pop out rugrats every other day. It's like the apocalypse hit and they're trying to repopulate the earth."

Sullivan laughed again, low and husky.

Christ, Liam had missed the sound of his friend's laughter. He'd missed his friend, period.

"They love you." Sully sounded sad. "You should go home more often."

"Yeah. I guess." Except he hated going home. His family was pure chaos. Liam had seven siblings, and he was in the middle of the age lineup. Not the oldest, not the youngest, just the forgotten fifth child. And when his folks *did* remember he existed, all he ever got was their disappointment and their disapproval, because he'd chosen a life of action instead of stability and family.

He had two brothers and five sisters, all married with children, and he was the odd duck. Always had been, and probably always would be.

Liam could only imagine what they'd say, what they'd *think*, if they saw him right now. Lying in bed, holding another man.

Christ. His relationship with Sullivan Port messed with his head. It *wrecked* him. He had no idea what he felt anymore, what he wanted, but deep down he knew that Sullivan was right. Their friendship was too important to destroy over something as trivial as sex, especially when Liam didn't know if he even *wanted* the sex. Sullivan might be bisexual, but Liam had always considered himself straight. Or at least he'd used to.

Now, who the fuck knew?

As tension continued to roil in his gut, he realized that Sully's breathing had steadied. He'd fallen asleep. Liam supposed he could have moved his arms, released his friend's body.

But he just held on tighter.

Chapter 23

Sofia found herself alone in bed when she opened her eyes the next morning. For a moment, she experienced a burst of panic, only to relax when she spotted D in the kitchenette. He was leaning against the small counter, gripping the cheap plastic motel phone in one hand and holding the handset to his ear with the other.

He was also naked as the day he was born.

Her breasts grew achy as she admired the smooth musculature of his towering frame. Every inch of him was hard, sinewy, *masculine*. And his face . . . God, for some reason it looked even more gorgeous to her this morning.

Maybe because she'd spent the entire night in his arms? Or because that perfectly chiseled face had gazed down on her with tenderness she never could've imagined while he'd moved inside her?

Something had changed between them last night. They were making progress. Real, honest-to-God progress. He'd opened up to her more than he ever had before. He'd held her in his arms. He'd made love to her with his mouth and his hands and his cock. Made love, not *fucked*. Fucking had left the equation when they'd had sex in the cell, and Sofia was well aware of that.

The question was—was Derek aware of it? Or did he still view it as meaningless screwing?

"For fuck's sake," D was muttering. "How the hell was I supposed to know that Morgan would send backup?" He paused. "Okay, fine. I'll own up to that—I should've checked in last night. But I was waiting for the heat to die down."

Sofia narrowed her eyes, easily spotting the lie. Then she felt a pang of guilt, because it was *her* fault he hadn't checked in with his teammates. He'd been too busy kissing her and touching her and talking to her. Actually *talking*. Who would've thought Derek Pratt was capable of stringing together actual sentences?

"Lay off, Trev," he snapped into the phone. "I didn't ask you to save my ass. I can save my own ass." Another long pause, and then an irritated crease dug into D's forehead. "Well, I apologize that you stayed up all night, coming up with an extraction plan. Maybe you can save the little notes you jotted down and use them for the next gig."

Sofia couldn't help but snort. God, this man was such an asshole. It probably wasn't fair to Trevor Callaghan and the others that she found that trait in D so ridiculously endearing, but she'd always appreciated the way he called it like it was. Blunt, honest, no beating around the bush with this man.

D went quiet again. "Ninety minutes. Got it. We'll be there."

Sofia offered him a dry look as he set the phone back on the end table. "The guys are pissed at you, huh?"

"The guys are always pissed at me. It's pretty much a given now," he grumbled.

Laughing, she slid out of bed and walked over to him. His eyes instantly smoldered, alerting her to her own nudity.

"You're very grumpy this morning," she remarked. "Do you need a lollipop?"

His eyebrows shot up. "A lollipop?"

Sofia grinned. "That's what I give the cranky kids who come to my clinic. Shuts them right up." Her tone went thoughtful as her gaze lowered to his groin. "But actually, I think there's another way I can help you."

A choked sound left his lips as she sank to her knees and grabbed hold of his quickly hardening cock. "We're meeting the team soon," he reminded her.

"You said ninety minutes. I heard you." She peered up at him and swept her thumb over the underside of his shaft, and was rewarded with a husky groan. "That leaves us plenty of time to"—she pressed her hands to his muscular thighs and swirled her tongue over his tip—"make you less cranky."

When she wrapped her lips around him and sucked, D's thighs clenched beneath her palms. "Oh Jesus," he hissed.

She batted her eyelashes at him. "I thought you didn't believe in God?"

Another groan escaped him as she closed her mouth over him. He was too big to take in fully, so she curled one hand around the base of his shaft and sucked down until her lips met her knuckles. His masculine flavor infused her taste buds, dampening her core.

"Fuck. Faster," D mumbled. "Suck me hard and fast."

Her eyes fluttered shut as she tightened the suction and took him as deep as she could, using her hand to pump him simultaneously. With each upstroke, she licked a circle around his crown before swallowing his length again, and soon his hips were rocking in time to the fast tempo she'd set. His velvety-smooth flesh pulsed on her tongue, and she felt an answering pulse between her legs.

The pregnancy had definitely changed her body, making it oversensitive and achy, short-circuiting her pleasure center so that each long suck on D's cock brought her closer and closer to her own orgasm—and she wasn't even touching herself.

As D's body tightened with impending release, Sofia wrenched her mouth away and bolted to her feet. "Inside me. Now. I'm about to come."

His brows soared. "You're about to—"

"God, get inside me!" She frantically hopped up on the counter, because the bed was too damn far and she was too damn overwrought. Her pussy tingled wildly. She knew if she so much as took a breath, the orgasm she was trying to stifle would break free.

D moved with swift precision into the cradle of her thighs, his cock jutting out as he gripped it in his hand. Without missing a beat, he brought it to her opening, nudged her with the tip, then drove into her wet core.

Sofia went off like a fireworks display. Oh sweet Lord. The rush of ecstasy that spiraled through her stole the breath from her lungs. She gasped, shocked by the force of the release, damn near blacking out as her vision turned into an entire universe's worth of stars.

D was right behind her, his cock plunging in and

out, then slamming deep as he came. His shoulders shuddered wildly.

"Fucking *hell*," he squeezed out. "You rip me *apart*."

Sofia barely had time to recover from that hurricane of pleasure before another sensation rose in her belly, a queasy rush that skittered up to her throat and flooded her mouth with saliva.

"Oh shit," she exclaimed.

D blinked in shock as she wiggled away from him and dove off the counter. She flew toward the bathroom and flung herself at the toilet bowl, sinking to her knees just as the nausea spilled over.

Well, look at that. For the first time since she'd learned about the pregnancy, she was actually experiencing morning sickness in the *morning*.

"Sofia?" D's gravelly voice wafted from the doorway as she threw up.

In the cell, he'd come up behind her and held her hair away from her face. This time, he stayed put. She wasn't sure what that meant, but when she'd finished retching and turned to look at him with watery eyes, her heart dropped. There was no emotion in his eyes. Zero. Just blank indifference.

So much for progress.

"Are you all right?" he asked brusquely.

She took a breath and waited for another wave of sickness, but it didn't come. Her stomach had settled as if someone had flicked a switch. But her knees were wobbly as she stood up. Robot D was back, and it scared her. Why had he come back, damn it?

Her heart pounding, she walked over to the sink and brushed her teeth with the toothbrush and toothpaste

D had bought at the store last night. Once her breath was minty fresh, she turned off the tap and slowly approached the door.

"Sofia?" he pressed.

"I'm fine." She brushed past him into the main room, hastily searching for something to wear. "It hits me out of nowhere, but after I throw up, the nausea just goes away. It's weird. You'd think I'd still feel sick, but it totally disappears. Everything just settles right up and I go back to feeling perfectly normal . . ." She trailed off when she realized she was babbling.

A dress. Thank God. She found a loose blue sundress in one of the plastic bags. And a pack of cotton panties. A pair of flip-flops.

Avoiding D's gaze, she threw on the outfit he'd procured for her and tried telling herself that maybe this was for the best. She would be going home in a couple of hours, and D would be going to his compound, she supposed. Or on another mission. Either way, he wouldn't be by her side after today.

There was no point in bringing up the subject. In D's eyes, the baby didn't even exist. She could count on one hand the number of times he'd mentioned the pregnancy since she'd tracked him down. So, no, what would talking about it achieve—

"I want you in this baby's life," she blurted out.

Shit. What the hell was wrong with her? She'd *just* ordered herself not to bring it up!

As expected, D's entire body tensed. Then, acting as if he hadn't heard her, he reached for the shopping bag she'd left on the bed and began tugging out items of clothing.

"Did you hear me? I want you in the baby's life." The crack in her voice embarrassed the heck out of her, but there was no hiding her distress.

D yanked a pair of black trousers up his naked hips.

"Derek, look at me."

He put on a clean white T-shirt, then pulled a belt from the bag and threaded it through his belt loops.

"Damn it, Derek," she said in frustration. "Don't be an asshole."

After he'd buckled the belt, he finally turned her way. "But I *am* an asshole," he said tersely. "A cold, ruthless asshole."

"That's not true," she shot back. "Some of the time, yes. But not always."

His jaw twitched as he stalked to the sink to pour himself a glass of water. "Why would you ever want me around a baby, Sofia? What the fuck do I have to offer a child?"

He drained half the glass before slamming it down so hard she was surprised it didn't shatter.

"Do you want me to teach him how to slit a man's throat? How to torture someone until they break?" Anger dripped from his voice, flashed in his eyes. "Should I cradle him in my arms and let him see the tats I put on my skin so I could hang out with *drug dealers*? Should I protect him from all the sick fucks in this world who might try to hurt him? Who might come after him because his father is a killer and has more enemies than a goddamn dictator?"

Sofia was stunned by the outburst. Every word he'd spoken sliced her heart to jagged ribbons, but he wasn't done yet. He wasn't done at all.

"I have nothing to offer him," D repeated. "Nothing to offer *you*. Just pain and darkness and violence. I am not a good man."

She stared sadly at him. "Yes, you are. You just can't see it."

D scowled. "I'm poison."

"You're *not* poison." She gritted her teeth. "You are good. You risked your life to save Sullivan. You risked your life to save *me*. You care about people, whether you want to admit it or not." Her heart started beating faster as something occurred to her. "Fuck."

"What?" he demanded.

You make me feel.

"That's it," she said quietly. "*That's* what you're afraid of. You said nothing scares you, but you're wrong. You're fucking terrified of *feeling*. Feeling anything— hope, joy, love, but especially fear. You're afraid of being *afraid*, because the last time you experienced true fear, it was at the hands of people you trusted, who were supposed to love you." An ache tightened her chest. "I get it. You were abused, Derek. I'm sure it was easier to shut down completely instead of letting yourself feel all those emotions. The pain and the shame and—"

"Stop psychoanalyzing me," he snapped. "It's a waste of time."

She met his furious eyes. "Did you ever see someone about it?"

D's features turned to stone.

"Did you see a therapist or psychiatrist after . . . after everything?"

"I had mandatory psych evaluations when I was Delta," he muttered.

"But did you talk about it?" she pushed. "Did you tell the shrink about your parents?"

"No." His tone went frigid. "Because there was nothing to fucking say. My parents liked to diddle their little boy—"

Sofia flinched.

"—and they enjoyed every second of it. But I got through it. I got over it, and I got my revenge. End of story."

"End of story?" she echoed in disbelief. "Yeah fucking right, Derek! You got your revenge on your parents—good for you. Congrats. But you never actually dealt with what they did to you. The feelings it evoked, the person it turned you into. You decided it was just easier to pretend that it didn't affect you. But it *did*."

Rather than answer, he stared right through her.

"I see you, you know," Sofia announced. "I see the real you under the mask. Not always, definitely not right now, but I've *seen* you. I've seen the man who loves his teammates so much that he'd put his neck on the line for them. I've seen the man who's kind and compassionate, who orders a pregnant woman to eat and rest because he genuinely cares about her well-being."

A muscle in his face jumped.

"I've seen the man who feels actual pleasure. You told me sex wasn't about feeling good and that it was just about release for you, but I *know* you feel something more when you're with me. I know you're capable of humor and laughter, because I've seen and heard it. I know you can be sweet when you choose to be. I know you, and I want our baby to know you, too."

She finished in a tired rush, but she might as well

have been speaking to a cardboard cutout of Derek Pratt. He was stiff and poker-faced, unblinking as he looked at her.

Time stopped. Silence fell.

Desperation filled Sofia's chest cavity, lodging itself in her heart, her blood, her entire being. "Give me that man," she begged. "Please, Derek, just give me the man I met in that cell, the man who shared my bed last night, the man I know you are. I promise you, I'll take good care of him. I'll always be there for him. Please . . . just let me have him."

God, what was she saying? What was she promising? *Why* was she promising it? She'd wanted to convince him to give fatherhood a try, but here she was, wanting him not just for their baby, but for herself.

Because . . . holy hell, was she falling in love with him? Had she *already* fallen?

Sofia felt weak as she frantically tried to sift through her feelings. But it didn't matter what she felt or what she wanted, because Derek Pratt was beyond her reach.

"That man doesn't exist," he said hoarsely. He broke the eye contact, stalked toward the door, and spoke again without looking at her. "Come on. It's time to go."

And with that, Derek Pratt couldn't have hurt her any more than if he'd pulled his gun from his waistband and shot her in the heart.

The team was already at the airfield when D pulled up in the truck he'd stolen last night. Sofia hadn't said a single word during the drive. She hadn't even looked at him. But maybe that was for the best. He'd hurt her. He knew that, and he couldn't stomach the thought of looking over and seeing pain in her eyes. Pain that *he'd* caused her.

She was wrong about everything she'd said about him. He was who he was. There weren't hidden depths to his fucking character, no lingering trauma twisting him up inside. He was a bad man who'd done bad things. That's all he was, and that's all he would ever be.

"Nice ride," Luke cracked as D hopped out of the driver's seat. "You make an adorable hillbilly."

D gritted his teeth and swept his eyes over the group, not stopping until his gaze landed on a familiar face.

Sullivan.

This morning over the phone, Trevor had confirmed that Sully was alive, but D hadn't really believed it until this very moment. At the sight of his teammate, he had to fight the massive wave of relief that crested in his gut and threatened to knock him over.

I've seen the man who loves his teammates so much that he'd put his neck on the line for them.

No. Sofia was wrong, damn it. He didn't love his teammates. He didn't love *anyone.*

He marched over to Sullivan. Hesitated. Then reached out and lightly slapped the other man's arm. "You made it out," D said gruffly.

Sully nodded. "I made it out."

An alarm went off inside him. Sullivan's voice was . . . different. His eyes were different. The person standing in front of D wasn't the cocky, no-care-in-the-world man that D had known for years.

He was looking at a stranger. A broken, shell-shocked stranger.

D drew an unstable breath. Didn't matter. Sully would

get help. Macgregor would help him. Morgan. Noelle. It wasn't D's responsibility to help the guy. He didn't fucking *love* the guy.

"Sully." Sofia came up to them, then wrapped her arms around Sullivan's waist and hugged him tight. "I'm so glad you're all right."

D didn't miss the way Sully flinched when she first touched him, but after a moment, the man returned her warm embrace. His forehead sagged, his chin resting on her shoulder as a heavy breath seeped from his chest.

The woman had that way about her, an innate strength that drew people to her, that made them relax in her presence. D's throat closed up as he watched her hug his friend, as he remembered everything she'd said back at the motel.

She'd been right about something, at least. He *was* afraid, and had been ever since he'd slept with Sofia. *She* had made him afraid. Because she'd left him wanting more after that first night. Because she'd showed up pregnant. Because she'd almost died on his watch. Because she *saw* him.

He didn't like that feeling. Fear. He didn't fucking like it, and he didn't *want* it. Maybe he had hurt her when he'd refused to give her what *she* wanted, but it was so much easier to just shut down, shut her out. He was good at shutting people out. He fucking excelled at it.

"All right, let's head out," Trevor announced, approaching the group with a black canvas bag slung over his shoulder. He glanced at Sofia. "We're going to the compound first, but someone will fly you back to the clinic after we land, okay?"

Sofia released Sullivan and nodded, not looking in D's direction even once.

"We're taking one of the smaller birds," Liam spoke up, his tone awkward as he gestured to himself, then Sullivan. "Franco already agreed to pilot for us."

Trevor's forehead creased. "Morgan wants everyone back at the compound."

"Sully wants to check on his boat first. She's docked in Portugal."

When Trevor opened his mouth to protest, Sullivan interrupted. "Don't bloody argue with me on this, mate. I'm going to Portugal."

After a moment, Trevor sighed. "If that's what you need to do, then all right."

Back slaps and handshakes were exchanged as Trevor and the others said good-bye to Liam and Sully, who were both oddly subdued as they strode back to the hangar to talk to their pilot.

The rest of the group headed toward the sleek white Gulfstream that waited on the tarmac. D hung back so he was the last one in the group. He stared at Sofia's back as she trudged forward. Her shoulders were slightly hunched, her long hair swaying midway down her back with each weary step she took.

Pain pierced his heart. Damn it, a part of him wished she would turn around and look at him.

The other part, the one that hated the way she made him feel, wanted her to keep staring straight ahead. To walk onto that jet and out of his life.

A phone rang just as Trevor and Kane reached the small flight of metal steps in front of the plane. It was

Kane's cell, and he stepped to the side to let Trevor board as he answered the call.

Three seconds later, he called out, "Wait!"

Everyone froze. Trevor shifted around, frowning. "What's wrong?"

Kane's features were tight as he searched the crowd before locking eyes with D. Then he held out the phone. "It's for you."

Tamping down his growing alarm, D marched up and snatched the phone from Kane's outstretched hand. "Yeah?" he barked into it.

There was a pause. Then a deep, satisfied chuckle.

"Derek, it's been a long time," Edward Bryant greeted him.

D's spine snapped straight, as if someone had shoved a steel rod into it. *Fuck*.

Before he could respond, the sound of multiple car engines echoed in the distance. Every man on the tarmac had his weapon drawn in a heartbeat, D included. He took aim at the black SUV speeding up from the left side, but shooting at it would've been a total waste of ammunition. The vehicle was armored. So were the other ones that appeared from all directions—two coming in from the right, another from the left, two more up ahead.

In a matter of seconds, the jet was surrounded. The only escape was the gaping entrance of the hangar, where Liam stood with an assault rifle in hand, his profile grim as he pointed it at one of the SUVs. But running toward the hangar would just trap the team inside the massive space.

D bit back a curse and focused on the voice in his ear.

"Tell your men to stand down," Bryant ordered,

sounding far more cheerful than he ought to. "My people aren't there for them."

"I guess that means they're here for me?"

"Of course." Bryant laughed again. "I have no issue with your little merc pals. Actually, I'd rather not order my guys to engage—I don't particularly want James Morgan on my back if I massacre his entire team. I just want you, Derek."

D inhaled a slow breath. "I don't work for you anymore, Bryant. I don't owe you anything."

"Maybe not, but you're still going to do what I say. Otherwise I *will* tell my men to engage, and then every person on that runway is going to die. I hear there's a woman there, too. Is she your girlfriend?"

He gritted his teeth, making a conscious effort not to look at Sofia. She would be able to see the fear in his eyes. She was the only one who ever fucking saw him.

"What do you want me to do?" he asked in defeat.

"Tell your friends to get on their jet and fly home. No harm will come to them. Tell your other friends, the ones in the hangar, to stay put, and no harm will come to them either. And you, Derek, are going to walk over to my people and surrender yourself to them."

"And then what?" he said bitterly. "They put a bullet in my head?"

"Of course not. Nobody is allowed to touch you until you and I have a little chat. They're just going to take you to another airfield. My plane will be waiting there for you."

"And if I don't surrender?" From the corner of his eye, he saw Kane's head whirl toward him in surprise.

"I just told you what happens if you don't," Bryant said irritably. "Your people die."

D studied the six vehicles parked strategically on the runway. He couldn't see through the heavily tinted windows, but Edward Bryant wasn't the kind of man who fucked around. Not the kind of man who bluffed, either. The men inside those SUVs were no doubt armed to the teeth, and they wouldn't hesitate to open fire if D didn't do what their boss demanded.

"So?" Bryant prompted. "What's your final answer, Derek?"

"I'll see you soon," he muttered into the phone.

"That's what I thought."

As the other man disconnected, D exhaled a steady stream of air, then addressed his teammates. "Get on the plane."

Nobody lowered their weapons.

"I'm serious." He swallowed his frustration. "You need to get on the plane. You need to go."

Trevor was the first to speak. "What the fuck is going on, D?"

"I have some business to take care of."

"Don't give us that vague bullshit of yours," Kane said angrily. "You just told that asshole you were *surrendering*. Who the hell was he? And how did he get my number?"

"He's resourceful," D retorted, his frustration levels rising steadily. "He's my former handler, and he wants to meet with me. That's all you need to know, all right?"

Ethan joined in, his hazel eyes narrowing. "You mean he wants to kill you."

"Probably, but I can handle myself, okay?" D spared

another look at the SUVs surrounding them, then glanced at each of his teammates. "I don't want you coming after me, understand? I'll take care of it, the way I always take care of shit. All you guys have to do is get on the fucking plane."

Nobody moved.

D's gaze rested on Sofia, just briefly, before shifting to Trevor. "Damn it, just go. Get Sofia back to the compound."

"We're not leaving you behind," Trevor snapped.

"Yes, you are. Because if you don't, my handler's men will kill every single one of you." His throat was so tight he could barely go on. "I'll be fine."

Every single pair of eyes remained unconvinced.

"For fuck's sake, get out of here," he burst out. "Get on the plane and *go*."

It seemed like an eternity before Trevor finally cleared his throat and nodded at the others, but he was visibly upset as he addressed them. "You heard the man," Trevor said woodenly. "Let's go."

Gratitude flooded D's gut as he met Trevor's eyes. "Thank you."

His teammate didn't answer. Nobody said a word, in fact. Not Kane or Ethan or Luke. They just stared at him in disapproval, as if he'd *asked* for Bryant's men to ambush them. As if he were betraying them by trying to save their lives.

Then, one by one, they trudged toward the metal stairs. One by one, they disappeared through the door of Morgan's jet.

Except for Sofia. Nope, the damned woman stayed behind, ignoring his orders the way she always did.

Her eyes bored into his face as she slowly walked toward him.

"You still want to tell me you're not a good man?"

He blinked. He'd expected condemnation, so the question surprised him. "I'm not," he mumbled.

"Really? Because it seems to me like you're sacrificing yourself—*again*—for the people you care about." Her expression took on a gleam of challenge. "Or are you still pretending you don't care about your team? About *me*?"

He clenched his teeth. "I don't."

"Because you're an asshole, right, Derek? You're a coldhearted bastard who doesn't give a shit about anyone but himself." She made a scornful sound. "Go ahead. Keep telling yourself that. Keep pretending nothing matters to you."

"Sofia—" he started hoarsely.

"No, I'm done listening to your bullshit denials." She let out a shaky breath. "I'm not going to try to change your mind about this. I'm not going to ask you to come home safe. I'm not even going to tell you I love you. Because it doesn't matter what I say or what I want. In the end, you're always going to take the easy way out."

"Easy?" he hissed at her. "You think giving myself up to Bryant is *easy* for me?"

"Yes." She met his angry gaze head-on. "It's easier for you to go off and die, because then you won't have to face how you feel or who you *are*. But I told you back at the motel, I *know* you, Derek."

His body went rigid as she stepped closer and pressed her palm directly on his left pec.

"I know there's a heart inside that big, strong chest of

yours. It's beating and it's real and it's fucking *there*. And I do love you," she said fiercely, peering up at him with those big green eyes. "A part of me wishes I didn't, but I do. I love you, Derek."

It suddenly got hard to breathe.

"I don't expect you to say it back. I don't expect you to say anything, actually." Her expression was sadder than he'd ever seen it. "You never do, right?"

D took a breath. Opened his mouth.

"Good-bye, D."

Sofia turned while the words were still stuck in his fucking throat. She didn't stomp or make a fuss or toss back some bitter parting remark. She just walked away, and watching her do it set something screaming in his head as loud as gunshots at close range.

She just *walked away*, taking his heart—the heart he hadn't realized he still had—right along with her.

Chapter 24

The building that had once housed Smith Group head-quarters was now in shambles. It was also the last place D expected Bryant's men to bring him after they landed at the private airport outside of Wilmington.

On the other hand, it made sense that this was the site Bryant had chosen. Bryant's whole life had revolved around the agency. D had destroyed the man's career after he'd failed to execute his mission all those years ago. In Bryant's eyes, it probably seemed fitting for them to face off in the one place Bryant had loved most in the world.

D winced as one of the stone-faced men yanked him out of the backseat. The zip ties dug into his wrists, which were sore as fuck after being bound for the entire four-hour flight.

He hadn't recognized the men who'd been waiting for him at the airfield back in Mexico. He didn't think they were former Smith operatives, but maybe they were. It wasn't like Smith Group had held company socials or holiday parties. D had met only a few other operatives during his time there, usually when he was being debriefed at headquarters.

The four men who'd accompanied him from Cancún flanked him as the group headed for the rear doors of the building. D studied the brick facade with a frown. The exterior was crumbling in some places, and there was an entire section missing near the door, revealing the pipes and beams and drywall that made up the skeleton of the building.

The walls inside were in the same run-down condition, boasting visible water damage from years of neglect, but the floor beneath D's boots was solid and the stairwell was mostly undamaged, except for the poorly done graffiti spray-painted on the walls.

D climbed the stairs, sandwiched between two of the men. Bryant's old office was located on the top floor of the building, which had only eight floors in total. Smith Group's headquarters had been low-key, situated in a quiet neighborhood that had once housed a variety of small businesses rather than in a flashy downtown high-rise that would draw attention. But in the past nine years, the area had deteriorated.

When they reached the set of doors in front of Bryant's office, D noted in amusement that the gold name plaque on the wall was still there.

EDWARD BRYANT, SENIOR CONSULTANT

He suddenly wondered if some gullible civilian had ever wandered into the building, somehow made it through the Alcatraz-level security, and then shaken his head in dismay when he'd realized he wasn't in a consulting firm.

"He's waiting for you." One of the men eyed D with no expression as he reached for the handle and opened the door halfway.

D stifled a sigh. Fuck. Might as well get this over with.

Having his hands tied behind his back limited his moves, but luckily, his legs were unbound and worked just fine. If he got close enough to Bryant, he could easily kick the man's legs out from under him. Get him on the ground and scissor his ankles around the bastard's neck. Snap it.

That would probably alert Bryant's people, though, and they'd come in, guns blazing. But D would deal with that when it happened. Right now, eliminating Bryant was his only concern.

The moment he entered the office, D's eyes widened in genuine shock.

What the fuck?

While the rest of the building looked like it was seconds away from being condemned, Bryant's office was in pristine condition. Utterly unchanged in the nine years since D had stepped foot in it.

Not one measly detail was different. The fancy drapes, the thousands of dollars' worth of furniture, the thick Berber carpet. Even the wet bar was fully stocked, with rows of liquor bottles gleaming in the soft glow of the desk lamp, which must've been running on batteries, because no way was there electricity in this building. All the wiring in the walls outside the office had been exposed, for fuck's sake.

"Derek."

He shifted his attention back to the commanding

desk, to the man who'd recruited him from Delta and coaxed him into signing away his life to Smith Group.

A silver pistol rested in the man's hand.

"Stay where you are," Bryant ordered.

D narrowed his eyes and studied his former handler. Bryant had aged, but not much. His shoulders were still broad, his torso still bulky as ever, and although his hair was now streaked with silver, he still had a full head of it. His hooked nose still seemed too big for his narrow face. His eyes were still the same dark shade of blue.

Absolutely nothing about the man had changed, same way his damn office hadn't changed.

"What the hell is this?" D finally asked, turning to examine his surroundings. "Jesus, Bryant. It's morbid."

Bryant's eyes flashed. "It's my office—that's what it is."

"Smith Group doesn't exist anymore. You don't have an office."

Now the man smirked. "Just because the government no longer funds or sanctions us doesn't mean we don't exist."

D's pity deepened. Was Bryant running ops out of this cesspool? Did he actually believe he still wielded any semblance of power in this world?

Bryant waved the gun at the plush gold-upholstered chair in front of the desk. "Sit."

D did as he was told, his gaze still taking in the pathetic sights all around him. The desktop shone as if it had been recently polished. Christ. This was seriously depressing.

Bryant pursed his lips as he searched D's face. Then those lips twisted in a displeased frown. "You truly have no remorse for what you've done, do you? I suppose that's my fault, though. I trained you, after all. I taught you how to ignore your conscience."

D cleared his throat. "This is pathetic. You realize that, right? This office, the furniture— everything. It's fucking pathetic."

"It's my life!" Bryant roared. "My legacy! Do you realize how hard I worked to get to where I am? Do you realize what you took from me when you couldn't do your fucking job like I ordered you to? Thirty years! I gave thirty years of my life to this agency. Not to a wife or kids or fucking *hobbies*, because *this* was my life!"

Bryant rolled his chair back and unsteadily rose to his feet. Then, standing behind his desk like an executive addressing his staff, he straightened his shoulders and lifted his chin. His tailored suit was starched, his tie perfectly knotted at his throat.

And seeing it made D profoundly sad. This was a sad, pathetic man, living in the past, clinging to an agency that had been shut down almost ten years ago.

His legacy.

Bryant had called this his legacy.

D's throat tightened as another thought flew into his head, one he'd never expected, something he'd never once wondered about.

What would *his* legacy be?

"I protected this country." Bryant was still ranting, still spitting out bitter words that D barely registered.

"I served it with honor. I took the jobs that every other agency was too fucking scared to touch, and I never demanded anything in return. I didn't need to be patted on the back or given medals. I didn't need recognition or phone calls from the president telling me what a splendid job I'd done. I didn't need any of that, because it didn't matter. I was already doing what *mattered*."

D's mind continued to spin. He was a soldier, a mercenary. He got paid to rescue people from sweltering jungles, he played bodyguard to government agents when they needed protection, he flew into war zones, took down rebel groups. But what did any of that really give him other than a way to pass the time? A way to keep from being bored, to keep from losing his mind over the lack of action.

"And you took it away from me!" Bryant boomed. "All you had to do was find that girl! Find her and then kill the man who abducted her! But no, you had to go and kill the son! You had to blow the whole fucking mission and turn my life into a circus."

The gun trembled in Bryant's hand as he seethed in anger.

D's hands were trembling, too. Seeing Bryant . . . this office . . . the man's desperate attempt to hold on to the past . . . It had shaken him up. Bryant had nothing. He had *nothing*.

But D . . . he had something, damn it. He had his team. He had Sofia. He even had a fucking kid, a *real* legacy.

Except he was too afraid to let any of them in.

"Did you know I had to answer to the president? That I had to stand in the goddamn Oval Office and explain to him why an agency that was supposed to be covert was suddenly being talked about all over Congress? Being debated in the Senate? Because that motherfucker Senator Richardson wouldn't stop screaming about how we'd failed him?"

Bryant seemed oblivious to D's inner turmoil. He also seemed oblivious to the fact that he was venturing closer and closer to D's chair.

D eyed the gun. The safety was still on. Bryant was too caught up in his own resentment, too focused on wallowing in the past, to notice his oversight.

It was a powerful thing, the past. It had turned a man who'd once been a legend in the intelligence community into a blubbering, pathetic amateur.

"And then that asshole tells me someone needs to take the fall in order to shut Richardson up!" Bryant was yelling. "And me, the man who served him for thirty fucking years—*I'm* the one who's punished? Because of *you*! Because of what *you* fucking did, Derek! Because *you* screwed up and—"

In the blink of an eye, D dove off the chair and tackled Bryant to the floor.

The two of them landed on the carpet with a heavy thud. The gun flew out of Bryant's hand and skidded underneath the desk as the man roared in outrage.

Straddling the man's torso, D brought his bound wrists to Bryant's throat and pressed down hard. But goddamn it, he'd been wrong—Bryant was no amateur. The man was still lightning fast, still highly skilled. His elbow shot up and connected with D's nose, and a sharp crack sliced the air as blood poured from D's nostrils and stained Bryant's suit jacket.

They were both breathing heavily as Bryant rolled them over, gaining the upper hand as he got on top of D. Meaty fists came down hard on D's face, bringing a bone-jarring jolt of pain that rattled his jaw. He blocked the angry blows with his zip-tied wrists, tried to bring his knee up to ram it into Bryant's groin, but the heavy weight crushing his torso made it impossible to move.

"You really think you can take me down?" Bryant grunted. His fist slammed into D's jaw again, while his other hand snapped out toward the desk, trying to slide underneath it in a wild grab for the gun.

D batted at Bryant's extended arm, causing the man's hand to slap the desktop instead. A flurry of items flew off the desk and rained over their heads. Something heavy, a paperweight maybe, knocked D in the forehead, and papers crumpled beneath his elbow as he attempted to roll again.

This time he succeeded in heaving Bryant off him, with such force that D ended up on his stomach, hands flat on the carpet. Something sharp dug into the center of his palm, bringing a sting of pain, a gush of blood.

"I *own* you!" Bryant yelled as his hand fumbled beneath the desk again. "I trained you! I'm *better* than you!"

With a triumphant growl, Bryant drew his hand back and emerged with the gun.

As adrenaline surged through D's blood, he grabbed the long piece of metal that had cut his hand. A letter opener, he realized. Fancy as fuck, with a shiny steel blade and what looked like diamonds glittering on the handle.

D heard the click of the safety, saw Bryant rise to his knees. He quickly twirled the letter opener around to grip it by the handle, then lunged at the other man just as Bryant pulled the trigger.

The gunshot was like an explosion in D's ear, probably because the bullet had literally flown by his ear. Heat seared the side of his head, but the pain he'd expected didn't come.

Bryant had missed. By millimeters.

The man realized it at the same time D did. With a furious growl, Bryant curled his finger over the trigger again, but not fast enough this time.

Because D had already plunged the sharp blade of the letter opener in the center of the man's neck.

A horrified sound flew out of Bryant's mouth. Blood gushed out of his neck, the arterial spray splashing D in the face as he leaned in and twisted the blade. Then he twisted again. And again and again, until Bryant's throat was slashed open like a grapefruit that had just been sliced in half. A mangled mash of flesh that still oozed blood even as Bryant toppled to the floor.

Dead.

D's ear was ringing like a fucking carnival game. Loud and continuous. Disorienting. He snatched the gun from Bryant's limp hand, then shot to his feet and aimed the pistol at the door, his breaths coming out in sharp pants. The men in the hall had to have heard the gunshot. Why the hell weren't they barreling through the door?

D's heart rate steadied as he spared a quick glance at his old handler's body. Blood continued to flow out of Bryant's neck, forming a sticky puddle on the beige carpet, turning the white collar of his shirt red.

The ringing in his left ear got quieter. He could hear out of it again. Thank fuck. For a moment there, he'd actually worried he might've been deafened.

D took a breath. All right. He needed to get the fuck out of here. He wasn't sure why the guards hadn't come to their boss's rescue, but they *had* to be out there. Patrolling the halls, watching the perimeter of the building.

It was fine, though. A-okay. He'd escaped from hairier situations before and come out of them alive. He just needed to focus.

Exhaling, he edged silently toward the door—just as it burst open.

D was a heartbeat away from pulling the trigger when he recognized the man who appeared in the doorway.

It was Trevor Callaghan.

Son of a bitch.

D's jaw fell open as shock crashed into him.

Looking amused by the reaction, Trevor lifted a brow and said, "What—you really thought we wouldn't come after you?"

Footsteps sounded from the hall, and then Kane sidled up to Trevor.

Kane studied D's face, which he knew was stained with Bryant's blood, then gazed past D's shoulders at the body lying on the floor by the desk. "Wow, you're such a badass, D," he cracked. "You killed *one* guy. We, on the other hand, just took out a fucking army out there. You're welcome."

D stared at his teammates. No, his *friends*.

Actually, fuck that. His *brothers*.

And then he started to laugh.

Chapter 25

"Are you sure you don't want to wait for D?" Abby's forehead creased in disapproval as she followed Sofia to the sedan parked in the courtyard.

It was the same car Sofia had arrived in at the compound three days ago when she'd come here to track down Derek. The realization floored her. Had it really only been three days? It felt like an entire lifetime had passed since she'd followed D to Cancún. Since the cell . . . and the motel . . . and the gut-wrenching goodbye at the airport this morning.

It was so strange. She'd known the man for years, and during that time the only feelings he'd evoked in her were curiosity and indifference. But three measly days at his side, and somehow she'd fallen in love with him.

Pain squeezed her heart and she swallowed hard, trying to ignore the hot rush of emotion twisting in her stomach. It didn't matter how she felt about him. She could love him until the day she died, shower him with that love, remind him of it every single day, but it wouldn't make a lick of difference.

Because Derek Pratt would always be too afraid to love her back.

"Just tell him to call me when he gets back," Sofia mumbled as she unlocked the driver's door.

When he got back, not *if.* She'd been so terrified earlier when she'd boarded that jet, convinced she would never see D again. And when Kane had called Abby from Delaware almost four hours ago, Sofia had almost bitten off her own tongue in panic, certain Kane would report that D was already dead. But she should have known better than to underestimate Derek Pratt. According to Kane, D had managed to kill Edward Bryant while *handcuffed.*

The man was fucking invincible.

But he was also unreachable. He was broken, and Sofia had finally accepted the bleak truth: she couldn't fix him.

D would just have to fix himself.

And she . . . well, she had a baby to focus on. It was overwhelming to think that she'd be doing it by herself, but she was strong, healthy, and determined. After years of being alone, she was finally going to have the family she'd been deprived of when she was a little girl. So what if it would be a family of two? She was going to love this child with all her heart. The two of them were going to take on the fucking world together.

"Thank you, by the way."

Abby's awkward voice jolted Sofia from her thoughts. She wrinkled her forehead. "For what?"

"For the Wilmington lead." Abby shrugged. "Even Morgan didn't know where Smith Group used to operate out of, so you saved us a lot of time with that lead. Made it easier to narrow the search."

Sofia couldn't fight a spark of pride. She liked knowing that she'd contributed to D's rescue. When his team had been scrambling to figure out where Bryant might have taken him, she'd suddenly remembered him mentioning Delaware in the motel, and tentatively offered it up as a possible location. And it had totally panned out.

"No problem," she answered, her tone sounding far more relaxed than she felt. "Anyway, I should really take off now. I'm anxious to get home."

"I wish you'd let me drive you."

"It's fine, Abby. Really. The rental company needs to pick up the car, so it makes sense for them to grab it at the airport instead of here. I doubt Morgan wants strangers driving up to his gate—"

She stopped talking, because the moment she'd said the word *gate*, two Range Rovers appeared in front of the gate farthest from the courtyard. She squinted in the sunshine, her shoulders tightening in alarm as she peered at the vehicles, but her wariness disappeared when she noticed Abby smiling.

"They're back," the redhead said.

Sofia's stomach roiled. Crap. She'd really, really wanted to be gone before D came back. She couldn't face him right now, not after everything they'd been through, everything they'd said to each other. Or *hadn't* said.

God, she'd told him she loved him, and he'd stared right through her.

As uneasiness gathered in her body, she watched as

the cars drove through the first gate. Then they stopped. An arm extended from a driver's window and punched in a code at the second gate. The cars rolled forward again. Stopped at the last gate. Another code entered.

And then the Range Rovers entered the courtyard, tires kicking up dust before the vehicles came to a stop.

Sofia jumped when the front door of the house flew open with a loud gust that could be heard in the courtyard. Morgan's daughter, Cate, hurried outside, her dirty blond hair whipping around her shoulders as she raced toward the vehicles.

The young woman threw her arms around Ash the moment he stepped out of the backseat of one of the SUVs, and Sofia hid a smile as she noticed the visible reluctance with which he hugged her back. Even so, there was also unmistakable pleasure in his eyes, which faded once he noticed the other men smirking at him.

"You're back." Cate Morgan was grinning from ear to ear as she peered up at the young rookie. "And you're alive."

Ash's voice was dry. "Yes, Cate. I'm back and I'm alive." His lips twitched. "You realize you say that every single time I come back from a job, right?"

The girl stuck out her chin. "I'm sorry for being concerned about your well-being, Ash. *So* sorry."

Behind Ash, Luke snickered, then moved toward the porch in a brisk stride. "Abs," he called over his shoulder. "Where's Liv?"

"Out back with Juliet and Izzy," Abby called back.

Luke immediately changed course, heading for the side of the house instead. Ethan and Trevor did the same at the mention of their wives, hurrying after Luke with no time to spare.

The eagerness in their expressions brought an ache of sorrow to Sofia's chest. And the way Kane approached Abby and kissed her on the forehead only deepened the ache.

Everyone was so happy to see their significant others. Even Ash, who was making an obvious effort not to stand too close to Cate, yet was so clearly pleased that she'd come outside to welcome him home.

Sofia finally found the courage to look at D. He was leaning against one of the Range Rovers, watching her with an indecipherable expression.

When their gazes locked, he straightened his broad shoulders and slowly walked toward her.

Her heart beat faster the closer he got. He'd changed his shirt. He'd been wearing a white one at the airfield in Cancún, but now it was black and stretched tight across his chest. The hard ridges of his abdomen rippled with each step he took, his chest radiating pure power.

When he reached her, the scent of copper instantly filled her nostrils. Sofia narrowed her eyes when she glimpsed a faint splotch of red under his chin. He must have tried to scrub it off at some point, but he'd missed a spot, and the caked blood on his skin triggered her concern.

"Are you all right?" she asked quietly.

Noticing where her gaze had gone, he awkwardly ran his palm over his chin, then shrugged. "I'm fine. Not my blood."

"Ah, okay. That's good."

He nodded. Went quiet.

From the corner of her eye, Sofia noticed Abby and Kane edging away. Discreetly at first, but then they quickened their pace, as if the tension in the air was too much for them to bear. Ash and Cate drifted away too, disappearing inside the house.

"You're leaving?" He gestured to the car keys in her hand.

"Yeah. Morgan arranged for a charter to take me back to the clinic."

D gave another nod.

"I should actually get going. I don't want to make the pilot wait."

Another pause, and then he cleared his throat. "Are you cool if he waits another ten minutes? It won't take me that long to pack."

Sofia blinked. "I . . . don't understand."

"I'd rather not have to replace my entire wardrobe when we get to Mexico. Figured it would be easier to just pack a few bags while we're still here."

His eyes revealed nothing. Absolutely nothing that could help her make sense of what he was saying.

Sofia gaped at him, her throat working overtime to swallow her confusion. "You're coming to Mexico?"

He nodded again.

She waited for him to continue. He didn't.

"Why?" she blurted out.

D dragged a hand over his close-cropped hair, and the movement caused his biceps to flex. "Because I'm not going to be one of those people."

Sofia was baffled. "What people?"

"The ones who leave you. You said everybody you care about leaves you. I'm not gonna fucking do that."

Her jaw fell open, damn near unhinging. Was this a dream? Some screwed-up fever dream? Or did pregnancy cause hallucinations in some women?

"D—"

"Derek," he cut in. "My name is Derek."

A frown touched her lips. "Okay."

"No, you don't get it. My name is actually Derek." A sheepish look filled his eyes. "That's the name I was born with."

Just when she thought he couldn't shock her any more than he already had, he threw her another curveball. Sofia's brain struggled to absorb the information. "Your real name is Derek? Derek . . . Pratt?"

"Porter."

Her brow furrowed. As she ran over what he'd just told her, a laugh popped out of her mouth. "You chose your real name as your *alias*? And the same *initials*?" The laughter came harder. "Oh my God, that's the stupidest thing I've ever heard! Aren't you supposed to be a *superspy*?"

D's mouth twitched with humor. "Of course it's stupid. Stupid enough to work, because how dumb would someone be to do that?"

Yeah, she supposed he was right. But why was he telling her this? And why had he said he was coming home with her? What did that *mean*?

"What's happening here?" she whispered.

D stepped closer, and her heart skipped a beat when he touched her cheek. His callused fingers scraped her jaw before absently toying with her bottom lip.

"You were right. I'm afraid to feel. And . . ." A ragged breath escaped his mouth. "And maybe I didn't deal with . . . everything that happened to me. Well, I mean, putting it behind me is one way of dealing with it, but maybe that's not good enough. Maybe I do need to talk to someone about it." His dark eyes met hers. "I was hoping you could help me find someone to talk to. A . . . professional."

Her knees grew wobbly. "Yeah." She swallowed. "I can do that."

Another nod. "Thanks. And listen. I don't want you to give me shit about the house, okay?"

Sweet Jesus, she'd never been more confused in her life. "The house?"

"Yeah. Your house. We need to get that front door replaced. New locks, too. And the window frame in the spare room is broken—I checked the last time I was there."

When had he been in her *spare room*?

"That lock doesn't work either, and there's no way I'm letting the kid sleep there until we fix it. And the fridge is fucking *gone*, Sofia. It sucks up way too much power." D's tone became stern. "We'll need a better security system, too. Motion sensors, alarms. I'd feel better if we installed some trip wires, maybe C-4 on the path from the clinic to the house, but that could be risky. I don't know how much freedom you give your patients. Do they wander around the property a lot?"

Sofia just stared at him.

"Fuck, fine," he muttered. "No, explosives. I'll figure something else out."

Now she shook her head. Again and again, because the cobwebs inside it were clinging to every corner of her brain. "Why are you saying all this? And what makes you think I'm going to let you move into my house?"

D looked startled. "Because you love me."

"Oh my God! *Yes*, I love you! But you said you didn't want me, remember?" She fought to calm her breathing. "You said you didn't want the baby! What the hell changed, Derek?"

"Everything," he said simply.

When he didn't elaborate, she growled in frustration. "You know what, *Derek Porter*? I've had it up to here with you! You can take your trip wires and C-4 and shove them right up your—"

"I love you."

Sofia's jaw hit the dirt. "W-what?"

"I, uh, love you," D repeated. He clumsily rubbed the back of his neck, then his cheeks. Either she was imagining it, or his fingers were actually trembling.

"You . . ." She trailed off, unsure how to continue.

"Should I say it again?" He looked confused for a beat, but then it turned to wariness. "I've never said that to anyone before. Am I supposed to give a longer speech or something?"

A laugh flew out. Oh God. This man was priceless.

Sofia finally found her voice. "You love me?"

"Yeah, I do. I probably should have led with that, but the state of your fucking house really pisses me off and I got sidetracked."

She swallowed another laugh.

"I'm not gonna lie, though. I'm afraid. I'm afraid I won't be a good father to the kid. I'm afraid I won't be good to *you*. And I'm really fucking afraid I might lose you one day because of it."

His stricken expression tugged at her heart. "You won't."

He blinked. "No?"

Sofia slowly shook her head, a smile lifting the corners of her mouth. "Don't you know me by now, Derek? I'm stubborn as hell. I would chain you up in the clinic before I let you walk away from me."

D's eyes gleamed with fortitude. "I'm never going to leave you. I can't promise not to act like an asshole or piss you off sometimes, but I can promise you that. I'll never leave you."

A ring of emotion circled her heart, flooding it with warmth, with *love*. Despite the joy overflowing inside her, she couldn't fight one nagging concern. Swallowing, she lowered her hand to her stomach. It was still too early to be showing, but the baby was there. Inside her. Growing and thriving.

"You can't leave him either." The thought brought a fissure of pain to her chest. "You have to promise to be there for him too."

The determination in his gaze burned brighter, and then he shocked the hell out of her by reaching out and placing his palm over her knuckles. Holding both their hands tight to her belly.

"I won't leave him," D said roughly. "I can't pretend I know how to be a father. I'll probably be fucking terrible at it at first, but I'll follow your lead, baby. I'll learn everything I need to know from you. I just . . . I want to be your family."

The love in her heart spilled over, gushing through her in hot, gooey waves. She took a breath. Then another. Then said, "Okay."

D searched her eyes. "Okay?"

She touched his face, skimming the scruff on his jaw. "You can come with me. You can do whatever you want to the house." She leaned up on her tiptoes and brushed her lips over his. "You can be my family."

He smiled.

Holy hell. He smiled a rare smile that actually reached his eyes, that lit them up and relaxed his entire face, and it was beautiful. *He* was beautiful. Still rough around the edges, still radiating strength and power and deadly promise, but there was more to this man than danger and violence. So much more.

He might not be the partner she'd envisioned for herself, but he made her feel safe and protected and completely at peace. He made her feel warm and weak-kneed and loved. He made her . . . *feel*.

"C'mon, let's go inside so you can help me pack," D said, reaching for her hand. "And I know you're in a hurry, but maybe we can grab some lunch before we go. When we called from the bird, Abby told Kane you only ate one slice of toast today."

Sofia sighed. "Are you going to monitor my eating habits for the whole pregnancy?"

"Yes. You should probably just accept it now to avoid any future arguments." D laced his fingers through hers, then outlined their plans in a brisk, efficient manner. "Okay, so we pack. We eat. And then we go home. Sound good?"

Sofia leaned her head against his shoulder as they walked toward the house. "We pack. We eat." Her heart was in her throat as she voiced the rest. "And then we go home."

Epilogue

Porto, Portugal

They'd barely said a word during the ten-hour flight to Porto.

Which was unheard-of for them—Liam couldn't remember the last time he and Sullivan Port hadn't had something to say to each other. It didn't matter the topic—sports, politics, frickin' TV shows. They'd been able to talk for hours about any old bullshit.

The distance between them made his chest ache, but it wasn't until they arrived at the marina that Liam realized it was only about to get worse. If the longing look in Sullivan's eyes was any indication, they were about to face a fuckin' *ocean* of distance.

"No," Liam choked out as he followed his friend's gaze.

Those gray eyes were glued to the gorgeous forty-five-foot sailboat in the nearest slip. Her sails were down, secured to the booms, but the way Sullivan was gazing at them, it was like they were unfurled and fluttering in the wind as the boat sliced through the waves.

"You agreed to go to rehab, damn it." Liam couldn't stop the accusation in his tone.

"This *is* my rehab, mate."

Sullivan slowly stroked the tattoo on the inside of his forearm, black lettering that spelled out one simple name: *Evangeline*.

The same name scrawled on the side of the gleaming white yacht.

"She'll make me better," Sully said hoarsely. "She always does."

Liam fought a jolt of panic. He suddenly envisioned Sullivan sailing into port, crawling the streets of some beachside shantytown, searching for someone to sell him H. Begging strangers on every corner for a fix.

As if reading his mind, Sully sighed. "It won't happen, Boston. I won't let it beat me." He raked both hands through his messy blond hair. "You can wait here with me while I call in a supply order. I'll get enough shit to last me for months. Just me and the water. Me and my girl."

Liam swallowed. "I can come with you."

"No." The answer was fast, inviting no argument. "I need to do this alone. I need to *be* alone."

Pain. Hot, gut-shredding pain. Liam could hardly breathe as he absorbed the rejection like a blow to the solar plexus.

But he understood where it came from, why Sullivan insisted on it. Sully had always been a loner. He'd grown up with no one. He opened his heart to no one. Not even Liam had access to every part of Sullivan Port. The man had allowed him to get close, probably closer than he'd ever let anybody else get, but Liam knew his teammate always held a piece of himself back.

"Okay," he finally said. "I won't fight you on this."

Gratitude filled Sully's eyes. Then it faded into hesitation, sorrow. Regret.

Liam's breath hitched as his friend stepped toward him. When Sully lightly rested his hand on Liam's shoulder, every muscle in Liam's body tensed. Time stopped right along with his heart. He searched the other man's face. Waited.

"I won't be radio silent. I'll keep in touch, mate. I promise."

Liam nodded, wholly aware of his friend's touch, the heavy weight of Sully's palm. Then Sully wrapped one arm around Liam's back and dropped his chin on Liam's shoulder.

The hug was brief. Too brief.

"I need to call my guy at the market," Sully said awkwardly, reaching into his pocket to pull out the burner phone Liam had given him.

"I . . ." His mouth felt like it was lined with gravel. "I'm not going to wait with you."

Sullivan nodded. "All right."

They stared at each other for a moment.

"Just . . ." Liam cleared his throat. "Stay safe, okay? And keep in touch."

"I will," his teammate promised.

They didn't hug again. Didn't speak again. They simply turned in opposite directions, Sully dialing a number into the phone as he headed for the boat, Liam walking on shaky legs toward the parking lot.

He fumbled for his own phone the moment he reached the car, his fingers trembling as he pulled up Morgan's name.

"Hey," he rasped when the boss picked up. "It's me."

"How's Sullivan?" was Morgan's instant response.

"Fine. He . . ." Liam bit the inside of his cheek. "He's checking himself into rehab."

"Good. You heading home now?"

"No. No, I, ah . . . I need some time off, Jim."

Suspicion thickened the line. "How much time off?"

"I don't know. A lot." His gaze strayed back to the dock. "I'm going home to see my family. My nephew's being baptized. And"—his heart caught in his throat as he saw Sullivan hop on board the yacht—"my ma's eager to see me, my whole family is. So, yeah. I need time off."

Morgan's tone became uneasy. "Why does it sound like you're quitting on me, Macgregor?"

He didn't answer. He was too busy watching the way the sunlight caught in Sullivan's blond hair.

"Boston, you there?"

"Uh." He tore his gaze off his teammate. "I'm not quitting, Jim. I'm just taking a sabbatical."

"A sabbatical." The boss sounded unconvinced.

"Yeah." He clicked the remote to unlock the car. "I've gotta go now. Need to make arrangements to get to Boston."

"Check in when you land," Morgan said before hanging up.

Liam slid the phone back in his pocket and leaned against the car, the cold metal frame barely registering against his body. Numbness was setting in. A blessed wall to block off the pain he refused to give in to.

He needed to go home. He needed to be surrounded by the chaos of his family, annoying and judgmental as they were. If he went back to the compound, he would see Sully everywhere he looked. It was better to distract himself. To listen to his sisters lecture him about being childless, his brothers rag him about not having a wife, his parents chastise him even as they hovered over him and showered him with love.

They would distract him from the sadness lodged in his chest. From thinking about what he really wanted.

And what he couldn't have.

Want to encounter a sexy new kind of alpha group from Elle Kennedy? Read on for a special excerpt from the first book in Elle Kennedy's brand-new Outlaws series,

CLAIMED

Available now from Signet Eclipse.

"I need to get drunk and laid—not necessarily in that order," Rylan announced as the group crossed the threshold into the bar.

Connor had to duck his head to clear the top of the doorway. So did the others. All five of them stood well over six feet tall, making an imposing sight as they entered the candlelit room. Every head turned their way, but fear dissolved into mild apprehension and disinterest once the patrons discerned that the men didn't have Enforcer logos on their clothing. Most turned away, refocusing their attention on their companions or the alcohol in front of them.

"And look at that," Rylan said in delight. "The bartender's cute. Must be new, 'cause I'd definitely remember those tits."

Connor followed his friend's gaze to the long metal counter tended by a thin blonde with serious cleavage. Yeah, Ry would remember screwing her. Skinny and big-busted was his flavor of choice. Blondie glanced up and winked at the men, her pouty red lips lifting in a sensual come-hither-and-fuck-me smile.

A sense of desperation hung in the air and mingled with the cloud of tobacco smoke hanging over the room like a canopy. Sex, booze, and cigarettes—rare luxuries these days, unless you knew where to find 'em. And hell, you didn't even have to pay to fuck anymore. Currency meant shit outside the city, and besides, most women were as eager to get screwed as the men who wanted to screw them. But Connor wasn't here for sex. He was looking forward to a nice date with Jack Daniel's. It'd been way too long since he'd felt the burn of alcohol coursing through his veins.

The bar used to be a morgue, and the compartments where stiffs had once been stored now contained bottles of alcohol and supplies that the owners of the establishment had amassed over the years. They'd brought in mismatched furniture, tables and old couches, splintered wooden chairs. No power in the joint, so they'd lit dozens of candles, which danced on the cinder-block walls and shrouded most faces in shadow. The small hospital on the floors above them lay deserted, because hospitals were a thing of the past. You got sick or injured, you died. *Population control*, the fuckers in the "government" called it.

Connor chose a seat that allowed him to monitor both the door and the smoky main room, while Rylan, Pike, and Xander scrambled for the rest. Kade got stuck facing away from the door, which meant he'd be the first one to get a bullet to the back of his head if trouble arose.

The tabletop was scratched and stained with shit Connor didn't even want to know about. Without any discussion, Rylan went up to the counter to order their drinks. That meant he'd be the one paying the tab, but he didn't seem to mind in the slightest. Blondie over there was right up his alley. In a barter-and-trade era, you sometimes paid a high price for whatever you were trying to acquire, but this was win-win for Rylan—he'd get the booze *and* the pussy. Which made him a damn lucky bastard, because the last time they'd come here, the bartender had been male and Connor had been forced to trade a rifle for a bottle of Jack.

Fate smiled on the attractive and horny, he supposed.

"So . . . do we move?" A trademark scowl twisted Pike's face as he voiced the question they'd all been thinking.

Connor rubbed the stubble coating his jaw. He wished like hell he had a razor, but the one back at camp had rusted to shit, and their next raid wasn't scheduled until tomorrow. "Don't know. I think we should wait it out. The rumors might be bullshit."

"Word is Dominik is heading south," Pike reminded him. "He did a sweep last week, cleared out an entire camp only a few hundred miles from here."

Bastard sure had, and damned if that didn't make Connor uneasy. Of all the Enforcers in the Colonies, Dominik and his band of bloodthirsty psychos were the worst. They were vicious, determined, and damn good at their job. Dominik answered only to West Colony's Enforcer commander, who in turn answered to the council members above him. The group's orders were simple: round up every last outlaw in the colony, force them to rejoin society, or kill them if they refused.

If Dominik really was closing in on them, the smart move would be to get the fuck out. Head for South Colony, or try to find a ship heading east, but traveling was a bitch these days. More checkpoints, more Enforcers, more bandits.

Kade spoke up. "I say we stick it out. We've got a good thing going here."

Connor couldn't disagree as he thought about the abandoned wilderness resort they'd been living in for the past year. Tucked in the foothills of the Rockies, the camp consisted of two dozen cabins and a main lodge nestled in the trees. After scouting the area for weeks, the men had claimed the old place and promptly turned it into a fortress. The resort was more secure than a military facility, just the way Connor liked it.

Rylan returned to the table with a full bottle of whiskey and five shot glasses, which clinked together in his hand. Unscrewing the bottle, he poured a stream of alcohol over the glasses, the excess liquid joining the other stains on the rotting wood.

"Hey, don't waste it," Xander grumbled. "Who knows when we'll have another chance to get shit-faced?"

Rylan flopped down in his chair, slugged back a shot, then poured himself another. "So what's the final consensus?"

Xander rubbed the thick beard covering his jaw. "Pike thinks we should go. Kade wants to stay. Con is undecided."

Rylan was quick to throw in his two cents. "I vote for staying. I like it here. And by the way, brother, what's with the beard? You know it's like a gazillion degrees out, right?"

"If your pretty-boy face were capable of growing a beard, you'd look like me too right now." Xander sighed.

"Shit. I hope we find some razors on the raid tomorrow. Maybe even an electric one."

"And candy," Kade added, brightening at the thought. "Some real sweet shit. It's been ages since we came across any chocolate."

"And some really filthy porn," Rylan added with a grin.

Connor didn't join in, mostly because he was scared he'd snap and piss everyone off. But seriously, chocolate and porn? A war had ravaged the entire globe, for fuck's sake. Bombs had fallen on cities like raindrops and eliminated entire populations, and those who survived were now prisoners—sorry, *citizens*—of the Colonies.

And Kade's biggest problem was that he couldn't satisfy his sweet tooth?

They're making the best of this shit.

Yeah, maybe. Maybe Connor was a negative motherfucker for dwelling on the chaos and destruction, but what was he supposed to do—act like everything was fine and dandy? Pretend that his life was filled with rainbows and lollipops?

Fuck that.

He raised his glass to his lips and gulped the alcohol. It burned his throat on the way down, heating his stomach in a familiar, welcoming way. Screw candy and porn—the only thing he wanted from the raid tomorrow was a crate of booze. Even cheap wine would do. Anything to numb the angry, powerless feelings swirling in his gut.

"You know what? Who needs porn when you can settle for the real thing?" Rylan scraped back his chair. "'Scuse me, boys."

Rylan headed to the counter, where he leaned forward

and murmured something that made the bartender giggle. A few seconds later, the blonde eagerly followed him toward a corridor in the back, but not before tossing a not-so-discreet look at Connor and the other men.

"Think she'd be down for some company?" Kade wondered aloud.

Xander grinned. "One hundred percent yes. Did you see the way she looked back just now? That hot little number is dying to be tag-teamed."

"Can you assholes forget about your goddamn cocks for one goddamn minute?" Pike snapped. "We've gotta make a decision. If Dominik's on his way here, I say we go."

"Since when are you scared of a fight?" Xander taunted.

Pike scowled at him. "Some battles aren't worth fighting. Let Dominik do his thing, as long as he leaves us alone."

And right there was the problem—Connor didn't *want* Dominik to leave him alone.

He was itching for a face-to-face with that bastard, and if he didn't have the other guys to think about, he would've taken off and fed his hunger for vengeance ages ago. But his men looked to him for guidance. Somehow, despite his many protests, he'd become their leader. They did what he said, even Pike, who didn't like to take orders from anybody. Connor didn't want any of them getting killed just so he could satisfy the bloodlust that had been poisoning his body for years.

Getting to Dominik was virtually impossible. Not only was he constantly surrounded by his legion of soldiers, but nobody knew where the West Colony Enforcers were headquartered. It wasn't in the city, where those who survived the war had been shipped off to after the Global Council took control. Rumor had it the Enforcers moved around constantly, never making themselves targets. This was the first time Connor had an inkling of where Dominik was going to be. It was an opportunity he refused to let pass, but . . . did the men who trusted him deserve to die during his own quest for revenge?

Uncertainties rolled through his head like tumbleweed, then faded as the creak of the door grabbed hold of his senses. His head jerked up, hand instinctively reaching beneath his jacket to hover over the butt of his pistol.

Even after he decided the threat level was low, he still couldn't look away.

The woman who appeared in the doorway held his gaze captive. Tall, slim, with wary gray eyes and long hair the color of warm honey. She wore tight black pants that showcased a spectacular pair of legs and a white tank top that revealed plenty of mouthwatering cleavage. A leather jacket and knee-high boots completed the bad-girl ensemble.

Connor's mouth went dry.

Christ, he wanted her naked.

It'd been a long time since he'd experienced such a sudden, visceral attraction to a woman. His cock strained against his zipper, but another look in the woman's direction and he knew the eager bulge in his pants wouldn't be getting the attention it demanded.

She might be dressed like a bad girl, but she sure as shit wasn't one. The fearful desperation clouding her eyes revealed her for what she was—a lost little lamb who'd wandered into a den of wolves. And yet . . . there was also determination flickering in her gaze. A sense of to-hell-with-you bravado that gave her a purposeful stride as she stepped into the room.

"Dibs," came Xander's low voice.

"Don't even think about it," Connor muttered.

He registered the surprised faces around the table realizing what his command had sounded like. Possessive. Like he was staking a claim. But that hadn't been his intention. His body might be throbbing like crazy at the moment, but he had no desire to claim the woman. Every instinct he possessed told him to stay away from her. To keep his guys away too.

He watched as she approached the counter and spoke to the young man who'd taken over for the girl who probably had Rylan's cock in her mouth at the moment.

The conversation was hushed, the blonde's shoulders going rigid as the bartender said something she clearly didn't like.

A flash of movement caught his eye. She'd slid something toward the kid, but Connor couldn't make it out. A moment later, the bartender tucked the item in his pocket and slid a beer bottle across the counter. The blonde took it and went over to a table in the corner of the room.

Connor tore his eyes off her. He was still semihard and not at all happy about it. He shouldn't be thinking about fucking, not when Dominik was finally within his grasp.

He could get off any damn time he wanted, but revenge? That was something he could carry with him for the rest of his life.